LOCUST
IN THE
SANDBOX

CYNTHIA GRAY

outskirts
press

Outskirts Press, Inc.
http://www.outskirtspress.com

Paperback ISBN: 978-1-9772-4639-4
Hardback ISBN: 978-1-9772-4831-2

Library of Congress Control Number: 2021920038

PRINTED IN THE UNITED STATES OF AMERICA

Everybody can be great because everybody can serve. You don't have to have a college degree to serve. You don't have to make your subject and your verb agree to serve. You only need a heart full of grace, a soul generated by love.

Martin Luther King Jr.

Table of Contents

A NOTE FROM THE AUTHOR

A BOMB IN a church. Four girls killed. It made no sense. On the television I saw smoke. Rubble. Chaos. Confusion. It was September 15, 1963. Who would kill children? Who does that? Who were these evil locusts and what children would be next?

Locust in the Sandbox is a narrative about children that started in my head the day I walked into the back room of my grandparents' home next door. Seeing and hearing a television broadcast by a voice familiar to me—Walter Cronkite—was confusing. He was talking about the bombing of the Sixteenth Street Baptist Church. Down South in Birmingham, Alabama, four girls had been killed on a Sunday morning, and two boys were murdered later that same day. Being close in age to the youngest murdered child, Denise McNair, age eleven, I was puzzled. Who would kill young girls? The other three children, each fourteen years old, were Carole Robertson, Addie Mae Collins, and Cynthia Wesley. And they were all gone.

Pieces of information would eventually come through our morning and evening papers, and my grandparents, avid readers, would comment in hushed voices. Those responsible had not been punished—although it was firmly known that the bombing had been orchestrated by the Ku Klux Klan. I could not get it out of my head.

Looking back, I vividly remember turning sixteen and being aware that the four Birmingham girls had not gotten to celebrate this milestone birthday. For them there had been no cakes or candles or teasing about being sixteen and not yet kissed. It remained a mystery to me why no one had yet been held accountable.

In 1967, I had a junior high history teacher who greatly influenced me. She loved history and wanted us to value it too. When she spoke, I hung on to her words. She taught history ferociously, but what she shared on the level of humanity and civil rights influenced me the most. She ignited thoughts about what was going on down South that had been tumbling in my mind. This gem of an educator frequently stated that if you don't know your history, you cannot move forward.

During my college years, in the early '70s, there were still no convictions in the Sixteenth Street Baptist Church bombing. I continued to question how justice could go so terribly wrong. Justice delayed. Justice denied. How do you *not* punish those who are responsible for a blatant, heinous crime? It was clear there could be no closure for parents, as well as the community still fervently attempting to seek justice for the children's murders. The case was reopened in 1971. In 1977 the first Klansman was convicted. It was reopened again in 1988, but one of the suspects died before being brought to justice. Finally in 2001 and 2002 two more Klansmen were found guilty and sentenced.

Once I had babies, I saw the church bombing through a different lens. As I experienced an incredible, newfound love for my children, I also discovered a newfound fear of something tragic happening to them. Realizing but not yet fully understanding how impossible it is to shield and protect one's children every minute of every day, you learn that you just do the best you can to keep them safe. And to pray. Constantly.

Six months after the birth of my first child, my cousin was murdered in Dallas, Texas. Barbara, a vivacious girl, was sitting in her apartment with two friends watching a football game when intruders entered the space. She was raped, tortured, stabbed, and strangled by two depraved and dangerous men. The date was September 11, 1980. The Park Lane Murders were chilling and would shatter the lives of parents and siblings, destroying their world as they once knew it. Rebuilding is a difficult process and moving forward a continuous one. Grief is a mixed bag of joy and sadness that comes with no instructions or time frame, and the journey of sorrow unwinds differently within each of us.

Although I will never know or understand what the Birmingham families felt and were forced to endure, I do know that to lose a child through a deliberate and violent act changes every aspect of your life, and that the heart can never fully heal. It's one thing to know true evil exists and is out there, but when it takes your children, it breaks you in ways you could never have imagined. And yet you have to figure out how to go on without them, praying to God you can find a way to exist in a world that they are no longer part of. No one wants their child forgotten. Their names are important, their lives unforgettable.

Locust in the Sandbox is a fictional story that started moving in my mind and inching its way into my heart over a period of almost fifty years. Sometimes there is no reason why we hang on to the things we carry from our childhood.

I have often wondered where the four Birmingham girls would be today and what they would be doing had the church bombing never occurred. These four girls were full of life and laughter, involved in and enjoying all the things young girls do. They had families and friends and were greatly loved. Bright as the stars that magnificently hang in the sky, I can only imagine that Carole, Denise, Addie Mae, and Cynthia are in the presence of their heavenly Father, singing and dancing with the angels.

It is my intent to share with an audience of readers who do not know the story nor the historical significance of the Sixteenth Street Baptist Church bombing. Sometimes living in different pockets of the country prevents us from being aware, let alone informed. I want readers to know and remember the names of the four young victims. It would be beneficial to check out more of the factual and historical accounts of this fateful terrorist attack before reading this book.

In 2011 a remarkable book by Carolyn Maull McKinstry, *While the World Watched*, was published. A personal accounting of the bombing, it connected the points of hard facts with answers to the questions I had wondered about over the years. The timeline was helpful as well as important. This book should be part of any American History course or required reading in schools. The inclusion of Martin Luther King's words was deeply meaningful as were other speeches and quotes. The layout and variety provide a well-written experience and education for the reader. It is a compelling book that you will want to read more than once. Its truths are timeless, its message powerful.

Another valuable source is Spike Lee's *4 Little Girls: The Story of Four Young Girls Who Paid the Price for a Nation's Ignorance.* This film documentary clearly depicts the oppressive challenges and atmosphere of life in the South during the civil rights era. It is an honoring tribute to Carole, Denise, Addie Mae, and Cynthia.

Locust in the Sandbox refers to the "locust" as that person, place, or thing that is not good or right or helpful. It holds us back from being the best version of ourselves, from who we were designed to be. It will eat away at our existence. Locusts devour, devastate, and destroy. They find the cracks in our armor and tempt or fool us in order to get a foothold into our thoughts and actions. Locusts prey on our weaknesses. They have two sets of mouth parts: one to chop us down and the other to pull us out. When left unrecognized and uncontrolled, they swarm together to become even a bigger negative force that becomes difficult to alter, change, or rein in.

"Sandbox" refers to that space where one lives, works, raises a family, eats, plays, attends school, goes to church, and everything in between. Our home. Our community. We need to protect the sandbox and understand what is in it. Morals. Values. Habits. Prejudices. The list is endless. If we don't know or understand what is sitting in our sandbox, we open our space to negative intruders—locusts—who will multiply and wreak havoc on our lives and the lives of others.

Take time to sift through the sand. Dig down deep in those corners. And ask yourself one question:

What is in *my* sandbox?

PROLOGUE

Do to us what you will, and we will still love you.
Bomb our homes and threaten our children, and as
difficult as it is, we will still love you. But be assured
that we'll wear you down by our capacity to suffer,
and one day we will win our freedom. We will not
only win freedom for ourselves, we will so appeal to
your heart and conscience that we will win you in the
process, and our victory will be a double victory.

Martin Luther King

ON SEPTEMBER 15, 1963, a 15-stick dynamite bomb exploded under the ladies' restroom in the basement of the Sixteenth Street Baptist Church in Birmingham, Alabama. The church was a central meeting place for civil rights activists and leaders and influential in all aspects of daily life for its members and community. A beacon in a city nicknamed "Bombingham," exploding bombs were a common occurrence in black homes, churches, and businesses.

At approximately 10:22 on that September Sunday morning, an explosion killed four young girls: Addie Mae Collins, Denise McNair, Carole Robertson, and Cynthia Wesley. The blast injured more than twenty others, along with Addie Mae's younger sister, Sarah, whose eyes were critically damaged from glass and debris. Equally devastating were the senseless deaths of two boys: Johnny Robinson, sixteen, who was fatally shot by a policeman during the confusion and unrest that followed the explosion, and Virgil Ware, thirteen, who while sitting on the handlebars of the bike his brother was pedaling was shot by one of two kids riding by on a motor scooter, after earlier attending an anti-integration rally. The deaths of the children rocked the community to the core, causing Dr. Martin Luther King to exclaim it was "one of the most vicious and tragic crimes ever perpetuated against humanity." President John F. Kennedy said, "If these cruel and tragic events can only awaken that city and state—if they can only awaken this entire nation—to a realization of the folly of racial injustice and hatred and violence, then it is not too late for all concerned to unite in steps toward peaceful progress before more lives are lost."

The racially motivated terrorist attack on the Sixteenth Street Baptist Church followed after the city's young people successfully participated in the Children's March (Children's Crusade) on May 2, four and a half months earlier. The children endured blasts from powerful fire hoses and attacks by vicious dogs. Law enforcement arrested approximately 1,000 children. These actions focused the spotlight on the South's volatile fight for equal rights and desegregation. Civil rights leaders and community members felt strongly the church bombing was in retaliation for what the kids had accomplished in their unified and effective march through the city just months earlier.

Suspected were four members of the Ku Klux Klan: Robert Chambliss, Herman Frank Cash, Thomas Blanton Jr., and Bobby Frank Cherry for domestic terrorism, but law enforcement made no arrests. Due to the influence of the KKK, which had infiltrated even law enforcement, the legal system was delayed and successfully evading justice. It wasn't until 1977 that Robert Chambliss was arraigned and convicted of first-degree murder. In 1994, Herman Frank Cash died without being charged in the bombing. It was 2001 before the judicial system finally pronounced Thomas Blanton Jr. guilty and gave him a sentence of four life terms. In 2002, the last of the four accused murderers, Bobby Frank Cherry, went to prison, also receiving four life terms. By the time the legal system had officially recognized the four perpetrators, thirty-nine years had passed since the bombing of the Sixteenth Street Baptist Church in Birmingham, Alabama.

It's impossible to comprehend what the parents endured struggling to work through the grief of losing their children while simultaneously fighting for justice and accountability for the acts of murder. They continued to move forward with grit, determination, and extraordinary courage.

Addie Mae, Denise, Carole, and Cynthia were talented, gifted, and dedicated young girls who brought joy to their families, friends, and church. They were taken by the hands of hate and racism in the most violent of ways. History will forever remember this sacrificial time period. These four girls became monumental catalysts towards significant change and equality reform in America. A long time coming, the Civil Rights Act was passed in 1964 and the Voting Rights Act passed in 1965. The senseless deaths of four innocent girls brought momentum, inspiration, and hope to the horrific struggles of the Civil Rights Movement.

The intention of the following work of historical fiction is to remember these young girls whose lives had been filled with the greatest of potential, acknowledging they would have been capable of becoming whatever they envisioned had their lives not been taken from them on that atrocious fateful day, September 15, 1963.

1

THE ATTACK ON HOPE

*Then from the smoke came locusts on the earth, and they
were given power like the power of scorpions of the earth.*

Revelation 9:3

SEPTEMBER 15, 1963

IT WAS A beautiful warm late summer day, but the sky had a sulky over-
cast with the sunshine only mildly peering out through the cluster of
foreboding clouds. It was almost as though the sun was afraid to send
its bold and luminous rays out to witness the tragic events looming on
the morning's tail. By all appearances it was a typical, chaotic Sunday
morning, adults and kids alike running around with many things to do
and places to be.

Josephine Bee Johnson awoke to the shrill of her Auntie Birdie's
voice at an octave she reserved only for Sunday mornings. Josie had
slept in on the Lord's day, and this was not acceptable.

Berniece Thomas was an icon in the community, to put it mildly.
She was revered by the entire family and practically sainted in the renowned Rosewood Street Baptist Church. The duly devoted leader of

the Hallelujah Circle, Birdie's home-cooked comfort meals were legendary, and the other group ladies suspected folks sometimes exaggerated their hardships in hopes of receiving some of her famous food. It had never been beyond Miss Birdie, as she was usually called, to serve up a real special meal before an important deacon or board meeting where issues about to be discussed might affect the Hallelujah Circle's enormous and growing budget needs. Truth was there was always someone somewhere who was hungry and in need of the Hallelujah Circle's healing food and fellowship. The Circle felt this to be the acute focus of their spreading ministry. Praise Jesus and pass the fried chicken, please!

Miss Birdie usually used her buttery sweet tone to influence others. She could diffuse anger, encourage laughter, and promote peace all without raising her voice, as if she were simply reciting her ABC's. Her soft lullaby voice was not present at this moment in time, however. Not once but twice Josie's older sister, Pearl, had rushed in to urge Josie to "rise and shine and give God the glory." Momma and Daddy had never been big churchgoers, but they certainly did not discourage Auntie Birdie from coming over whenever she was inclined and snatching both girls for a Sunday school experience or revival jubilee.

"Pure joy to be in God's house!" Auntie would enthusiastically exclaim after passionately waving her hands in the air anytime she wanted to emphasize how grand it was to be going to God's official place of worship. She would have been palms down the best waver in the Macy's Parade—had there been a Macy's Parade for the colored. Pearl idolized Auntie Birdie for her charisma, enthusiasm, and sincere kindness for others.

With nearly four years between them, Pearl had taken great, big-sister care of Josie Bee from the time she was born. Pearl rejoiced in Josie's little victories, cried when she was hurt, and covered for her whenever she crossed the line. Having a willful personality, baby sister frequently and deliberately pushed the boundaries. Momma had occasional headaches that kept her confined to bed so she generally did not notice. But when Daddy caught wind of Josie's bad behavior, Pearl, who preferred a calm environment with rules and boundaries respected and in place, would take the blame and accept the punishment.

It was during Josie's preschool years that Pearl had carved out a special place for her younger sister that comforted and quieted her wandering spirit, keeping her out of conflict with Momma and Daddy. The girls shared a room, and although the bedroom was small, it contained a large wardrobe. Pearl did her best to make the closet a sacred spot where they could escape, shelter down, and enter into a happy existence in their created world. It was rare that the girls did not daily go inside their special space and spend time playing. Pearl had painted the wardrobe the prettiest shade of blue with paint leftover from when their old next-door neighbor Mrs. Russell had painted her front porch. From that very first layer of sky-blue bliss, a peace settled in and the girls' world became a little calmer and brighter.

"Young lady, you best be praying for a set of wings so that you might fly out of that bed this very second," shouted Auntie Birdie, the high-pitched tone in her voice jerking Josie back into reality.

"Auntie Birdie, please calm down," pleaded Josie.

"Josephine Bee Johnson, your lack of discipline and care for others is . . . well, it's a disgrace! You promised the girls, your friends, you would be at their church today. Then you disregard my rules and here you still be," said her Auntie, gasping for air.

Auntie Birdie's breathing was labored. All because of Josie's careless behavior she was close to hyperventilating, which scared Josie. Josie Bee glanced over at Pearl, hoping her big sister would bail her out. But Pearl didn't budge a muscle. Josie was on her own. The disapproval in her eyes hurt almost as much as Auntie Birdie's unexpected outburst.

Suddenly Josie ached for her parents, missed living in her old house with the crabby neighbors next door, and crawling into the safe haven of their old wardrobe. Pearl was the one who had always made everything better, who loved Josie more than she could ever love herself. Pearl allowed her to feel safe. Josie's heart had such a big hole in it that it couldn't hold much of anything these days. Her beloved aunt was the only person in the whole wide world both girls had. She took them in and provided abundantly when their parents were senselessly killed— an act of selflessness that was both personally and financially challenging for her. But Berniece proudly marched to the beat of her God's drum, never shying away from family obligations. An inspiration of charity, Auntie's sacrifice and adoration for her baby sister's children was a vision of both commitment and love. Pearl and Josie would never forget what love in action looked like.

Now Josie Bee had managed in a short period of time to test Auntie Birdie's spirit and aggravate her only sibling. It was a disappointing start to what otherwise had promised to be an interesting day at church. With the youth group in charge of the morning service at the neighboring Sixteenth Street Baptist, watching the kids playing adults was all fun and games for Josie. However, Pearl recognized how dedicated and committed they had been on prior youth Sundays.

"Auntie Birdie, I hear you and I will make it up. Right this second, I will get dressed lickety-split and make it to church for the youth service. I promise," said Josie. She wasn't looking for a miraculous makeover, just to be somewhat acceptable.

Josie knew this was a stretch. Getting dressed and ready for worship was a big ordeal in the church ladies' Sunday-morning lineup. Besides ironing about everything imaginable, hair preparations got well underway on Saturday evening with final touches being expertly performed on Sunday morning. Then it was necessary to choose the right jewelry and complete the look with the perfect matching hat, gloves, and pocketbook—a total presentation purposefully set in place to reflect the importance of going to the house of God. Producing your very best, giving special attention to detail and ornamentation, reflected style and gracious manners. These women took great effort to model proper etiquette and to dress their young ladies in church attire acceptable for a lifetime of service in both God's house and, one day, in their very own homes.

"Pearl, might I count on your efforts to salvage this situation and get your sister to the church in a timely manner?" Auntie asked. "I have my own commitments at Rosewood."

"Yes, ma'am," Pearl gently replied. "Most certainly."

Auntie Birdie inhaled and slowly exhaled. Instantly composed, she wanted to make sure Josie knew that Pearl was sacrificing her time in order to get her moving and to church on time. Poor Pearl, she had been up at the crack of dawn with Auntie for morning coffee and prayer. And now she would be running late, thanks to Josie. However, it was the best that could be done under the circumstances. Auntie announced she was taking the automobile, this being the one time she would allow the girls to walk to the church. No lollygagging or stopping to talk to neighborhood acquaintances or friends. Auntie's instructions were crystal clear, and the ever-obedient Pearl Opal was ready to carry them out.

The sound of the door's firm closing signaled that Berniece Thomas was gone, and the girls flew into action. After what seemed like a small eternity, Pearl and Josie were on their way, half-walking, half-running out of the apartment complex and onto the busy street. Auntie Birdie would not have been thrilled with either of their appearances, but her frequent reminder that "the Lord is more concerned about what is inside your heart than what is on your back," reassured them both. It would not have been a stellar idea, however, nor the right moment to bring that up to Pearl, who wore a scowl on her face and kept her lips tightly pursed. So Josie kept quiet and picked up her pace.

As they walked, Josie observed the noisy neighborhood, a beehive of activity. Big people and little people, young and old, walked down sidewalks as cars pulled out of garages, the impatient honking their horns. Children lined porches as if emerging from assembly lines. Morning light flooded the landscape with a vibrancy and energy that exclaimed celebration on this special day of worship. Those not on their way to church were casually dressed, starting lawnmowers, warming up grills, or whistling along to their favorite tunes on the radio.

The view was like an elaborate symphony of excitement and delightful diversity, lulling Josie into thinking all could be well in her world, despite being fully aware of the strained silence between her and Pearl, whose stillness was unsettling. It wasn't like her sister not to be checking on Josie's feelings or trying to smooth her feathers. Today Pearl looked exceptionally lovely. She wore a strand of pearls, a gift from Auntie Birdie in honor of her high school graduation four years earlier. Pearl Opal Johnson had excelled in school, was considered a shining star and voted Peacemaker of the Year. Pearl was a true gem in every sense of the word, and in comparison, Josie reflected a rough stone or chipped rock. But Pearl had faithfully loved her sister without interruption and in spite of her childish character flaws and ongoing immature ways. Josie was really sorry she had upset Pearl and desperately wanted to make up with her. As they were coming into view of the church, Pearl's focus was getting there on time. Josie Bee would make peace with her sweet sister later. For now, she could live with a bit of silence.

Then—*kaboom!*

A deafening blast knocked Josie and Pearl off their feet. Their noses were filled with what felt like a fine powder. As they coughed and gasped for air, their mouths were filled with dust that tasted like metal and smoke. The girls' throats were suddenly parched. Stinging tears burned their eyes, as they clutched their ears with both hands. The fuzziness in their eardrums was indescribable. Their every move was filled with hesitation. Uncertainty. Indecision.

There was heavy pushing, uncontrolled panic, and ear-piercing screams. The air space was polluted with incoherency and desperation. Breathing was hard. Destruction lay ahead of Josie, behind her, and encircled the two girls like a wake of buzzards. It continued to be near impossible to catch a breath. Nobody had any idea what was going on. Josie couldn't think straight. Everything was jumbled and disconnected. Josie felt like she was having an out-of-body experience. Just then she recalled a recent sermon by a visiting pastor who had spoken at the church. Brother Long had captivated the congregation with his description about a plague of locusts. Exodus 10, or something like that. What did it really matter? Why was his saying the locusts were already among us coming to mind? Was this about locusts? This preacher said they were calculating our every move, anticipating the opportunity to damage our very existence and devour our minds, bodies, and spirits. It is their nature. He urged the congregation to be vigilant and aware that the climate was dark. Although Josie sensed his sincerity, she had brushed his message off. Now she wasn't so sure. This brother was way-over-the-top dramatic, and she wasn't sure whether she believed him much anyway. Brother Long strongly encouraged follow-up readings in Exodus, but Josie disregarded his suggestion with an inward smirk, not interested in the Bible at all. Yet now his words depicting swarming and evil forces flooded back, tumbling continuously in her dismantled mind. Why this connection was clicking, Josie couldn't really explain. It just was. It made her skin crawl as she winced at the possibility of truth in words that forewarned of tragic events. Josie was a nasty mess, her mind jumping all over the place. She was wondering why her parents weren't there. But they were gone, right?

Pearl and Josie struggled to their feet and stumbled back toward each other. They had to find Auntie Birdie. Maybe she already knew. That is how things worked between the two churches, especially being blocks apart. Something happens at one church and the other church was already involved. Sister churches worked like that, and Sixteenth Street Baptist and Rosewood were no exception.

But should Pearl and Josie stay put and assume their Auntie was looking for them, or should they hightail it back to Rosewood in case she had not been alerted? Holding one another for support, the sisters decided to go in search of their Auntie Birdie.

Going forward, the scene was one of mass confusion. People were injured, those attending to them demanding space and clearance. Pearl and Josie were becoming inconsolable. They could not find Auntie. Nothing made any sense and they were at a loss for what to do next.

Then the girls heard the familiar and desperate sound of Auntie's shrill voice piercing through their uncertainty and bewilderment. "Oh, dear Jesus, precious God Almighty, thank you, thank you!" she cried. Auntie Birdie was a big fountain of tears. She clung to Pearl and Josie as if she would never let them go, her head bobbing up and down as she wept with unrestrained relief.

In the heat of the moment and in the midst of the tragedy at hand, Josie Bee vowed to do better by her steadfast Auntie Birdie, giving her the respect and love she had earned. Generously she had offered her and Pearl a home and an opportunity to be safely taken care of after losing their parents only six months earlier. Auntie Birdie had been a part of their lives in the good times and the bad. Auntie was the gift that kept on giving and serving, reliable and safe, and for that both girls were grateful.

In this time of the unknown and the unimaginable, Josie thought about what she had been taking for granted. It made her heart wobble and her insides ache. How dare she be so careless in her attitude and attention to God, to her Auntie, and to her devoted sister? A new sense of appreciation washed over her and took hold in her heart.

Josie Bee was also scared to death. Nothing made sense at all. Nobody seemed to know anything more than Josie did about what had just happened, at least not for sure. But everyone knew enough to understand that Sixteenth Street Baptist Church had been violently attacked. Coming to a full understanding of the evil and wickedness that was released that fateful mid-September morning, one that had begun with sunshine and was ending with irreparable darkness, would take a lifetime.

Soon it became clear that a bomb had caused the explosion. It had been placed below the girls' restroom in the basement of the church. That's what everyone was saying. Members immediately began searching for victims, covering themselves in layers of white powder and shattered glass, hoping to find signs of life amid the destruction and rubble. Tragically, what they found were the splintered and crushed bodies of four young girls: Addie Mae Collins, Denise McNair, Carole Robertson, and Cynthia Wesley. The girls had been in the restroom finishing up preparations for the youth-run morning service, tidying their hair and smoothing out their dresses, when the explosion happened.

What appeared to be a deliberate act of violence leveled at the church's congregation—and specifically at children—was beyond comprehension. The disbelief and raw shock of an apparent bombing and subsequent confirmed casualties created chaos and confusion, producing riots with uncontrollable actions. More than twenty others were seriously injured in the blast. Addie Mae's ten-year-old sister, Sarah, suffered irremediable damage to both her eyes. She would remain in the hospital for two months, eventually losing one eye. The wounds would last a lifetime. There were also two separate tragedies later that day with violent outcomes involving two young boys: Virgil Ware, a thirteen-year-old, and Johnny Robinson, a sixteen-year-old, were killed during the mass upheaval following the explosion. One was shot by a policeman, the other in a drive-by shooting as a result of the ongoing civil unrest. The murders of the children ripped deeply into the hearts and souls of the weary community, continuing to burden their already exhausted spirits.

The ceaseless fight for equal rights was taking a dramatic toll on Birmingham and its citizens. Hate had seemingly and successfully reached into the beloved safe haven of the church and all it represented. The church had continuously built its people up as life outside was brutally trying to tear them down day by day. It was the enforcer that the hopes and dreams in the hearts of the church family would come together and emerge one day into a better tomorrow. It provided the needed refuge in which to keep believing, to keep moving in the right direction for change. It mourned, it cared, it celebrated, it sacrificed to bring restoration and peace forward. And now it was compromised and violated. The depth of sadness and disbelief was shockingly off the charts. The Ku Klux Klan had been responsible for bombing after bombing, and now they had somehow done the unimaginable: murdered and destroyed young, innocent children in their beloved church. Trying to bring the KKK to justice would be a tremendously difficult ongoing process. It would be filled with more disbelief, frustration, and continuous agony for all suffering from racism, inequality, and the failures of the justice system. Weighing heaviest and hurting most would be the unresolved and irreplaceable loss of loved ones.

On the unforgettable morning of this Birmingham church bombing, the Sunday school lesson taught was "A Love That Forgives." Is there a limit on the depth of forgiveness or the type of love that can forgive? Do we have to forgive? Josie Bee had her own issues of trying to forgive others for their deliberate acts of destruction. Missing her Momma and Daddy, she didn't have to look far to find pain and sorrow. The loss of both parents was cruel. Josie's bitter heart had no room for pardon for those who had struck her parents only six months earlier. No one had been arrested or held accountable for the hit-and-run car accident that claimed both their lives. Simply crossing the street after a Friday night at the movies proved deadly.

How on earth could the parents of these promising kids forgive these horrific murderers? Josie Bee couldn't wrap her head around the possibility. The Klan had poured continuous deadly poison into many, many lives, and the damage was indescribable. There were steps to that type of ongoing forgiveness that would be too much for Josie to understand. She wouldn't know where to begin. Her hardened heart was not interested in letting anyone off the hook for anything. She had already been in a state of anger and bitterness, and this bombing pushed those feelings to a new level of darkness.

In these days of severe unrest, Josie still knew there were good people out there—there just had to be those who would help others continue on. The women of the Hallelujah Circle at Rosewood would be heavily involved in the painful days to come assisting their Sixteenth Street sisters and brothers, taking care of the brokenhearted with outstretched hands, compassionately preparing meals before, during, and after the upcoming funerals. The churches supported one another. It was what they did. Like the sun coming up every day, you could count on the Circle sisters to show up and give their best to those in need of their assistance. They considered it an unspoken honor to demonstrate their love through support and prayers for the hurting families of the children and the victims of the horrific explosion. This kind of tragedy, one that purposefully claimed the lives of innocent children, affected a multitude in ways unimaginable and unforeseen. In the meantime, however, being nourished and fed remained a necessity, in order to gain the strength and stamina to persist in getting through what needed to happen. They needed to continue standing in the aftermath of this great loss. They knew they were in for the battle of a lifetime in securing justice for the innocent lives lost. Like glue, food brings people together, holding them in support and unity. The Hallelujah Circle's job was to make the best comfort food possible and to serve it with tenderness and compassion and without any judgment whatsoever. It was how they worked.

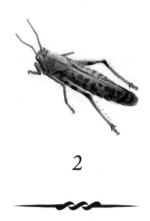

2

———

THE CHALLENGE

Man must evolve for all human conflict a method
which rejects revenge, aggression, and retaliation.
The foundation of such a method is love.

Martin Luther King Jr.

MID-JULY 1965

THE HALLELUJAH CIRCLE at Rosewood Street Baptist Church was
again meeting to do what they did best, creating and serving meals
that soothed and comforted the heavyhearted, broken individuals and
families within their cherished community. Today the ladies were preparing for a funeral.

These kinds of funeral preparations were a regular event and they
expected it. However, funerals were not the only time they produced
incredible and creative foods. The Circle celebrated with great magnifi-
cence happy events in the church as well. Dinners, baptisms, weddings,
and other celebrations were always elaborate.

While God was ultimately the head and inspiration for the large
kitchen ministry, Berniece Thomas was His commander-in-chief.

Outstanding leader that she was, the efficient Birdie fully understood the importance of encouraging and uplifting each of her ladies in their recognized gifted area.

It was understood that Eunice Wilson was to be the one who scrubbed the enormous black-and-white-checked linoleum flooring that eye-catchingly popped amid the textured lemon-yellow painted walls. The tool of choice in her cleaning box was a denture toothbrush, which Miss Eunice used to relentlessly scour the floor's corners, resulting in an immaculate and spotless reflection.

On the other hand, Delphina Porter operated in a haphazard way that obviously lacked that quality of detailed neatness. After greasing down cookie sheets and baking pans, one was captivated by the joyous jig Delphina performed when sprinkling the flour on top of the well-oiled bakeware. It looked as though the holiday snow machine got turned on and then nobody switched it off. The newly sifted white powder wafted through the air, softly settling on counters and appliances.

Each and every participant recognized their invaluable contribution, and together as a team the Hallelujah Circle utilized one another's gifts and talents to further advance the kingdom of their Lord and Savior.

Private concerns and sensitive issues could also be brought into the protective kitchen by those seeking the Circle's confidence. It was a safe place to vent. It was unthinkable that any of the ladies could work next to someone and not notice pain or sadness, let alone go about their business and pretend it didn't exist. When one member was troubled, it disturbed the entire unit. That being said, rule number one—and it stood firm—was that there was not to be intentional gossip brought in at any time. Requesting prayer for someone as a lead-in to dumping the latest bit of scandal into the ears of others was strictly prohibited. If you felt the need to spill some beans, you best have been praying and checking your heart with what Jesus might do and be clear on your intentions before releasing sensitive material. Doing so risked the justified irritation of the Circle. Nobody looked forward to becoming the subject of the group's scrutiny or the embarrassment of a scolding by Berniece Thomas. Birdie was always respectful and kind but simultaneously firm.

Rules were in place, spoken and unspoken, to prevent uncontrolled outbursts and bad behavior in general. This was to promote gentle hearts for the common good and well-being of the entire Hallelujah Circle family. The melodious coexistence the many women shared was the result of a well-tended, ongoing effort. It was like keeping the weeds out of the garden before they could take hold and flourish. Certain buds had to be nipped, and Birdie was the designated bud-nipper.

The women of Rosewood's Hallelujah Circle never viewed any situations as obligations or burdens but instead as valuable opportunities in which to carry out their mission. To the best of their abilities, individually and collectively, the Circle warmly accepted all requests regardless of their size.

It had been close to two years since they had assisted with the meal preparation for the funerals of the precious girls murdered in the September '63 bombing at Sixteenth Street Baptist Church. The expressions of shock locally, nationally, and around the world apparently were not enough to compel either local law enforcement or the Federal Bureau of Investigation to pursue justice for the men responsible for the murders. The Klan was notorious for their cowardly and intimidating acts of violence and racial hatred. It was strongly suspected that the bombing was in direct retaliation for the success the Birmingham kids had earned during the May Children's March, which had taken place just four months before the church bombing. Josie would never forget the way in which she and the other participants had been treated. The police were not their friends and went to great lengths to abuse their power, show their irritation, and lash out in anger toward them.

The peaceful walk across town had been meticulously organized to demonstrate the need for civil rights and equality. The efforts resulted in roughly a thousand children being arrested. It both captivated and enraged the nation as a whole. More importantly, this event placed a direct spotlight on the struggle and brutality of the civil rights movement raging in the South, which then permeated the entire country. When people saw the mistreatment of children, it was explosive, providing urgent fuel in moving the nation forward toward recognizing and resolving these issues. The kids bravely demonstrated persistence in the face of violent blasts from powerful firehoses and attacks by large, vicious dogs. The horrendous tactics used by those in government roles and positions of authority were shocking.

Who attacks children? Who does these things and why do good people turn their heads? Or are they not really good folks after all? How can others pretend they don't see evil and why are the guilty not convicted? The questions just didn't stop. Justice was absent from the lives of the innocent, and surely the locusts of racism were unleashed, enabling the shameless and the wicked to carry on. It was crushing to Josie that the killers had not been brought to justice. Nor had there been evidence of progress being made in the nearly two years since the 1963 church bombing. Justice was neither prevailing nor ringing true in Birmingham, Alabama. The broken wheels of the legal system remained unfixed. The stalling prevented justice and closure for the victims' families, the church population, and the entire city.

One of the most anticipated events of the year was the Sweet Sixteen Jubilee at Rosewood Street Baptist every September, with preparations already beginning now in mid-July. The women of the Circle usually had a ball experimenting and creating the cakes for it. The ladies were experts at producing impressive results with their varied efforts.

This was the year, however, that Addie, Carole, and Cynthia should have been celebrating their sixteenth birthdays with their families, friends, and church community. And now they wouldn't be. They had been vivacious, beautiful, and aspiring girls of faith. Smart, funny, and bursting with a limitless spectrum of talent and aspirations, they had the potential and ability to tackle anything. The tragic events that unfolded that fateful morning of September the 15th, Youth Sunday, 1963, resulted in the loss of these promising young girls and traumatized a multitude of others. A bomb does that; it changes everything.

That was why many of the fallen girls' friends, children and adults alike, thought it would be a sweet act of remembrance to celebrate the three oldest girls and to invite their parents, family, and friends to Rosewood's Sixteenth Jubilee. Usually reserved for Rosewood's girls only, this celebration would demonstrate how special the four girls were and would be a true time of acknowledgment—a testament to their lives and time at Sixteenth Street Baptist Church. The sense of unity and support between the churches was second to none. Pearl led the action to make their requests a reality. She expressed the sincere thoughts and hopes of many to make this addition to Rosewood's 1965 Sweet Sixteen Jubilee to include Addie, Carole, and Cynthia. It was also noted to honor Denise in three years, and to invite her family and friends as well. It was humbly and readily accepted by the Circle planners.

Members of Rosewood Street Baptist Church highly anticipated the sixteenth-birthday celebrations. The older girls were excitedly over the moon looking forward to meeting individually with the Hallelujah Circle's cake committee, which provided the cakes for the Sweet Sixteen Jubilee. The Hallelujah Circle had a great deal of fun providing this meaningful and celebratory service recognizing and honoring their young ladies. The church, along with families and friends of the girls, created what were called Sweet Memories, which celebrated each girl's unique, special qualities. These memories would be read aloud in front of those attending the festive gala. How bitterly sad that three of this year's celebrants would not be there to hear their memories read. They would not get to taste the cakes of their choice. The young ladies would never be forgotten, but hearts were still split wide open. Tears of deep sorrow mixed with frustration continued to flow. The fact that the shattered wheels of justice still weren't moving only made things worse.

Maybe that was part of the reason why Pearl's announcement of her desire to join the Hallelujah Circle a few months earlier had meant so much to her Auntie. She knew the coming months would be especially heavy and burdensome, and Pearl's offer gave her a sense of strength. Birdie was taken by surprise when Pearl gently rose from the Wednesday night prayer service to humbly offer her permanent involvement in the Circle. "Amen" and "glory" flew off the tongues of the ladies, and with hugs and squeezes, Pearl was readily accepted into the sisterhood. Auntie Birdie was overcome with emotion to be able to share her passion in ministry with her beloved niece. She had longed for this moment of commitment, to work side by side with Pearl.

"This means the world to me, Pearl," Auntie Birdie exclaimed. With the group's members nodding in agreement, she continued, "The

Circle is both delighted and honored. Goodness knows we are not getting any younger and relish your talented hands and sweet spirit."

More "amens" resounded throughout the group.

"It is my sincere pleasure to assist the Hallelujahs in their mission
to serve others, and I take my entry into this crucial ministry very seriously. I am in awe of your dedication and continued faithfulness to
others," said Pearl. "Thank you for your example, and for allowing me
this opportunity to serve."

This development came as no surprise to Josie, however. Pearl had
shared her intentions with Josie beforehand about making it official.
She had consistently been available to help Auntie and the ladies out
when needed and knew it would please them when she made her participation permanent. Once again, Pearl knew exactly what to say and
how to graciously and humbly place adoration on others. This kitchen
commitment was certainly never going to be Josie's thing. All those
ladies in one room made Josie a bit claustrophobic. Plus, there was a
lot of time and work involved, and Josie wasn't a fan of commitment.
This bit of information about the Circle, Josie would realize later, was
one of the last things Pearl would openly share with her.

As the Circle began preparations for the upcoming funeral dinner,
Pearl became an instant hit. She readily took direction from others,
had an engaging and easygoing personality, and was a hard worker.
Accepting her role as a floater, Pearl moved around and filled in wherever she was most needed. Auntie Birdie continued to praise her dili-
gence, repeatedly expressing her thankfulness at having Pearl in their
midst. She was an inspiration to the ladies, and they in turn were grateful for her calming presence regardless of the task at hand. She was such
a sweet addition, and the group felt blessed, wishing there were a dozen
more like her.

Auntie Birdie and Pearl had double-teamed Josie Bee to persuade
her to help with the overwhelming preparations for an exceptionally
large funeral party. Chuckling, they both figured Josie would be just
grand at washing and peeling the roughly forty pounds of potatoes
that awaited them. It would give Josie something to do, and the others

were delighted too. Trying hard not to let their giddiness at avoiding this unpopular task slip out, they agreed that Josie Bee's rambunctious energy would be put to good use.

The workplace experience quickly started to wear on Josie Bee. She nicked herself with the paring knife right at the beginning. Her back ached, and her eyes were tired of looking at the buttery-yellow walls. In fact, they were making her eyes swim, causing her to feel somewhat nauseous. She rolled her eyes. The whole service thing was not her cup of tea, and she couldn't foresee it being any part of her future. Josie wasn't sure what she wanted to do with her life, but really, what was the big hurry? Sometimes she felt indirectly pressured by her Auntie, but she understood that Auntie Birdie wanted only the best for her. Josie Bee loved her for that.

Josie desperately wanted to go home. Looking around, she noted that the average age in this kitchen had to be close to seventy. Josie marveled at the ladies' ability to forge ahead. To get their jobs done and to do it all without any mumbling or complaining was astonishing. Josie's head throbbed.

"Pearl, hey Pearl," Josie whispered. "Do you think I might be able to slip out in just a few? I'm feeling a bit queasy."

"Throw-up queasy or tired queasy, Josie?" Pearl said, rolling her eyes in a way that indicated her guess was the latter. "Really, we're almost finished."

And with that Josie Bee knew she best complete what she had reluctantly started. There would be no messing with any of these people, Pearl having been her best shot at cutting short the potato process.

Josie turned back to mindlessly peeling the spuds and fell to thinking. These days Pearl just wasn't herself. Josie, who knew her sister inside and out, wasn't sure what to make of it. Josie felt like Pearl wasn't as interested in her feelings and opinions anymore. Sometimes Josie felt like Pearl wasn't even aware she was in the same room. This had been going on for a while, but now Josie was getting more curious. She felt as though she were prying when she looked into her sister's eyes for any length of time. She just didn't know what she was looking for. When there *was* a chance to talk about things, Pearl seemed uninterested or distracted. Even though Pearl was always in control with an even display of emotion, Josie could tell when she was thinking about something, and that seemed to happen frequently these days. And what's more, the tiny one-syllable sound she made when she quietly coughed was becoming more frequent. Pearl had had this little quirky but cute outtake of breath for as long as Josie could remember. It probably was more habit than anything and nothing to be concerned about. Just one more thing that made the unassuming Pearl simply more adorable.

Josie finished a potato, tossed it into the sink, and started another.

Also, she thought, there had been sightings of Pearl in strange places, allegedly with a young man by the name of Jumpin' James Black. Nobody put much stock in the rumors. Jumpin' wouldn't have been Pearl's type anyway, even if she were interested in dating relationships, which she wasn't. She had made that quite clear. There had been and continued to be plenty of young hopefuls who vied for her attention, all of whom the beautiful Pearl abruptly dismissed. This probably pleased Auntie Birdie, leaving her with one less thing to worry about and a dependable companion to accompany her to church activities. Many of which were surely created to keep the mature ladies occupied and entertained. Rosewood Baptist had something going every day of the week. The church doors were never officially closed, although after the Sixteenth Street bombing, security had had to be added and observed across the board in all the churches. The history of the church was divided into two eras: before the bombing and after the bombing. Auntie Birdie was always grateful for an escort and thankful for Pearl's willingness to accompany her. Josie preferred other activities, usually appearing busy but in reality purposefully concealing her plans.

Josie Bee wasn't quite sure what she did and did not believe in as far as church went and was not willing to commit in one direction or the other. Josie was more comfortable hanging out with the friends she had developed over the past year or so, ones interested in real change and set on doing something about the unrest and lack of true advances in the civil rights movement. These were the doers that had Josie's attention. She felt as though she had purpose and hope, that these determined activists counted on changing something. They weren't going to wait, and she wanted that too. Josie knew she was one of the sole reasons Auntie was on her knees much of the night at times, but goodness, she didn't ask Auntie Birdie to drop down and petition on her behalf. But she did. Josie rolled her eyes. Whatever.

If Josie had heard it once, she had heard it a hundred times. Auntie Birdie's daddy was remembered for his direct go-to instruction: "If you don't have holes in your pants you aren't working hard enough or you aren't praying hard enough!" Followed by a stern "Let's visit that." Daddy Thomas also said, "Get an education—no one can take that from you." It wasn't surprising his middle daughter had a storehouse of snappy responses in her repertoire. Auntie Birdie was quick on words and wisdom. But Josie had thus far put into practice neither of those pieces of instruction given by Auntie Birdie's daddy.

Someday Josie Bee would be mightily reminded of the tender acts of Auntie Birdie's faithfulness and devotion to her Lord and deep concern for Josie's soul. To continuously be at the forefront of one's mind, to be thought of day after day in this way, is indeed a powerful gift of love and commitment. Josie would have much to learn about matters of the heart. But at this point in time, her heart was in a different place than her Auntie's, and Josie was okay with that.

Pearl, for her part, went along with the entire church scene, although there had been a time when she was a bit more detached and off on her own. It was during that time that she encountered Jumpin' James quite by accident. She found herself unexpectedly distracted by his striking good looks and overtaken by his charm and gregarious personality. Pearl, best known for her gentle and graceful movements, all but tripped over herself. Like a dancer with two left feet.

No one could have been more surprised at the kaleidoscope of butterflies flurrying in the depths of her belly that day than Pearl herself. The sensation was unfamiliar but not unpleasant. She wanted to cup her mouth for fear the butterflies would escape, and then everyone in the room would know that the reserved and elusive Pearl Johnson was falling for the likes of Jumpin'. That chance encounter would prove to be a game changer, sending Pearl on the ride of her life.

Pearl had bumped into Jumpin' at the Corner Bookstore, which was created and supported by the Colored Reading Council. It was a great asset to their community and an enjoyable place to pick up exciting reading materials and current books. Pearl popped in to check out a book on sea glass that a previous teacher had strongly recommended. Browsing and absorbed in the shelves of reading material, Pearl was taken aback by a deep voice that seemed directed at her.

"Hello there, Miss Pearl, fancy bumping into you," the readily recognizable James Black commented. Pearl knew who Jumpin' was, but it was the fact that he called her by name that jarred her. She found to her surprise, however, that she didn't mind being unsettled.

"You must forgive me, but have we met before?" Pearl inquired. She had seen him from a distance several times and was well aware of his reputation as a ladies' man. Tall, dark, and incredibly handsome, he was something to look at in person.

"You mean formally or informally?" Jumpin' said in a toying way.

Pearl liked the sound of his buttery smooth voice. It was calming. Soothing. And Miss Pearl felt as though she could at any moment melt into a puddle on the floor smack in front of the bookstore and everyone in it.

Pulling herself together, she extended her hand. "Pearl Johnson, and it is a pleasure to officially meet you, Mr. Black."

"Ahhh, so you do know my name." He grinned.

"And you know mine. I don't know which of us should be more surprised," Pearl teased. "I must say, I am curious about what kind of reading material it is that you might find interesting and worthy of your time?"

"Pearl, are you doubting my ability to invest in a good read? Surely you know that one should never judge a book by its cover, right?" Jumpin' was totally in his element and enjoying himself.

Pearl was completely caught up in the newfound magic of Jumpin' James. When he glanced at his watch and softly stated that he hoped to catch up with her again real soon, Pearl didn't know what to say. When she finally spoke, he was already gone.

Not quite sure what to make of the encounter, Pearl kept it entirely to herself. She anxiously looked for Jumpin' everywhere she went for several days after their encounter at the Corner Bookstore but then settled down and tried to dismiss the situation altogether. She realized she was acting like a silly schoolgirl and scolded herself for being vulnerable. Six days later Jumpin' again was able to take her by surprise and reduce her to mush.

Pearl had decided to treat Auntie Birdie and Josie to a box of doughnuts from Crawford's, the best bakery in their part of town. She spent a few minutes enjoying the view of the big storefront window, knowing exactly what she would get once she went in. As Pearl entered, Mr. Crawford greeted her, saying he would be right back. Responding to the beeping timer, he headed to the back to remove some things from the big oven. Sitting down at one of the corner tables, Pearl was happy to have a minute to herself and leisurely kicked back.

"Is there anything sweeter in this shop than you, Pearl Johnson?" Jumpin' asked.

Startled, Pearl lurched forward. "I am most certain there is," she replied. "What kind of sweets are you hankerin' for?" This time she was more prepared to banter.

"Something incredibly different, I guess," James sincerely responded.

"Might you care to join me? Mr. Crawford is detained in the kitchen," said Pearl. It was unusually quiet in the normally busy bakery. "I had no idea you would have such a sweet tooth, James," Pearl playfully cooed.

"And I had no indication that I would have the pleasure of this encounter," he shot back.

"Really? And how often do you come here?" Pearl quizzed.

James seemed to ponder his answer. "I can't exactly say that I do on a regular basis, but I may more often in the future. In fact, I am sure of that possibility and thank you for asking."

"Why do I get the feeling you might be following me, sir?"

"Maybe I'm just watching out for you, Pearl," Jumpin' offered.

"Is that good to know? I'm not sure I know precisely how to take this newly discovered information. Do I need your eyes on me? Do I need extra protection?" Pearl sweetly inquired.

"I think we all do. It's always good to have others watch out for you," James insisted.

"Are there big bad boogeymen out there, James?" Pearl asked.

"Always. You need to be aware of that. I will watch out for you, Pearl, I mean that," James said. "And I will do my best to keep an eye out for your curious little sister too."

"Josie? I'm not sure what you mean, but she *can* be a handful. Thank you, I appreciate knowing you are out there," Pearl said.

Pearl unconsciously toyed and twisted with the bow tied at the neck of her pale-yellow blouse. Jumpin' reached across the table and lightly steadied his fingers on hers. "Have I said too much? Do I make you nervous? Uncomfortable?"

Pearl wasn't sure what to say. Her desire to convey only exactly what she wanted to say created a lapse in her response.

"Pearl?" James softly prompted.

"I'm sorry. No, not at all," she honestly replied. "I'm just not used to someone looking out for me is all. I am genuinely touched. Thank you."

Charles Crawford stepped back in behind his pastry-filled showcases just in time to witness the tender moments between the two young adults. He smiled. Then he tactfully popped back into the kitchen to allow the kids a few more moments to enjoy themselves.

With time seemingly standing still, the feelings passing between Pearl and James were electric. Pearl was aware of Jumpin's hand so close to her heart. Surely, she thought, he could feel how fast it was beating.

"Jumpin' . . . ," Pearl began.

"Shhhh, Pearl . . . you are not only the sweetest thing in this shop, you are by far the sweetest thing in this world."

Pearl was tempted to place her other hand on top of his, but Mr. Crawford noisily came out of the kitchen. Clearing his throat, he apologized. "I am very sorry to have kept you waiting. Now what may I get for you, Ms. Johnson?"

And just like that the charm and play came to an end. James gave Pearl a wink and stood up. Pearl Opal was befuddled and out of sorts.

That was then.

But here and now in the church kitchen, under control, Pearl was operating in the venue she was most comfortable with—being the person everyone else wanted and needed her to be. She had no energy or desire to hop onto the merry-go-round of emotions Jumpin' sent spinning around in her. Right now she wanted to stay in her zone and do what she could to be available to Auntie Birdie and the busy ladies of the kitchen. From time to time Josie needed Pearl's attention, but even now Pearl felt freer to let her go, to let her impetuous younger sister experience life in any way she wanted. And this evening she could read Josie like a novel, almost word for word. Josie had been ready to check out hours ago and was not enjoying her given assignment. Eventually, however, she did finish, and now the ladies were eager to call it a night and go their separate ways.

There was a scattered chorus of "amen" and "hallelujah" from the ladies, followed by an under-the-breath "about time" from Josie, as they all headed for the door. Auntie Birdie and her two tuckered nieces beelined it to the parking lot, where even the old Buick looked tired and ready to split the scene.

A day wasn't complete without sitting down to watch Walter Cronkite on the CBS evening news. He was the man folks trusted to deliver the day's news. How he handled the 1963 church bombing tragedy would never be forgotten. Cronkite had read a column written by Gene Patterson, the editor of the *Atlanta Constitution*, that was brutally honest regarding what happened in the Sixteenth Street Baptist Church. Cronkite asked Patterson to read it on the air. Patterson urged the world to "never forget the Birmingham, Alabama, church bombing or the mother who held her dead child's shoe." For Berniece Thomas and many others in Birmingham, Cronkite became a symbol of truth and compassion and a daily fixture in their lives. Auntie faithfully watched his program each and every evening. And tonight would be no different.

As the girls got ready for bed, Auntie Birdie watched CBS and then prepared her nightly chamomile tea. She retired to her room earlier than normal. Everyone was preparing for an early night's sleep. Beating Josie to the bathroom, Pearl forfeited her routine evening bath in order to quickly get in and out. Josie did not dawdle much either. She was exhausted and had a sense of emptiness overall. Time spent in the Hallelujah kitchen wasn't one bit what Josie had in mind for an exciting or meaningful experience, but she had chosen the path of least resistance in giving in to Auntie Birdie and Pearl. At least her participation seemed to make Auntie happy. Josie felt that Pearl saw through her flimsy attempts to fit into their expectations. As she hopped into bed, she vowed to stay out of the kitchen in the near future.

All three women sought a much-needed, peaceful night's slumber. A dark sky had been lingering on the horizon, but it looked to be a quick hitter and not a problem for the night hours. Each dropped off to sleep the moment her head landed on the goose-down feather pillow.

The next thing Josie knew, a thunderous sound followed by a loud crackle and pop splintered through her short-lived peaceful quiescence. Josie Bee instinctively popped up out of bed and stood up. It was as if she was being involuntarily pulled toward the window. Once there Josie gripped its frame with both hands, peering out at the great amounts of rain furiously running down the panes. The sound was somewhat soothing to Josie, which surprised her. She wondered if this was how the tears and heartache of others in pain and sorrow might collectively look, rolling and rolling with no beginning or end in sight. She recalled hearing someone say when she was a child that when it rained it meant angels in heaven were really sad. When they cry you would see the raindrops and know it was so. Stick your tongue out and you would taste their salt. The rain picked up and intensified, pounding sharply against the glass. Josie was mesmerized.

Almost as quickly as it had started the rain stopped, the thunder ceased, and an enveloping hush of silence filled the room, quieting the earth. Gone were the hundreds of pooling tears against the windowsill, and the darkness was replaced with a ray of light shining from the heavens above. A spectacular moon hung in the sky, breaking through the clouds. In that moment Josie had a personal connection with the Almighty. God spoke to Josie Bee Johnson. Clearly and simply. It wasn't a frightening or a booming voice, but one filled with gentleness, compassion, and direction meant for Josie's ears.

Since the bombing at the church, Josie's anger and frustration had focused on the loss of Addie, Denise, Carole, and Cynthia. It landed there because she could relate to someone being in the wrong place at the wrong time. But how could it happen in a church? Their church. She blamed God for failing to protect the girls. If He didn't do it for them then, why should she trust Him with her life? They had it all going on, were poised for success, and Josie paled in comparison. She could never be as good as those girls were, even if she lived to be a hundred years old. Angry thoughts and feelings had been growing, beginning with the loss of her parents and intensifying by the deaths and devastation caused by the Klan's bombing.

Now captivated, Josie listened as God spoke clearly to her.

"I love you, Josie Bee. I love you too much to not allow you the opportunity to find your true heart and purpose. I see your pain and understand your hurts. I have a challenge for you, Josie, and you will never be alone through this. Listen to my servants. You must trust me, and you must trust them. Because they know me, they can help you."

What God was proposing made no sense to Josie. Did this have to do with the church bombing? She couldn't get her head around it. What did He mean by "a challenge"? Josie was no Moses nor was she some kind of miracle worker. Given her evident lack of faith, she was not a practical or probable candidate for anything orchestrated by God. She barely even knew who God was. All Josie's pent-up anger came rushing to the surface, flowing into her fists as she let loose, banging on the window.

"Are you kidding me, God?" she cried out. "The answer is no, no, and more no!"

Josie Bee was taken aback by her blatant boldness. She glanced over her shoulder toward Pearl, who was amazingly still sleeping through Josie's spiritual conversation. Or maybe Pearl was pretending not to hear because she didn't want to get involved in the craziness.

"Dang it, Pearl, help me out here," Josie said over her shoulder. "C'mon, I know you can hear me."

Then God spoke directly and clearly to her again. "The decision is yours alone, Josie. I love you. I will wait for your answer. There is no rush."

And that was the last thing Josie heard God speak. She never doubted for a minute what she had heard. So, was she off her rocker? Or was God off His?

Josie ceased her assault on the window. She was drained and exhausted, wanting only to run and hide. Pulling herself together, she ran to Pearl, who had gotten up and was now crossing the room, coming toward her with open arms.

"There, there, baby girl, everything's going to be okay. I promise you that," Pearl whispered in her ear.

Holding her tight, Josie told Pearl all she knew, exactly what she thought she had heard, and the challenge God had mentioned.

"I told Him no, over and over, Pearl," gasped Josie. "I meant it. I can't do this, I don't get it and I won't do it! Please, Pearl, I have to go to my safe place, and I need to know I am not going crazy," Josie whispered to her sister.

Together they huddled in the bottom of the closet atop Momma's quilt, the one that had been loved and handed down by their great-grandmother Rose. With its yellows and blues, each square containing lovely detailed flowers, it had always made them feel comforted and special. Pearl slipped a pillow under Josie's weary head, cradling her like a helpless infant as she had when Josie was a baby in need of comfort. Half-embarrassed and half not believing what had just taken place, Josie clutched Pearl. The tears rolled down her cheeks. Pearl cried too, and together they tasted the salt of their mingled tears.

"I need to know you believe me," whimpered Josie.

"And you need to know I believe in you," replied Pearl.

And with the wardrobe door wide open, moonlight peeked in and rested on the faces of the two sisters as they slept gently, undisturbed throughout the night.

3

The Kindness of Others

*Sometimes those who give the most are
the ones with the least to spare.*

Mike McIntyre

Josie woke up in the corner of her impromptu safety spot on the closet
floor. It had been in another lifetime when she had last been on the
floor of a closet. Josie Bee was alone, which immediately set off warning bells. How late was it and where was Pearl?

Recalling the previous evening's experience with God, Josie felt help-
lessly exhausted, wondering what to do next. It certainly had not crossed
her mind to withhold any of what she had experienced when babbling to
her sister. She didn't tell Pearl not to share it with anyone because surely
she didn't need to. Pearl would recognize it was a private conversation
between them, albeit a confusing one. Josie had confided everything she
could remember to Pearl. She had been on the edge of hysteria, and her
trusted anchor, Pearl, had come to her rescue. Josie Bee was still in a state
of semi-disbelief that she had firmly and unconditionally spoken to God.
And she instinctively had said no. "No" as in "not me." No, you have the

wrong person. And no, I still have not changed my mind. This was insane, and Josie was not going anywhere to do anything that was suggested to her during a storm in the middle of the night. Not now and not ever. Period. Exclamation mark. End of story.

However, something wasn't right. Josie's immediate fear was that Pearl had gone to Auntie Birdie and unloaded the fragmented story complete with her disrespectful response to God. If that happened, all heck would break loose. And fast. Truth be told, right now Josie was more afraid of Berniece Thomas than she was of the Almighty God.

"Let me think, let me think," Josie chanted over and over, not wanting to believe her sister could have betrayed her. What if Pearl had taken the situation to Auntie and had already spoken about the not-intended-to-be-shared drama with her? This would not fare well for Josie no matter how you sliced it. Josie had to hold it together and stand her ground, whatever that meant. It would be considerably easier if this situation stayed between God, herself, and Pearl. And if it didn't, Josie had no idea where to turn.

What to do next? Josie remembered that Pearl had mentioned a dental appointment for ten o'clock that morning with Dr. Tibbs. If she wasn't home, she had probably already left for the dentist's office. Josie could zip over to the waiting room and snag Pearl to ensure that their previous night's conversation stayed between themselves. The good doctor routinely ran thirty to forty-five minutes behind, and Pearl always arrived a half hour early with a book tucked in her purse. Another one of her excellent qualities. She was well-read and made good use of her time. Pearl had been a Girl Scout and took the oath of being prepared to heart, along with all the other rules and regulations. Josie had never had any success with the Brownies, which explained her short-lived involvement in the overrated organization, never going on to the desired Scout level.

Where was I?, Josie wondered. She was getting off track. *Ah yes, what to do next?* "Get yourself dressed and get your butt out of here," she told herself out loud. Her mind made up, she made for the bathroom. A few minutes later, with brushed teeth, mediocre but presentable dress, and unruly hair, Josie flew out of the bathroom like a bat out of hell.

It looked like the coast was clear. Josie sailed through the dining area. She just had to grab her coat off the hall tree and she would be on her not-so-merry way. With a sigh of relief and imminent victory in hand, Josie was clutching the doorknob when Auntie Birdie's voice called her out.

Josie could not catch a break.

"Not so fast, young lady," Auntie exclaimed with her index finger shaking in the air. How did her finger move so rapidly? When she got all worked up she could get her hand to flutter like a tireless hummingbird.

"Josephine, you just back yourself right up," she demanded. "And I mean at once!"

No longer having any question about whether Auntie Birdie knew, Josie became intent on finding out exactly how much she knew. With her back pinned against the closed front door, all she could do was hope that Pearl had not revealed every little detail to their Auntie. Josie's wishful thinking was short-lived.

"Pearl told me all about your late-night discussion with God. Would you like to share any of those details with me, Josie? I am wondering what you must have been thinking speaking to our Lord so pointedly, if I understand your responses correctly?"

What followed shook Josie. She expected anger and condemnation but her Auntie was filled with concern, hesitating as to reconsider her directness and tone. Josie noticed that Auntie Birdie's eyes were misted over. She softened and quietly whispered, "I just don't know what to do with you, baby girl. My best has not been good enough, and I fear I am losing you. I apologize that I have failed you. May God forgive me. I've tried my best."

In the midst of the enormous silence that engulfed the room, Auntie Birdie walked over to the corner desk and picked up her shiny black faux lizard pocketbook. She had carried the same purse for as long as Josie could remember, and yet it looked almost brand-new. It was a testament to her detailed care, which was reflected in everything she tended to and in those she cared for. Poking into the handbag she seized her keys and despondently walked out to the car. There was nothing more that could be said at this moment. Auntie's stooped shoulders and weary demeanor spoke volumes. Berniece Thomas was broken, defeated, and now on her way to the shelter of her beloved church.

Birdie had set the prayer chain in action that very morning. Thankful for Pearl's forthrightness in confiding in her, Birdie nonetheless felt overwhelmed, inadequate, and too emotional to confidently address the situation on her own. Maybe she had called the group more for her own benefit than Josie Bee's. She also let Pearl know that, for some time now, many had been praying for and were deeply invested in Josie's spiritual well-being. Thus, it would be necessary and reasonable to include the Hallelujah Circle in the process of guidance and support for their beloved Josie although the situation was not fully understood at this point.

Berniece started the chain notification process with the Circle's two call warriors, twin sisters Maylene Parks and Marlene Pitts. Both ladies had magnificent phone manners, efficient coordination skills, and success in ringing members in order to collect and organize the chain links of intercession. By the time Birdie walked through the doors of the church, the ladies had set up the hospitality room with several pots of coffee and plates of homemade chewy gingersnaps and chunky peanut butter cookies. They were ready to listen, absorb, and initiate prayer. Birdie was eager to unload the specific details and present the circumstances as clearly as possible.

Referring to Josie's experience as "the Challenge," Birdie gave a fairly accurate account of the facts and particulars, to the best of her ability. When finished she was surrounded by overwhelming support and understanding, yet there was a peppering of disbelief that their Josie, contacted, would possibly not consider something proposed by the Almighty. The women certainly could understand Birdie's predicament. She had more than plenty on her plate. She had been concerned with the ever-blossoming budget needs of the food pantry, the health of her sister Gertie, and the future of her nieces should anything happen to her. Josie had always been a handful, and now the warriors were determined to help guide a headstrong and misguided adolescent trying to process a remarkable interaction with God.

Next on the agenda would be bringing Josie into their circle of love for the mere opportunity of gathering together as a unit of faith. Birdie readily agreed that she would speak with Pearl and together they would come up with a gentle approach to encourage Josie. They wanted her to understand she owed it to her Creator, and to herself, to reconsider the direction of the conversation and not sell either party short. The group agreed to reconvene during the service that night and help Josie figure this whole thing out.

Meanwhile, Pearl returned home from her dental appointment to a very irritated younger sister. Josie was madder than a hornet and instantly lit into her.

"I didn't expect you to be such a big tattletale, Pearl," Josie shouted at her.

"Grow up, Josie. Honestly, you are such a drama queen. You can't always be the baby, have your way, and expect everyone to fall into your whims and whines," said Pearl, tossing back the sharp words faster than you could lick a stamp.

Josie had expected her to back down a bit, but that wasn't going to happen now. Big sister was on her high horse and was just about to let her opinion roll when in marched Auntie Birdie. The spat was on hold. All three of them seemed to be short on patience, weary with unanswered questions and possible misconceptions. Auntie announced that both girls were expected to be at the church promptly at 7:00 p.m. to collect their loose thoughts and feelings on whatever happened the night before.

"Do you think you can do that for me, Josie Bee?" questioned Auntie Birdie. "Be on time, that is. Attending is not an option."

"Sure can—I mean, Yes, ma'am," said Josie, knowing it best not to say another word and trying very hard not to roll her eyes. She retreated with a pout to the bedroom to prepare her case for the cross-examining she surely would be facing from the inner workings of the Hallelujah Circle. Those lady commandos took no prisoners, and she wondered how she would hold up. Josie Bee had not changed her mind about last night's decision, but she owed it to Auntie Birdie to appear before her friends and co-conspirators. Embarrassing her by not doing so wouldn't be right or acceptable in anybody's eyes. Josie didn't want that; she just wanted to move on. She wasn't even sure how to put everything into words but was certain that, although she was dreading the upcoming confrontation, she would face the Circle and then that would be the end of it.

The gathering started promptly with prayer.

These persuasive women were in position and ready to defend God's divine intervention with every breath they had. Their sincerity was obvious and their devotion undeniable. The concern they shared regarding Josie's life and the opportunity afforded her, whether or not she chose to go forward with it, would touch Josie in ways she couldn't have seen coming. As they gathered, Birdie made it clear there were more questions than answers and it would be best to speak with Josie and hear her story for themselves, assuming Josie would do that.

Now that the church family appeared to know about it, Josie Bee felt it would be best to face the earlier encounter, resolve it, and put the whole thing to rest. So, when Auntie originally asked her to speak with the group, Josie considered the meeting a formality, not the investigation of an open question. Present and facing the ladies now, Josie wondered what she had been thinking. And then things got started.

Delphina Porter began with, "How did this contact with God make you feel, Josie?"

"I surely didn't expect when I went to bed that I would wake up to have a conversation with God," Josie replied.

"Could you understand what He was saying to you?" asked Miss Eunice.

"Yes. He told me he loved me and that He understood my pain and my hurts. He told me He had 'a challenge' for me. He told me to trust Him. And He told me to listen to His servants," Josie said. "But I am not sure exactly what God meant by any of that."

Maylene Parks raised her hand, adamant on asking the next question. "How did you respond to the Challenge, dear . . ." with sister

Marlene finishing her query ". . . and how can we help you?"

Josie decided to be straightforward with them. "I told Him no."

There was a collective intake of breath.

"And since I told Him no," Josie continued, "I don't have a need for assistance, although I surely do appreciate your concern on my behalf. I truly do, but at this time it isn't necessary. I think I expressed to God my feelings, and He understood my reluctance to become involved."

"And why did you tell Him no, dear?" Marlene asked.

Josie decided that since she was already being honest, she might as well keep going. "Because I don't trust Him."

Another intake of breath.

"I don't trust Him," Josie continued, "because He let those girls die in the bombing. How am I supposed to trust a God who lets people kill children?" What Josie did not mention was that she had become involved in a resistance group. This group, she knew, was powerfully sincere in its collective efforts to move their agenda forward, and was willing to fight fire with fire.

"We love you, Josie, and we don't want you to sell yourself short, nor do we want you to feel overwhelmed or alone in any endeavor you might choose to participate in," Maylene said.

Josie wondered whether that would be true for the resistance group.

"Josie's youth should not be held against her or minimize what God is offering her," stated Peachie Parsons. "At eighteen I was married, pregnant, and working as a waitress, and not particularly in that order. Josie has experienced a lot in her young life, but at twenty she has qualities that will serve her well in whatever she chooses to do. We don't need to push her, but I don't want to be a part of holding her back, either."

Then Grammie Beulah spoke up. She was the oldest member in the entire church. When Grammie spoke, everyone listened. "To make a difference in the lives of others is what we as followers are all about. It is our purpose and privilege to influence others in order to help make their lives richer and their journeys lighter. Our opportunities to share God's message of love come in a variety of ways, and it looks different for each of us. But God bless the person who reaches out to lift someone else up." Grammie Beulah was on the edge of tears. "Josie,

I am going to go out on a limb and tell you what I think God wants you to do. God was there with those girls on the day of the explosion. And God was there with you too. We don't know why the good Lord allows things like this to happen. But we do know he uses his children to bless others. I believe that you are God's child and that God wants you to become involved in the lives of four little girls and to bless them in honor of your four lost friends."

It was a moment of Holy Spirit inspiration. The older women nodded; the younger women looked in awe at Grammie Beulah. After a few moments of silence, Berniece thought it was a good place to stop for the time being and let Josie chew on their words for a few days. It was a lot to expect out of a young person who was still trying to sort out what she had experienced and think through its implications. Best to bring a close to the meeting and reconvene later.

Everyone after the meeting was upbeat and excited, suggesting that Josie take some time to searchingly reflect and consider what this proposed experience could mean in the lives of others. In chatting among themselves after the meeting, several women encouraged Josie to look at the Challenge as they felt God surely intended: an opportunity to bless the lives of four little girls in honor of Addie, Denise, Carole, and Cynthia. Wouldn't they be delighted in knowing they were being remembered in this unique and God-directed way? The ladies couldn't say exactly how this was going to play out but assured Josie Bee that they would walk with her and support her with their finances, prayers, and friendship in the Lord. These were not empty promises but overwhelming gifts of compassion and hope, offered to Josie Bee from a community that demonstrated authentic love.

Josie Bee had no defense for the genuine love focused on her spirit by the Inner Circle. She didn't feel as though they were breaking down her declaration but building her up toward positive consideration of some type. Josie was touched, but she still resisted in her heart. She was not ready to receive these things and remained steadfast in refusing the Challenge.

The next morning Josie woke up to a quiet, empty house. It was perfect. She needed time to figure out her next steps in order to convince the others to give her their blessing in letting this Challenge thing go. Josie figured some fresh air would do her good as the warm rays of sunshine would take the chill out of her rattled bones. Deciding to head out the door toward the nearby Liberty Park, she was already deep in thought searching for a much-needed plan of action.

Josie did not keep track of time and walked haphazardly on her way. After a while she casually glanced up and saw in the near distance a colorful merry-go-round she had joyfully spent countless hours on during her early years. Many good and unforgettable memories were created in that exhilarating wonderland. Exploring the grounds, holding hands with Momma, swinging and climbing with Pearl. The huge set of swings and the massive jungle gym were coming into view too. It was no longer the intimidating piece of equipment Josie had once thought it to be. But her favorite thing in the whole park had always been the extraordinarily large sandbox with its mounds of imported white sand. Sheltered from the hot sun with a massive, colorful canopy, it also sat under the arms of a far-reaching oak tree. Josie constantly begged Momma to please take Pearl to the swings and allow her to remain in the happy box picking up and sifting the tiny grains of sand over and over and over again. That was where she wanted to be now, sifting and lulling herself into oblivion. Yes, Josie Bee wanted to go to the sandbox, most of all to figure out everything cycling through her head. She was hoping for a clear fix while sitting on a pile of sand.

As Josie approached the park's entrance, she was drawn to a weathered lady sitting on the metal green bench surrounded by birds. She seemed to be as much a part of the area as the equipment itself. Funny, Josie had never before given her much thought. There had certainly been plenty of rumors floating around for as long as she could remember—about who the lady was and what she was actually doing, always sitting there on the long metal seat. Although it was alleged she was blind, some said she could see everything and was the park's protector. Others said she wasn't a woman at all but a figment of one's imagination, and that could be either a good or a bad thing.

Josie hadn't particularly realized she was slowing down her pace until she noticed how close she had gotten to the lady. Although she was instantly drawn to the woman's face, Josie looked around. These days it wasn't a good idea to take up with strangers on a whim. However, the lady had a pleasant demeanor and did not seem visibly unsettled or concerned by someone entering her space. Josie considered asking permission to sit down. The grooves in the woman's face looked like a roadmap of a life etched with pain and sorrow. There was also evidence of abundant laugh lines and kindness in her clouded eyes. The difficult and the joyous had taken up residence in this face, and Josie couldn't help but be attracted to it.

"Are you going to speak or just stand there gawking?" the woman asked.

"I didn't realize . . . how did you know?" Josie stammered.

"I've been around and observing others for a very long time. Initially it's in the footsteps and the approach," she replied.

Before Josie knew it, she heard herself saying, "Excuse me, ma'am, I was wondering if it might be okay to join you." She certainly looked like a real person, complete with a cane hanging off the end of the bench.

"It's a public place and not mine to claim. Feel free to sit down. Might I ask whom I have the pleasure of sitting with?" Her voice had a soothing rhythm to it, and Josie felt comfortable stepping into her space.

"Josie Bee Johnson, thank you very much," Josie replied as she reached out to grasp her hand.

"My name is Regina Reynolds. My friends call me Reggie."

"Do you talk to the birds?" Josie asked.

"Not near as much as they talk to me. Birds always have plenty to say." She grinned. "So, Ms. Josie, what does the *B* stand for?" asked Reggie.

"Excuse me?" Josie wasn't following.

"In your name, dear."

"Oh that. My middle name is Bee, B-E-E. It was my mother's way of naming me after her idol, Josephine Baker. My father didn't think it would be proper to use 'Baker' as my middle name. Do you know who Josephine Baker was?"

"I do," Reggie confirmed. "An activist second to none and a beautiful one at that. Word is she sings like an exotic bird, if you can imagine that. She is a woman ahead of her time, and she is bold and courageous as well as incredibly talented. The world could use a million more like her," Reggie enthusiastically remarked.

And just like that, common ground developed between the two, allowing Josie to feel secure and content in the presence of her unassuming new acquaintance. "My momma would certainly agree with you, Miss Reggie. Wholeheartedly!" gushed Josie Bee.

"And do you feel a connection with Miss Baker due to this association by name?" Reggie asked.

"No. Not really. Maybe, I don't know, I guess I haven't given that much thought before now," Josie stammered.

"What is on your mind today, Josie Johnson? What made you come this way and actually stop?"

"That's the crazy thing. I do have something on my mind, and I was headed to the sandbox to think through it. I hadn't planned on stopping anywhere. Or maybe I am avoiding it," Josie said. Here she was in the presence of a woman she just met, on the verge of unloading her burden, as odd as that sounded even to her.

Miss Reggie laughed. "You know, sometimes it just seems a lot easier and safer to share with those that don't know us well enough to question our perspective or point of view. Human nature, dear."

And then Josie went on and spilled her entire story into the lap of Miss Regina Reynolds. Her parents' deaths, the Children's March, the bombing, the girls, her anger, the resistance group, the Challenge—all of it. There was no doubt Miss Reggie had the gift of listening. The wise woman allowed Josie to unfold her entire bundle of burdens without interruption. When Josie reviewed everything that happened the night of God's contact with her, she expected Reggie to have a multitude of questions or a good hearty chuckle at her expense. But she only had a few thoughts.

"Do you believe in God, Josie?"

"Yes ma'am, I think I do. Most of the time," Josie added.

"And do you believe God reached out and spoke specifically to you?"

"I do."

"Is your heart in a good place, Josie Bee?"

"I am not sure what you are getting at," Josie answered.

"Let me try and rephrase that. How do you feel about who you are?" Reggie softly asked.

"I don't know how to answer that, ma'am." Josie sighed.

"Maybe it would be helpful to start there. It sounds to me like you have folks who are truly interested in your well-being and would do anything to help you. That makes you very fortunate indeed. And at the same time, the loss of your parents and your life as you once knew it has caused you irreparable pain and your sense of belonging appears muddled. I can see that. I can hear the confusion in your voice. To belong or not to belong. To do or not to do. Always gonna be something. Please try and remember this, Josie Bee: life is not fair, and it is not perfect. You cannot change anything that has happened. If only we could."

Josie wanted to keep soaking everything up like a sponge, but she felt she had taken in all she could for the time being.

"I'm not sure I know any more than I did before I plopped down, but it was nice sharing the bench with you, Miss Reggie."

"The pleasure was all mine, young lady. Still headed to the sandbox, Josie?" Reggie asked.

"Nah, you have done tuckered me out," Josie said with a chuckle. "But maybe we can have one of these chats again sometime." And Josie left the bench.

Josie was drained. Sharing with Reggie about her parents and the four girls at church brought back feelings of deep sadness, regret, and fear. She was afraid of branching out, being forced to trust her life to strangers and not knowing what to expect. Josie Bee had not received a mapped-out course with the Challenge and had not the foggiest idea of how working with four girls she did not know could possibly honor her lost church acquaintances. Maybe that was also what was eating away at Josie. She could have paid more attention to those younger girls. Being much older, she knew they looked up to her in their own little ways, but Josie had not gone out of her way to be involved with them.

They were friendly but not close friends. Pearl had been more readily available to them because she was in the church loop and involved in almost everything. But that did not stop Josie from unleashing her fury for everything that followed their tragedies. She was angry that the girls and their families could not expect justice in this world and that the Klan had gotten clean away with murder. Josie continued to doubt the legal system and to question God. She was uncertain what the future held for her.

A few days later there was another meeting of the faithful prayer warriors of the Hallelujah Circle. They warned Josie that doubt was a thief and would delight in robbing her of confidence. Josie Bee wasn't sure she had much confidence, but they were right on the money because what confidence she *did* have was quickly slipping away. The group reminded Josie that God had indeed reached out to her. Four girls somewhere were in need of something God felt Josie was fit to do. So, the "no, not me" and "I can't do that" argument was obviously not going to fly. Through the steady influence of the Hallelujahs' confidence, Josie's "no, no, and more no" began to sound absurd to even her. What had she been thinking when she responded so quickly and negatively? Josie felt a slight tipping of the scales toward God and His faithful prayer posse.

Josie saw no satisfactory way out of her predicament. The hardest part to reconcile was that she didn't have all the details. When one of the ladies mentioned the possibility of a "mission trip," Josie panicked. Would she be going across the world to a country where they ate bugs and lived in huts? Possibly having to leave Birmingham? She couldn't imagine leaving the only home she had ever known. More of concern was the possibility of going anywhere without Pearl. Truthfully, she did not know whether she could function in any type of situation without Pearl. All these unknowns piling up overwhelmed Josie, and her pent-up tears knew no bounds. She placed her hands over her face and wept.

The sympathetic ladies recognized that it was too much and decided that the best thing for all of them would be to eat another cookie and call it a night.

Another day, another meeting to discuss the Challenge. This one, apparently, was urgent. Back-to-back prayer get-togethers like this were extremely unusual, an indication that the group felt God's business could not wait.

Josie prepared herself for the dramatic—a lot of swaying and break-out singing going on in the hospitality room. Usually that was both entertaining and fascinating for Josie to witness. But being the subject of all this action by the sisters put a different slant on it. Despite her softening feelings toward the Challenge, Josie decided it would be best to nip it in the bud before the ladies got too excited and worked up. That would be the right thing to do. Let them down quickly but gently.

Another quiet drive back to the church did not tip Josie off to what was about to go down. As usual, the meeting got off to a punctual start beginning with prayer. It was all very normal and routine—until, that is, Birdie stood up requesting a couple of minutes to bring everyone up to speed on another pressing situation. Josie had no idea what her Auntie Birdie was referring to. So she was absolutely caught off guard when Auntie delivered her news: Gertrude Thomas, her older sister, was in dire need of someone to come as soon as possible to Florida to care for her. Gertie had been bravely battling lung disease for quite a while now, but at this point needed around-the-clock care. Nursing-home services were not financially feasible, nor was her sister able to afford in-home nursing. Birdie had known this situation was coming for several months now. After much consideration and petitioning for God's direction, Auntie Birdie and Pearl had come to the conclusion that Pearl should be the one to go to Jacksonville.

Josie glared at Pearl, but her sister displayed a calm exterior and a complete lack of surprise. Pearl had obviously known about this for a while now. Josie gave into her anger, clenching her jaw and crossing her arms, while feebly attempting to pay attention. Pearl, Birdie went on, had answered the call for help with a willingness to do whatever was best for Auntie Gertie during her stressful and difficult time.

Josie was reeling inside, feeling like she had been kicked in the stomach. Pearl was going to leave her. How could she? Why the big secret? Anger and hurt welled up inside Josie, like a balloon ready to pop. She didn't know if she even wanted to control her response. If she were to let her anger fly out on the Circle, certainly the group would then finally understand that Josie was not a good choice for service to God. Then they would hopefully cut her loose. Josie was absolutely not a good fit for anybody or anything regardless of the circumstances.

The fact that Pearl had not even found it necessary to share her decision before this public moment was painfully crushing for Josie.

"What is going on, Pearl?" Josie tossed the words in her direction through gritted teeth.

"Later, Josie, please," Pearl replied with those big doggy eyes of hers.

"You couldn't even take a tiny minute to let me in on your big decision? Fine, just peachy," said Josie, and she let it go because the group was about to delve into her business, and she wanted to give them her listening ears and not miss a single point.

To begin with, the ladies pointed out to Josie that she had been out of school almost two years with no job, she was not enrolled in any further type of education, and she was definitely not engaged in service to others. Nothing was holding Josie down in Birmingham. There would be no interruptions or hardship due to an upcoming absence on her part. Stopping short of recapping further details, and declaring Josie's empty state of affairs, they rested their case. Now it was Josie's time. The floor was hers.

"I remain confident that without more information or details, I cannot in good conscience accept something I don't believe I am capable of doing," Josie insisted. "Trust me, God doesn't need me to accomplish any of His plans." She delivered her message firmer than she had intended, but under the new circumstances of Pearl's plan to leave home to help Aunt Gertie, Jodie's head was spinning and her patience plummeting.

"But Josie, we don't see it that way at all. There is nothing you will be *forced* to do," one woman said. And from someone else, "God doesn't work that way. He's not a bully."

Eunice piped up, "Can't you place some of your trust in God, as

He has in you?" Several women were talking over one another saying similar things. And from Josie's beloved Auntie Birdie, "If you need more time, we surely understand, dear." From mouth to mouth and face to animated face, Josie felt the ladies' genuine faith reaching into her heart and wounded spirit.

As they talked she pondered. Would doing something different be that big of a deal? No one was asking Josie to cut off her arm. What if she did what no one really expected her to do? If Pearl could make a change, why couldn't Josie? They both could be involved in other things for a while, then they could reconvene and go back to what they were used to. How long were they talking about? Weeks? Maybe a few months? Half a year tops? The details in both areas were sketchy at best. On the spot, Josie decided to relent for the time being and then figure out the rest as she went. She generally chose the path of least resistance, especially when she felt there was no reasonable way out of a pressing predicament. *Okay, Pearl,* she thought. *You got the ball rolling, now I'm going to catch you off guard too.*

"I will go with the Challenge and do my best," Josie announced.

Those ten words caused an uproarious commotion.

Josie repeated her words. "I will accept the Challenge. I will do my best."

In this moment Josie felt a strength that seemed to stand up to her previous doubts and lack of confidence. Maybe Josie was doing what she was designed to do. She hoped these new vibes would carry her through the opportunity she was accepting. Doubt would certainly have to be dealt with as the process unfolded. But for now it was time for celebration. The ladies were shaking the room and praising the Lord in every octave available, singing and dancing joyously in the Spirit. Many of these gals would wake up the next morning and wonder what they had done to bring on their stiff backs and necks, but would recall this night of victory and think it was well worth it. The prayer warriors had poured courage into someone who needed it, helping Josie make the decision—and in their view, the right decision—in God's favor.

The women reiterated with astounding determination and unanimous resolve to do as they promised. Each woman congratulated Josie Bee, all of them sealing their delight with tight, encompassing hugs and squeezes. Josie was told to go home and get some well-deserved rest. She had had a long day. The Hallelujah Circle would take care of all the details. At the moment Josie was not worried, not one teeny tiny bit, about anything.

But that wasn't the case on the Hallelujah's end whatsoever. Speaking among themselves earlier, they knew they had a clear-cut responsibility and direct need to assess Josie's options sooner rather than later. Wanting to have a quick discussion with Birdie, one of the ladies suggested that Pearl and Josie run out into the kitchen and enjoy a Coke. They were aware of Josie's penchant for the dark cola and knew she would happily consume one with her sister. Goodness knows God had purposefully left things in the Challenge open-ended for their involvement and direction. It was an ideal time to quickly share a few thoughts and ideas and not put any pressure on Pearl as well. Birdie was on board.

"Let's first tackle the possibility of Josie working with young girls," prompted Eunice.

"Josie Bee Johnson? Our Josie Bee working with teenagers? Really, you all think that's a good idea, ladies?" said an exasperated Delphina.

"I see your point quite clearly. In fact, I can't help but remember how trying it was for our Josie to finish peeling those potatoes not too terribly long ago," remarked Maylene Parks with a sheepish grin.

"And we must keep in mind that Josie will not have Pearl at her beck and call, let alone there to prod and guide her through each and every assignment," continued Marlene, who routinely finished her twin's thoughts and sentences.

Berniece sharply cleared her throat. "Friends and sisters, I think we all can agree that an opportunity has been placed in the path of my free-spirited niece. That is not up for debate. It is God's suggestion Josie Bee become involved in the lives of others for multiple reasons," Birdie stated. "I think God has given latitude in order for us to help shape this unique opportunity."

"I couldn't agree more," confirmed Grammie Beulah. "Most certainly God does not want to see this young lady fail and it is our duty to explore what might best suit Josie Bee and give her the needed guidance to see this situation through in the very best ways possible."

What was moving around in the minds of the Hallelujahs as this discussion played out was that they were not specifically sure of what Josie was even capable of. Because she would be involved with others in order to honor the four girls murdered in the bombing, she needed to be qualified to run the race set before her. And to be poised for success.

"I know we are just talking aloud but Josie was helpful at Vacation Bible School and seemed sincerely taken by those younger children," piped up Eloise Price. "Josie actually seemed to enjoy herself."

"And Pearl said she was helpful with the preschool kiddos on Sunday mornings," remarked Birdie.

"Maybe we should steer ourselves in the direction of helping and assisting young children for Josie's service," Grammie Beulah reflected.

Birdie replied, "For a variety of reasons, we have allowed Josie to remain a child in many ways and as such, we now need to allow her to grow up and become the woman God intends her to become. I put most of the blame on myself," she said quietly.

Peachie Parsons sat there silent as a church mouse, tightly clutching her hands. She badly wanted to remind everyone how overwhelming her situation had been when she had been just a little younger than Josie. She made it. Josie could very well do the same thing if she put her heart and mind into it. The Hallelujahs took Peachie's hand and walked with her every step of the way, carrying her brokenness when her husband left. They would do the same for Josie no matter what came her way. It's what they did. And Peachie would be on this journey too.

Birdie was bringing the session to a close. ". . . And we have much to consider and pray about, ladies. It's been a long night and now we take our desires and hopes to God on bended knee. Amen?" she suggested.

And then everyone scurried out with more purpose and promise in helping to develop God's best for Josie.

As soon as it was feasible, Pearl would head south to Jacksonville, Florida, to care for Auntie Gertie. Pearl wondered if she would be able to spend time exploring the beaches. She had been interested in sea glass for as long as she could remember, checking out every book available from the library. Pearl was amazed that broken glass with sharp jagged edges went into the waters and after being tossed and turned returned to the beaches all smoothed out and absolutely beautiful. She felt like sea glass, her edges rougher than they appeared. Pearl felt confident the ocean would become her newest safe haven, offering a compensation of peace and healing for her own wounded heart.

On the car ride home after the meeting with the Hallelujah Circle, Auntie Birdie, Pearl, and Josie were reflective and silent. Each one realized that their lives, separately and together, were about to change drastically. Neither Pearl's assignment nor Josie's Challenge came with a set time frame. In reality, the unknown was unsettling for both sisters. They had never lived apart from one another. At the end of the day the girls counted on each other, and that closeness provided them with a binding love like no other.

Once the prayer warriors got working on Josie's situation, she would be heading somewhere in search of four little girls. The group in fact had already been checking on options before Josie's decision had even been confirmed. Funds would need to be raised. Josie expected there would be bake sales, Friday-night donation dinners, and who knows what other creative money-makers the resourceful ladies would come up with. But they would get the task done.

Next on Josie's list was to corner Pearl and get some alone time with her to find out what was going on. Something was off. Her indifference had been troubling. It wasn't like her not to dote on her baby sister nor to purposefully keep things from her. Pearl had been mysteriously occupied and nowhere to be found, then like the flip of a coin she was back, and out of the blue joining the Hallelujah Circle. Maybe Josie was making too much out of this, but then maybe again she wasn't. Pearl's behavior had been different the last four months, or so it seemed. Initially Josie just hadn't been paying attention. Pearl had been holding back, and Josie was strongly beginning to think it could have something to do with Jumpin' James. What if the sightings and the rumors about Pearl and Jumpin' had some truth to them? Now that would be worth pursuing.

4

Moving Out

Nature makes the locust with the appetite for crops;
man would have made him with an appetite for sand.

Mark Twain

IT WAS OFFICIAL: Josephine Bee Johnson was on a mission, and how it was going to unfold was anybody's guess. But she was going somewhere. Of course, God had it all arranged in His schedule, but Josie and the others were not yet privy to the specifics. Not wanting to appear whiny or give in to the panicky feeling in the pit of her stomach, Josie was now in the position of having to depend on others coming through for her in support of the Challenge. This assignment already had her hoping it would get started and completed in a relatively short period of time. Step by step Josie Bee would do what needed to be done to move forward in the fashion everyone expected and to do it as well as she was capable of.

For now, Josie's attention, not to mention her building curiosity, was focused on her big sister. Pearl had been too tired to talk when they returned home from church the night before. And she had left earlier

in the morning to pick up and drop back off some much-needed items
for the pantry at church. She would be returning shortly, and Josie, like
a stalking cat in search of its prey, was ready to pounce. It didn't sit well
with Josie that Pearl had failed to share with her the Florida plans. Josie's
feelings were strained, straddling concern for Pearl's well-being and sus-
picion because of what she appeared to be holding back. Josie could
beg and guilt her sister into sharing or rush in and hope to catch her off
guard. The element of surprise, she thought, might be the better of the
two options, and with a game plan of sorts, Josie was ready to roll.

"I'm home," Pearl said cheerfully as she entered, softly closing the
heavy oak door behind her.

"Great," Josie quickly responded. "Can we talk?"

And without the slightest hesitation, Josie promptly launched into
attack mode in search of answers to clarify what had been going on
with Pearl and to make up for the disconnect in their relationship.

"What's been going on? Something's up and I can't figure it out.
Have you been keeping something from me? Are you okay? Help me
out here, Pearl."

"Slow down, you're overreacting again. There's nothing to tell,"
Pearl half-heartedly insisted.

"C'mon Pearl, it's me. Don't you trust me anymore?" Josie was
tearful.

For someone who had never cried much, Josie Bee had sure done a
lot of bawling in the past week. And that is probably exactly what got
to Pearl. Once the tears started trickling down Josie's cheeks, Pearl's
shoulders dropped down and her demeanor visibly softened. With a
certain resignation in posture, Pearl's face looked like it was flooded
with unrestrained relief. Josie didn't know if she should be apprehensive or grateful that Pearl could possibly be forthcoming with the particulars. On the one hand, Josie didn't want to give her time to change
her mind or think too much about what she was about to share. On
the other hand, she couldn't afford to be pushy and didn't want to rush
Pearl either.

"Is it true about you and Jumpin'?" Josie could not hold back.

"That is a very . . . complicated question, baby girl, and I just don't
think you need to know all my business, let alone try to process it,"

Pearl mechanically replied as if she had been practicing the response.

Josie, in turn, moved by Pearl's sincerity in struggling with what to share, could see how painfully difficult this conversation was for her sibling. She recognized that most likely her big sister would not confide much, and she was disappointed. But more than that it was disturbing. Josie couldn't leave it alone and asked one more question that had been haunting her.

"Did he hurt you, Pearl?"

"Hurt me? Never. James loved me. I will always be sure of that. He loved me with all his heart, and I loved him back with all of mine," Pearl softly replied. "But now we both have lists and lists of things to attend to." And with that, sensible Pearl was back, doing what needed to be done whether she felt like it or not. Josie instinctively felt her eyes roll, something she had been in the habit of doing since she was a toddler.

"At least you know where you are going and who's house you will be sleeping in. I'm scared, Pearl," Josie whimpered.

"'Course you are, silly goose. You're supposed to be. But as long as you get up every day and try to put a foot forward, you will be fine, Josie. God's grace will always be with you. Kindness will find you in ways you could never imagine. Accept it and say thank you, God."

But it was Pearl's next words that Josie would never forget. "Protect your heart, but you gotta open it up, because you are so much more than what you are holding onto, baby girl. Do you hear me, Josie?"

Josie Bee could barely nod. There was an achingly tight lump in her throat. She tried to take in more air, relax, inhale and exhale, pull it together. Pearl's sweet words and sisterly advice were hitting Josie hard. Like she had always done, Pearl was attempting to soothe the panicking inner child. Despair taking hold, Josie could not imagine living life without her anchor, not for anything.

Today they were chatting somewhat like they used to, and although it was a fairly short conversation, it affected Josie in several ways. She had not expected Pearl to unload every detail or feeling she had been experiencing over the last few months or so, but what she did share about Jumpin' took Josie by surprise. She saw Pearl in a way she had never seen her before. Passionate. Vulnerable. Brokenhearted.

Josie couldn't have known that Pearl didn't have the information to adequately explain what she had been going through. Pearl didn't have the specifics herself, and she feared they might never come. Pearl was contemplating where to go and how much to expose of the relationship, but she feared it would only invite more questions. She just couldn't go there again. Maybe never. But she also did not want to be purposefully untruthful or misleading, feeling it best to say as little as needed to satisfy her sister. Something would be better than nothing, as Pearl's most intimate details were hers alone.

Pearl missed Jumpin' so much. She was convinced he would never have chosen voluntarily to leave her. No doubt whatsoever. She feared that some unspeakable thing had happened to the newfound love of her life. Pearl was desperately stumbling. Without James life continued on but with little meaning and no direction or hope. James had not just taken a piece of her heart, he had disappeared with all of it. Pearl would continuously ache for the man who had allowed her to grow up in unexpected ways. Having no answers to his disappearance or whereabouts was excruciating. She had gone from crayons to perfume, from being a child to behaving like a woman. James had given her a new identity. When Pearl was with Jumpin', she felt adventurous and bold yet safe. She hadn't realized how mechanical and mundane her life had been. James taught Pearl how to love freely and unconditionally. He treated her like someone mighty special. She hadn't felt that way since her Daddy died. Not once. Now that both men who had lit up her life were gone, she was overflowing with mounting despair, becoming a shell of a human being. Completely hollow without James. Shaking off her own sense of hopelessness, Pearl closed the curtain on any further discussion with a dramatic shrug of the shoulder.

Josie was accustomed to Pearl fixing things for her, but there was something she couldn't have known. Pearl had come to realize it hadn't always been in Josie's best interest to give her what she wanted. For the past few years, Pearl had been trying to compensate for the loss of their parents and the upheaval it caused for the two sisters. Maybe it was too much and it was time to change gears and just coast. Pearl was tired. Sometimes one needs to stop and go in a different direction, because that's how it's supposed to be. And there are periods when you have to be the one to go in order to get that other person where they need to be. Life was like living on a checkerboard: move here, move there, get jumped. Lessons of the heart wouldn't come easy for either Pearl or Josie, but in time, hopefully there would be healing for both. Josie needed to learn that the heart is the thermostat for what is done and not done. Josie would have to learn how to cultivate and regulate hers and then claim the results. And she would have to get out on her own in order to do so. Pearl, on the other hand, just wanted to survive her brokenness. Now she had a job to do, and that brought a measure of stability and direction.

Hard to believe that it had been Pearl's heart that was isolated and regimented, but when it flew open, her life became magical. It seemed like such a long time ago. Pearl sometimes wondered if it really was as she experienced it. Her head had been such a mix of fact and fantasy that the lines of reality were at moments blurred. Jumpin' had swept Pearl off her feet. The ride was so dang exhilarating, to borrow a favored word from Josie's vocabulary, although Auntie Birdie had repeatedly asked her not to use it. As unsuspectingly ready as Pearl was to discover love, once it was in her heart, she was in no way prepared to let go of it. She had heard once that it was better to have loved and lost than never to have loved at all. Really? Pearl didn't know whether she agreed with Alfred Tennyson or not. She was wounded, maybe beyond repair. Her precious James made her feel safe, the way she felt when she had been in the closet. This empowering sense of security was like a shield that made Pearl feel invincible and that all things would work out as they had dreamed. She never for a second imagined life without James in it. And here she was living that reality.

It was not enough that Pearl could sympathize with Josie's confusion and insecurity in leaving. That was the easy part. It was stepping back and loving her younger sister enough to not hold her back that was difficult. Both girls needed to forge forward and in the process tackle their unresolved personal issues. It needed to be done away from one another, which was the kicker.

∼∼∼

TWO WEEKS LATER

From day one the Hallelujahs had been putting out feelers and correspondence to families and friends locally and across the country about Josie's experience. They knew God would lead and direct as their options materialized. It never occurred to the Circle that Josie would not accept God's request. Most of the ladies were instantly partial to situations and opportunities that were coming in, familiar with and eager to bring their efforts to the group. It was understood—and communicated—that the Challenge involved Josie stepping into the lives of four young girls to be of some type of service to them. Exactly how that would look was still unclear, but that didn't hold the resourceful women's group back from trying to figure out what they could. They were on fire for the Lord and committed to supporting Josie Bee in working out the details of this mission. They had worked hard and had much to show for their initial efforts.

After days of visualizing things, discussing, and pursuing dozens of scenarios, the group was about to bring its findings to a final vote. They had turned over many stones. After yet another night of prayer and deliberations, they had narrowed it down to two opportunities: one in the Midwest and the other one set in the heart of Dixie, their beloved state of Alabama. Everyone knew the Hallelujahs were buzzing like bees, which meant things were at a tipping point. The combs were filling up and they could taste the honey. When Josie Bee was initially asked if she would like to be involved in the process, she had the wherewithal to stand aside and trust them with her destination. Had she needed to think that much about everything, it would have been too real and Josie would have been uncomfortable and impatient and probably would have gotten in the way of their well-intended efforts. Better to trust the ladies, get her assignment, and get on with it. Pearl readily agreed with Josie, although she had not been directly involved because of everything she was trying to tie up on her own end. Birdie had asked that whichever way the choosing went, that she first be allowed to take the information home to Josie and Pearl. The ladies fully understood the tenderness of this moment and wholeheartedly granted Birdie's request.

The final debate between the sisters of the Hallelujah Circle was well prepared and chock-full of passion. The women split into two groups, one representing the Midwest connection, the other voicing support for the local Alabama option. Each member had her say and expressed her point of view. After deliberations, the group silently voted. As the ballots were distributed, Birdie's heart did flip-flops. Each woman prayerfully marked her choices and dropped her ballot into the box. Grammie Beulah read the results one by one. Then Birdie was anxious to get home to her girls with the news.

Pearl and Josie were in their rooms packing boxes and sorting through giveaways for the local shelter. Neither heard the door open or close when Auntie Birdie came in. They were aware that their Auntie was at the church and that the Hallelujahs were very close to arriving at a decision on Josie's placement. Josie had more interest in knowing the decision than enthusiasm for where it would take her. This would make it all too real. But the excitement in their Auntie's voice was undeniable as she shouted, "Girls, I'm home! Pearl? Josie?"

"Coming, Auntie!" Pearl shouted back.

The Hallelujahs had made a surprise congratulations cake and slipped it to Birdie on her way out of the building. It was such a lovely expression of thoughtfulness and support. Auntie Birdie placed it on the small kitchen table. The girls arrived in the kitchen, and instantly both of them had tight lumps in their throats. Auntie meant this time to be special and had no intention to move quickly through it. Both girls knew how important it was not to rush her. Josie was just trying to hold it together but was focused on letting Auntie Birdie unpack the information as she saw fit. This decision was a big one for her too.

"Auntie, sit down, I'll make the coffee and get the plates," Pearl offered.

"The three of us have had a lot on our minds, and it'll be good to resolve some of these things. Do I hear an 'amen'?"

Classic Auntie Birdie.

"Amen!"

The girls knew their Auntie loved them as her own and had their best interests at heart. Pearl cut into the pink-iced Neapolitan crème cake and served it up. When the coffee was ready she brought it to the table for herself and Auntie Birdie and pulled a Coca-Cola from the fridge for Josie. Content to savor the moment, the ladies stayed silent for a few minutes. Each had different thoughts swirling through her head, and it was nice to have a few quiet moments to let the contemplations go their separate ways.

Auntie Birdie broke the silence. "I am happy to inform you both that the Circle has reached a near-unanimous decision as to where you will be going, Josephine. We also have a thorough backup situation should there be a substantial request for a change of venue. We are assuming this won't be necessary, but in case it is, we have provided for such."

Auntie was building her story, and evidently it was going to take a while to hammer down the forthcoming details.

"After going through all those possibilities and options, that brings us to the chosen place, now doesn't it, girls?"

Auntie Birdie was gearing up to release her precious information. Josie was now growing more anxious to know exactly where she was headed. Pearl seemed to be holding her breath. Auntie, they hoped, was about to let the cat out of the bag.

But she wasn't. Auntie Birdie pressed on. "Girls, life is like a ripple. One ripple runs into another, and then that one goes on to touch the next and so on and so forth. It all started because one initial splash set what followed into motion. One of Eloise Price's nephews has past history with our church and with the Hallelujahs. In fact, he would be the first to tell you that his relationship with Rosewood Street Baptist changed his life and that of his family."

"Auntie, I'm not sure what you're getting at," Josie said. *Goodness, where is this going?*, she wondered impatiently.

Pearl piped up quickly. "I think that Auntie Birdie is letting us know that wherever you are going might have something to do with Miss Price's nephew. Educated guess."

"Thank you, Pearl, that makes it crystal clear now," Josie said, tongue in cheek but as demurely as possible.

"Always happy to help the dense and uninformed baby sister," she smiled back. Josie rolled her eyes but smiled as Pearl grinned at her. It was hard to believe how much Josie would miss this sisterly banter.

"Yes, that is correct, and we couldn't be more pleased," Auntie Birdie said. "We are like bees in clover. The Circle is confident it has done its homework and has reached the best results possible."

"Auntie, you have us entirely on the edge of our seats. We are ready for some answers please!" Josie urged.

"Well, okay then. Josephine, you are going . . . to Sand Haven, Indiana!"

Josie felt her heart go kerplunk.

Indiana had not been on her radar. Noooo way. But it was a means to an end, and right now she did not want to disappoint Auntie with a sad face or, worse yet, a breakdown in tears.

"Oh Auntie, this is really starting to feel like . . ." and Josie struggled for words.

"A bona fide adventure," Pearl said, finishing her sentence. "Is that what you are trying to say, Josie?"

As Pearl automatically responded to cover Josie's stammering loss for words, Josie felt the reality of their journeys taking them both far away from Birmingham.

The reality of going away was a punch in the stomach for Pearl as well, only she dared not show it. She wanted to continue her search for James because a part of her believed he could still be out there somewhere. Maybe undercover, it hadn't yet been safe for him to contact her. She missed him so much it made her appear numb. Inside she was totally twisted in knots. Pearl knew it was possible James had encountered really bad trouble and it may have gotten him silenced. There was that constant stabbing in her heart. Those were her fears day in and day out. It was the reality of the unpredictable and volatile climate in which they lived. The very last night Pearl and James had seen each other, they held one another tight while dancing under a bright full moon. At ease, Pearl had relaxed in his arms in total contentment. She remembered every gentle word that was spoken between them.

"Pearl, have you ever considered living someplace other than home?" Jumpin' asked.

"For heaven's sake, no," Pearl said.

"Why not?"

"I have never been alone. I lived with my parents and sister, then with my Auntie," she said. "I really can't imagine anything else." But in truth, she was beginning to.

"You've never dreamed about living with a man before?" James asked.

"No, I really haven't," Pearl said as she shook her head. "I don't have time for those kinds of thoughts. Life is complicated enough." But suddenly Pearl knew she would absolutely contemplate such a situation if she got the chance.

"To make it simpler, let's just call those thoughts 'dreams,' Pearl," Jumpin' said.

Pearl leaned in closer yet and whispered, "And then what, James?"

"It's my dream that someday in a perfect world you and I would be together, and I would make it my life's mission to love and protect you for always. That's my vision, pretty lady."

"Maybe I can meet up with you in your dreams," Pearl suggested playfully.

"It would be a good starting place, now wouldn't it? Just say a little prayer for me, would ya, Pearl? For us. That would mean everything."

"I must admit, you are full of surprises, Mr. Black," she said. "What might cause you to be in need of prayers?"

"You are missing the point, Pearl. I don't need just anybody's prayers, I need *your* prayers."

"You're being serious, aren't you, James," Pearl breathlessly remarked.

"Real serious. Lots of bad stuff goin' on out there and I want you to know I am committed to proving myself to you, making good on those dreams. I'm hoping they will be *our* dreams, lovely woman," whispered Jumpin'. "As presumptuous as that might sound."

Pearl held on to every word he spoke. She never wanted to forget what she was hearing. It was tender and genuine, and Pearl knew then that she had fallen completely for James Black. Her heart was opening wide for this man, her head spinning. This surely must be what it feels like to tumble into love head over heels. And just like that, Pearl released her heart to James. She didn't want this time to end. Pearl Opal Johnson felt alive and thirsty for more. She purposefully tightened her arms around James. She felt committed. But she also felt a strong sense of urgency that she couldn't explain, and it was unsettling. She couldn't put her finger on it.

"Pearl, you still with me? Pearl?" asked Jumpin'. "Thought I lost you there for a minute."

"I am," said Pearl.

"And you think there's a chance for us?" he asked knowingly.

"I do," said Pearl.

James grinned. "Pray for me when I'm away from you, knowing I always intend to return," said Jumpin'. "Just saying there are times when things don't go the way we want them to. It is a dark and crazy world we're living in. Things are not going well for our people these days."

Sadly, Pearl understood.

"I know you probably feel like I'm talking in circles, but for now all you need to know is how important you are to me. The boogeymen are real. I am in need of your prayers, so just pray. Okay?"

"I will. I want you in my life, James." Pearl knew she hadn't felt safe or cared for in that way since her daddy had been run down. She also knew she couldn't afford to lose James too. Certainly God would grant her the desires of her heart.

"Are you sure you're still gonna love me tomorrow?" Pearl asked. Somewhere the Shirelles crooned in the background as they danced.

He nodded. "From now till eternity."

"That sounds like forever to me," cooed Pearl.

"Hope so, pretty lady. I truly hope so."

Those would be the last words Jumpin' would say to Pearl.

Pearl was brought to the present by the sound of Josie's voice. "You read my mind, Pearl. I am grateful for this opportunity and all the time and investment everyone has put into this Challenge. I really am." At a loss for what to say next, Josie reached for Auntie and squeezed her tight. When Pearl joined in, Josie thought it was perfect.

Auntie wanted to give more details, but it was Pearl who insisted that she needed to give herself some time to absorb the news as well. But Auntie Birdie was excited to share just one more particular.

"In moving forward the Circle is putting out an announcement as we speak. For everyone's immediate attention . . ." With a copy of the invitation in hand, she continued reading: ". . . there will be an upcoming community and church potluck—stay tuned for date and time. The Hallelujah Circle is counting on the support and aid of the faithful in assisting the nieces of Berniece Thomas. Pearl Johnson will be headed to Florida in order to care for Birdie's ailing sister. Josephine Johnson will be accepting a challenge to go to Indiana to work with children. Time and funding are urgently pressing. Thank you, and may God bless all contributions, big and small. Every little bit helps tremendously in these acts of faith."

Josie never doubted that the needed money would come in. The potluck fundraiser would be the beginning of many, but this first one would predominantly benefit Josie. Folks might be more generous if supporting two girls instead of just one young lady on a mission. Already there were bake sales and a mystery shoebox exchange scheduled, both happening the very next week. The most efficient way for the girls to travel would be by bus. Tickets would be purchased through Greyhound as soon as they had the money in hand.

Money did not trickle in—it flowed like a river. The bake sales were completely sold out, and the mystery boxes were so successful that the Circle decided that the project would become a regular fundraising effort in the future. The potluck dinner brought in record-breaking amounts, mostly out of gratitude and thankfulness for all the years Birdie and the Hallelujahs had given to the community. Now Birdie needed some help with her nieces and sick sister, and people wanted to show their appreciation and dug deep into their generous pockets.

In the midst of all the accelerated activities in preparing for their departures, Pearl and Josie were thoroughly grateful to be able to attend the Sweet Sixteen Jubilee at Rosewood that Saturday in celebration of all the girls. Tears welled up in both their eyes when it came to honoring Addie Mae, Carole, and Cynthia. There wasn't a dry eye in the house. It looked to be an emotional weekend all around. Now they were close to experiencing a Sunday celebration of their own.

The church had planned a farewell gathering for the afternoon before the girls were to leave. In the morning service Pearl and Josie were recognized as servants who trusted God with all their hearts, gifts, and talents. And although Josie felt that might have been a bit of a stretch on her part, with Pearl paving the way, they gracefully thanked the congregation for taking care of them and sharing their prayers and finances.

At the afternoon send-off, Pearl and Josie were given matching Bibles with pale pink covers, as well as gold cross necklaces. They were also given drawstring bags with their names embroidered on them, containing notes and letters with months of good wishes, advice, recipes, encouragement, and lots and lots of Scripture verses. It had been a whirlwind time of packing, saying goodbye, and tying up loose ends, and both girls were exhausted, making them extremely tearful. The women enjoyed the display of emotions around them, indicating that they would be deeply missed. Auntie Birdie tried mightily to keep her feelings in check and to continue being the stoic, no-nonsense kind of leader others could expect to hold it together.

After saying goodbye with hugs and squeezes, Auntie Birdie and her nieces gathered up their things and eagerly headed home. They were all relieved to be able to let down and get to last-minute details. The atmosphere was bittersweet. The three women knew this would be the very last time they would all go to bed and wake up together in the same place for a very long time. And that was probably the hardest detail, not knowing when they would be together again.

Everyone was exhausted. Knowing it would be best to get to bed as soon as they could so they might be somewhat rested for their trips, the girls did not dillydally. After kissing Auntie goodnight and sharing how much they loved her, Pearl and Josie walked to their sweet room. Holding on to one another as they had done throughout their lives together, words were not needed to demonstrate how they were feeling. Quietly crawling into their beds one last time, they both sighed before attempting to fall asleep.

After lying awake for close to an hour, Josie just wanted to reach out to Pearl. Because she could. Still wrestling with why she was having to leave the nest and go who-knows-where, she was overcome with feelings of fear.

"Hey Pearl, you awake?" asked Josie.

"I guess I am now," her sister responded. "What is it, Josie? Do you need something?"

"Why did they have to die, Pearl? The girls? And the two boys? Was God just taking a break?" Josie's voice was breaking up. She was scared and overwhelmed with emotion.

"You know it doesn't work like that," Pearl gently whispered. She, too, felt the unavoidable reality of leaving Birmingham and being separated from Josie Bee.

"Then explain it to me, would ya? How does it work? Because even now I'm not getting it. Can you hear me?" Josie cried out in a panic. "Pearl, I don't get it!"

"I wish I could tell you why. I really do, but I can't. Either way, it's not my place to say," replied Pearl.

"Say what?"

"Speak for God as to why He allows these things to happen," replied Pearl, trying her best to be patient with Josie. At times she was frustrated as well. Pearl had no answers, and if she did, she would definitely be asking God about James's whereabouts. "I think God wants us to trust Him as much as we can. Maybe sometimes it's in our best interest not to have answers," Pearl offered.

Josie reflected for a minute. Typical Pearl—yet again. But she felt somewhat better just calling out to her. Boy was Josie going to miss Pearl. As she would eventually learn, taking the high road isn't easy or fun, but it's usually the right thing to do. It was going to be harder than Josie had even first imagined.

As scheduled, the girls boarded their designated buses the next morning. Both had decided to sleep as much as possible on their drive. Pearl had roughly 460 miles on the road, and Josie 605. As the crow flies, Josie's trip was 530 miles, which somehow sounded better. Physically and emotionally, Pearl and Josie were drained, and they were both looking forward to sitting still and doing nothing more than trying to rest. Each carried identical large baskets filled with stuffed cream-cheese-and-tomato-rye sandwiches, orange slices, fresh veggies, tall thermoses of icy cold lemonade, and sweet tea. Auntie tucked her renowned moist butterscotch scotchies and her great-grandmother's chewy oatmeal raisin cookies inside worn red-and-white-checked tins to prevent breakage.

The girls hugged before their departures, vowing to write weekly and pray for one another daily. The praying part would be a stretch for Josie Bee. Pearl and Josie also promised to keep in touch with their Auntie Birdie as much as possible, realizing it would be a difficult change for her as well. Josie and Pearl knew they meant the whole world to their Auntie, and she had fashioned hers around them.

Quickly after Josie got seated, her thoughts started drifting and she flippantly allowed them to go their ways. She attempted to give some thought to the types of employment she would be qualified for and interested in pursuing once she got settled. But she couldn't think straight. It was clear that Josie was expected to help out and contribute a small amount financially toward her host family's expenses. Eleanor and Delbert Price had moved to Sand Haven several years earlier with their two little girls, Paula and Patsy. The Circle had made their move possible, and the Prices were eager to pay it forward as they anticipated bringing Josie into their home. The entire family would be there at the bus station to pick Josie Bee up when she arrived. Auntie Birdie had told her they were excited to meet her. Josie wished she felt more optimistic. Now that the extreme busyness of packing and getting ready to go was over, panic and doubt were creeping back in. She was hoping some sleep would help her wimpy disposition. But Josie Bee just could not see any traceable evidence of the courageous convictions she needed to follow through on her commitment. She had been warned.

Dang locusts.

5

THE MELON DANCE

*And those who were seen dancing were thought to
be insane by those who could not hear the music.*

Friedrich Nietzsche

WAKING TO THE boisterous and much-too-cheery chatter of the
bus driver in the guise of a formal announcement, Josie heard the
Greyhound spokesperson declare they were less than thirty minutes
away from their destination, Fort Wayne, Indiana. Then she would
depart for a twenty-minute car ride to Sand Haven with people she
had never met before. She didn't know what to expect, and growing
up in Birmingham, Alabama, could make you suspicious of almost
anybody. Not a fan of meeting strangers in general, Josie realized she
would quickly have to do some work in masking her issue of general
mistrust if she was going in search of finding four girls she could help.
She desperately wanted to get the Challenge off the ground. All she had
to do was be willing to go forward and trust that instructions would
fall into place as she needed them. Or something like that. She felt like
a toddler learning to walk: you get a wobbly start and stumble and fall

over. Then you try it again. Maybe you sit down and throw a good old-fashioned temper tantrum, which gets everyone's attention quick, and then somebody will tell you what to do. Josie had ample experience with that method.

True to their word the Price family was waiting for Josie. They seemed genuinely happy to see their new houseguest, warmly greeting and embracing her. It would have been more than slightly uncomfortable and awkward for Josie had it not been for the squeals and unsuppressed giggles of the Prices' young daughters. The youngsters were real icebreakers. Paula was seven and Patsy was five. Eleanor and Delbert immediately made it clear that they preferred Ellie and Del over Mr. and Mrs. Price.

Delbert was the nephew of the dear and proper Miss Eloise Price, and as such he fully understood the ways of the South and how one was expected to address their elders: formal and respectful was the rule of thumb. As Eloise's favorite nephew, Del knew better than to speak carelessly or without reverence in her presence. He took great care in displaying flawless manners and basked in the pleasure it gave his Auntie. Del appreciated Auntie Eloise's unique interest in him, making it easy for the other cousins to tease him about buttering her up like an ear of corn.

"Looking back, I guess those manners had something to do with bringing us to Indiana," Del chuckled. "They certainly captured my Aunt Eloise's attention, and we have remained extremely close and involved in one another's lives since I was a little one."

Josie couldn't help but mention how important manners were to her Auntie as well. "My Auntie always had plenty to say on the subject and the lack of it in others. She always used to say that manners are an outside mirror of who was operating on the inside." Auntie Birdie would have been titillated if she could hear Josie quoting her. And rather surprised.

"So, here's to impeccable manners and this wonderful opportunity to meet you, Miss Johnson," Del said.

Josie couldn't help but grin.

Common ground is a wonderful thing. A sense of relief flooded over Josie as she realized these were truly nice people and that she liked them already. Her time in the Price home would not only be convenient but most likely comfortable, and she couldn't wait to tell Pearl. Instead of calling out "Hey Pearl" in their home, she would be writing "Dear Pearl" in a letter. Hopefully, this experience, off to a good start, would move along rapidly. Josie looked forward to getting back South sooner rather than later.

The Prices were thoughtful tour guides, giving Josie bits and pieces of essential and interesting information throughout their drive home. Sand Haven, a fairly small town with roughly fourteen thousand residents, was located east of Fort Wayne and situated on the southern banks of the Maumee River. The family enjoyed the slower pace of small-town life and appreciated exploring outlying rural areas. The girls enjoyed visiting local farms and animatedly told Josie all about pigs and goats, crops and haystacks, and everything in between. Once they had the floor, Paula and Patsy competed against each other to see who could tell Josie the most in a single breath. Ellie called a time-out to ask Josie when she had last eaten and whether she was hungry. Josie Bee suddenly remembered the basket from home filled with good Southern food and readily offered it up. The girls noisily clapped from the backseat and suggested going to Cranston Park for a picnic. Everyone agreed this was a super idea.

Within minutes they arrived at the community park, the girls begging to go to their special play spot. There were tables close by, and the adults unpacked and started munching while the girls released all their pent-up energy. Josie was famished and knew the Prices would enjoy the potato salad and sandwiches, among everything else Auntie and the other ladies had lovingly prepared for her trip.

Josie wandered away from the table and, arriving at the big sandbox, was unexpectedly touched with memories of times spent at their local park with Momma and Pearl. It also brought back recollections of the gigantic sandbox at the church and the Sunday school lessons taught there. And now, with several different things going on throughout the area, something caught Josie's attention. A tall blonde lady was leading a pack of twenty or so quiet youngsters neatly organized in a single file. She looked like a mother duck wearing bright red heels and had an undeniable swagger. They, too, were headed for the huge sandbox, which sat under a big maple tree with generous, sprawling, leafy arms. It would be one big happy sandbox party. As the others approached the box, Paula and Patsy naturally folded into the group, clomping into the sandy area. They all laughed and played together. Their simple joy was infectious.

After the adults had eaten all they possibly could, the parents called the girls to the table to eat. Then out came the cookies, which was a great way to end the meal. The next stop would be the Price home to unpack and settle in before the day ended. All in all Josie could not have hoped for a better start to her first days in Sand Haven.

Once back at the house, Del and Ellie showed Josie her new room. She was thrilled with the space. The wallpaper had Alabama yellow roses with green stems and leaves that delicately popped against a white background. The painted walls were fresh and naturally earthy, providing Josie with a backdrop of sunshine that was comforting, yet charming. Josie could hardly contain her delight when she opened up the wardrobe to find it, too, freshly painted with a bright lemony-colored textured interior. She felt the lump in her throat expand when she realized Pearl would not see this lovely closet, but if she had, she would have been delighted.

It appeared many things in her room had been refurbished in white and yellow with touches of moss and apple green. No sooner had Josie hopped into the white wrought-iron bed and snuggled under the floral handmade quilt than there was a soft knock on the door.

It was Ellie. "Might I be able to come in for a minute or two, Josie?" she asked gently.

"Please," Josie said as she pushed herself back up in the bed.

"We just want you to know how happy we are you have chosen to come to Sand Haven. We will support you in any way we can. Already, you have blessed us."

"Blessed you?" Josie heard herself reply.

"You are very brave to make these types of changes all at once and to open yourself up to total strangers. It must be scary."

Josie felt exceptionally understood, and in that moment, she felt a full measure of safety and security. "Thank you," she choked out.

Ellie was holding a pack of index cards. She handed it over to Josie Bee and explained that some of her neighborhood and church friends had a few job suggestions, which were written on the top five cards, should she be interested.

"Of course," Josie replied. She certainly was interested. Ellie wished her good night and left the room. Josie easily drifted off to sleep appreciating that she already had a handful of possibilities for her future employment.

The next morning Josie immediately reviewed the list Ellie had given her. First up was a dog-walking position for a local veterinarian at an animal clinic called Pet's Choice. Second on the list was Posie's Flowers and Pots, which boasted the best and freshest florets and blossoms in the entire state of Indiana. The third opportunity was a prep position at Barney's Bakery, which specialized in doughnuts, breads, cakes, and pastries for all occasions, with a possibility of promotion to a bakery assistant position. Number four was a clerical position in a "prestigious" accounting firm that promised to be exciting, exceptional, and educational. The fifth entry, and least appealing of the bunch, was a domestic position in the home of Mrs. Henrietta Whittaker with endless openings for advancement. *Where might one advance to?* Josie wondered.

All in all, a good variety. Josie called the first three numbers listed and was able to book three interviews throughout the day. She scheduled interviews four and five for the next day. Easy peasy. Josie couldn't believe how smoothly things were unfolding.

Josie arrived promptly at Pet's Choice. The crowded reception room was packed with a variety of pets and, noticeably, look-alike owners. Josie was whisked off to the Doggie Day Room, where she was instructed to wait. Another applicant ahead of her had just received a white toy poodle and was attempting to attach a leash to Poopsie's rhinestone collar. After the applicant had left for her trial walk, Josie waited and was assured in the interim that her dog, Sugar, was a larger canine but was considered the gentlest pooch in the place.

However, Josie was not prepared for being in the same room as the biggest German Shepherd she had ever laid eyes on. Flashbacks of the Children's Crusade just over two years earlier flooded Josie's memory as she shook with fear. The threatening growls, the bared teeth, the angry dogs pulling on their handlers' leads while jumping and knocking children down left and right—it was more than Josie Bee could handle. There had been bites, torn clothes, bloody flesh wounds, not to mention spewing firehoses. One of the officers had shouted that his dog preferred *dark* meat. At the time, his statement hadn't registered. Josie was more alarmed at the viciousness and authority in his tone. Only later would those words come back to Josie's mind, with the full understanding of what he had spat at them. Josie knew she needed to revisit these memories at some point but on her own terms when she was ready. This unexpected thrust into her volatile past sent her fleeing Pet's Choice faster than a speeding bullet. She was not the person for the canine-walking job. If she never came in contact with a huge dog again, it would be too soon.

Collecting her scattered thoughts and trying to suppress the disturbing intrusions from her past, Josie headed for Posie's. At least flowers didn't have teeth. Arriving ahead of schedule, she casually strolled the beautiful, calming gardens. Located on plots in every color of the rainbow, mixtures of multi-flowered scents wafted through the warm air, pleasant and sweet. Josie sneezed. Then she sneezed again. And again. Now her nose was visibly running. When Mrs. Posie Powers greeted Josie Bee, the owner quickly recognized that Josie was having an allergic reaction to the environment. Josie Bee's eyes were red and irritated and tearing profusely. There would be no need to go further into the specifics of the job. It could not work out well—the proof was splashed across Josie's puffy face.

Two down. Feeling frustrated, Josie reassured herself that she still had Barney's. She felt the bakery might end up being her best shot. The Hallelujahs had taught Josie many useful things, and she knew her way around a commercial kitchen about as well as anybody. She felt she could compete well in this arena. Josie Bee could stir, sift, blend, and grease pans thoroughly and efficiently. Although it would be extremely tedious, Josie wasn't looking for any inspiring or thought-provoking

employment at this point. She needed to make enough money to contribute to the Price household on a regular basis and that was all the
Hallelujahs had required.

She arrived at Barney's Bakery. The job looked promising and
the interview started out well. What Barney's was looking for was a
responsible person who could dependably prepare and clean up and
oversee an enormous kitchen. No doubt Josie was somewhat capable
of performing the specified duties. The process continued to go like
clockwork until Josie was informed that she would be expected to
report to work at 4:30 a.m. Since Josie Bee did not own a car and
had no possible rides to and from the business at that time, she was
reluctantly forced to decline. She was given a doughnut of her choice
for her interest and departed with a delicious crème-filled pastry in
hand, and no job.

Josie was disappointed, but there was always tomorrow, and she
had two more scheduled appointments then. Ellie was waiting for Josie
when she popped off the community bus. She offered to help Josie get
ready the next morning by smoothing out her unruly hair. Ellie also
had a dress and shoes Josie could borrow if she wanted, which would
give her the professional, I-am-ready-to-go-to-work look that should
impress potential bosses. Josie wore her one and only pair of black
pumps but took Ellie up on the black dress with matching suitcoat
and Ellie's suggestion to add the string of pearls that had been her
grandmother's.

"And don't fret if none of these jobs work out, Josie Bee, because
this is only a beginning," Ellie said. "Or look at it as practicing for
when the right job does comes along. Even if it hurts some, usually
that's an indication that God has something better in store for us."

"Well I am not even thinking better. I just need something on the
side to do as soon as possible," Josie lamented. In her heart she just
wanted to get back to Alabama.

"Be patient, Josie. Everything will fall into place when it's supposed
to," Ellie gently reminded her.

"One can only hope," Josie replied.

The next morning was lighthearted as Ellie and Josie had a nice time playing dress-up. "You look professionally striking, Miss Josie, and I do mean mighty fine, girl!" Ellie said, stepping back and admiring her work.

Glancing up and down in front of the floor-length mirror, another thoughtful touch from the Price family, Josie shot back, "Yes, ma'am, I most certainly do!" Josie wished everyone back home could get a peek at her at this moment. They wouldn't believe their eyes. Already feeling successful, Josie Bee had high hopes for the next interview, her confidence soaring higher than an eagle. By the time Josie left, she felt positive that today would be the day she would find that much-needed job.

Stepping off the downtown bus, Josie checked her directions and turned toward the business district. Within minutes she had arrived at the parking lot located outside the building of her interview. Strolling past parked cars and folks jostling with their car keys, Josie had a feeling she was being observed. She looked up at the building, and a woman was peering at her out of one of the top-floor windows. As soon as Josie noticed, the window's large shade was pulled down. Josie shrugged it off and continued on.

Quickly, Josie found herself standing in front of a tall and daunting brick structure that, according to the signage, housed several law practices and two governmental agencies. She entered the stately double doors and saw in the directory box to the right that her destination was located on the fifth floor. Choosing not to stand in line for the elevator, Josie hit the stairs, being careful not to twist her ankle or break a heel. Heart thumping, Josie Bee felt winded by the time she rounded the corner of the fourth staircase. Taking a minute before popping onto the fifth-floor landing, Josie ran her hand over her hair and then got out the compact Auntie had given her. Reapplying rosy red lipstick, Josie rolled her lips together for that evenly perfect look. Josie opened the door onto the fifth floor and looked for her destination. Ahead of her she eyed the designated door and approached it. As her right hand clutched the doorknob, she noticed a yellow sheet of paper with what looked like a hastily scrawled, handwritten note: "Job Filled. No Need to Apply." It didn't look like the kind of sign that would land on a professional business door. Instantly Josie recalled the lady at the window, and with chills up and down her arms turned on her heels and promptly exited the building.

Coincidence? Josie had no concrete proof that it had anything at all to do with her. But it didn't sit well, and immediately Josie felt suspicious and somewhat on edge. Once again, she felt the unseen eyes of Birmingham following her. Old ghosts are hard to let go of. It was tough being a woman of color back home with all the civil unrest, but it was going to be hard here in Indiana too, with the lack of brown faces. Now Josie was getting herself all worked up, and over what? It was all out of her control. "Be a big girl," she could hear Pearl saying.

"Shake it off, shake it off," Josie mumbled to herself.

Josie Bee could only hope she qualified for something at the Whittaker household. She wanted to be done with the job-seeking process. How bad could a domestic job be? When you ask a question like that you can usually expect to get smacked with whatever comes your way next.

Arriving ten minutes early and noting that her Auntie would be proud of her for doing so, Josie knocked the brass "W" harder than was probably necessary. When the door was promptly opened by an older gentleman in all-black attire, Josie was taken aback by his formidable presence and formal inquisition of her reasons for being at the residence. Josie confirmed her identity and appointment time, feeling not only uncomfortable but in some way out of place from the get-go. Josie passed the initial interrogation and was curtly invited into the home.

"Mrs. Whittaker is expecting you. She will see you in the front parlor, Miss Johnson."

"Thank you . . . sir," Josie stammered.

"Walter Windom. It is my pleasure to meet you." And with a slight wink and whisper he added, "Good luck, ma'am," as he closed the door.

Stepping into the room, Josie had not five seconds to reflect on what might come next when a nasal-sounding voice bounced off the dark and dreary walls.

"I am Mrs. Henrietta Whittaker. I am most curious to know if you can properly read, young lady? I am referring to the job description listed regarding this position in my home. I am waiting, Miss Johnson," she demanded without giving Josie a chance to respond.

"Yes, Mrs. Whittaker, I'd like to think I am an excellent reader. Reading is an important—"

"Because it is apparent you do not comprehend what the position encompasses, and it was clearly spelled out in the wanted ad. Details are important. You are not going to a party nor are you interviewing for a frivolous secretarial position. You are completely and inappropriately overdressed. In fact, you look rather ridiculous, Miss Johnson," Mrs. Whittaker sneered.

"I apologize, Mrs. Whittaker. Where I come from it is thought to be important to dress well when meeting with a potential employer regardless of what the dress code may entail at a later date." Josie managed to say this without rolling her eyes.

"And where *do* you come from?" asked Mrs. Whittaker.

"I have just arrived here recently from Birmingham, Alabama."

"Well then, that explains many things. I see you do have a lot to learn, and I will overlook your presumptuous error in judgment this time," she said as if she were giving Josie a real break.

"I appreciate that, ma'am," Josie responded.

After a series of insignificant and mundane questions, Mrs. Whittaker, to Josie's surprise, seemed somewhat satisfied and offered her the position. Because it was only part-time and temporary, Josie felt she could give it a shot. With only a brief moment of hesitation, she accepted the job in lieu of having to go through any more interviews. The sooner she did what she had to do, the sooner she could go back home where she belonged.

Mrs. Henrietta Whittaker continued on with a few dangling details.

"Might I need to remind you, Miss Johnson, to certainly find sensible black shoes before returning? And here is your uniform, which will need to be crisply pressed and the collar starched." She handed Josie a bulging dry cleaner's bag. "Do note that this attire is to be worn at all times on the premises, which includes coming to and from the workplace. And be punctual. I think that is all for now, Miss Johnson."

And it was over. With a dramatically flimsy wave of the hand, Josie was dismissed.

Josie Bee was to report to work at 9:00 a.m. the next day and not be one minute late. Mrs. Whittaker had an afternoon luncheon to attend and would be needing several items for a fresh fruit salad she would be taking with her. Josie was to familiarize herself with Marshy's Market, which was where the Whittaker family's shopping was conducted. Mr. Windom would drive her to the grocery store that morning and wait for her in the car until she was finished. This would be Josie's first assignment and a test of her ability to follow instructions. The pale pea-green one-piece dress with white collar and cuffs was going to be a real pain to keep clean and pressed, not to mention the white lace-trimmed apron. *Ridiculous* was the only word that came to mind, but Josie knew better than to question her uniform.

Wearing practical and freshly polished work shoes, Josie reported to duty the next day with a smile fixed on her face. Resolving to be pleasant and simply nod when she had nothing positive to say, Josie found herself nodding constantly. Mrs. Whittaker was eager to send her to the market to collect the needed items, especially the four succulent cantaloupes. Josie was directed to find ones that were sweet, not too ripe, and not too hard. "You can do that, correct?" her employer asked several times. Her repeated questions suggested to Josie that she was not convinced Josie was capable of picking out good cantaloupes. After the market, Mrs. Whittaker would be waiting to walk Josie through slicing and scalloping the melons, then placing them on her finest Lenox china for the pleasure and scrutiny of the Women's Garden Club. Because it was "more fashionable to eat at one o'clock than at the traditional noon hour like common folks," Josie's boss needed to have her fruit salad in hand and be on her way out the door at 12:30 on the nose.

Once at Marshy's, Josie intended to pick up the requested items on the handwritten list and put a check next to each completed entry as instructed. She wasted no time in heading to the produce department in search of the cantaloupes.

She was overwhelmed with how tricky this whole thing might be. Not only were there mounds and mounds of melons, but they all looked alike. Josie Bee had no idea where to begin or what to look for in choosing a good melon. She was completely out of her zone and felt sheer panic coursing through her body. As if on cue, up pranced a woman in an extremely tight-fitting, clinging coral sweater. How she got that piece of clothing to stretch over her head and situated below her neck was baffling to Josie Bee.

Then it hit Josie like a jolt of thunder that this was the very same lady who had been leading the children to the sandbox at Cranston Park. She had been striking from a distance and was even more so up close, in a theatrical kind of way. The way she moved through the fruits and vegetables with her well-heeled swagger appeared effortless. The woman made it a point to acknowledge Josie's presence in the clearest, sweetest, most cheerful voice: "And how are *you* doing today, Miss?"

Taken aback by the woman's sincere and friendly demeanor, Josie shot back with her dilemma. "Just fine except I am stuck trying to figure out how to choose a perfect melon."

"Well, I can certainly help you right now and right here with that, young lady." Her enthusiasm suggested that she knew something about melons and was confident she could help. Josie nodded, saying nothing. The woman was apparently eager to coach her and asked, "Ready?"

"Yes, ma'am."

"Soooooo, you grab a ball of melon and you immediately start squeezing while preparing to take your stance. Legs and feet about two feet apart. Stand fairly straight. Lift the fruit to your face. Now with your sniffer—that's your nose, dear—inhale slowly, S-L-O-W-L-Y, and concentrate on exactly what you are smelling while squeezing the fruit from all directions. Just like I am doing, please follow me. If you have any questions just go right ahead and raise your hand and we will pause. Don't be shy. Are we okay? Do we need to go through this again? Now this melon is fabulous. And that is how we find a perfect cantaloupe," cooed the melon whisperer. "You probably can tell I'm a teacher," she proudly declared.

Quite frankly Josie couldn't wrap her head around that vocation for the woman, but she *could*, stifling a nervous giggle, easily envision her in the dancing or entertainment business. She was mighty attractive and charismatic.

By now the lady's demonstration had drawn a small crowd. A few men clapped and one whistled. One of the men remarked, "I am going to have to rent me some grandkids to place in that Fiesta School of hers." A buddy laughed, although not everyone was amused. Several of the women were visibly annoyed. Snickering and with wide eyes rolling, they practically ruptured their necks from jerking their noses so quickly into the air.

"Sister, you got some real good moves. Can't thank you enough. You just saved my job," exclaimed a grinning Josie. "Would you mind snagging me three more good melons, please? I just don't think I can compete with your nose and expertise."

"No problem, happy to help," she said while handing them over one at a time.

"Thank you again! Gotta run. Have a nice day!" And Josie was off to fetch the other items on her list.

As she rushed toward the checkout lanes a thought hit Josie like a ton of bricks, and she came to a full stop with her cart. *Oh my goodness!* she thought. Was this her idea, or was God trying to garner Josie's attention again? Josie Bee had to find and introduce herself officially to the melon lady and get some scoop on the Fiesta School. It would only make sense that this school could be a starting place for Josie and the Challenge. The age of the children had never been specified in the chat with God but the Hallelujahs were directing her toward young children. Granted, Josie Bee was to connect with four girls, whenever and wherever that might be. Doing this to honor Addie, Denise, Carole, and Cynthia was the easy part. Finding those girls was the hiccup.

At this moment Josie felt the Challenge taking root some way inside her, and she felt a desire to explore in this direction. She knew she had to talk to the lady from the Fiesta School before she slipped through her hands and out of the grocery store, but she would have to move quickly.

As Josie placed her quivering hand over her heart, she wondered how scattered she must appear. Mere minutes earlier she hadn't known the lady in heels, and now she didn't want to lose her. Josie whipped past the meat counters, flew past the dairy section, and tore down aisles with soups and canned fruits and vegetables. She passed the baking goods and cereals, the crackers and cookies, the paper towels, toilet papers, plates, and napkins. Only one aisle left and that would complete the tour of the store.

Where had she gone? Had Josie really let a possible opportunity slip through her fingers? As Josie Bee approached the very last aisle, something on the floor caught her eye. A packet of cherry Kool-Aid. Josie bent down to pick it up. She took a few steps and noticed an orange packet, followed by green, and after that two purple packets of grape. Like following a trail of breadcrumbs, Josie picked up packets until there stood the Fiesta School leader right smack in her line of vision. The packets had been slipping out the side slots of her cart.

Heading directly toward the melon lady, Josie threw both her hands up in the air in a gesture of relief. Realizing she had not officially introduced herself, she extended her right hand and announced, "My name is Josie Bee Johnson, and I just recently relocated here from down South. Birmingham, Alabama, to be specific. I wanted to properly thank you for being so nice to me back there and for your assistance with the melons. I have been trying to catch up to you ever since. Please excuse my lack of manners back there!"

"And I am Faye Lewis, director of the Fiesta School, and it is my pleasure to 'officially' make your acquaintance, Miss Johnson." She said "officially" with both hands making dramatic air quotes.

"Please call me Josie Bee. Practically everyone does."

Handing the Kool-Aid packets to Miss Lewis, Josie noticed that her cart was filled to the tip-top with boxes of Kleenex, several bags of Krunchie's dry cat food, numerous bottles of Tom's Vodka, countless tubes of Ben-Gay, and even more Kool-Aid. Director Lewis was doing some serious stockpiling. Josie wondered whether there was a sale on those specific five items. There were no actual consumable food items. Josie wasn't sure what to make of it.

Noticing the puzzlement on Josie's face, Miss Lewis chirped in that she was just picking up a few personal items and that her assistant and cook, Nola, did all the routine shopping for the school.

"Again, I apologize for not introducing myself back there," Josie said, gesturing toward the opposite end of the store. "The melon demonstration, by the way, was wonderful, and I learned a lot."

"You are sooo welcome," gushed Miss Lewis. "I really enjoy helping others as much as I can, which is why I really, really enjoy teaching."

"Yes, ma'am, I can see that. And while we are on the subject of school, I am very interested in early childhood education. I actually saw you and your class of youngsters at the sandbox in Cranston Park. I was wondering if I might be able to drop by sometime to visit—that is, if you don't mind visitors."

"I wouldn't mind in the very least," Miss Lewis sweetly replied. "Just want to warn you that at the onset of the visit you may be led to believe we are a disorganized, chaotic bunch of ragamuffins, but I can assure you we are anything but. I take treeeemendous pride in the daily steps my students take in going forward as we are all works in progress. Wouldn't you agree? We will plan on seeing you sometime soon, Miss Josie Bee." Miss Lewis gave Josie a number to call.

Saying their goodbyes, Josie hightailed it to the nearest checkout counter as fast as she could to pay for the groceries. She felt confident Mrs. Whittaker would be happy with the melons. While waiting in line Josie Bee overheard two women and remembered seeing both of them at the melon dance in the produce department. The two women were whispering like the devil, as Auntie Birdie would have classified it. Top secret it was not. Josie heard one of them say clear as a bell, "That highfalutin woman has a big drinking problem." Josie privately hoped either they were talking about someone else or were mighty wrong about Miss Faye Lewis.

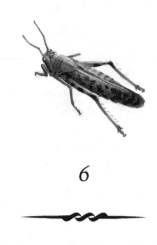

6

FIESTA SCHOOL

*The child who has felt a strong love for his surroundings
and for all living creatures, who has discovered joy
and enthusiasm in work, gives us reason to hope
that humanity can develop in a new direction.*

Maria Montessori

ONE WEEK LATER, LATE SEPTEMBER

JOSIE WAS WARMLY greeted at the front door of the Fiesta School by a pleasant woman she assumed to be Nola Greene, Miss Faye's assistant. Josie felt comfortable by the mere sight of the older, brown-skinned woman. Josie wasn't sure what she was feeling, but she almost wanted to reach out in some way to the lady with kind eyes. There was something about her that Josie gravitated to. It was like being greeted by someone you were familiar with from somewhere else in your life. Josie couldn't quickly put her finger on the situation before Nola gestured her to come in.

"I hear you're from my neck of the woods or so to speak, Miss

Johnson," she grinned.

Josie felt a deepening kinship with the woman with a true Southern accent and gentle manners who warmly and graciously welcomed her.

"Oh please call me Josie or Josie Bee, everyone back home does," she instantly responded.

"I might have to think a minute about that, young lady," Nola responded. "But it is certainly nice to make your acquaintance, and anything I can do to sweeten your time here in Sand Haven will be my pleasure."

"Oh, I don't plan to be here very long." Josie was almost too quick to answer. Sensing her abruptness, Josie added, "It's just that I already miss Birmingham and I pretty much just got here." She paused, and then asked curiously, "And where are *you* from, Miss Greene?"

"I was born and raised in Mississippi. The climate got to be a little complicated for me and I decided to try something new and had family in these parts . . ." she said as her voice trailed off.

"I bet you want to go back someday," said Josie. "Right?" She felt homesick and ready to head back South now if she could.

"I don't believe you are here, Miss Josie, to observe me," Nola said, suppressing a grin. "Shall we go into the classroom and find Director Lewis and the students?"

"Yes, ma'am, that's what I'm here for." If they only knew what had really brought her to their community in the first place! Josie was mightily hoping this was the experience she needed to get her butt back home. And probably for everyone, the sooner the better.

Nola guided Josie into an open room filled with long, connecting tables and a variety of colorful miniature chairs. School was actively in session. The bright yellow apron tied firmly around Nola's waist reminded Josie of the church ladies, which brought her a measure of comfort and familiarity. Josie Bee missed each and every one of them— even those who seemed to consider it a sport to scold her. Auntie Birdie would have eagerly recruited Nola, signing her up for the Hallelujah Circle and putting her down on the schedule before you could swat a fly. Nola would've been a nice fit for the Circle because whatever it was she was baking in the kitchen off the main room, its delightful promises permeated the air with currents of cinnamon and nutmeg. Within her walls, Josie was crumbling like cornbread, homesick and missing the fragrant foods and fine folks back home. Josie Bee was here because she had a job to do and she hoped this was where her new journey would begin. Motioning Josie to take a seat, Nola whispered that Miss Faye would be with her at the first available break in the schedule and if she needed anything to let her know.

Hearing the sweet sound of twenty or so children reciting the Pledge of Allegiance was uplifting and inspirational. Each child appeared to make a sincere effort to clearly and accurately state every word. They seemed to truly understand what they were actually saying. It was surprising that these particular children had only been in preschool a few weeks or so and already had mastered the Pledge. Josie knew she was in the midst of a very different type of learning experience from her own. When the children were finished, Miss Faye encouraged the kids on to the morning's next exercise.

Next up was the "Star-Spangled Banner," and with little hands covering tiny hearts, these pint-sized individuals sang unrestrained with the fervor of the Mormon Tabernacle Choir. Josie couldn't believe her ears and was completely taken aback by their efforts. Touched by their pure innocence, Josie heard herself softly murmur, "Glory." Josie had not expected this organization or control. She had just assumed that a preschool would be filled with rambunctious children chasing one another, coloring on the walls, bouncing balls, and shouting. There was none of that business going on, and this appeared to be their normal routine.

Next the voice of the director cheerfully rang out. "Young ladies and young gentlemen, we have a very special guest with us today. Miss Josie is visiting our very own Fiesta School. Could you please show her a warm Fiesta welcome?"

The eruption of clapping, foot stomping, and cheering that ensued made Josie Bee feel like she was a rock star! Heavens to Betsy, these little minnows made Josie feel like queen of their pond, and she was caught off guard yet again. Sporting personal name tags around their tiny little necks, the kids all beamed at Josie. One of them even presented her with her own name on a lanyard. Miss Lewis apparently thought of everything.

"Well I declare, thank you for such a wonderfully nice welcome. I am looking forward to enjoying this day with each of you," exclaimed Josie, genuinely happy to be in the center of the kids' attention and a part of whatever was to happen next. How these youngsters were going to fit into the Challenge was anybody's guess. Maybe the Fiesta was just a starting place and not a place of actual implementation. Josie remembered Ellie's suggestion to let things unfold in their own time, and she made an effort to stay focused on the moment. Patience was not a virtue in Josie's world, nor was it even in her toolbox.

Miss Faye did an excellent job keeping things moving without cutting the kids' enthusiasm short. She encouraged the youngsters to share during show-and-tell, but there was no pressure if anyone preferred not to participate. Nola, leaning toward Josie's ear, explained that Miss Faye felt that allowing the kids to share something helped establish a pattern of contribution, stability, focus, and buckling down on whatever had to be done that day.

In that moment Josie recognized the distinct smell of Ben-Gay. She thought back to her church in Birmingham. Several of the elderly folks had used it, and when they all congregated together, it smelled like a revival of menthol and camphor. Now Josie took notice of Nola's distinctive limp, thinking back to the grocery-store visit and the numerous tubes of Ben-Gay she had seen jumbled up in Miss Faye's cart. It all made sense. So maybe other things in the basket had been purchased for Nola as well. "Presumption can be one of the devil's favorite tools," Auntie Birdie would say often in the kitchen at church when someone was gossiping. It was always entertaining to watch someone fall into the pit of presumption in front of Auntie, then try to scramble back out before they got pounced on.

Also in that same cart at Marshy's had been several bags of dry cat food. As if on cue, a feline the size of a miniature poodle territorially strolled across the room. The children had just finished up when one of them spied the cat. Chaos did not erupt, as Josie would have expected. Nola leaned in and explained that only one child could approach the cat, Mister George, at a time. They had important things to do, needed to keep moving, and Mister George was not a fan of group handling.

Miss Faye took great pride in teaching her preschool students. She felt it demeaned her intentions when she was casually referred to as a glorified babysitter or nursery school aide. Faye Lewis was saturated with purpose. She prided herself on her high standards. It was her job to provide children with a positive and healthy start to their ongoing educational experiences. She wanted to help equalize the playing field for them when they arrived at kindergarten in the year or two following their Fiesta experience. Miss Faye wanted to give these kids the tools and skills needed to feel confident about themselves, developing into kind young students while still enjoying the learning process. There were many skills to develop both social and personal, as well as many practical day-to-day habits to introduce and reinforce.

Sharing time moved quickly and gave Josie insight into several of the children's lives, some who might qualify for the Challenge list and others who appeared happy-go-lucky and carefree. She immediately noticed one little girl who looked as though she wanted to speak but had tears in her eyes and was unable to let go of a box of tissues. Josie would remember those sad eyes and the nervous eye-dabbing with the Kleenex. Then there was another child who kept sneezing and saying "oopsie," seemingly every other minute as if she couldn't help herself. Josie was fairly sure her name was Esmeralda, which was a mouthful for anyone. Then there was Joey, a funny and personable little guy. He charmed them with all the different faces he could make. He was a goof!

Next it was time to move on to math stations. Josie was invited to assist the kids if she wanted to. Today's math class consisted of addition up to the number five. Instead of beads or tokens or any other number of items, the kids were each presented with a bowl containing five grapes. Although most of them seemed familiar with the activity, a boy named Ernie proceeded to eat all five grapes as soon as they were placed in front of him. Josie was petrified because she feared he was going to choke before her very eyes. Before she could motion for Miss Faye, Nola was there gently handling the situation. Funny thing, Miss Nola then gave Ernie another chance, a fresh bowl of grapes, and the exact same thing happened. Only this time he held them in both of his bulging cheeks like a proud chipmunk. Nola whispered to Josie Bee that Ernie was having an attention-seeking moment that she could remedy. Announcing she could use Ernie's assistance counting out cat food, together they headed toward the kitchen. Little man would have no desire to stuff his mouth with kitty crunchies, and he would still get his counting practice in. Brilliant plan. But it was certainly not a punishment, as Ernie had the biggest grin on his face when he passed by Josie on the way out of the learning center area. Then Ernie attempted a wink specifically leveled at Josie Bee. This had been the little stinker's plan all along. To share some one-on-one time with the nurturing and jovial Miss Nola and possibly a fresh-baked cookie tossed in—it was well-concocted on the little guy's part. Josie couldn't help but smile, secretly giving him two thumbs up.

Josie unconsciously scanned the room to see whether there were any kids that might stand out in some way, shape, or form for the Challenge. Josie wasn't really sure what she was looking for, and it got her wondering if she had any wiggle room to interpret God's short message. She would have to take these concerns up with God at some point, although it hadn't yet crossed her mind to actually have a conversation with Him. Josie Bee made a mental note to herself to consult God when needed. Failure to do so might result in a redo, causing a delay in getting back home to Birmingham, which Josie did not have time for.

The morning's break included snack time. Nola served up miniature cinnamon rolls topped with gooey coating. The tiny mounds of warm puffed pastry with almond icing dripping down from its highest peaks were served with icy cold milk. No store-bought Hostess pies or Little Debbie cakes for these special young-uns. For the rest of their lives the preschoolers would fondly remember the lovingly prepared confections and homemade goodies. Miss Faye and Miss Nola reminded the kids of the importance of putting napkins on their laps, not making crazy noises while eating, and saying please and thank you, which showed that you weren't demanding but grateful for your food. Manners were very important at the Fiesta School, and Miss Faye was a firm believer in the importance of being courteous and polite. She knew it was her purpose to give each child the gift of value, worth, and hope. What she could do for the youngsters at home was not in her control, but by golly, for the nine months they came to her school she would do the best she could to give them unconditional love in a healthy environment. Miss Faye and Miss Nola were a part of the kids' forever team. Forever loved, forever believed in, forever valued, and forever in their hearts.

Josie Bee was astonished at what a day entailed at the Fiesta School. Organization and routine in the morning kept things moving. Sign language was next on the agenda, and that would finish out the morning's activities and lessons. Miss Faye had the kids cover their ears, and when she spoke she only mouthed the words so they thought she was speaking but they couldn't hear her. The reactions were interesting, and in some instances flat-out amusing. Several of the children shouted, "I can't hear you," and when their teacher did not answer them, they only got louder and more impatient. Josie Bee was fascinated. She wondered how the lesson was going to work, but as Miss Faye taught them the hand motions, Josie realized she shouldn't have been surprised at all. The kids took to speaking with their hands like ducks taking to water. Using their hands was just another way to talk. Today's vocabulary words were "help" and "bathroom." The students easily picked up the new words. Miss Faye used role-playing to build on the importance of helping others.

It was what followed the signing lesson that brought tears to Josie's eyes. Miss Faye was using the example of how some people might feel when they are unable to hear or talk. After a short discussion, the children were asked what made them feel different or left out by others. Not expecting these little ones to be able to express those feelings and hurts, Josie was surprised when they did just that.

Agnes felt like an elephant because she ran into things and was clumsy. She also said she was dumb because that's what someone told her. One of the boys called her a retard. Josie couldn't believe it. Agnes Jones was such a little thing to be labeled with those hurtful words. Josie knew how it felt to be called ugly names, and there would always be words that stuck somewhere for a very long time. Agnes had wrestled with math that morning, and Josie wondered if she was slow or not very bright. The lesson was simple. At first Agnes just looked puzzled, but she grew frustrated. It really didn't seem like a big deal at the time, but maybe there was something to it. Or not. Josie didn't want to get too excited because this was a one-day visit. But maybe they could use a volunteer or tutor of sorts. Josie Bee was definitely getting ahead of herself, not to mention everyone else around her.

A little girl named Penny spoke up next. "Someday when I grow up, I am going to be a princess. I will be a happy princess. I will have a magic wand. It will be my favorite color purple and have lots and lots of sparkles. It will have very, very special powers. I will touch everyone, and they will be happy too. I might have to touch some people more than one time," Penny said while holding up her index finger. Then energetically shaking it, she said, "Nobody will cry anymore or be sad, I promise. Not even cats and dogs." And when she was finished, Penny looked pleased as punch, as though she had been thinking about this for a while and it felt good to let her thoughts out.

Tentatively raising her hand, the little girl in the blue-dotted Swiss dress, who was unable to speak at the show-and-tell session, now wanted to say something. Again though, as hard as she tried, she couldn't get out a single word. Her name tag said Patty-Jo. She was still hanging on to a box of tissues. A few tears trickled slowly down her cheeks and off her chin. Tuckered out, Patty-Jo took her reliable box of Kleenex and plopped down like a discarded ragdoll. She seemed to be carrying the weight of the world on her shoulders. Josie was curious about what was bothering this little girl so much that it caused her tiny frame to droop. At the very least, these half-pint individuals were full of surprises and secrets. But then again, most everybody had something they hid and tried to keep locked up inside.

The character-building lesson had struck a chord in Fiesta's tender hearts, big and small. The morning's lessons wrapped up, Miss Faye decided they would slide into an early lunch. The chatter around the tables was light and childlike with lots of grins, giggles, and glee. After finishing up and using the bathroom, the kids enjoyed a half hour of rest time. Josie wished she could join, pretending to be the little girl under her great-grandmother's rose quilt, next to Pearl. Josie shook off the emotions tugging at her heart and went into the kitchen to see whether Nola could use any help.

Miss Faye was already resting on her own mat, and if she wasn't taking a power nap, she appeared to be miles away. Should Josie be allowed to stick around, she would inquire about getting a floor mat of her own so she could enjoy rest time too. Funny how napping as a youngster had been a daily battle of resistance, but now Josie would welcome it. Miss Faye was right when she said that everyone in the room was a child. Some were big, some small, but everyone was the same when it came to needs and wants. Worn out, Josie was already entertaining thoughts of dropping into bed early at the end of the day. Work tomorrow at Mrs. Whittaker's would come quicker than Josie wanted, but that is how things rolled in her new working world of domestic employment and adult responsibilities.

Out in the kitchen Nola had an efficient system of her own. Having lunch cleaned up, she was preparing brown paper sacks containing a small clementine, a square of co-jack cheese, and a chocolate chip cookie for the afternoon break. Mark Nola's words, after an hour of play in the sandbox, the children would devour the treats as if they hadn't eaten a thing all day. It was a warm afternoon, and the two-block trot to the park after rest time would be invigorating. The fresh air and breezes swirling the leaves would energize them all.

Cranston Park was one of the community's most loved treasures. The genuine delight and excitement of the kids as they neared their destination affected Josie too. Miss Faye brought them to a halt close to the sandbox and gave last-minute instructions and reminders.

"Please remember that we will not be taking food into the sandbox and we will not throw sand while we are in the sandbox. Please be kind and thoughtful while playing with others in the sand. Everyone got that?" Miss Faye paused and then gave the five magical words the kids had been waiting for: "Now go and be free!" Those words prompted the class into a fit of giggles and applause as they took turns entering the sandbox. The class jumped, hopped, crawled, wiggled, closed their eyes, and turned around, and one future gymnast hopeful, Tabytha, even did a cartwheel.

Josie sat outside the box smiling as she thought of her own adventures at the park and inside the sandbox at church. She guessed she was only beginning to realize how much learning she had done among her peers in the sandbox, a place where dreams, big and small, took flight. Who didn't remember how comfortable they felt and how many things they could ponder in the midst of all that glorious sand? Josie spent countless hours trying to imagine where it all came from and how it got into their box. She believed the Sand Fairy was responsible, holding mounds of tiny grains in storehouses all over the world, just waiting for distribution to empty boxes in need.

Josie watched the children play, more than a tinge regretful that she hadn't gotten into the sandbox and burrowed down in the sand with the youngsters. She knew she missed out on something by not feeling the sand running through her fingers or allowing her red painted toes to disappear beneath its grainy surface. But she was happy that the students could have this kind of time to explore and kick back. Instead, Miss Faye was enjoying being in the midst of their laughter and silliness, and Josie chose to converse with Miss Nola. While helping unload snacks onto the picnic tables and setting up the Kool-Aid station, Nola shared a little more with Josie about her childhood in Mississippi. Josie wondered if Nola missed her home half as much as she herself did right now.

The children were contented and happy. Even Patty-Jo, box of tissues tucked carefully into the sand, seemed to relax. If Josie got another chance to participate, she would get inside the sandbox with the animated youngsters. Hopefully Faye and Nola would consider allowing her to become involved in the school in some capacity, but Josie wasn't sure how she should approach them. The ladies had no idea what her motives entailed. How was Josie going to explain it to them so they could understand? She really hadn't needed to break it down or put it into words before now. Everyone back home had done that for her.

All too soon it was time for snacks before heading back to the school. As the kids approached the picnic table, Josie noticed pushing and shoving going on between one of the boys and Agnes. Josie instantly realized that the male child was the instigator and Agnes was looking intimidated. Feeling okay about intervening, Josie let him know she was aware of his behavior. When he appeared to ignore her, Josie gently tugged on his arm to get his attention. When the lopsided ball cap fell off, Josie Bee was surprised to see that this boy was actually a girl. The scruffy jeans and stained tee had given her an appearance of being one of the boys.

"What's going on, Miss Josie?" Miss Faye asked.

"Not quite sure, just trying to find out if Agnes is okay," Josie replied, looking toward the other child. "She looks a bit scared to me."

Already Josie sensed something special about petite Agnes. She also felt the need to reach out, instinctively wanting to protect her. Agnes looked as though she could be Josie's little sister, and there was something comforting and familiar about that too. Josie was smitten.

"Charlie, are you not being kind to someone?" inquired Miss Faye as if she wasn't at all surprised. Faye suggested Agnes run along and get her snack, and she took Charlie off to the side. When the chat ended, Charlie ran over to Agnes and apologized but didn't look very remorseful. Clearly the situation had little impact on "Charlene," as she jumped into line and attempted to grab two snack bags. Nola was all over it. Seemed like pushy behavior for such a small pint, but maybe Charlie, as her nickname suggested, was more of a tomboy. Or maybe she was really hungry or just out of sorts. You never could tell with kids.

What followed next rocked Josie Bee to her core. Penny, the princess-to-be, was still sitting in the sand pulling her blouse's long sleeves down when the left one stopped just short on her skinny little arm. The area was visibly black and blue with what looked to be serious bruises. It was all Josie could do to hold herself back and not rush over and ask Penny what had happened. And what would the child say? An accident? Or worse yet, that someone had done it on purpose? Josie was crazed with disbelief but calmed herself and slowly moved toward Penny, tenderly bringing the sleeve down. Speaking softly Josie asked, "Can I help you out of the sand, Penny?"

"No thank you, Miss Josie," she said as her eyes turned away. Josie's thoughts were scattered. No doubt this little person would be the type of child that she might be able to work with if she got a chance here at Fiesta. Josie was determined to find an explanation for such a young one having bruises like that anywhere on her body. No one ever deserved to carry around marks inflicted by others. Dang, dang locusts. Josie had to get them away from Penny. Maybe she was jumping to conclusions, but what if this little one needed her help in some way? Josie hoped she was overreacting and that there was an explanation for what she saw. The feeling deep down in the pit of her stomach steered her in that direction. Josie Bee pulled herself together, meandering about as if nothing had happened. But the "nothing" had changed everything.

Snacks completed, the group formed a single line following Miss Faye back to the school without any further issues. Once back they started the end-of-the-day pickup and getting personal items collected so nothing would be left behind. Each child had a specific task, and Josie marveled at their ability in doing them to completion. Only a few weeks into school, they had the routine down pat. When finished and after the tasks passed inspection, the students gave each other high fives.

"Yes, give yourselves a big hand! Way to go! I am so proud of all your hard work today," Miss Faye exclaimed. "Here at the Fiesta School we enjoy our time together! We learn. We laugh. We share. And we have a lot of fun, right kids? Celebrate the moment!" The young students nodded and clapped.

Once all the kids had been picked up, Josie found that she felt wiped out. "How do you do this and still have so much energy at the end of the day?" she asked both women.

"Seeing what we can accomplish each day elevates us . . . most of the time," Miss Faye replied with a smile. "Sometimes the kiddos can run us ragged, but it's always worth it."

"I can see that. I really do. I mean, what you are doing is so important, and what you are doing for these children is amazing. I am overwhelmed, and I've only been here a single day," Josie remarked.

"Glad you enjoyed your time with us, Miss Josie. Nola and I appreciate your interest and hope this has been a helpful experience for what you want to do next," said Faye.

"And that brings me to a very important point I had been hoping to make," Josie began. "I am about to bust at the seams. This has been a super day for me. I am wondering if it would be possible to sit down with the two of you very soon. I really want to share more about what prompted me to visit the Fiesta School in the first place. But more pressing, there are several reasons why I am hoping—wondering, that is—if there is anything I can do to become more involved in your school." Josie felt as though she might be jabbering excessively, throwing too much out there too fast. *Slow down, girlie.*

"Why, Miss Josie, I am surprised that you are so taken by our small preschool in such a short span of time," Faye declared, with Nola nodding in agreement.

"But I surely am interested. A volunteer position, job shadowing, just about anything that might allow me to spend some time here. Though I'm not trying to put either of you on the spot right now," Josie said.

"You seem to have a lot of ideas. What else might you be thinking?" asked Faye.

"This being Thursday, I have to work tomorrow at a part-time job. So . . . it would be perfect if I could meet with you on Saturday sometime," Josie stated. "I'm sorry, but I have to run, or I am surely going to miss my bus."

"How about we plan on seeing you mid-morning Saturday?" Faye asked. "Is 10:30 okay?"

"It sure is, thank you," and Josie was out the door.

Arriving at the Price house, Josie found a note from Ellie hoping Josie's day had been successful and letting her know a letter from Florida had been placed on the pillow in her room. The family was at a PTA function with the girls, and Josie's dinner was wrapped in foil, keeping warm in the oven. Other than that, Ellie wished Josie a good night, and should she be resting when they returned, they would be eager to see her in the morning at breakfast.

Josie Bee was not in the least bit disappointed that the house was empty. She was too tired to make conversation. Josie would never have fathomed that spending a day at school with little kids could exhaust her this much. Josie's mind was jam-packed. First things first, she just had to get involved with the Fiesta. She liked just about everything she saw at the school, plus Nola and Faye were fun to be around. Second, this was the perfect place to easily choose four children that she could get involved with. After meeting Nola, Josie wondered if the Prices knew her or of her experiences at Fiesta. It seemed feasible. She'd ask them, although it seemed a lot of things were basically on hold until Saturday.

For now, Josie was happy to be in her new home. After eating her dinner and readying for bed, she attempted to put a close on her crazy day, knowing her big sister would be proud of her efforts to do what she had promised to do. Even though Josie still felt she had been co-erced to accept God's Challenge in ways she could not fully explain, on some level she knew it was a good thing to do. Doing something specific to honor the lives of Addie, Denise, Carole, and Cynthia car-ried real purpose. Their age difference had affected Josie's relationship with them, as they participated and ran in different groups. But the girls' deaths overwhelmingly affected both Josie and Pearl. Pearl had known them better because of her involvement in their church with the interchurch mentoring program for young girls. So it had surprised Josie that Pearl hadn't been the one designated for God's plan. After all, she had experience and enjoyed spending time nurturing others. But Josie guessed Pearl was the best suited for stepping in to care for Auntie Gertie and would not have been available to assist in the Challenge.

The letter from Pearl was now about to become the very best part of Josie Bee's day. She needed this contact with her sister. Knowing she wasn't going to be able to share her daily experiences or connect with Pearl at bedtime was already hard on Josie. Wasn't that one of the best parts of accomplishing something, sharing it with someone who knows and understands your heart and journey? Not to mention your struggles and sacrifices.

"Pearl, I miss you so much," Josie said to herself, wanting to sob. Her sister had always been the most important person in her life and the center of her universe. Pearl understood and knew Josie's heart, especially the difficult parts. And faithfully she watched over and had truly cared for her. Now the closest thing that Josie Bee had to precious Pearl was the envelope she held tightly in her hands.

7

ANGEL LIST

If you can't fly then run, if you can't run then
walk, if you can't walk then crawl, but whatever
you do you have to keep moving forward.

Martin Luther King Jr.

CLUTCHING THE PALE pink envelope postmarked Jacksonville, Florida, Josie got situated in her cozy bed, propping herself up for the letter's grand opening. With great care and anticipation, Josie Bee slipped her finger under the flap, gently lifting the scented rose paper. Only then did she realize that she hadn't even stopped to consider how things might be going for Pearl. How was she getting by? Josie had been so preoccupied with her own concerns that she had just assumed Pearl would do what she had always done—be a brave little soldier making the best of any situation. Holding her breath, Josie began reading.

My Dear Baby Sister,
    I hope this letter finds you rested, settling in, and adjusting well in your new home with the Price family.

I miss you terribly but am proud of you, Josie. I know you must be scared silly, but you are stronger than you think and always have been. Truth be told I was shaking to my core when I boarded that bus, but I know this is what I am supposed to be doing. Auntie Gertie is really grateful, and that warms my heart.

Was so excited to tell you I made it to the beach. It is my hope we can go together sometime. I think you would be mesmerized by the sun, sand, and water. It is a whole new world unlike anything we have ever seen.

My first piece of sea glass is so beautiful, mint green in color. I picked it up for you, Josie. A peace offering of sorts? I am sorry I didn't share everything with you before and hope you know I did not purposefully set out to hurt you or push you away. It just happened.

Please write when you can. I know you have a lot going on right now. I am praying for you as you try to figure things out.

I love you to the moon and back,

Pearl

Josie was relieved and happy for her sister. Pearl sounded hopeful. Saying she was sorry meant everything. Not because Pearl had to, but it reaffirmed to Josie that she loved her. Josie knew there had to be more, mostly stuff she would probably never be privy to. It was okay. Everyone has things they don't want to share. Or can't.

The next morning arrived all too quickly. When Josie awoke to the sound of her alarm, she was still comfortably resting in the room she shared with Pearl. But her peacefulness popped like a balloon when she realized she was not in her old bedroom with her sister nearby. She felt like she was imprisoned on the other side of the world. Josie reluctantly put on her crisply starched, ugly uniform. She would make it to work on time and try her hardest to please the finicky and demanding Henrietta Whittaker. Zipping past the kitchen on her way out, Josie Bee waved and told Ellie to have a good day. Someone needed to have one, and Josie knew that it wouldn't be her. Wearing her sensible shoes, she darted to the bus stop.

The ride gave Josie time to think about the Challenge. She didn't have a handle on all the details, but she was hoping to find a place to start. Then Josie could begin sorting out her role in helping others and how she might do it. What did that mean? Josie had no defining ideas. This was where she was beginning to realize the importance of getting advice and guidance from others. Faye and Nola would be great allies and role models. Helping kids was what they did. Knowledge gained from years of caring for children would be invaluable to Josie and her mission. If she could somehow gain their support, Josie Bee felt her direction would become clearer and more practical. It was not lost on Josie that Faye and Nola were two formidable women who already had things handled. In fact, the duo might very well prefer not having an outsider come in and muddle up their smooth operation. Josie knew she needed them more than they needed her. What could Josie really contribute that they didn't already have? She needed to give that some serious thought before her Saturday morning meeting.

Josie arrived at her place of employment and was greeted by a whispering Walter. "Mrs. Whittaker is having another one of 'those' days."

"Of course she is," Josie replied. In the short amount of time she had been working at the house, Josie knew that Mrs. Whittaker was incapable of being nice or pleasant on any given day of the week. "Thanks, Mr. Windom. I surely appreciate the heads-up."

"Yes, Miss Johnson, it's my pleasure," he said with a wink.

Josie expected her day to be spent performing more superficial duties. She could easily do any of them with her eyes closed. And it would allow her to think about what she had to do to get ready for Saturday's chat. Josie needed this job, meaningless and insignificant as it was. She felt Henrietta Whittaker was more interested in the representation of hired help than the actual petty tasks she had Josie doing. The job was a means to an end, not a permanent career move.

"Good morning, Mrs. Whittaker," Josie cheerfully exclaimed. "And how are you doing?"

"How I am doing is really none of your business, Miss Johnson," she curtly replied. "I would suggest that your off-the-cuff comments cease, young lady. Do I make myself clear?"

"I believe so, ma'am." And so began another day in Whittaker paradise for Josie Bee Johnson.

"And please do something with that *nappy* hair of yours, Miss Johnson. You could frighten a ghost!"

What? Did she really just say what I think she said? Josie was speechless.

"Or maybe we should invest in hairnets," Mrs. Whittaker smugly suggested.

Josie knew it best not to answer, even though her employer's comments did seem a bit racist. And no, Josie would not be wearing a hairnet if she had anything to say about it.

Needless to say, Josie was relieved when she was sharply dismissed at the end of her workday. Getting out of the toxic environment almost made Josie giddy as she inhaled the fresh air. Thinking about going home to dinner at the Prices' made her realize she was famished. She hadn't eaten anything all day. Mrs. Whittaker did not permit lunch breaks. Josie had to snatch a bite here and there between chores. Today, however, she had forgotten to pack any food at all.

Joining the family at the dinner table was extra pleasant and gave Josie a time to relax and refuel before heading to her room to figure out tomorrow morning's game plan. Chitchatting with Paula and Patsy was easy. The girls were never at a loss for words and were well-behaved and sweet, which was a relief to Josie because it meant no uncomfortable periods of silence to try and fill. As Josie's thoughts were beginning to come back to the Challenge and how to approach the Fiesta staff, she helped clear the table then excused herself. Josie Bee had intended to share a little with Ellie, but she was busy getting the girls ready for bed, and looked tired herself. Besides, as Josie was seriously leaning toward fudging the facts of her story, she hardly wanted Ellie to know she was possibly going to be disingenuous and misleading in tomorrow's meeting. Things were just beginning to roll in Josie's mind, and she hoped they would take her somewhere good so she could be confidently prepared and ready to go in the morning.

With the embossed notebook she had received from the church
ladies at the Rosewood send-off celebration, Josie quickly wrote down
a description of the situation, starting back on the night when God
first spoke to her. After recalling the facts, Josie noted that the weather
had been fixin' to blow up a storm that evening, but everything was still
quiet as she hunkered down for bed. But true to the forecast, a storm
kicked up with lightning flashes and thunderous booms that normally
would have chased Josie deep beneath her rose-covered quilt. This time
it was different. Instead, something gently woke her and drew her up
toward the window. Outside the trees swayed in the powerful gusts of
wind. The branches did backbends, their limbs sweeping the earth's
moist floor. The lulls brought the fluctuating and graceful movements
to a standstill, and the dance suddenly ceased.

Mentally reviewing her circumstances of that stormy evening, Josie
knew now the weather was an exceptional backdrop for an extraordinary intervention by the Almighty God. In the moments when she
heard God speak to her, He clearly let Josie know He loved her and
wanted to challenge her to become involved in the lives of others, specifically four young girls. He wanted to challenge Josie to do something
in honor of the four promising girls who had perished in the tragic
church bombing close to two years earlier. God knew that Josie Bee
had not healed from the loss of her parents, and the deaths of Addie,
Denise, Carole, and Cynthia only made Josie angrier and more vulnerable. Josie wanted revenge, to "settle the score." Corrupt law enforcement failed to bring to justice those responsible for killing Josie's
parents or the church bombers. There had been no closure for anyone.
Justice was a joke.

Josie had begun to dabble in underground resistance groups, and
was close to taking the next step of total commitment with one organization in particular. While others were praying and petitioning for
equality and peace, Josie Bee was fired up with the group's eye-for-an-
eye mentality. Josie felt accepted and affirmed by them, wanting to
commit and join their movement. One female member in particular,
Angela, was especially encouraging. Josie felt Angela understood her
frustration and was grateful for the support.

Josie had always heard and was frequently reminded that God

worked in mysterious ways, but His speaking to her directly was an over-the-top spectacular experience. Funny thing, Josie hadn't felt alarmed or frightened during the conversation, but once it was over, fear did surface. And like the locusts it began gnawing away at her as if she were under attack. With her own thoughts and questions, Josie started to tremble that night as the doubts came in waves crashing over her. Like doubting Thomas, Josie Bee quickly became skeptical, defensive, and inconsolable. It was Pearl who came to her side, cradling her like a colicky baby, soothing her sporadic emotions and calming her troubled spirit. It was one of the most tender moments of Josie Bee's entire life, and she never wanted to forget the intense security and unconditional love she had experienced in the arms of her sister. Hunkering down in the corner of their beloved closet, Josie felt safe and protected.

Now, putting the information down on paper helped Josie focus her thoughts. She needed to present consideration for the school and confidence in her mission. Faye and Nola had such big hearts, and Josie Bee was counting on those hearts warming to her journey when she presented it to them. Josie planned on sharing God's Challenge before petitioning for involvement in the school. Josie hoped that by gauging the vibes in the meeting she could avoid giving too much information about the Challenge while providing just enough to get her by, no more and no less. That was the best she could do.

On the way out the door for her meeting the next morning, Josie was handed a huge plate of festively wrapped chocolate chip cookies from Ellie. They smelled heavenly and looked like bakery creations.

"Thank you so much, Ellie. These are really special. But how on earth could you know I needed a little—okay, a whole lot—of something to take in with me?" Josie asked with a squeal of excitement.

"It never hurts, Josie Bee, in putting your best foot forward, that your hands also demonstrate just how nice and thoughtful you can be," Ellie replied with a smile. "Remember that a little bit of sugar can help just about everything. We've been rooting for you, Josie, and even the girls have tossed in a few words to Jesus on your behalf. Not to mention the extra chocolate chips." She grinned.

"Aw, thanks," Josie replied.

"Good luck, baby girl."

Josie was touched by her words. It was something Pearl would have said to her too. These were really good people whose actions danced with their words, a reflection of their faith in action. Josie was grateful to be on the receiving end of purposeful kindness with no hidden agenda.

Once inside the bus and settled in her seat, Josie thought through the finishing touches of her approach to Miss Faye and Miss Nola. Since she hadn't quite gotten around to speaking with God, she hoped that what she was about to say would somehow meet with His approval. She made a mental note to check in with Him possibly on Sunday. The Hallelujah Circle, and specifically Auntie Birdie, had told Josie Bee that they expected her to regularly attend services at the Second Street Baptist Church with Ellie and Del and the girls, eventually participating in church activities. She fully understood this was part of the deal and that in accepting God's Challenge and the ladies' funds, she had an obligation, a duty, to represent everyone as best she could.

The bus dropped Josie a few blocks from the Fiesta and Faye Lewis's residence. Josie felt more unsure of her presentation with each step she took toward the school. Her instinct to flee was kicking in, but Josie kept moving forward. She knew what she had to do. With cookies in hand, Josie reached for the door knocker just as Nola opened the door. Were they charily waiting for her? Hoping she wouldn't show up? Josie reminded herself that presumptions were never good.

"Good morning, Miss Josie. I saw you marching up the sidewalk as if you were going off to war, and by golly I felt sorry for you. But I must admit, the sight of those goodies piqued my interest even more," Nola said kiddingly. "Thought I would save you the trouble of knocking. Miss Faye just adores the color yellow and calls this door her sunshine entrance. She sees to it that a fresh coat of paint is applied every spring whether it is needed or not." Nola smiled. "And while we're at it, please come on in. The treats will go perfectly with the coffee we have waiting." And with that she limped off to call Miss Faye.

"Thank you kindly," Josie whispered, more to herself than anybody else. Telling herself to get it together and be a big girl, she silently thanked Pearl again for giving her that advice, most likely hundreds of times throughout their years together. Just thinking about Pearl right then gave Josie a surge of *parakletos*, a favored buzzword at church meaning "encouragement." The Greek word literally meant pouring courage into someone who needs it, and Josie needed a vat of it. Her courage appeared to have a mind of its own, coming and going as it dang well pleased. Ooooh, Auntie Birdie would not have appreciated hearing that and would have sternly told her to control the rough language and behave like a lady.

"Helloooo, Miss Josie." Faye had a Southern twang that was sweet as honey but overexaggerated. Yet it disarmingly made Josie feel comfortable and welcome in a way she appreciated in this moment of sheer trepidation. Josie Bee needed to get on the Fiesta team in any way possible so she could get her mission up and moving forward. Yes, the Challenge was the assignment Josie had recklessly dismissed, reluctantly considered, and eventually accepted. But once finished she was heading back home faster than you could slap a tick.

Sitting down and looking directly at Faye and Nola, Josie felt her resolve and organized explanations slipping away. Taking a deep breath, she tried to center herself. Then she began the meeting with her vision to work with young children. As she started to roll, however, she clearly failed to clarify God's role in the process. In fact, she avoided giving God any credit for His intervention. Josie didn't want these folks to think she was delusional or strange, or worse yet, a religious fanatic.

"I believe this fascination with younger children began with my time spent at Rosewood Street Baptist Church back in my hometown of Birmingham, Alabama. And it has continued to blossom tremendously in recent months," Josie began.

"And what do you attribute this growing fascination to, Miss Josie?" It was Nola who surprisingly spoke first.

"Something inside me is urging me to explore my options in this area," Josie replied.

"And does this have anything to do with your relocation to Sand Haven?" Faye questioned.

"In more ways than one, it certainly does. Actually, I have an organization funding me so that I may be here and be somewhat available and flexible."

"Is this an educational or business group of sorts?" Faye wondered.

"Trust me when I say this is a well-organized combination of over-achievers. And these women mean serious business. You don't want to fail where they are invested, and I am somewhat accountable to them, if you know what I mean," Josie said.

"I'm not sure I do. But was it necessary to leave Alabama?" Faye asked.

"I had options. It was strongly suggested that it would be in my best interest to come here to Sand Haven, and here I am," Josie declared.

Nola laughed. "Yes, we can see you plain as day."

"Thank you for allowing me to visit earlier this week. It was one of the most interesting days I have had in a very long time," Josie admitted. "You two make quite a team, and the kiddos are really lucky to have you both in their lives. You are like tireless, high-spirited cheerleaders."

Faye was quick to respond as Nola nodded her head in agreement. "Thank you, Miss Josie. It was fun having you underfoot. We appreciate your interest in our little ones, and they seemed to be taken by you."

"Which is exactly why I think this is where I am supposed to be," Josie said.

What Josie didn't mention was how desperate she was to use the school to help her meet the requirements for the Challenge. She wanted to get started now so she could go home. Half-truths quickly formed into little white lies that ran into one another as Josie spoke. Josie went as far as to say that she hopefully would be able to incorporate much of what they were doing in a teaching facility of her own one day. Now that was a whopper. A gigantic taradiddle. Effortlessly combining truth with fabrication, Josie was in her zone. She went on to explain how the Hallelujah Circle was sponsoring this mission, allowing her to come to Sand Haven, which included free room and board with a host family, a healthy weekly allowance, an emergency fund, and monies designated toward helping children.

"It is my goal to learn more about young children and at some point, to specifically reach out and support four kids in ways even I have not defined at this point," Josie sincerely said.

"It sounds like you have given this a lot of thought and traveled quite a distance to work this out," Nola said. "I left my home and I am aware of how difficult it can be in such a different place. It can be a real challenge."

"Something like that. It's hard to put into words," Josie reflected.

After taking a big breath and holding her flat palms up and outward, Josie indicated she would like to continue on and finish her spiel, hoping they would be patient with her and humbly consider her requests.

"And you might ask, what does the Hallelujah Circle hope to receive from their generous and unfailing support?" Josie asked. "Glory. It all comes down to one word: glory. Glory to God, glory for what He has done. Glory for what we can do for one another, glory in remembering those who have gone on before us." With each "glory" Josie's speaking became more animated and passionate. "For these committed ladies, it is all about His glory." And that was pure truth!

If Josie didn't quite feel the conviction of these words in her bones, she thought they would at least help further her case with these ladies. Staring at Faye Lewis as if her life depended on it, Josie went on, "Like the ray of sunshine you and Nola are in the lives of these precious students, my hands are out, pleading to stand in the light with you both." And firmly if not dramatically clasping her hands, Josie rested her case. "And I think that about covers it," she declared.

"Well, butter my biscuits, Miss Josie!" Faye chirped like a bird. "Thank you for sharing from the innermost sanctuary of your heart. It is obvious you are serious about becoming a part of our school family. At the same time, I am most certain you understand that an issue of this great importance must be thoughtfully and reasonably deliberated. Nola and I will need a weeeeeeee bit of time to consider your request," Faye said in her most Southern drawl yet. "We will review every single thing you said and render our decision Monday after the school day has ended." Josie was relieved not to have an answer johnny-on-the-spot. It meant they had some things to think about and discuss, and that seemed to be a positive thing, instead of a quick "thanks but no thanks."

"I'll see you then. Thank you," said Josie.

"You are most welcome," Miss Faye said as Josie shuffled toward the sunshine door.

Once outside, Josie Bee reviewed everything she had and had not said. She planned on eventually telling the women everything about the Challenge if it came to that. But if Miss Faye didn't allow her to be involved in the school, it wouldn't be necessary to tell them the entire story anyway. Either way, Josie felt she had covered her bases and could easily live with her minuscule fabrications and fill in the blanks later. And as she had heard on many occasions from the Hallelujahs, it was now out of her hands and on God's plate.

Speaking of God, Josie didn't feel much like having a conversation with Him quite yet, although she knew the time was coming. What if He asked her why she left Him out of the discussion? Or what intentions was she referring to? Josie Bee would have to chat about the Challenge sooner or later. In Josie's mind she had been committed to choosing only girls, but what if that was up for grabs? She figured it wasn't, because it made perfect sense to pick girls to honor Addie Mae, Denise, Carole, and Cynthia. But Ernie the grape stuffer and Jupiter the line jumper made Josie smile. She had instantly recognized Jupiter as being the little guy she saw trying to move up in line at Cranston Park the day she was with the Prices after her arrival in Sand Haven. The way the redheaded boy was creeping up the line made both her and Ellie giggle. Best yet was when he was noticed by the two women in charge and quickly removed to the back of the line. Jupiter's expression was priceless. Josie was seeing that boys could be interesting too. Josie Bee felt whoever she would be looking for needed something special and unique in their lives. Something God wanted her to provide. Josie knew she couldn't contribute to the needs of every single child at the school, but she *was* expected to find four. If Miss Faye accepted Josie's offer to help at the school, she felt it would be difficult not to become attached to numerous children and then have to narrow it down to only four. How do you pick one child over the other when you don't know their stories inside and out? Josie was feeling dumbfounded and dense. And overwhelmed. One day at a time.

Josie Bee had planned on going to Cranston Park after the meeting to hunker down in the sandbox to ponder. But instead she opted for going straight back to the house and reflecting in the comfort of her little room. The Price family would be attending an event at the county public library and wouldn't be home until dinner. It was the perfect time to sit down and reach out to Pearl.

Hey Pearl,

Had every intention of properly starting this letter like Auntie Birdie taught us, but I wanted to make it sound like we were just rooms apart instead of in two different states. I really miss you!

So much to tell you, but I really think the most important thing is thanking you for taking such good care of me my whole life. I guess I am only beginning to realize what you've done for me. There could be no better sister than you. And I know you are meeting Auntie Gertie's needs left and right. That's what you do, Pearl. I really admire you.

The sea glass sounds really cool, and I can't wait to hold it in my hands as a reminder of when you were thinking of me. That meant a lot.

Everything is fine here in Indiana, and the Price family is super nice. Paula and Patsy are the sweetest little girls, cute and well-behaved. Going to church tomorrow with them. Don't want to get on the bad side of the Hallelujahs by not following their rules. Ha! I have a part-time domestic job if you can believe that, and the Circle will be thrilled about it too. Hoping to volunteer at a local preschool. Will have to get back with you later on that situation.

Will give more details next week and don't ever forget how much I love and miss you.

Your baby girl,

Josie Bee

The next morning's Second Baptist Church experience was strikingly similar to Rosewood Street Baptist, only on a much, much smaller scale, but every bit as friendly. It was comfortably familiar, and Josie felt thoroughly welcomed. Greeted with many warm hand squeezes and genuine smiles and a pair of fragrant hugs from two very jolly ladies, Josie did not feel out of place at all. The huggers reminded her of Ethel and Edna Singleton, spinster sisters from back home. They both enjoyed applying tremendously generous amounts of Ambush perfume, which announced their presence in one's nose long before one actually encountered them. At the beginning of the service, Josie Bee Johnson and Carl Watkins, referred to as "Big Carl" due to his six-foot-six stature and generous girth, were asked to stand and be recognized as the newest faces in the sanctuary. Pastor said it was an honor to make their acquaintances and to have them as a part of the church family. When the congregation was asked to give the newbies a Second Street Baptist welcome, you would have thought they had just won the lottery. The applause was deafening and took both Josie and Carl by surprise. They laughed out loud, delighted by the enthusiasm and support of their fellow worshipers.

After church, Josie went home with Ellie and Del and the two best-dressed little girls in church to a succulent and juicy pot roast complete with mashed potatoes and gravy, scalloped corn, black-eyed-pea salad, and lightly browned, buttery cornbread. Ellie had insisted on preparing the feast all by herself, and the girls set the table with the good china, a wedding gift twelve years earlier from Del's Auntie Eloise. Miss Eloise was a classy lady with exquisite taste. Josie was reminded of how important food was to each and every one of them gathered at the table, tightly holding hands, giving thanks to God for His goodness in providing for them in such a mighty and magnificent way. With bowed heads and closed eyes, everyone in the room eagerly contributed to a hearty "Amen!"

The Hallelujah ladies had prepared countless meals and banquets and potlucks knowing what it meant to others. They understood not only the necessity but also the powerful emotional ties and memories connected with food. Josie Bee was only beginning to understand the gifts of family, food, and friendship but would eventually carry these sentiments and practices for the rest of her life. But the most important thing about all those mealtime get-togethers was the atmosphere of belonging and fellowship that joined folks one to another. Everyone craves that connection of fitting in with others and feeling accepted unconditionally. And today was another example, not an exception, of designated and deliberate hospitality. Josie Bee felt she was being treated as an honored guest but also felt part of this special family.

In those moments of reflection Josie realized this was exactly what Faye Lewis was accomplishing at Fiesta School. Gifted with hospitality and a desire to serve others, she gave her students the opportunity to enjoy food and fellowship daily with one another. The little ones looked forward to those meals. The laughter around the table and the social skills being developed were important. Faye Lewis, the butt of jokes in some circles around town, realized more about bringing others together and celebrating individuality, Josie mused, than possibly anyone else in the community. It was a concept almost too basic, too simple. All people regardless of age desire love and security on some basic level. Meet their physical needs, bring them in, encircle them with acceptance and unconditional love, and you have created an atmosphere of trust. Fiesta School was trying its best to provide for the children, attempting to give them the things needed to more easily walk through life. Faye and Nola knew more than most people gleaned in a lifetime about this kind of thing. The kindness and respect they demonstrated day in and day out for the most vulnerable, impressionable, and tender young students was blowing up in Josie's innermost being. Her desire to fulfill the Challenge as God presented it to her had been the initial driver sending Josie to Fiesta. But already she realized the mission was starting up in ways she had not anticipated. And she began to believe she was placed in this community for a reason.

Josie Bee envisioned the endless hours Nola spent in the kitchen preparing what the kids loved to eat, encouraging them to try new foods, and she was gently humbled. Josie could see in her mind Miss Nola bending over the kitchen counter peeling potatoes, her elbows occasionally resting on the aqua Formica top for stability. Josie remembered how little she liked that job of skinning spuds, how quickly her back ached after only a short period of time when helping out in the church kitchen, and she cringed. What a whiny baby she had been. Knowing Nola's arthritis was likely more painful and far more severe than she let on, a more considerate Josie recognized and applauded her efforts. Both Nola and Faye had a level of grit and unexplainable determination that made Josie want to know more about their stories. The funny thing was, she really was becoming interested in others. Josie Bee had accepted most things in life, at least so far, at face value and with very little hesitation or reflection. Now the questions were popping like kernels of corn, and she knew few if any of the answers. But she was curious.

What sparked this desire to provide and serve the smallest of individuals in a school community? How did these two very different women become such a dynamic duo for education and young children?

"And how could they afford all those nice things, the tables and chairs, the bookcases, the food, and so on?" Josie asked out loud.

All the Prices looked at her in confusion.

"Oh, sorry! Just thinking out loud," Josie said. This talking out loud was getting to be a real habit!

Even Josie, who knew so little about the ladies' work, would have felt disrespectful and dismissive of what they did if she had referred to it as "a typical nursery school." There's nothing wrong with nurseries, but this was a deliberate school for solid early childhood education. Josie wondered what initiated this purposeful journey for each of them. For the moment, it was safe to say that only God knew that, 'cause He knew everything, and Josie quietly wondered if sometimes knowing everything saddened Him. Or caused Him pain? Disappointment? Did He feel sorrow and shed tears?

These thoughts kept Josie preoccupied as she did the dishes and cleaned up the kitchen for Ellie. It was the least she could do for all the hospitality and care they had already shown her. Josie Bee would then be ready to visit the sandy "think box" and get down to the business at hand, which was staring her in the face. Just like when she joined the Children's March, she realized she "had a job to do." Those words were painfully productive and yet magical. They also continued to spring Josie into action when she dared think about them.

Pearl always said, "Sometimes you just know what you have to do, and it is best to get to it." The world according to Pearl was practical and reliable. Sometimes Josie's imagination went crazy thinking about her reserved sister with the wild likes of Jumpin' James. It was like the meeting of a delicate raindrop and a hurricane. At least Josie hadn't gotten wind of it, and she was fairly certain Auntie Birdie hadn't known about it either, or there would have been a commotion second to none. Auntie would have placed the Hallelujah Circle on notice that Pearl was in need of an intervention faster than double-struck lightning. On the other hand, Auntie seemed to know about everything going on in her hometown and her church. Now that was another something to ponder. Once somewhat annoyed and intimidated by the Hallelujah gals, Josie now saw them in a different light, and welcomed their influence. This formidable unit had the inside track to God, and Josie certainly needed their assistance.

Walking to Cranston Park was refreshing. Josie felt the sun on her back and a bounce in each step as she came closer to her destination. Looking forward to the sandbox, Josie needed this uninterrupted time to clear her head and pull together what she did know. Entering the sandbox, Josie relaxed her tight muscles, consciously letting go of the tension and worries she had felt. Contentedly sitting in the sand, Josie's thoughts began shifting and she started to feel more like a vessel instead of the ultimate decision maker.

"A peace that passes all understanding" was the best way to sum up Josie's present state of being. She felt a calming wash over her. Josie Bee's breathing relaxed as she felt the pressure from the heavy load she had been carrying being lifted off her shoulders.

Unexplainably, Josie began feeling connected to this plan of God's. She didn't have many details, but she did know it was no mistake that circumstances had delivered her to Faye Lewis and the steps of Fiesta School. Things were unfolding, but Josie couldn't be sure of the outcomes. She felt she had been led to make the connection with Faye, and that would suggest that Josie might ultimately become involved with the school. That made her feel excited and substantiated. The four children she hoped to find were right there within those school walls. She needed to be patient and positive, trusting that things would be revealed when they were supposed to be.

Josie realized she was uninformed and trying to figure out too much too quickly in her driving urge to get back home. She wisely recognized she had the time to begin searching for the designated children, and would have to exercise patience—this was not her strongest virtue, as her family would wholeheartedly confirm.

Josie hoped that God had a plan. But had He been directing and reassuring Josie all along and she wasn't tuned in? Because if that was the case, Josie needed to improve her listening skills. But God wasn't finished. He had more to say. And she wanted to get her listening ears on.

8

THE GIFT OF SIGHT

*There is no better way to thank God for your sight than
by giving a helping hand to someone in the dark.*

Helen Keller

STILL SEATED IN the sandbox and basking in her newfound confidence,
Josie reflected on the Challenge and its purpose. She would choose four
girls, hopefully from the Fiesta School, each one in memory of one of
the four promising young girls that were killed in the 1963 Sixteenth
Street Baptist Church bombing just over two years earlier. Murdered by
hate and racial prejudice by the Ku Klux Klan, the girls had been taken
by a deliberate and brutal tragedy so unimaginable it was still hard for
Josie to get her head around it. Intense anger and thoughts of revenge
had been gnawing away at her heart since the death of her parents six
months before the bombing. No one had been held accountable for
either crime, and law enforcement had quickly closed the case on the
Johnson family. Josie wanted better than that for her Momma and
Daddy and had been filled with deep loss and a raging anger that drove
her toward more vengeful options to right the wrongs done. There was

no justice for anyone, or at least not anyone in Josie's world.

Now two years since the horrendous bombing, no progress had been made in bringing the evil perpetrators to justice. Josie just couldn't seem to get past the loss of the girls and the lack of accountability for the murders. It wasn't enough to let things go, so she edged toward retaliation and revenge. As Josie neared making irreparable mistakes, God reached out and suggested in a most convincing and creative way that Josie remember those girls by helping four others in their honor. His intervention gave Josie something new to focus on, placing a temporary halt on Josie's bad thoughts and desires and the destructive path she was snowballing down. God was offering an alternative direction for Josie. And now it was imperative that she pay attention to God's nudges. Listening and being open would not be listed among Josie's virtues either, but there was hope for developing those characteristics. After all, she was a work in progress.

And then it hit Josie—an eye-opening moment in understanding the inner workings of the Challenge mission. Clearly it was not Josie's responsibility to find and fix broken children but to assist the chosen in discovering and developing their God-given strengths. Not to be distracted by difficulties or obvious problems but to search for and focus on the positives in the kids' lives. Josie was not enlisted to save anybody but to walk alongside and encourage them. This brought her tremendous relief and a welcome strength. Addie, Denise, Carole, and Cynthia had been living out glowing versions of themselves when their lives were abruptly ended, and Josie would be assisting these little girls in trying to do the same. To shine. To be comfortable in their own skin. To celebrate as if there was no tomorrow. Because, simply put, sometimes there wasn't.

This day was full of God's grace. Josie's heart was stuffed, experiencing an overabundance of blessings, relief, and gratitude for what had been accomplished. Today God walked with her and revealed that which she was unable to do for or by herself. Then He brought forth clarity and confirmation; it was beyond helpful. All Josie could say was, "Glory!" Tomorrow afternoon Josie Bee would pop into the school after work to find out Faye and Nola's decision about her working at Fiesta, but she wasn't too worried. God had been preparing her for this task. It was enough to have experienced the unexpected resolutions, and Josie would let tomorrow take care of itself. Or at least she was trying to do so.

The next afternoon Josie practically pranced up Fiesta's walkway, happy to be finished with her domestic duties, anticipating good things. The kids' silliness and giggles slipped out of the half-cracked windows and made her heart frolic. They would be picking things up, overstuffing their backpacks, trying to remember whether they had worn a coat or sweater to school that morning. Or not.

Josie desperately wanted to clear her conscience with Faye and Nola—to give them the entire story minus the fabrications and omittances from Saturday's time of sharing. She also wanted to speak with them before they could relay their decision to her. Initially, she had considered telling them the total truth only if they were going to accept her. But now Josie felt conflicted, realizing that complete honesty and transparency, regardless of whether it affected the Fiesta outcome, might be the right thing to do. How could she tell students it was important to tell the truth and be honest if she herself was not? She would admit her wrongdoing, which sounded better than saying "lies," letting the chips fall where they may and hoping for the best. That's what happens when you lie. You have to cover and uncover a whole plethora of things, trying to keep them straight and crossing your fingers that it somehow makes sense and works out in the end.

Barely opening the yellow front door, Josie peeked in the crack but was instantly spotted. "Hi Miss Josie," she heard several of the kids say. They clustered around her, jumping up and down like she was a superstar. Josie loved the attention, knowing they were sincerely delighted to see her. And she was excited to see them too. This type of reaction was a new experience for Josie, and she was starting to really like it!

Judy asked Josie to help her look for Ginger the Giraffe, who had been missing most of the day. Josie headed for the oversized toy box. Judy, tired and exasperated, was heading toward a bona fide meltdown. A child in crying mode when the parents arrive to pick them up doesn't look good. The children could be fine for a good stretch of time, then one little snafu could mess up a perfect record. Josie found Ginger stuffed into a pickup truck but otherwise unharmed. A joyful moment. Judy was thrilled, and Josie felt victorious in avoiding an onset of tears. Funny how quickly youngsters can turn those tears on and even more quickly shut them off. Like magic! Unbelievable.

Faye held up one finger to indicate she'd be with Josie shortly, so Josie made herself useful by picking up what hadn't yet gone into backpacks. There was a laundry basket labeled "leftovers," and Josie Bee dropped her findings into the bright red container the kiddos were supposed to stop and look through before leaving (although more often it was the parents who checked it out). The day ended and departures went smoothly as the little people filed out, hand in hand with their big people, until the school was empty.

"All righty, Miss Josie, Nola and I are ready to chat," Faye said as she offered one of the children's chairs to her. Josie took a deep breath.

"Would it be possible first for me to explain a little more of . . . um . . . um, what I may have accidentally left out when we last spoke?" Josie asked, the sound of her breaking voice indicating how important this was to her. "Pretty please?"

Josie was surprised at what came out of her mouth. She hadn't used the words "pretty please" since she was a toddler.

"Shall we put some sugar on that, dear?" Faye asked. She seemed tickled by Josie's apparent nervousness and childlike words.

"Do you really think that is necessary? Nola and I don't beat around the bush, and we have readily accepted your request for placement here at Fiesta School. The only question is whether you can afford to be involved. There is no money available this current school year to adequately compensate you for your time or efforts. On our part, this would be considered a temporary volunteer position, an apprenticeship providing on-the-job training for your potential future employment in the field of childhood education. Would that be agreeable with you, Miss Josie?"

Josie was tempted to bite her tongue and readily accept her good fortune without saying anything that could jeopardize this victory. But she knew what she had to do. Without hesitating, Josie launched directly into the initial interaction she had with God.

"About three months ago I had a conversation with God in the middle of the night. There was a storm with lightning and thundering and lots of wind and rain. It got my attention, and I went to the window to see what was going on. Suddenly everything stopped and there was this big hush." Josie took a breath. "Then out of nowhere God spoke to me. I didn't initiate the communication. It was all on God. But I clearly heard every word He said."

"Josie, stop, you seem flustered talking about this experience. Do you need to go into all these details?" asked Faye.

"Yes and no, depending on your point of view, I guess," Josie offered. "I just want to be as up-front as possible about why I am here. I may have left out or skipped over some pertinent information when we last spoke."

"Okay, then by all means continue if you think you must," said Faye.

"So, the gist of the conversation was that God wanted me to do something and I said no. Then I told my sister about it because I was somewhat rattled, and she told our Auntie Birdie. Then the thing started snowballing after Auntie told her church ladies about the interaction. Before I knew what to do next, everyone thought it would be a good idea for me to go on a mission trip of sorts and work with children." What Josie had said still sounded somewhat sketchy and aloof. Trying to be more transparent, she continued.

"They decided that not only should I work with children but that I should choose four girls in particular. They dubbed it 'the Challenge.' This is where it gets—"

"The bottom line is," Nola interrupted, "are you here because you want to be or feel an obligation you cannot escape, Miss Josie?"

"I am here because I know I'm supposed to be. Plus, I really want to be here," whispered Josie. "I really, really do."

"Then hold your horses, pulllllease, I think we have plenty of information for now," Faye replied. There was that exaggerated drawn-out twang again, but Josie was happy to hear it coaxing her to stop.

Josie saw no point in continuing on. She could live with what she had and hadn't yet shared. Right now Faye and Nola seemed to get it and appeared confident that they knew all they needed to bring Josie on board. They seemed to understand what she was trying to explain, and nothing as far as they were concerned had changed. These generous ladies were going to actually allow Josie Bee Johnson into the Fiesta School. Nodding their heads in sync, Faye and Nola reiterated their goal to provide their unique and gifted student body with the necessary tools to enable their future educational successes. Both women strongly recognized the difference Josie's energy and assistance had brought to the Fiesta the day she visited. And Josie, who was delighted to provide an extra set of eyes and hands in working with the children, brought the gift of youth and excitement to everyone.

"Do you understand our goals, Miss Josie?" Faye asked.

"Absolutely," she replied.

"Can you identify with and conform to what we do here?" Faye continued.

"Affirmative," Josie responded.

"Then we would like to officially welcome you to Fiesta," Faye squealed.

Together the three women formed a joint hug, and the Fiesta Circle was created and confirmed. Faye quickly informed Josie that both she and Nola had seen in her something they were actually missing at the Fiesta School. Her youth, the ways the kids interacted with her, and Josie's intense desire to be at the school told them all what they initially needed to know about her. After the previous Saturday's appointment and Josie's intriguing request, the two women had no doubt Josie would be coming aboard. Faye and Nola immediately started putting together a folder of school information.

The first thing Josie would need to do was memorize the first and last names of the twenty-one students: twelve girls and nine boys. In case of an accident with the children or if Josie ever needed to take charge, it was imperative she have the enrollment list in hand. Josie would later pull out the list to read the following names:

1. Adams, Ernie
2. Baker, Tabytha
3. Barker, Beanie
4. Beard, Johnny

5. Carson, Josiah
6. Cross, Elijah
7. Flack, Judy
8. Harper, Charlene (Charlie)
9. Higgins, DeeDee
10. Hill, Esmeralda
11. Jones, Agnes
12. Lawson, Peggy
13. Links, Joey
14. Martin, Jupiter
15. Miller, Moshe
16. Perez, Rosita
17. Redmond, Etta
18. Schmidt, Polly
19. Tucker, Patty-Jo
20. White, Penny
21. Wynn, Tommy

There also was a bright red card file box that contained all necessary information such as addresses, phone numbers, birthdates, and contact person in case of an emergency. Faye and Nola advised Josie to take her box with pertinent information and highlighted instructions home and thoroughly devour its content. It was agreed that Josie could start the next afternoon after working for Mrs. Whittaker in the morning and be there on her two days off, for the time being. Josie Bee needed to sit down and discuss a new schedule with her stiff boss, already surmising it would not go well.

"I'll be back soon and ready to go, ladies," said Josie. "Please bear with me. I'll be the first to admit I'm not sure how this is going to unroll, but I look forward to your input." She continued with a grin, "And twenty-one students. That's a lot of . . . pretty much everything." She was thinking about snacks, trips to the bathroom, wiping noses, picking up, and everything else that went on at Fiesta School.

Faye, trying to interject some lightheartedness and humor into Josie's unintended sigh, said, "Twenty-one. I guess that at least makes us legal!" She chuckled to herself as Josie organized her things and got up. As she turned around to wave goodbye, Nola pulled Josie back and gave her a tight squeeze.

"Thank you for coming our way, Miss Josie. You are bringing new life and challenges to us. Everything is going to work out; your trials are ours now as well. It feels good to acknowledge God is on the throne, and although we may come and go, He is indeed in control. I have missed God since I left Mississippi. I am thinking He has missed me too. He sent you here, Josie, make no mistake about that. He loves you dearly. We are all His works." Nola smiled.

Josie certainly hadn't seen this coming. Yep, Nola was Hallelujah material for sure. Josie felt a kinship, but she couldn't pin down why. It was just there, this feeling of acceptance and understanding. Josie felt Nola probably had almost as much to do with getting her into the school as God did. Maybe not quite as much, but close.

Riding the bus home gave Josie time to unwind and do some reflecting, which was something she had never needed or considered doing back in Alabama. She enjoyed the soft rumbling under her feet that sometimes tickled, lulling her into a state of peaceful oblivion. Josie was able to gaze out the windows, not focusing on anything in particular. Mostly she liked just sitting there and not needing to carry on a conversation or search for an appropriate response. Letting her mind drift was like being in the clouds, gently folding into the sky and sailing. She was like a little boat bobbing in the big sea, letting the water's movement have its way with no cares about what would be coming next. Memories of sweetness shared with Pearl in the closet began fading in and out, wrapping invisible arms around her that felt tenderly familiar. Thoughts of her sister were moving in her heart, and while it was wide open, they came tumbling in.

Josie stepped off the bus and beelined it to the Prices' house. Arriving back to their household was becoming second nature. Josie liked being considered part of the family and couldn't wait to tell them her good news.

"I'm home, everybody," Josie announced when she got in the door. "And I have the BEST news ever 'cause I got the J-O-B!"

"How could they not love you, baby girl," Ellie exclaimed with a high five followed by a hug. Paula and Patsy had gathered around Josie too, jumping up and down like grasshoppers.

"Yay Josie!" they shouted over their shoulders as they disappeared back into the kitchen.

"How about some happy dogs for dinner, Josie?" Ellie grinned.

"What?" Josie asked.

"Well the girls were absolutely positive you were getting the job! They have been busy as bees making tonight's dinner in your honor. One of their specialties are hot dogs with smiling faces," Ellie giggled. "They're pretty cute and tasty!"

"Aw, how yummy," said Josie.

"I made your favorite cake, Josie Bee, and the girls are just putting on the finishing touches. They are kind of picky, and this is really important to them. It may take a few more minutes. They really adore you, Josie," Ellie remarked. "I guess we all have a soft spot for you."

"The feelings are mutual," said Josie.

After dinner and dessert Josie Bee trotted off to her room. On top of her pillow was another letter from Pearl. Ellie had wanted Josie to have one more surprise to cap off her successful day.

Dear Josie,

How's my baby sister doing?

Auntie says the Hallelujahs are praying for you and have an upcoming bake sale with all proceeds going to your mission Challenge.

Making toasted chocolate coconut birds' nests in your honor. Once the nest is purchased there are very special edible eggs that can be bought separately to place inside the nest. Each one will represent time spent in prayer for you. Auntie Birdie encourages them to remove an egg after each intercession, the goal being to have an empty nest. Sounds yummy and different.

Do you remember smarty-pants Eugene Stump from the Young Whirlybirds class? He got wind of the nests from his

Grammy Jane and said it was surely a rip-off if he ever heard one. Auntie Birdie said he threatened to buy peanut M&Ms and sell them twelve for a dollar, a real good deal, calling them "painted petition prompters" to remind people to pray. A lot cheaper than the Hallelujahs' singularly sold handmade specialties! He thought parents might be interested in purchasing twelve for the same price as one fancy chocolate egg. Berniece Thomas did not, for one single minute, appreciate being upended by an obnoxious too-big-for-his-britches six-year-old.

Auntie Gertie is getting slightly weaker by the day. The doctors are going to try treating her with a different medication. That little cough tickle I have always had, you called it a coo-coo, seems to be becoming a bit more frequent. Gertie says she will bring it up to her doctor at some point, and we have fun going back and forth about who is the patient and who is the caregiver. You would enjoy her so much, Josie! She is a spunky and spirited dear, dear soul. A lot funnier than Auntie Birdie, and the stories she has to tell, well, you wouldn't believe all the trouble our Auntie B caused! She was a handful and would be intensely mortified if she knew what Auntie Gertie has been sharing. What a hoot!

Not much else happening. I am going to the beach regularly but have been unable to coax Gertie to the sandy shores, and that is okay. I really enjoy exploring by myself and searching for sea glass. It is miraculous how it gets broken and comes back refined and beautiful. I get totally lost, and sometimes I feel myself drifting out to sea and wish you were here experiencing this feeling too. So peaceful. Sea-glass pieces are like snowflakes, no two are alike. You will know what I am trying to say when you see those snowy ice crystals for the very first time. Don't forget to stick your tongue out and catch a few. I have my sea glass and you will have snowflakes, baby sister.

Looking forward to one day being together and sharing our adventures. You are always in my thoughts, and what you are

doing, Josie, is amazing. I could never be that brave.
    I love you,
    Pearl

That was all she wrote. And it was more than enough. Josie was so glad Pearl thought she was brave, even though Josie didn't feel that way most of the time. But she couldn't stop thinking about smarty-pants Eugene, who was headed for real trouble if he had already gotten the attention of the Hallelujah Circle. Sounded like it was time to give him a dose of his own medicine. He was always causing a commotion at the church, but he was no match for any one of the Circle's dutiful enforcers. Josie was sure that some of those ladies lived for the opportunity to "assist" a headstrong member of the younger generation in choosing to think before they acted with careless disregard toward one of the Hallelujah's fundraising endeavors. A real big no-no. Josie was sure he would be spending time on his knees in the big kitchen with the bright checkered floor, learning a thing or two about not bragging up his own thoughts and ideas. Leave it to Pearl to give her a good laugh.

Later that evening, Josie Bee's heart began tenderly turning to the selection of the four girls who would be chosen for the Challenge. Class list in hand, and with a new sense of clarity, the possibilities were carefully being revealed to Josie, forming in her mind and somersaulting into existence.

She began writing down the names in her notebook. Her heart beat furiously, and when she had finished writing, she flailed both her arms over her head in joy. It was one of the most unrestrained moments Josie had experienced. In her excitement and relief, she wanted to jump up and down on her bed and shout, "I have names. I know their names. I know WHO they are!"

Acknowledging the four girls had now been chosen, the Challenge was taking shape. Josie had to give God full credit. He was calling the shots, and she was ready to obey. Josie had wrestled with doubts about how to move forward, and she had felt inadequate and overwhelmed.

Now she firmly believed God was lifting her up, filling her head and heart with direction. In partnering with Josie, they would together share the Challenge and eventually steer the mission to its ultimate fruition and purpose. This was no longer just a list for the Challenge; it was now the Challenge's official Angel List. Thinking of Addie, Denise, Carole, and Cynthia, Josie Bee could only say, "Oh my" and "Glory!"

She had not expected this type of revelation. Josie's life was once again proof that when God intervenes, it is not only unexpected but spectacular. Josie now had what she needed to get started, knowing the other details would drop into place soon enough.

Josie Bee couldn't take her eyes off the notebook she held tightly in her hands. It contained the four names she had written down: Agnes Jones, Patty-Jo Tucker, Charlie Harper, and Penny White. Days earlier Josie had been leaning toward others, including two boys, Jupiter and Ernie, as well as several different girls. But God had directed, and now confirmed, the choosing of four little girls. His hand was in the particulars.

She now felt it important to let Faye and Nola know that the four girls had already been chosen but found that would be the most difficult part to explain. It seemed downright presumptuous to have chosen the girls after only being at the school a short time, but the truth was that God had selected them and revealed their names to Josie in His own way.

ONE WEEK LATER

The minute Agnes Jones appeared on the Angel List, Josie connected her sweet spirit to that of Carole Robertson. Carole had been such a friendly young girl and was nice to everyone she encountered. Had she encountered little Agnes, she would have picked her up and taken her under her wing. Filled with an extraordinary amount of confidence, Carole would have poured some of that self-assurance into this small gem, building her courage and strength. Thinking of Carole, Josie went from sad to mad in a matter of minutes. Carole's life, which had been so promising, was taken from her by the hands of hate. Josie Bee knew it was easier to hate and wondered whether she could ever have the kind of strength Carole had been known to have. There was a deep temptation orbiting Josie's soul, one that made her want to leap out and hurt bad people. It was so strong it sometimes scared Josie. The church and the families of the four bombing victims had stated continuously and believed in their souls that only love could trump hate. Josie hoped that was true because if there was any other way, she guessed she would have seen it by now. Like Carole's sparkling spirit, Josie saw a similar spark in Agnes that was second to none.

Agnes remained sweet and kind even after being picked on by others. The teasing had been light, but it appeared to Josie that the kiddos surely didn't realize they were making Agnes feel bad when she ran into things and they called her a clumsy elephant. She resisted being mean back, pretending she didn't really hear the comments, and possibly she didn't fully understand their meaning. Josie wasn't sure if this was anything to worry about or not but was going to bring it up to Faye and Nola at some point. She wondered if there was anything preventing this sweet child from hearing or seeing properly. Maybe Agnes had something going on at home or health issues, because sometimes this child existed as if in a fog, stumbling quietly in her own space. Josie had a lot to learn.

What she did know was Agnes's middle name was Grace, after her grandmother who lived in their home and was legally blind. It was Agnes's second repeated year at the school, and while Agnes struggled especially with math, most subjects were challenging for her. She had difficulty interacting with other students and did not generally join in. Agnes Grace Jones did seem to bump into and knock over many things, which is why the kids compared her to an elephant. But Agnes was always willing to assist others if she could and when they needed it. This little girl was soft-spoken and patient, thoughtful and considerate, and she never forgot to say her pleases and thank-yous. Though she was a real sweetie pie with a tender heart, something was off, but no one at the school had witnessed any specific red flags. Maybe Josie's eyes on the situation could be helpful.

Josie had learned from Faye and Nola that Agnes's parents, Jackie and Jay, had accepted that she was "slow" because that is what they were told by one of the temporary practitioners at the Child Discovery

Center, a clinic that specialized in identifying and diagnosing early learning disabilities. However, they had not been helpful in addressing Agnes's delay in learning. The Joneses knew not a single thing more when they left the clinic than what they had known going in—a very disappointing and expensive experience. Mr. and Mrs. Jones hoped Agnes's issues were age-related and she would simply outgrow them. They also feared they were possibly making a fuss over nothing and that another year at the Fiesta School would work wonders for their one and only child. Because they did not want Agnes to be any more self-conscious than she was, Mr. and Mrs. Jones overlooked everything and questioned or pointed out nothing. Faye and Nola both noted that this girl was very much loved and cared for, and that her home life was stable.

Within a short time, Josie had already learned something special about Agnes. Even though she was struggling in many ways, this little girl was still able to see and recognize the needs of others. What a gift! Josie was not seeing disadvantages but marveling at the advantages Agnes offered her classmates. This was something remarkable. Whatever was holding Agnes back from getting all that she may be needing or what others wanted for her wasn't hampering her success in helping others. The difficulties were effectively cultivating Agnes to an awareness and understanding of what others around her needed.

"So then, what could be wrong?" Josie whispered to herself. It was now officially her job to find out, and she hoped God would work out the details as only He could, which would be a tremendous help to Josie Bee. Agnes already had a good heart filled with kindness and compassion. And that was a sweet advantage.

In troubleshooting with Ellie about Agnes one evening, Ellie shared with Josie Bee that one of the deacons, an eye doctor, volunteered his services to perform free eye exams for those in the community who couldn't afford them.

Josie and Faye had been putting their heads together and, even with Nola's input, couldn't quite figure out what was going on with Agnes. She definitely could not focus on the easiest of assignments, and even after contacting the Joneses, the ladies were stumped. Grandma Grace was doing well in their home, and everything was good between her and Agnes. In fact, Agnes persistently watched out for her grandmother and doted on her. They had a tight bond. There seemed to be no explainable worries or changes that would cause Agnes to be anxious or fear losing her own eyesight. Jackie and Jay, extremely caring parents, agreed that it might be a good idea to check her vision and see if there were any concerns that the school could address. After the Joneses' experience at the Discovery Clinic, Josie thought they would not mind a second opinion if it didn't cost them anything. Ellie was certain W. Clark Decker would be more than happy to assist Josie and do the eye exam for Agnes. All Josie had to do was ask, and Ellie reminded her it wouldn't hurt to share her role and mission in accepting God's Challenge. Josie still wasn't sure about that part of the request but would include whatever was needed to get Dr. Decker on board.

Josie was attached to this sweet-spirited little one, finding out that a kind heart knows no age or limits. Sometimes Josie Bee was sure that Agnes was the teacher and she the pupil, which amused her to no end. Go figure.

9

THE GIRL WITH THE TISSUES

*There is a sacredness in tears. They are not the
mark of weakness, but of power. They speak
more eloquently than ten thousand tongues.
They are the messengers of overwhelming grief,
of deep contrition, and of unspeakable love.*

Washington Irving

ANGEL NUMBER TWO, Patty-Jo Tucker, was a perfect match to honor
the life of Addie Mae Collins. Little Miss Addie by all accounts was a
sweet-spirited and gentle young lady. Addie Mae, whose loveliness was
apparent in her calm and serene ways, had a quiet nature. A child who
did not engage in conflict of any kind, she was a true peacemaker at
heart, which made her extremely easy to get along with. Always willing to help, Addie was doing just that when the bomb went off that
fateful day in Birmingham. Addie Mae was one of eight children, and
her family suffered greatly after Addie's death, a suffering compounded
by the horrible injuries that her younger sister Sarah experienced from
the blast. The loss of one of Sarah's eyes, along with the psychological

trauma from the bombing, marked a life of added difficulty and sadness for the Collins siblings and their parents. It was an excruciating burden that weighed permanently and heavily on all the survivors. To carry such an overwhelming load of intense suffering each and every day for the rest of your life is beyond description.

Reflecting on the pain the parents of the deceased young girls carried in their hearts, it was remarkable how they refused to give in to their intense emotions and continuous disbelief, at least in public. No one wanted to believe that this type of vicious crime could be inflicted on innocent children. Now they only wanted justice for their babies. They spent countless hours on their knees praying to keep peace with God's Word and respectfully serve Him. They held their heads high. These folks carried on, determined that if they could be fair and obedient, then they would beat hate. Their tears continued to flow, but they strove for balance. How they did this Josie and others did not know. Setting an incredible example, these believers walked the walk, supported by their families, friends, and the church. Local law enforcement and legal watchdogs, along with the FBI, fell short in any concrete efforts or commitment to bringing the guilty parties to judicial accountability. This was where the constant weariness of not being able to fully heal came into play. The delay fueled the fires of anger and distrust of the legal community, governmental agencies, and others in authority.

Patty-Jo Tucker reminded Josie of Addie Mae and brought feelings of loss and remembrance to the forefront of her mind. Who could purposefully hurt children? None of the victims had or could have done a single thing to warrant such a savage attack. Nor could they have prevented it, and that is what haunted Josie Bee almost as much as the deadly bombing itself. Who is allowed to strike God's holy, anointed, safe haven? Why did God not prevent this everlastingly painful and tragic event in His own house? It was a sacred place of refuge for its members and families, not to mention everyone involved in the struggling civil rights movement. It was obvious that the sick and twisted murderers were still running free as birds, a fact that continued to tear Josie up and keep all wounds open and unable to heal.

Josie Bee felt that her perspective was justified. She had been free-falling and spiraling downward prior to the bombing. In May of 1963 Josie and Pearl eagerly participated in the Children's March, and it had been a life-changing eye-opener. Wanting to support parents, leaders, churches, and the movement for equal rights, over a thousand children peacefully demonstrated by walking across the city of Birmingham together. Their mantra: "We shall overcome." Experiencing the wrath of law enforcement and fire officials and those in about every government position, the demonstrators were attacked with batons, foul language, water hoses, and vicious dogs. The powerful force of the streamed water damaged the eyes of many of the children, even pulling hair follicles from their heads. Along with cuts, broken ribs, and severe bruising from the physical abuse, mental anguish and fear were off the charts.

"Who attacks children? Who does this?" Josie screamed as Pearl was knocked to the ground by an out-of-control German Shepherd. The snarling and the bared teeth of the aggressive and uncontrolled dogs would remain an atrocious memory in Josie's mind forever. She and Pearl had never been exposed to prejudicial hate and racism on that kind of level. Or if they had the girls were too young to recognize that "whites only" and "coloreds only" signs were to keep them legally and physically separated from white folks. It was what they were used to, not asking why or questioning the circumstances. Looking back, Momma and Daddy had protected them in so many ways by keeping them out of places or situations that would have warranted explanation. Momma always made sure she had little sandwiches packed in her oversized pocketbook should they get hungry when out and about running errands. Daddy constantly warned his daughters not to go off by themselves, urging them never to talk back to anyone and especially not white folks. Ever. When he shook his rigid finger and said "ever," Pearl and Josie Bee felt his unexplained anger. His voice had authority, and knowing Daddy meant business, they never considered disobeying or questioning the rules. Pearl would demurely nod her head after such discussions, while Daddy would scold Josie, "Don't you roll those little brown eyes at me, baby girl! I'm serious about this." Marcus Johnson knew he would not always be able to protect his daughters and that pained him deeply.

The Children's March and what followed marked a violent and anxious time for people of color in Birmingham, Alabama, and across the Deep South. The plan to allow youth to present the message and stand up for their rights and the rights of others culminated in an event of great meaning and courage. It also focused the national spotlight on the unjust and inhumane treatment of people of color in America's Southland, ironically called the "Bible Belt." "Do unto others as you would have others do unto you" meant nothing.

The attention to Birmingham and the state of Alabama complete with photos and press coverage of the horrifying, unforgettable treatment of children appeared in papers throughout the country. Suddenly, it was as if the country had awakened from hibernation and wondered, "What's going on?" Apparently they didn't wonder enough to honestly or morally consider one another's basic human rights and needs, let alone to then act accordingly. This soured Josie to no end, further developing and advancing her distrust of white people in general. Everything around her was affecting this irritable state of mind. And with the suspected "payback" bombing, Josie Bee bitterly questioned, "Why?"

Extending far down the scale of emotions, Josie's distrust and anger had fostered a cold heart. The locusts were right there gnawing at her, and Josie Bee could feel their presence as she began looking for others who felt like her. That is what the locust does, seeks out others just like themselves. When they band together, they become bold and aggressive, an appropriate description of the Klan and its mentality. The KKK preyed on the hatred and white superiority others like them felt entitled to, which attracted like-minded members, making their numbers increase. Acts of hate toward people of color escalated because the Klan incited fear in any who opposed their views, intimidating those folks who did have a conscience to turn their heads and do nothing. No one welcomed a confrontation with the notorious haters, but one never knew for sure who privately and secretly participated in their organization. It was safer to simply pretend not to see what was going on, trying to be easygoing and non-opinionated in public. But Josie was developing her own inner desires to push back. The feelings ran deep, culminating in her desire to connect with an underground resistance group, one of many that had gotten Josie's attention. She was on the fringe of cultivating her rising anger, taking steps forward in that direction and deliberately connecting with others who also wanted justice. Josie, too, had the beginnings of similar behaviors much like the locust.

It was at this exact and critical time that God divinely intervened, catching Josie Bee with the rescuing net of the Challenge as she was about to take a deliberate plunge. Josie began to recognize that she would have been no better than the Klansmen if she had continued on the destructive path she was considering. Josie still questioned; angry feelings roused themselves when she looked back on that fateful Sunday morning in September. But she did know one thing: she never wanted anyone to forget the murders and tragic loss of Addie, Denise, Carole, and Cynthia, victims of racial hatred and brutality. Her recollections of these four girls were filled with love and promise, and it was Josie's mission not to allow them to be forgotten or their memories to fade. Her commitment to assist the four designated angel girls at the Fiesta School to recognize their worth and value was a privilege. Setting aside her unresolved feelings, Josie wanted to encourage and cheer these sweet girls on.

Josie Bee realized that there was absolutely nothing she could do to heal Birmingham or any of those who experienced and survived the church bombing. But she could certainly walk with Agnes, Patty-Jo, Charlie, and Penny in honor of the victims. Josie knew God had a plan, and now she was a part of it. To honor her friends she would do the very best possible to bring their character and uniqueness into the lives of the Challenge's Angel List. These little girls might have some troubles and sadness in their sandboxes, but they could overcome. Josie suspected at least one of them was dealing with a locust, and Josie knew something about that kind of destruction. If there was anything holding these girls back or chipping away at their joy, Josie was determined to identify them and then get to work.

Here was Patty-Jo Tucker, Angel Number Two, looking like she was carrying the world on her shoulders. Patty-Jo looked tired and frazzled. Much of the time her big blue eyes were filled with tears, where there should have been sparkles. What Josie wouldn't give to see a relaxed expression. Patty-Jo smiled when encouraged, but the forced grin was visibly tight. In spite of her burdens, Patty-Jo was thoughtful and considerate in ways that demonstrated sincerity, which was endearing at such a young age. Josie could honestly say she did not see a white girl with issues; she saw an innocent child's hurting heart, and it had no color. Josie secretly wondered if she could have done this just months ago when she despised white folks in general, eagerly wanting to band with others who held similar contempt and disgust. God was working in mysterious ways, and Josie's heart was softening a bit. But she knew she had a long way to go.

Patty-Jo was the girl with tears in her eyes and a box of tissues in her hands. She clutched that Kleenex like others held on to their blankies or beloved stuffed animals. The grasp was visibly firm. Patty-Jo could not let go of it or leave those tissues out of her sight. It had been the very first thing Josie noticed about this delicate child, and then she saw her reddened and tear-filled eyes. Patty-Jo was totally connected to her tissues. She looked sincerely distraught, although she was able to put her feelings aside when working with others.

For all the emotion this child displayed, Patty-Jo Tucker was a quiet soul. She did not blow loudly or noisily into her tissues, choosing instead to delicately wipe her nose. Nor did she make a spectacle of her wet eyes and cheeks. It seemed to be as much a part of her daily routine as breathing or speaking. It was the way things were. Patty-Jo seemed to enjoy the quiet nap time provided. Loud noises sometimes caused her to cover her ears as if it were too much on top of everything else going on. Josie Bee didn't know what caused the constant tears. But it was certainly something to look into. Hoping to receive some flexibility with her job at Mrs. Whittaker's, Josie absolutely needed to spend more time with Faye and Nola after hours in order to gather much-needed information. Josie didn't know if she needed to be on their team as much as she needed them on her team. Josie was hopeful things would then start falling into place. She was eager to begin connecting the pieces.

Finally, after several requests, Josie got the chance to speak with her employer. It was no surprise to Josie that her hopes of rearranging or reducing her hours fell on stubborn and reluctant ears. Henrietta Whittaker was not pleased. Clearing her throat not once but three times, she expressed her complete and aggravated displeasure at Josie's suggestion to tweak the work schedule.

"Selfish and absolutely inconvenient, Miss Johnson. Out of the question," Mrs. Whittaker snapped.

"But Mrs. Whittaker, I was hoping—"

"Young lady, it's not as if you aren't paid abundantly well for menial work and substandard results," exclaimed Mrs. Whittaker.

"I had no idea you were unhappy with my work," Josie replied. She was crushed.

"Of course I am not happy. How could I possibly be? It's apparent my standards are quite a bit higher than yours. And even the lovely uniforms I have generously provided for you cannot begin to improve your disastrous appearance," she continued. "And it is no mistake that I do not entertain guests when you are present in my home." She appeared finished but, as if that were not enough venom and ugliness, Mrs. Whittaker added one more hurtful comment: "You embarrass me, Miss Johnson."

By the grace of God and pure fear of the Hallelujahs finding out, Josie did not spit, snarl, or storm out of the Whittaker residence. But she did immediately begin collecting her things. She was about to calmly announce that she was leaving when Mrs. Whittaker stopped Josie in her tracks.

"And if you think, young lady, that you are going to disrespect me by quitting, you have another thing coming. I will make sure you never work again in Sand Haven," she hissed.

"And what is it you would have me do?" Josie asked in a voice she did not recognize as her own.

Mrs. Whittaker replied, "It is my sheer pleasure to fire you! Miss Johnson, you are hereby terminated." With another flippant wave and curt snap of the hand, Josie was dismissed. Mrs. Whittaker left the room, and Josie finished picking up her belongings. While she was on her way out, the ever faithful Walter trotted down the sidewalk with one last message from Josie's former employer.

"I am sorry, Miss Johnson, but Mrs. Whittaker is requesting you

dry clean and have both your uniforms pressed and promptly returned
to her on hangers," he said. Uncomfortably caught in the middle,
Walter whispered she had done an admirable job and wished her the
best in the future. Josie momentarily felt worse for this gentle person
having to continue working for such an unkind and spiteful woman.

And then Josie Bee remembered. She would have to explain to her
sponsors back home how she had been fired from a demeaning and
servile job that hadn't even paid minimum wage.

Not wanting to go straight home, Josie stopped off at the Fiesta to
quickly tell Faye and Nola about what had happened. Upon hearing
the news, Faye said with a wave of her hand, "Well, good riddance to
the old bat." Her dramatic flair made Josie laugh. It wasn't until then
that she realized how good it actually felt to know she didn't have to return to the Whittaker home. It had been oppressive. Her employment
terminated, Josie had to figure out what to tell the Hallelujah ladies
and when to share the news with Ellie and Del. It felt good letting the
cat out of the bag with Faye and Nola, but telling Auntie Birdie and the
church warriors could probably wait.

"Now that the 'old bat' has let me go, I hope you two will allow
me to be here as close to full time as possible," Josie remarked. "I really
want to work with the kids and learn more about my four girls so I can
get going on the Challenge."

"Of course," said Faye. "Let's start meeting after hours to get you
caught up and on the same page, girlfriend!" The word "girlfriend"
sounded so good to Josie. She was grateful to have these friends. Josie
Bee was feeling acceptance and love at the Prices' and at the school.
Both were becoming her safe havens.

"And by the way, Josie, we gave Agnes a magnifying glass today
during numbers time. Just a guess that maybe her eyes were not seeing
all the blueberries. It did seem to help her focus when she remembered
to use it. Either way, we might want to look into this eye thing some,
with her grandmother's history and all," mused Faye.

"Nice job, Miss Faye. That is awesome," Josie excitedly responded.
"I'll hit base with Dr. Decker at church on Wednesday."

"Please, call me Faye. If we'll be working together nearly full time,
I think it's only fitting to be on a first-name basis, don't you?"

Josie was in time to go to the sandbox with the kids. It seemed an ideal place to be on a day like this. The kids marched single file with Faye leading the way. Nola grabbed the box of individually bagged snacks and they were off to Cranston Park. The gift of play was going to be especially wonderful today, and the warm sun was a welcome bonus.

Miss Faye had everyone take off their shoes before entering the sandbox. There was something magical about wiggling one's toes deep down into the soft coolness. As she released the tensions of the day, Josie felt herself becoming a bit silly. Everyone felt carefree and spontaneous. Doing nothing meant everything to the students. For these moments everyone was safe, and every single person appeared happy and content. They were building moments of joy together in a box of white sand. Not one child was asking about what was next. No one needed a thing, and they succumbed to pure wonder and delight. Josie wished she had a camera to capture this perfect picture. Some of the children were allowing the sand to filter through their hands, others had their faces tilted upward toward the sun, and many were jiggling their toes out of the sand and into the air. Smiles and giggles filtered through the air with abandon. This had turned into a glorious day. Even Patty-Jo temporarily forgot about her tissue box and seemed caught up in the fun. Josie Bee's heart was full. She wanted to cherish forever the happy photo she had just taken in her head. A sandbox filled with laughing kids, safe and secure, the warm sun, the cool sand. The afternoon was unforgettable, and no one wanted to see this time come to an end.

After school Josie informed Faye and Nola she'd be back tomorrow and would plan on staying afterward to start pulling their plans together. Josie wanted to head on home and start figuring out how she was going to support her end of the bargain with the church and explain this new predicament to everyone who would want to know. Arriving to a quiet house was more normal than not, and Josie enjoyed the emptiness, knowing it would be buzzing again shortly. It gave her an opportunity to regroup and kick back. Grabbing a banana, Josie hustled to her room to get a letter off to Pearl.

My Precious Pearl,
    I am wondering how you are? How is your coo-coo? Baby

talk is fun sometimes.

I had "a dilly of a day" to borrow some verbiage from Auntie Birdie. Almost makes me want to say "dang" so she could sit down and have a chat with me, set me straight and all.

I miss you both so much, but I am making progress on my mission and moving forward possibly quicker than I could have imagined. I will be closer to full time starting tomorrow at Fiesta School. You see, Pearl, I actually lost my domestic job today. Frankly, I was downright in-your-face fired. It's important to me that you know I really tried my best to make Mrs. Whittaker happy, and it was not in any way, shape, or form possible. I gave it everything I had, and it was never enough, not once. My former boss said I was an embarrassment. You do believe me, right, Pearl?

I need help in figuring out how much I should reveal to Auntie Birdie and the Hallelujah ladies. I already feel ticked off about losing the job, but I really don't see the point in giving them all the information. The truth would be a bit shocking if I shared the details of my treatment at the Whittaker house. We all know things could be worse. I just need to figure out a way to make some money so I don't have to ask the group back home for more. They have already been extremely generous as you know. I can't let the Prices down either. Living with them has been a huge blessing.

I chose my four little angel girls and want to share all of them with you and will put that in the next letter. For now I can tell you their names: Agnes, Patty-Jo, Charlie, and Penny. They all need something special, but of course I don't know what that is yet. But I can tell you the Fiesta School is exceptional in every way imaginable, and I have made two friends to boot, Faye and Nola. Will share more later.

I hope Auntie Gertie is hanging in there. Bless your heart for being with her. She is lucky to have you, Pearl. We are all very lucky to have you. You are my special angel!

And finally, I hope you are taking time to go to the beach and wiggle your toes in the sand and feel the warm sunshine on your beautiful face.

You know you were always the "prettiest" sister! I can almost see your perfect smile!

You are the best, Pearl. As Momma always said, you were her gem and I was the rabble-rousing diamond in the rough. I am thinking Momma knew exactly what she was doing when she named you after a precious gem and me after Josephine Baker. Tell me about your latest sea glass pieces? One day we will stroll those beaches together, and maybe someday we can build a snowman too.

Sisters forever!

I love you so much!

Josephine Bee

Being named after Miss Josephine Baker was something Josie was growing prouder of by the day. Momma had a great imagination and a stubborn will, so when Daddy said no to Josie being named Josephine Baker Johnson, Momma said fine. Then she went right ahead and declared Josie would be named Josephine Bee Johnson and that was the end of that discussion.

Momma had viewed Pearl, her first child, as a precious gem and was enthralled with her sweet name. Pearl was an exquisite baby with delicate pursed lips. Marcus and Monique doted on their firstborn, and Pearl felt secure and loved in her daddy's strong arms where she would peacefully and quietly sleep for exceptionally long periods of time. Momma commented many a time that she "wished the little princess would do that for me!"

"It's all that singing you do, dear. It could keep the dead awake," Daddy retorted amusedly. It was no secret that Momma fancied herself a superb vocalist, although she was generally off pitch. Monique had always envisioned herself as an actress on Broadway. Most of the time she was conspicuously overdramatic. She preferred to make a scene, and you could generally count on an outstanding, jaw-dropping performance.

Sweet Pearl had been an only child for almost three and a half years when one day Momma excitedly announced she was going to have another baby. Pearl, not quite sure what that meant, thought *she* was the baby. Daddy always called her his honey sweet baby, so was Momma having something else? Maybe a cat or a bird? After a lot of explaining and drama, Pearl finally understood the situation. She had been taking care of baby dolls for as long as she could remember, and suddenly taking care of a real one seemed much more interesting and fun. Seeing the twinkle in her daughter's eyes, Momma immediately appealed to Pearl's new interest. Like schoolgirls, they chatted up ideas and plans for this "cupcake in the oven." Indulging Pearl with a lifelike dolly, Momma had the two of them attend pretend parenting classes so Pearl would be ready to help with the new baby when it arrived. Pearl took these instructions very seriously, becoming efficient at changing diapers, giving baths, and warming bottles. Burping was one of her favorite things to do, and baby doll was constantly being patted on the back and bounced up and down over Pearl's tiny shoulder.

When the big day finally arrived, two weeks earlier than expected, Pearl was overjoyed and unbelievably relieved that she received a baby sister. Momma said the little gem had been quite concerned that her unborn sibling might be a boy. She had practiced only with girl dolls. Josephine Bee was a handful from the very beginning. But Momma was thrilled with Josie's spirit, feeling immediately she had the makings of an actress and/or activist. Her aspirations for this newborn were high. Momma felt confident her Josie, like Josephine Baker, would have the ability to not only endure and succeed in this difficult life but also to command the stage with beauty, charm, and direction. Momma had been enamored and starstruck when she first saw pictures of Josephine Baker. Miss Baker was a shining star, a woman of great talent and heart, a true champion for equal rights for all. Momma welcomed any opportunity to share about Josephine Baker when anybody inquired about her daughter's name. Momma would spare the listener Daddy's refusal to allow her to use *Baker*, instead launching into her dedication and commitment to fight one of the biggest locusts of all: racism. And when asked, Momma would theatrically say, "Goodness no, Josie Bee does not sting and is not named after an insect!" Some people had no imagination, and Momma was impatient with their silly questions. If it is true that a child can grow into the significance of their given name, then Josie was already blessed with more truth and inspiration than she could have ever dreamed of. Marcus and Monique saw both their girls as gifted and special, commanding promising names. Pearl and Josie would carry that knowledge, names that held significance, with them for their entire lives. Back in ancient days one's name defined you. It was who you were, where you came from, and where you were going, and it was carried with honor and pride.

Make no mistake about it, Momma and Daddy were extremely proud of their firstborn, Pearl. When she entered their world everyone from the doctor to the nurses to family and visitors remarked that this child was the most beautiful baby they had ever laid eyes on. Born with a full head of dark curly hair and a button nose, Pearl looked like a perfectly sculpted doll. Her skin was flawlessly smooth and radiant, as if she had already been gently kissed by both the sun and the moon. Pearl's appearance was breathtaking, making it difficult to turn your eyes away from this glorious wonder. It was surreal that this much sweetness and contentment could be contained in the tiny, delicate body of a newborn, and the proud parents beamed at all the attention bestowed on their precious baby girl. Originally, Marcus and Monique were going to name her Pearl Agatha after a beloved friend, but once she arrived, they knew she was a gem in a category of her own, and *Agatha* just did not fit. Daddy recalled another gem, the opal, and how it was believed in the ancient world that opals contained lightning and fell from the sky only during thunderstorms. Pearl Opal didn't drop out of the sky, but the heavens graciously opened their doors and gently placed her on the earth. She was very much loved and adored.

Thinking about Momma and Daddy and their life on Woodstock Street in their creaky but cozy little house made Josie homesick for everything that had been safe and familiar. Even when the church was compromised, its heart kept beating, just as Josie's and Pearl's did after the death of their parents. Strange how broken hearts survive when the world around them is devastated and dying. Josie would ask God about that someday along with a whole list of questions. She wondered if God would mind being questioned, or was He expecting it?

Josie enjoyed the after-school time she spent with Faye and Nola. The ladies had many things they wanted Josie to help with, and Josie diligently sought more information on the four angels on the Challenge list. The past few days Josie Bee had gotten whiff after whiff of Nola's Southern cooking and was tempted to invite herself to stay over for dinner. Tonight she could smell the chicken and hear it crackling in Nola's black cast-iron skillet. With a side of fried okra and buttermilk biscuits and gravy, Josie would have been in hog heaven. Instead, she was packing up to go home, with not as much information as she would have liked, and a growling stomach. A bit disappointed and somewhat crabby, Josie knew you can't rush trust even if your tummy is egging you on. Sooner or later they would ask her to join them. She just wished she knew what was holding them back.

Josie had her things packed. She was saying her goodbyes while heading out the door when Faye hollered, "Hey Josie, want to have dinner with us tomorrow?"

Josie about had heart failure but quickly recovered and shouted back, "You bet I do!" Filled with joy and anticipation, she knew tomorrow evening with Faye and Nola was going to be a whopping bonus of a night.

After arriving back at Fiesta the next morning, Josie was busier than a centipede at a toe-counting contest. The day went smoothly, and Josie was feeling more and more grounded in the lives and activities of the preschoolers. She was able to share an activity with Agnes and Patty-Jo, and Josie marveled at how they interacted and shared with one another. They actually had many things in common. Both girls had good manners and gentle temperaments, and both enjoyed wearing dresses with matching socks and hair bows, which made them as cute as a pair of buttons. Josie felt like she was advancing and learning more about each of them with every day that passed. Agnes's struggle with staying focused continued, and Josie felt on the cusp of narrowing down the possible issues. Patty-Jo was still attached to her tissues at this point, and Josie Bee was trying to evaluate whether the Kleenex was a necessity or just a habit.

As the school day wound down, Josie turned her focus to what was going on in the kitchen. Once the kids were gone, Nola got busy with dinner preparations, and Josie Bee helped Faye finish up the growth charts. As they worked to complete the individual poster boards signed by the children, Faye and Nola chatted and Josie picked up new information that would prove to be helpful. Josie, smelling meatloaf, scalloped corn, and mashed potatoes, was finding it hard not to be distracted by the upcoming meal. Hopefully Nola would be making some gravy, but if not, maybe they could heat up the creamed chicken sauce from the night before. Auntie Birdie always said she wondered why people didn't like to mix birds and cows, like putting chicken gravy on pot roast or beef gravy over Cornish hens. Whatever the case, it was a certainty that her Auntie would approve of anything Nola Greene concocted in her kitchen.

Josie did not need to be called twice for dinner. She looked forward to devouring everything in sight as she eagerly sat down. Feeling as though she had waited a long time and had to earn this privilege, she was going to appreciate every single bite. This was one of those meals that forever would be lodged in her mind. Everything was cooked to total perfection. It meant everything to Josie to be sitting at the yellow Formica-topped table with matching chairs. Josie felt like she had entered yet another type of sanctuary, where she felt safe and cared for.

Nola prayed, sweet and direct. The food, delightfully Southern, made Josie feel as though she were attending a mini potluck back home. How on earth did Faye stay so slim and trim eating this high off the hog? In honor of their guest, Nola created a special meatloaf with extra sides too. Josie felt pampered and celebrated. This was more than worth the wait.

Josie grabbed what appeared to be cherry Kool-Aid, prompting Faye to explain it was a "special drink" that Josie was not yet old enough to partake of. Josie recognized the familiar bottles of Tom's vodka, the ones she had seen in Faye's cart at Marshy's Market, sitting on the countertop. The beverage in the iridescent green Mosser glass pitcher was disappearing as fast as Faye could drink it. Josie wasn't quite sure what to make of it, but it did seem Miss Faye was drinking far more than what she was eating. Her plate had hardly anything on it. Josie had so thoroughly been enjoying the meal that she hadn't initially noticed. She didn't know what to think. But Josie was now more intrigued with watching Faye kick back and let her guard down. Nola encouraged Faye to eat something, respectfully acting like a mother who wanted her child to eat all her peas. Josie could sense that Nola cared deeply for Faye Lewis, and it was obvious that they shared a tight and protective bond. Faye made herself another pitcher of vodka and Kool-Aid at the counter and, returning to the table, almost missed her chair when she plopped down.

"Easy going, sweetie, maybe you could try eating a little bit of this meatloaf. It's one of my best," cooed Nola. But Faye didn't want to eat anything and literally guzzled her next two glasses of juice. Although they were by no means large, the content was potent.

"Really, Faye, must you drink so much?" Josie timidly asked.

"Thank you very much, I certainly must! As if it's any of your concern," Faye assuredly announced. "Why would I want to remember what I have been trying so hard to forget?"

Josie was temporarily at a loss for words. Then she gently prodded, "Is there something you want to tell me, Faye?"

"I will tell you this, Josie Bee. I wish I was more like Patty-Jo. I wish I could let my tears escape, running and running until they all ran out, but I don't know if that is even possible. Why start what can't be finished?"

Josie looked at her questioningly, wondering what she was referring to.

"I am not convinced it can work that way. I absolutely don't think I need to say anything about it—it just wouldn't be worth it. I don't want to open that can of worms, dear. Nola understands, and she doesn't judge me. As far as needing to confide my issues, Nola has always been enough for me."

Nola remained silent. Josie's warning bells started going off as she unintentionally held her breath. "Might there be anything else you don't want to tell me?" Josie whispered. If Faye heard the question, she didn't bother to answer.

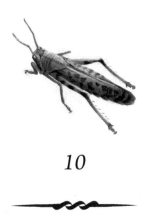

10

HAND-ME-DOWNS

*She didn't know her clothes were hand-me-downs,
or that her home wasn't a mansion.
She had a family, friends, a cat and lived in
the best place ever: it was called Innocence.*

z2z

JOSIE DIDN'T WANT to beg or irritate Faye, but she really felt this was the time to open up and start to develop some personal trust. She was getting very attached to both Faye and Nola, and far be it from her to judge anyone at this point. Josie Bee knew how darkly twisted her thoughts and desires had gotten, so much so that God had put the brakes on, bringing Josie to an involuntary, reflective stop.

"C'mon, Faye, please don't keep me guessing," Josie pleaded.

"Not now, Josie, and probably not ever," Faye replied. Nola gently shook her head, and Josie realized she should let it go, at least for the moment.

"Okay, I really wasn't trying to pry." Then Josie gushed from her heart: "I just love you two to pieces! I truly do, and you are about the only friends I have in the whole world." The softness and sincerity in

Josie's voice moved Faye. Having had more than plenty to drink at this point, she was loosening up, beginning to relax while slowly letting her guard down. Nola started clearing the dishes, and Josie instantly jumped up to assist her. Faye had a faraway look about her, seemingly not noticing that she was sitting at the yellow dinette all by her lonesome. At the counter Nola gave Josie a warm pat on the back as if to say, "Take it easy, it will work itself out." Josie returned the kindness with a quick hug, mouthing "thank you" in silence.

When they returned to the small table, Faye did not appear aware of or interested in the hot cinnamon apple pie with puddling ice cream. Josie was eager to sample the irresistible dessert when she glanced over at Faye and noticed her glassy eyes. It was obvious Faye had consumed way too much alcohol and she was feeling chatty.

Once Miss Faye got started, Nola let her tell her story, tapping the top of her hand for support and acknowledging that what she was about to say was going to be difficult. Josie had no inkling what was about to be revealed, but she saw that Faye's hands were trembling. Josie patted the other hand, and there was strength in the circle of three, confirming safety and support for one another—a strand of three cords that would not easily be broken. The words, barely above a hush, began tumbling out as Josie leaned in to catch each and every one of them.

"Let me begin by saying I never knew my daddy, but Edie, my mother, had many boyfriends, each one meaner than the last. Then Edie met slick-talking fancy-pants Earl Carter, the man of her dreams. It was never like I mattered much anyway, but when she went out with Earl, leaving me home alone, I became scared of most anything that moved. But Moon Pie, the sweetest black-and-white cat ever, was always by my side. He was my best friend, my only friend. I always thought Moon Pie would scratch the eyes out of anybody who would try to hurt me, and he became my imaginary defender. My worst fear was when Edie worked night shifts at Billy Bob's, a local bar, and Earl would be at home watching me. I would run upstairs to my tiny room, slipping under the bed the exact minute I heard the front door close.

"Then one evening Earl started calling my name, and I woke up in an awful sweat, knowing something bad was about to happen. I heard Earl's heavy footsteps coming closer and closer toward my hiding spot.

Clutching Moon Pie, I hoped with all my might my cat would stay still. I had to protect him too. Earl found me and grabbed my ankles so hard I thought he was going to break them. He began pulling me out—" and Faye gasped, covering her face with both hands, sobbing uncontrollably. Nola let her cry, painfully watching the rising and dropping of her chest, releasing the shame. Josie felt her throat constrict, and her stinging eyes overflowed with tears running down her face.

"Faye, it is okay, there is no need to go on," Nola softly murmured. "Please, sweetie, I think you've shared enough. Josie understands what you are trying to say." But Faye took a deep breath, determined to continue.

"I don't know if I blacked out when I hit my head on the bed or if it was after Earl viciously tore Moon Pie from my arms, but he kicked my baby boy straight into the wall. Hardly recognizing my own screams, I saw the lifeless pile of black-and-white fur and knew in my heart Moon Pie was dead. Earl Carter had killed my everything. He somehow made me stop screaming. Although I can't exactly remember what happened next, when I was older, I was able to put the pieces together, and it wasn't a pretty picture.

"A few months later I was in the bathroom with dry heaves and thought I was coming down with the flu. Edie was still working nights at Billy Bob's and Earl was already in bed. I thought I would slip downstairs and get a few saltine crackers and some soda. I was at the top of the staircase when all of a sudden I felt a crunch in my back. I toppled all the way down the twenty-four splintered wooden steps. I hit the bare floor like a ton of bricks. Earl always had a penchant for kicking things, and I clearly heard him say, 'That should take care of that.' I was only thirteen years old, Josie, and at the time I had no idea what he meant. Years later while living with my Aunt Pauline, during a doctor's appointment, I was told I would never be able to have children. In putting all the splintered fragments together, we had a frightening but clear picture of what had actually happened to me those years before. It forever changed my life when I finally figured out what Earl had done. I felt so worthless and broken, like a piece of no-good junk."

"That's enough, Faye, please. We can finish this later if you still want to," said Nola, reassuring her. Looking entirely exhausted and brokenhearted for Faye, Nola grieved that her beloved friend carried such tormented and cruel memories.

Putting her hand on Nola's arm, Faye reassured her. "It's okay, Nola, I'm okay." And after pausing she went on. "It hurts so much that others look at me like I am not as good as them or that I am just plain stupid, as if I don't hear their whispers or see their condescending actions. I decided a long time ago that I would treat children with the respect and dignity they are all entitled to. I also wanted to give them a place where they could be safe, feel really good about themselves, and have a variety of wonderful food to eat—not like the Spam I grew up on. My brokenness finds healing in being with these children and loving them as if they were my very own, at least for the short period of time they are in my care. When a child comes to the school my heart opens up and I feel worth and a real sense of hope.

"I am deeply committed to Fiesta School and so grateful for Nola's friendship and unconditional love. I don't know what my world would look like, would feel like, without Nola. And I feel the same way about my Aunt Pauline. When my mother ran off with Earl, it was her older sister Pauline who came and took me in. Her husband had passed just a few years earlier, and she had been alone ever since. Never able to have children, she welcomed me into her life and home with open arms and a great big heart. Pauline truly cared for me, and she spoiled me. We were a family, just the two of us. Aunt Pauline left everything to me when she passed, and she generously provided the funds for me to follow these dreams," said Faye, as her hand gestured toward the class-room area. "She knew my heart and understood my hurts. My precious aunt believed in me, and I am forever grateful. Then when I met Nola Greene, I knew she was someone special."

"Oohhhh Miss Faye, you know that it was you that picked up this old bag of achin' bones and breathed new life into me. I love you as my own!" Nola ardently exclaimed. "You have been my world, and who else would keep me overstocked with Ben-Gay?" she chuckled.

"And that reminds me, we absolutely need to get you to a doctor and find out what really is the problem with your right knee, dear!" added Faye. "Yes, you do love Ben," she murmured, and Josie saw her contagious smile for the first time the entire evening.

"I have Ben and you have Mister George, so I guess that makes us both pretty lucky," Nola remarked. "And now we have Josie too, so looks like we have hit the jackpot!" she declared with a grin.

"Time will tell, now won't it," a punchy Faye contributed. Heavy emotions, drink, and conversation had taken its toll on all three women as they ended their time together.

In the days to come, Josie Bee continued to reflect on what Faye had shared and how difficult it had been for her to reveal the sad and painful part of her story. Faye's young life began with a childhood that had not been fair or just or kind, but by the grace of God she survived. Josie realized that she had been fortunate living in a home with a mother and father who did the best they could for as long as they were able. When they were killed, Josie and Pearl were blessed to have a new home offered to them. It truly was incredible that the two girls were able to continue life together, living with their wonderful Auntie Birdie. Berniece Thomas's willingness to include her nieces in her home and love them well was a tribute to her faith and generous spirit.

Josie Bee was only beginning to see how God's hand was in all the segments of her life. He knew Josie needed Pearl, who had done everything possible to make her feel special, safe, and loved after the loss of their parents. Pearl had added such sweetness that Josie couldn't even imagine what she would be like without the influence and support of her precious sister. Pearl was selfless, an angel, a lovely spirit that seemed incapable of selfishness or questionable acts. Missing Pearl, Josie broke up her reflections with a mischievous thought and then a chuckle. Perhaps her older sister had gone out on a limb with Jumpin' after all. Maybe Pearl and James had danced under a shining moon and shared "what-ifs" while making plans to run off together. At least Josie Bee could hope Pearl had been deliriously carefree, chasing her heart and having a ball. It would have been even more entertaining to see Auntie Birdie's reaction and that of the Hallelujah Circle, had they somehow known about the mysterious and questionable relationship.

Speaking of the Hallelujahs, Josie had still not shared the loss of her "overpaid dream job," as Mrs. Henrietta Whittaker viewed it. It was not a disastrous situation. Josie actually counted her termination as a blessing in disguise. But she still needed a source of income in order to honor her commitment to contribute toward room and board with the Prices. A new part-time position? A weekend-only job? This was a priority, and Josie would be picking everyone's brain to get it figured out as soon as possible. Then she could fully concentrate on the Challenge.

Figuring out the needs of Angel Number Three, Charlene Harper, was next on Josie's plate. She sat on her bed after dinner with the Prices one evening and looked at her list of four girls. She was eager to know more about Charlie and clarify to herself why she was designated to be on the list. On the surface she appeared to be a rough child with tendencies toward bullying. It seemed to Josie that it had to be a learned behavior, because why would a child want to intimidate or be cruel to another child? Children tend to be more forgiving and accepting of others unless they are taught differently. Maybe rough-and-tough Charlie was mimicking someone at home or one of her brothers. Or she could be protecting herself in a strange way, throwing up walls so others couldn't get too close.

Josie also knew that spunky Charlie was not the clotheshorse that her friend Denise McNair had been. Josie had chosen Charlie in honor of Denise, who from a very early age had enjoyed dressing up and was the apple of her parents' eyes. Her daddy was a milkman and also had a photography studio on the side, taking great pleasure in his pictures of photogenic Denise. A perfectly dressed young lady at all times, she thoroughly enjoyed coordinating with many accessories. Denise was a strikingly beautiful child with a spirited personality. A real spark plug. Strong-willed and feisty, Denise carried herself with confidence and poise. She was particularly fond of her collection of dolls and spent hours and hours playing and changing their outfits. One of her favorites, Chatty Cathy, had been Pearl's best-loved dolly too.

Charlie, however, consistently came to school in soiled denim jeans and well-worn T-shirts. Josie Bee had no idea who handed the clothes down to Charlie, but they were awful. Several times her clothing was so tattered and stained that Josie secretly wished to take and dispose of them where they would never again be seen or worn by anyone. Auntie Birdie would not have approved. Who allowed this child to leave the house in the mornings looking so ill-kept and neglected? Were they blinded or too busy to notice? It was then that Josie envisioned what this little girl, whose appearance suggested she was a boy, would look like in a dress. Every day Charlie wore a red-and-blue ball cap, and Josie wondered what her hair would look like freshly washed and curled. Young Charlene never played with the dolls or engaged in the tea parties at school. She preferred playing cars and trucks with the boys. It was obvious Charlie and Denise were very different, but the space between the front two teeth of both the girls made Josie smile. Charlie didn't smile or laugh that much, so Josie hadn't noticed her gap at first. When she did finally see it, she thought right away of Denise. After learning that the space was celebrated in some countries as a sign of being gifted and special, Denise had been delighted. Josie had secretly admired Denise's determination and ability to fit in with the older girls, even though she was three years younger than Carole, Addie Mae, and Cynthia. Josie had always struggled fitting in with peers, let alone older kids. Competitive and popular, Denise was only eleven when her life was ended in the church bombing. Denise's being the baby of the group, Josie related the most to her and had constantly wrestled with her death.

Almost daily, Charlie Harper had to be gently and firmly reprimanded for some type of questionable behavior, even if it was minimal. Although Charlie could be intimidating and pushy, many times several of the boys would clump together, taunting her. They weren't being particularly cruel but when they fell into a teasing pattern they didn't quite know when to stop. The Fiesta ladies, always looking to intervene when necessary, were on it.

"Charlie is a girl, Charlie is a girl," the boys would chant in a singsong rhythm. And as small boys commonly do, they would say it over and over and over, tediously repeating themselves until Charlie reacted. Most of the time, Josie noticed, she was more threatening than physical, raising her fist as if she were going to swing. She seldom seemed out of control, but when they said other things such as "Charlie smells like a skunk," or "Charlie is creepy," the little girl's tolerance would drop drastically. Josie felt her embarrassment and frustration at not somehow fitting in with the girls and then being teased by the boys. What was Charlie to do? When she got backed into a corner, she handled things with frustration and a threatening defense. Wouldn't anyone else do the same?

Josie didn't see her behavior as being all that bad. When given limits or questioned, Charlie seemed to listen and respond according to what was required of her. Josie had planned to talk with Faye and Nola to better understand her family dynamics, but it had gotten temporarily pushed aside. At least Josie was getting a feel for and noticing more specifically how Charlie was handling her situations. At first glance, Charlie appeared to be the culprit, but there were other outside circumstances, and it would take some time to figure out what was what. One thing Josie knew, bullies are never sure of themselves, and Charlie was no exception. She could use a big helping of the kind of confidence Denise McNair had demonstrated. Denise was a terrific force enclosed in a petite and tiny frame, confident in who she was.

Riding the bus home from Fiesta on Wednesday, Josie looked over her to-do list, which was growing rapidly, faster than she could keep up. There didn't seem to be enough hours in the day to complete even half of what Josie wanted to scratch off her notepad. Since it was Wednesday, she had to go to church for sure. The Prices would be waiting for her when she got home from work. Josie had considered asking Faye if she could check out a little early, as she had wanted to arrive at the church before Bible study and prayer group got started. But she quickly thought better of it. Best to stay put and finish what was expected of her.

As she got off the bus, Josie couldn't wait to get to her room and see if there was a letter from Pearl. With great joy, she saw that there was.

Dear Josie Girl,

How is my baby sister really doing?

My goodness you have had your hands full!

Please have no doubt about it, I am beyond proud and OF COURSE I BELIEVE YOU! You are growing up in my absence, Josie. I am not sure how I feel about all of this. It makes me miss you even more.

I have an idea on how to solve your money issues. I have not used nor do I need any of the money the Hallelujahs have kindly given me. So, in the little enclosed envelope please find all the money forwarded me, thanks to the generosity of others. I need absolutely none of it, Josie Bee.

Auntie Gertie continues to give me money, and I have no expenses at all. Sweet Gertie is continuing to struggle, and it is breaking my heart. I see her sleeping more and more, and I fear one day she won't even wake up. I have never watched anyone die. Josie, I don't think I am that rock you think I am. Some days I realize I am losing everyone I have ever loved. And I am scared. I wish you were here, or I was there. I am sorry, I don't mean to sadden or burden you.

Your willfulness has always encouraged me.

Auntie's doctor has taken me under his care and has been running tests on my increasing coo-coo issues. It seems to have gotten a bit more active since arriving here in Florida. I don't know if I am fatigued because I am constantly worried about Gertie or if it is due to the humidity and heat. The results should be back sometime soon.

I can hardly wait to hear about the four girls on your list. They must be so special! Addie, Denise, Carole, and Cynthia will live on in others, and that is glorious. We are all so very proud you had the courage and strength to go on this journey, Josie.

And I don't see the need to share with the group back home anything about your previous employment. Let's keep this between us, like we used to always do.

I love and miss you,
Pearl

Josie opened the small envelope and almost fell off the bed. The cashier's check was for more than Josie could ever have earned. It was amazing! Pearl had done it again and fixed everything. Josie didn't know what she would ever do without her precious sister in her world.

She was her rock! And Josie couldn't wait to get moving through the Challenge so she could meet back up with Pearl. Josie had felt somewhat hoodwinked by the process and backed into a corner by the persuasive church ladies. But once she realized that Pearl was going away and hadn't bothered telling her first, Josie's defiant and rebellious self decided then and there she'd go away too. Josie Bee was committed. And Josie had no wiggle room in which to back out and no way would she bring shame or embarrassment to her Auntie and her backers. So, the best Josie could do was to tackle the Challenge. And she wanted to complete her assignment to the very best of her ability and then get her butt back to Alabama where she belonged. Pearl had the dream job in Florida with beaches and living in a large diverse community, predominantly black. Josie was still adjusting. But when she initially arrived by bus into Sand Haven, the sight of the mostly white community made her feel cautious as more walls went up. Josie would have preferred working the Challenge in Alabama among her own people. Her plan was to embrace the process, see the mission completed, and get herself out of Indiana as soon as possible.

Arriving at Fiesta before her scheduled time on Thursday, Josie couldn't wait to tell Faye and Nola that she had garnered a to-be-scheduled evaluation with the eye doctor for Agnes. Her introduction and meeting with Dr. Decker at church had gone well the night before, and Josie was still ecstatic. The doctor assured Josie Bee he would be more than happy to check out the struggling Agnes Jones. Soft-spoken and genuinely concerned, the doctor said Josie could book an appointment with his receptionist. Handing Josie his business card, he encouraged her to call sooner rather than later, as they were generally booked weeks in advance. Dr. Decker said he would instruct his staff to immediately put her on the schedule. Josie could not have asked for more and was thrilled at the doctor's willingness to help.

Josie also couldn't wait to share with Faye and Nola about Pearl's unexpected gift. She still had to pinch herself. It was another miracle and would instantly take the pressure off everyone involved. It would also allow Josie to be at the school full time and not worry about picking up another job. There would be extra dollars to put toward whatever was needed to assist the girls on the list and for the class as well. Josie was grateful to be able to meet her minor but significant commitment to the Price family too. Faye and Nola were thrilled to hear both bits of news, and all three women celebrated together.

That afternoon, with rest time almost over, the youngsters were eager to be called to line up for their daily jaunt to Cranston Park. It had been a productive morning at Fiesta from the start. The students were focused and worked exceptionally hard. Every day was jam-packed, filled with lessons and activities that kept the kids three-dimensionally busy: mind, body, and spirit. It was intentional and deliberate that the school address all three areas, as they were interconnected on every level. A special presentation by a local nurse was a big hit. The kids were enthusiastic and listened well when she spoke. For doing so, they were given tongue depressors and colorful Band-Aids. Afterward the kids showed their appreciation by giving the guest a genuine—not to mention loud—round of Fiesta applause.

Hearing the high-pitched sound of the whistle that signaled to the kids it was time to head for the park, they excitedly lined up behind Miss Faye in single file. She took the lead, and Josie placed herself in the middle of the line. Nola would trail behind, carrying two shopping bags of homemade treats and juice packs, singing like a bird. Josie's heart was light and her spirit soaring. When the class arrived at Cranston Park, the students found their way toward the large sandbox. This was one of the best parts of the Fiesta school days for both students and staff. Josie was realizing over and over again the importance of play in the lives of youngsters. Faye had stated repeatedly, "You must give your brains and bodies time off. There is no better place than in a big box of sand to embrace your imaginations and launch your dreams!" After much practice the children knew to wait until Miss Faye said the magic words: "Go be free." After being officially released, they entered the box with unharnessed gusto, unrestrained giggles, and sheer joy. Faye and Josie were equally thrilled, instantly finding a nice place for themselves in the sand.

The air was cool, but the sun was out and shining bright, providing the needed warmth to make it a comfortable time at the park. Josie Bee had been casually glancing around, taking in the happy faces, when the cringing face of Penny White caught her eye. Josie followed her down-turned head and tear-filled eyes as the youngster pulled up one of the sleeves that had been covering her thin, bony arms. But it wasn't the scrawniness that alarmed her. Instead it was the colors and sizes of the fresh welts and bruises littering Penny's tiny limbs that punched Josie in the stomach. She wanted to vomit and scream and scoop this baby up and run. Run until she couldn't run anymore. Keep her safe because there only seemed to be one plausible explanation for this kind of hurt. Josie Bee was hot. She wanted to hurt the monstrous locust who did this unspeakable thing. Poor Penny. She caught her young teacher's piercing stare and began tugging furiously to slide the sleeve back down. Josie was absolutely frozen with anger and disbelief. She had no idea what to do next.

She held her breath, placing her hands quickly and deliberately over her mouth. There were kids all around, and Josie tried to calm herself and garner some much-needed control. The locusts were here, and it was frightfully unsettling. Josie could hear her Auntie Birdie say, "When life throws you a devastating gut-wrenching locust, get rid of it, and then drop to your knees and ask forgiveness." In one instance she used the words "destroy them," which had made the Hallelujahs uniformly gasp and sputter. It never made much sense to Josie Bee back in those early years in Birmingham, but here in Sand Haven, Indiana, she was about to get a lesson in what her dear and wise Auntie was referring to. Josie was filled with anger. And Josie was ready for a fight.

11

BAD PENNY

Childhood should be carefree, playing in the sun;
not living a nightmare in the darkness of the soul.

Dave Pelzer

JOSIE STILL FELT as though she couldn't breathe or move, stuck in her once comfortable seat in the sand. With the happy feelings gone, Josie didn't know what to do next. Her mood had shifted to a different place, and she was in turmoil, gripped with confusion. Fear tightened her throat. Penny was already scooping and sifting the sand playfully through her dainty little fingers. The jarring moments, at least on Penny's end, appeared to have passed, but Josie Bee was locked in a state of fear and disbelief. *Breathe. Breathe. Breathe.* Josie could feel Pearl's hand softly swirling her back while whispering calming words over and over again. When critical moments unfolded, Pearl had always been there to soothe her baby sister, striving to make her feel safe and secure. What would Pearl do? How would she choose to help Penny? What was Josie going to do? She felt ill-equipped to say or do anything. Josie was furious. Could it even be possible that Faye or Nola had *not* seen markings on Penny's arms before? Or had they? Whatever this *was*, did it happen at home? Josie could hear Auntie Birdie warning about the danger of presumptions but Josie couldn't help herself. She knew she could be jumping the gun but previously she thought she had seen something. It had made her feel uncomfortable. Either way, Josie felt she now needed to place her immediate focus on Penny White.

Angel Number Four needed what Cynthia Wesley had in her life before the fatal explosion. She had a loving father, and Josie suspected Penny had a cruel and violent one. Cynthia's dad was a wonderful and well-respected elementary principal at one of the local Birmingham schools. Supported and adored by both her parents, Cynthia was a happy and well-adjusted young lady. Penny likely had a troubled and unpredictable home environment. Cynthia was such a tiny little thing, with delicate arms just like Penny's. Josie wanted to hear Penny laugh, the kind that jiggled your tummy. Cynthia was always laughing, and maybe Penny could too. Josie, if her suspicions panned out, couldn't get Penny a new father, but hopefully something could be done to protect this little girl.

Josie was still in a daze when Faye blew her whistle. "Pack it up kids, it's time to roll," Faye called out cheerily. Now was not the time to have a showdown with Faye or Nola, so Josie did one of the things she just was not very good at: holding her tongue. As she helped the kids get back out of the sandbox, Josie's thoughts kept going back to Angel Number Four, precious Penny. She had to shake this off for now and concentrate on what she did know and go from there.

Earlier in the morning Josie had gleaned what information she could from Nola regarding her third angel, Charlie Harper. The ladies were quite familiar with her family as two of Charlie's older brothers had come through the Fiesta School in its beginning years. Charlene was the baby sister of four older brothers. Given the brothers' reputation as "rough, tough, and all boy," Charlie's behavior made some sense to Josie Bee. Out of the four angels, Charlie looked to be the easiest to work with and Penny the most difficult. Hopefully, with prayer and support, it would not be an impossible assignment. Josie needed to keep moving.

Josie had not even entertained the thought that she could fail.

Would God allow her to fall flat on her face? What would it mean for her if she was unable to intervene successfully in Penny's life? Josie could not fathom what that would look like for this innocent girl's future, if she even had one. The four girls in the bombing had been pure, innocent, guiltless, and blameless too. They were gone, and Penny could be critically hurt as well. The Challenge, which Josie had at times taken flippantly, had evolved into a form of seriousness that Josie didn't know how to handle. God help her, she had to somehow discuss this potential crisis with Faye and Nola. Josie Bee was in over her head.

By the time they arrived back at the school, Josie was less certain she could restrain herself. She was impatient to talk to Faye. Everyone had routine jobs to perform before packing up and heading out the door. Josie's questions and growing accusations were going to have to wait. It seemed like a slice of forever until the last kiddo had gathered their possessions and exited the Fiesta. Seconds later and without hesitation, Josie jumped Faye.

"So, Faye, how long have you suspected Penny's abuse and why haven't you said a single thing? Anything else you DON'T want to tell me?" Josie hardly recognized the defiant tone and high pitch of her own voice. She found herself shaking and pushing back tears.

"Not now, Josie, we need to discuss this later, please," Faye pleaded.

"If now isn't convenient, then when, Faye? I'm asking you, how long have you known and how long do you want me to wait? Until something uglier and bigger and more violent happens? Maybe when it's too late? Will that be a better time for you, Faye?" Josie was on the brink of hysteria.

"I'm saying not this very minute. Because you think it needs to be done right now doesn't make it so," she stated, firmly holding her ground.

"I may only be an inexperienced rookie in your eyes, but I'm not stupid, Faye," Josie hissed.

"I never implied that you were, Josie," she said.

"What are you implying then? Am I one of your mistakes, Faye?" Josie's voice was rising. She was about to go off the deep end.

"That's really, really not fair, Josie," Faye said softly.

Josie knew her words had stung.

"Nor is it called for," Nola said, joining the discussion for the first time.

Josie Bee turned toward Nola. "Tell me, what am I missing here?"

"Miss Josie, this nasty attack is not going to help anybody. Please lower your voice and settle yourself down," Nola firmly cautioned.

"I hear you just fine, both of you, loud and clear. I don't think I am capable of settling down, and quite frankly, if it's all the same to you, I'll be back in the morning. Would an hour before the start of school be acceptable? Or do you need to discuss that first too?" Josie just couldn't hold her words. She grabbed her bright yellow backpack and left without receiving an audible response from either Faye or Nola. It didn't bother her in the least.

When Josie had first joined the school on a full-time basis, she was touched and peacock proud to be given a beautiful bag with "Fiesta School Staff" embroidered on it. The gift indicated acceptance and unity, cementing their togetherness in serving the school's community of young students. Josie was honored each time she hoisted the bag onto her back. When she was out with Faye, Nola, and the students, Josie Bee felt like a member of an exclusive club. The feeling she got from being part of something bigger and more important than herself was strangely new and exhilarating. Josie Bee relished being on this team, trusting both ladies enough to have shared with them about her true mission and the Challenge. Or at least a good part of it.

Oh, my goodness, what just went down? What have I done? Why did I practically rip the head off of the nicest white woman I've ever met? Not to mention my sharpness with Nola. Auntie Birdie's words about "presumption being one of the devil's favorite tools" continued to echo in her ears. What if there had been circumstances that Faye and Nola were planning to share regarding some of the inner workings at school but the time hadn't yet been right? Josie hadn't calmed down, she had flown the coop. What if they never wanted to see her again? What if she got there in the morning and was let go? From self-righteous accusations to crumbling doubt: just like that, things had flip-flopped. In a matter of a few loose-tongued minutes Josie had jeopardized her position and credibility, attacking the only close friends she had in Sand Haven. Her presumptions had gotten the best of her. But then again, they usually did.

~~

On what was most likely the worst bus ride ever, Josie resented the quiet hum of the oversized vehicle. It was so peaceful when she was anything but at peace. What was once an escape was now like a cage on wheels, transporting a wild and crazed lunatic. Why had Josie not taken some time to explore her imploding thoughts and bite her scathing tongue before unleashing on Faye and then Nola? Josie had sucker punched her coworkers. They never saw her attacks coming. Then again, Josie hadn't intended on things going that way. Josie Bee's sharp and quick responses had constantly gotten her into trouble since she had been knee high to a grasshopper. Even then it usually took the finesse and assistance of Pearl to rescue her from the consequences of her disrespectful comments. If only Josie Bee could bounce this off Pearl before going back in the morning. She was already deeply embarrassed but couldn't figure out why all the guilt landed back on her. Josie Bee was disturbed and for good reason. But being out of control and demanding had not gotten her any answers or insight into the circumstances. It was what Josie didn't know that was scaring her. There had to be something else going on. Faye and Nola had been nothing but kind and generous to her, and in return Josie had unfairly spewed her anger on them.

Thank goodness the Price household had gone out to Tito's for the weekly Tuesday taco competition. Little Patsy had been proud of setting a personal record for consuming six consecutive tacos over her older sister's barely being able to knock down four the week prior. Josie figured she could use the extra time to sort things out and share with Pearl. Josie would have preferred a phone call but was afraid Pearl might find it wasteful. It was hard to beat written correspondence when a first-class stamp only cost five cents.

My Dearest Pearl,
    I don't even know how to begin this letter.
    I want you to know that you are the best angel of a sister in the world. The way you have always taken care of me humbles

me. I don't even know what to say about your unbelievably generous check, but I thank you from the bottom of my heart. It really
is not enough to thank you for what you just did for me and so
many others. You are a gift from God that I don't deserve. I am
not sure I deserve a single thing at this point.

   Out of my four little angel girls, I was planning on telling you
about three of them in this letter. Then today I saw my fourth angel covered in welts and bruises while in the sandbox at the park.
I lost it, Pearl. I thought I could, for lack of better wording, handle
what I saw. I was working, so I did wait until after school to share
what I saw with Faye and Nola. But I got crazy mad and started
questioning the ladies. Quickly it became accusations, and it continued to snowball from there. I couldn't stop. I am embarrassed.
I am sad. I messed up. I don't know what to do. How do I get
through this without you, Pearl? I am ashamed to be such a pest.

   Did you get your tests back? How's your cough? Auntie
Gertie? What if you get sick too, Pearl, who is gonna take care
of you?
        Pray for me?
        I love you,
        Josie

                           ∽∽

   The next morning, Josie Bee felt small and insignificant as she tried
to navigate the walkway leading up to the school. Josie knew that she
had not spoken reasonably, professionally, or kindly the day before. She
had not acted like an adult but more like a child throwing a tantrum.
Faye and Nola had deserved better than what Josie had given them.
Josie not only needed to apologize, she wanted to. Then she would
throw herself on the mercy of the Fiesta court.

   Normally Josie would've let herself in, but today she planned on
knocking. She felt more like an unwelcome guest than a valuable member of the team. Nola, watching Josie from the front picture window,

moved toward the entrance and opened the yellow door before Josie had even tapped on it.

"Please come on in, Miss Josie. There was no need for you to knock in the first place," she said.

It was calming for Josie to encounter Nola first. She was relieved Nola hadn't demanded she go away and slammed the door in her face. But of course, her Southern friend was too civilized for that kind of nonsense. In times like this, formal politeness and manners sure did go a long way in setting the stage for a civil interaction. Soon Faye entered the room, greeted Josie with a nod of her head, and they all sat down together. Josie felt a hint of panic.

"We are sincerely pleased for this opportunity to sit down and discuss our situation," Nola said. Josie Bee cringed at the formality. It stung. Maybe it had crossed their minds that Josie would be a no-show, fueling doubts they might now have about her. What exactly were they thinking? That they hired a spoiled brat? It wouldn't take long for Josie to have an answer to her questions.

"Josie, how are you feeling today?" Faye politely inquired. Josie wasn't sure how honest she ought to be. Faye was certainly making an attempt to be professional and courteous, but putting Josie Bee at ease was not on the agenda. In an effort to be lighthearted and break the ice on her end, Josie replied, "Just trying to get myself down off the cross I've been hanging on."

"Make no mistake about it, Missy, you put yourself up there. And, Josie, for future reference, that type of disrespect and immaturity will not be accepted here or tolerated anywhere in the school. Is that perfectly clear?" There was no Southern charm, exaggerated or not, in the tone of her words.

"Yes, ma'am, and for the record, I am very, very sorry about my careless and unprofessional outburst. In fact, I am downright mortified at my behavior yesterday. I mean that, Faye, Nola . . . it's just that I don't get it. But that's no excuse, and I apologize. Even now, I really don't know what to say. I was raised better than that. I have no idea where to go from here."

"C'mon, Josie, you've been here for just over a month, and we have been running the school for years. You just can't expect to be informed about all we have experienced and witnessed. It doesn't work that way, and you are in no way entitled to that information. Nor are we required to tell you anything, let alone everything you seem to think you deserve to know," Faye firmly stated. "Entitlement is not pretty."

Glancing up at the oversized industrial clock on the wall, with its bold and prominent ticking sound, Josie felt as though it, too, was scolding her.

Ticktock, naughty girl, ticktock, naughty girl.

Loud and clear.

Ticktock, naughty girl, ticktock.

Clicking her fingers, Faye suggested to Nola she grab the pot of coffee so they could get started. The kids would be arriving before they knew it, and they needed the java. Josie was as ready as she could be, eagerly bobbing her head up and down in agreement. She could sure use a cup of crazy, as her momma called morning brew. In fact, Josie thought maybe even two cups would be best.

"Since it now seems to concern you," Faye said, "let me tell you about the White family. In a nutshell, the family of Penny White has always been an extremely complicated unit. Beginning and ending with little Penny's overbearing and aggressive father, Frank. Frank rules the roost with an iron hand, and there is no easing up and no letting down. Do you know what I mean, Josie?"

Josie couldn't help but notice the deep furrow in Faye's strained forehead and the gripping tightness of her delicate jaw. Josie's heart was beating a mile a minute as she realized this was only the very beginning of a seriously messed-up story. This one affected sweet Penny Ann, and Josie felt the gravity of child abuse staring her smack in the face, its ugliness pugnacious and revolting. Not to mention scary.

Faye continued, "This problem exists throughout the entire family, starting with Mrs. White. Alice is a very kind and decent lady, but she can't seem to do a thing to help those kids or herself. They need her there, and Alice dare not stand up to Frank. He is meaner than a deranged polecat and doesn't think twice about knocking his wife around, or anyone else for that matter. Alice tried leaving once and ended up at the hospital in pretty bad shape. Frank's done it before, and he will do it again. It appears it has always been his way or the highway, and efforts to change things have not, shall we say, been successful."

Nola then recounted a conversation Alice had shared recently that was tearing her up. When Penny had come home from school one day the previous week, Frank was there, irritable as ever, and started ripping right into her. His words were intentionally cruel.

"You ain't even worth a halfpenny, girl!" His rough voice was louder than normal. "You are like a bad penny! I am here to remind you of that every day. That's my job. Not worth a single cent, do you hear me, kid?" Then Frank threw down a dirty tarnished penny, instructing his youngest child to pick it back up. And fast. "I wanna hear you repeat exactly what I just told you. And if you don't, we'll do it as many times as it takes to get it into that thick little skull of yours. You got that?"

Alice held her breath as she fiercely clasped her fingers together till her knuckles turned white. She secretly hoped Penny could get it done quickly, for all of their sakes. Scared out of her wits, she knew what Frank was doing wasn't right, but she was no match for him. It broke her heart to see her sweet girl with tears running down her face and her tiny hands shaking—yet again.

"We don't know what to do, Josie," Faye lamented, "but we have considered many options, and legally our hands, at the moment, appear to be tied." The way Faye dragged out and emphasized the word "legally" caused Josie to temporarily reflect on what other "options" may not have been thoroughly explored. "Isn't that right, Nola?" said Faye, turning to her for support. Nola solemnly nodded, and Josie could see on the women's faces concern at their predicament.

"Again, I was wrong, and I am asking for forgiveness from you both. I need you to forgive me," Josie insisted.

"You want to know if we are letting you off the hook, am I right?" Faye asked.

"I guess so. I know that things aren't like they were, and I don't know how to fix that," Josie said.

"And I can't fix it for you either." Josie saw the hurt in Faye's eyes. "But that's part of growing up and accepting the consequences of one's behavior. Both Nola and I realize this is a very new and unusual experience for you. You have been under a lot of pressure for some time now, Josie. We recognize this. Moving away from home, let alone such a great distance, is not an easy thing to do. You are missing your loved ones and your comfort zone. Nola reminded me of how difficult it was for her to leave Mississippi. She understands the persistent ache in your heart. Nola has advocated for you from the very beginning because she understands many things I just don't know or will never fully grasp. Between us, we do understand. Nola and I see you beginning to really care about the students, and that is what grabs our hearts. You reacted the way you did because what you saw scared you. But most of all, you are genuinely concerned and worried about our precious Penny, and that's what is most important to us."

"I don't know what to say. I'm speechless," Josie said.

"Sometimes that's not a bad thing," pitched in Nola.

"It's reeeaaalllly going to be okay," Faye promised. And there was that Southern twang thing again. It sounded good in Josie's ears to hear Faye's drawn-out syllables. Sweet and soothing. Josie also knew that Faye had one of the biggest hearts she had ever encountered and would not purposefully hold the previous incident against her. And Josie Bee was thankful for Nola's behind-the-scenes support, which spoke volumes. Most of all, Josie was relieved she hadn't been asked to leave. She needed the Fiesta in many more ways than one. Especially now. She still had a lot of learning to do.

And probably some growing up as well. Josie couldn't help but think back to a conversation she and Pearl had once had. Big sister had been trying to keep a straight face while attempting to explain one of the facts of life with her, probably for the umpteenth time.

"Someday, Josie, you will have to grow up," Pearl had lamented.

"Why would I want to do that?" Josie flippantly replied.

"Because if you don't, things are going to be very hard for you one day," replied Pearl.

"I don't much care 'cause you'll probably be there, too, fixing it for me. Right, Pearl?"

"I wouldn't count on that. I'm not a magician and I don't have a magic wand, baby girl. It would be better for you if you started recognizing that, Josie," Pearl cautioned. "Everyone else does—has to grow up, I mean." Pearl stifled the urge to laugh. Used to getting her own way, this would be a tricky process for Josie Bee.

"Yeah well, whatever you say, Pearl," said Josie as she rolled her eyes.

"And you best be working on controlling that habit, too," said Pearl.

"Anything else you want to get on your high horse about while we're at it?" asked Josie.

"Honestly, sometimes I have to ask myself why I bother," replied Pearl. "So, no I guess not."

Josie missed their playful banter. Entertaining and lively, her sister was always trying to offer her suggestions to make her life easier. She sure could have used Pearl for this last round of consequences due to her inability to keep herself in check.

"Oh Pearl, sometimes I want to grow down, not up."

As the youngsters started arriving, it seemed like a natural place to break and refocus. All three ladies turned their attention to the children. Josie had a contented sense that what specifics hadn't been shared about Penny's situation would be shared when the time was right and there was more of it. Faye and Nola were willing to work with her, and that was enough for now. The grace they afforded her was priceless.

Josie quickly reminded Faye and Nola that it was Wednesday and that she wouldn't be staying after school, which she had intended on doing as much as possible. She explained that she absolutely had to be in church that evening to attend a weekly class commitment. Josie Bee dared not cross the Hallelujahs on this requirement. She suspected they had their ways of checking up on her. Their involvement included a monetary investment they took serious responsibility for. Accountability was everything to this group of supporters. Josie got that loud and clear.

Being patient was not Josie's strong suit, so waiting for Penny's details was going to weigh hard on Josie Bee. But it wasn't going to stop her from working on some ideas of her own since it was clear that Faye and Nola were aware of Penny's bruises and they weren't making any progress. It was something to think about. Each day counted, and there was no way Josie was going to be able to keep her mind off Penny.

Having mentioned church, Josie knew exactly who she could trust to bounce her thoughts off, and that would be Big Carl. Carl Watkins had joined the church family at the same time as Josie. During the strongly suggested weekly newcomer's connection class, they became fast friends. With no teacher in attendance, it was an unstructured and pressure-free situation they were thoroughly enjoying. It was a surprise bonus that they were the only two newcomers at the time. Both had been transplanted into a predominantly white community, so they shared similar feelings and experiences. Being grateful for the interest Second Baptist took in nurturing and meeting their newly acquired needs provided common ground. Josie and Carl felt like church "projects," getting many chuckles out of that joint observation.

Putting thoughts of sharing with Carl on the back burner, Josie was just happy to be focusing on another day at Fiesta School. What she thought she had come close to losing meant even more to her, and Josie vowed to work even harder to prove that she was worth it. It seemed like she was trying to prove that to the whole world.

Josie got goosebumps watching the students standing upright proudly reciting the pledge and hearing them singing the national anthem. Ready to soar, the kids went to their learning stations filled with energy and excitement. Nola was already baking something in the oven, and its scent was fragrantly floating through the air. Catching Agnes Jones out of the corner of her eye, Josie was mindful of needing to give the eye doctor's office a call and snag that initial appointment for Agnes. Josie was eager to find out whether her vision was an issue. And if it wasn't, she could check it off her list.

Patty-Jo and her tissues fascinated Josie. The past weekend Josie had gone to the local library and done some research on "object obsessions" and learned that if you bring attention to these types of things it could make a person more attached to them. But even if you can get the child to start dropping the objects, you still may not get to the root of how or why the initial obsession began. The article suggested immediate professional intervention. Josie didn't even understand how that process would work. She didn't feel particularly convinced or enlightened one way or the other and decided to go with what little gut instincts she had. This meant trying to figure out what it was that made Patty-Jo cry.

It seemed logical that if you cried, you would need Kleenex and a box of tissues in hand for convenience. Josie had an idea she wanted to bounce off Faye or Nola. She wanted to introduce a hard-boiled egg. If Patty-Jo coddled something in her hands, it might make her less apt to clutch a tissue box. It seemed a whole lot better than giving her a hamster or something like that to fuss over. It was a crapshoot either way. Auntie Birdie never did approve of any form of the word *crap*. This is probably why Josie purposefully let it slip out here and there, for the sheer enjoyment of hearing Auntie's exasperated remarks. The egg was worth a try, but Josie wasn't too optimistic. She wasn't a shrink and didn't even know one, so getting into the head of a four-and-a-half-year-old was a real stretch. But Josie wanted to try *something*. She wanted Patty-Jo to care for the egg as if it had something special inside. Hopefully Patty-Jo would take care of it and not try to eat it.

Snack break allowed Josie the perfect time to ask Nola if she wouldn't mind calling Dr. Decker's office to schedule the first appointment for Agnes. With the way things had been going Josie half-expected some reluctance, but Nola agreed to call right away. For a minute there, Josie felt like she had a personal assistant. Josie overheard her on the phone and could only hope that one day she might sound that professional. Nola was a real gem. Josie Bee knew Pearl would have adored this woman to pieces, which reminded Josie that she should be receiving a letter from her dear sister in the next few days.

"Enjoying your snack, Josie?" Faye winked.

"It looks like you are as well," Josie teased back.

"Hard to beat Nola's mini oatmeal pies! Surprising how many kids like the raisin ones over the chocolate chips," she mused.

"I am officially a fan of the apple ones, and anything else Miss Nola whips up in her culinary department."

"We are blessed to have her talents in the kitchen, and she loves doing it!"

"You are right on."

"Oh, by the way, I'm expecting the volunteer I mentioned earlier to be stopping by today sometime. Back from family business and ready to assist the staff of the esteemed Fiesta School," said an excited Faye. "Just wanted to give you a heads-up."

"I appreciate that, since you haven't mentioned any volunteers," said Josie.

"Then file this information as just 'needing to know.'" Faye giggled.

"Will do, Boss, thank you." Josie gave Faye her best pretend smile. "And by the way, you look exceptionally festive today. Like kind of gussied up."

"I always want to be an example to the students that it is important to care for one's appearance, and thank yoooooouuu for noticing, Miss Josie."

The break over, Faye moved on.

Finishing up the last activity of the morning with lunch looming, several of the kids squealed when a visitor walked in the door. Although his hands were full, the guest immediately received a warm hug from Nola and a huge squeeze from Faye. Josie was puzzled at the presence of a man in their midst. His visit certainly brought about a good measure of excitement and intrigue. He approached the unsuspecting Josie in a friendly manner.

"You must be the new addition to the Fiesta staff I've heard so much about. Welcome, Miss Johnson. My name is Archie Wilson, and it's my pleasure to meet you," he said.

"Thank you, Mr. Wilson." Josie flushed, not sure what to make of this suave man who popped into the school with several brown papered luncheon bags filled to the brim.

"Let me put these down. A little something for the students," he said while handing all but two of the bags off to Nola. "Now don't fuss, Miss Nola, this sugar will not put the kids on the ceiling if it is doled out properly." The bags were filled with all kinds of candy: Smarties, Swedish Fish, Astro Pops, Starbursts, Sixlets, and the kiddos' all-time favorites, Pixy Stix and Candy Dots on Paper.

"And don't think I'd forget what my two big girls like," Archie said as he handed a bag to Nola and slipped the other to Faye. "I haven't been away that long."

"Charleston Chews, Black Jack Taffy, Chick-o-Sticks, and Caramel Creams are my favorites, Mr. Wilson," Nola exclaimed, digging through her bag. "And you always remember that," she said with fondness. "You are too good to us."

"Ooooohh, my turn," said Faye. Peering into her bag she found Bit-O-Honey, Sugar Babies, Banana Split Chews, and in the very bottom, bright red Wax Lips. When she spied them she said delightedly, "Oh Archie, you make me laugh."

"My pleasure, ladies, and next time I'll bring you your favorites too, Miss Johnson," he promised.

Josie smiled.

"Just popping in to let you know I am home, alive and well, and looking forward to getting back into the swing of things here at the school. Have you missed me?" Archie asked with an impish grin.

"I guess so. Can we twist your arm to join us for lunch?" responded Nola.

"You sure can. I accept. I was afraid you weren't going to ask," he said.

"You bring us our sweets, how could we not. It will be our pleasure," said Nola.

"It certainly will. And we *have* missed you," said a beaming Faye.

Josie didn't know exactly what to make of Mr. Wilson. He was good-looking, friendly, and seemingly a favorite with everyone at Fiesta. She wondered what he did at the school when he was around. Didn't he have a regular job? What Josie Bee would learn was that the big clock that hung in the open classroom had been a gift from Archie Wilson. Five and a half years earlier Archie had retired from Magnavox in Fort Wayne, Indiana, a manufacturer of radios, TVs, and phonographs. His coworkers in the plant gifted him with an industrial clock, as his punctual arrival at work was legendary. In fact, they had removed it from the entranceway into the factory in order to give it to him. While Archie appreciated his friends' enthusiasm, there wasn't much he could do with it because of its enormity. So he and his wife, Althea, thought it more practical to donate it to a hospital or some other large facility. Shortly after his retirement, Faye Lewis moved in next door to the couple, and they both took an instant liking to their new neighbor. After sharing her plans to open a preschool in her home, Faye was delighted when they asked if she could use their big wall clock. She eagerly accepted. Within a few months the rezoning permit had been acquired. Faye, with Althea and Archie's support and blessing, officially opened the Fiesta School, with Nola joining her shortly thereafter. Faye couldn't imagine better neighbors, and a budding relationship between the four began to blossom. However, within eight short weeks Althea was diagnosed with cancer and passed away six months later. Faye was heartsick. The two women really enjoyed one another, and Faye was thrilled about their growing friendship. Archie and Althea had been unable to have children, and both looked forward to seeing kids at the new school, as they lived a good distance from family. After Althea's passing, Archie grieved aimlessly and alone until a close buddy contacted him to ask if he would consider helping out by driving truck for a few months while an injured employee recuperated. Archie agreed to give it a whirl. At first an interesting distraction, a busy few months turned into a tedious few years. Archie, resigned and ready to move on, initially spent a good portion of time visiting family and old friends out of state. Once settled back home, he did whatever was needed to help out his neighbors and the school. He started with general repair work. There was always something to do. He enjoyed the atmosphere and kids at the Fiesta, and Faye and Nola were most appreciative and complimentary of his efforts.

When Faye first moved in next door to the Wilsons, Archie immediately became the envy of his buddies and about every other man in their subdivision. Just as quickly, however, Clara Kravitz, president of the smug Neighborhood Association, had the wives buzzing like bees. In her mean-spirited and petty gossip, Clara presented Faye as the enemy who had just taken up residence in the association's very own backyard, someone to keep their eyes on. Suddenly the ladies went from knowing nothing about Faye to knowing everything. They were less than kind in their assessment of the woman. Who did she think she was? And with a colored housekeeper! Nola was not a domestic, but the ladies secretly accused Faye of thinking she was above them. These women always had plenty to chatter about, but the sight of Faye took Clara Kravitz's inner circle to a new level of insecurity. Unfortunately, Faye's hopes for a normal life complete with real girlfriends, friendly neighbors, and long-anticipated outdoor gatherings would not be forthcoming. Faye was considered a threat. She was tall and thin with gorgeous blond hair, baby blue eyes, and an outgoing and electric personality. Not to mention that sliver of Southern drawl and her sass. Faye was labeled a menace. And as far as Nola went, she had zero chance of becoming part of the neighborhood niche. But this did not bother her one iota. Nola was just fine not being part of their shallow group.

The sad thing was, Faye had gone through a friendless childhood, consequently developing a seasoned desire to reach out to anyone she came in contact with. She never felt confident or worthy of anyone's attention. During Faye's second year of high school, a caring and nurturing counselor named Priscilla Rogers took her aside. Mrs. Rogers told Faye that life is a stage and she an aspiring actress. The audience only knows the performance given at the time. "Be worthy of the accolades and give it all you have. You must act as though you believe you are a wondrous star! It is always your prerogative to shine bright and feel accepted for who you have been created to be. Even if you don't feel like it, you can pretend. No one will know the difference. Don't let anyone steal what is not theirs to take from you."

Even though Faye dropped out of high school at sixteen after an especially rough time of harassment and ridicule from the mean girls, Mrs. Rogers's comforting and wise words affected her in a forever way. Faye took them to heart, and they would someday make all the difference in the world. Even though it took a long time to figure it out, Faye knew she had to believe in herself because there wasn't anyone else in her life that did. Not one single soul.

So, with a whole lot of determination and defiant persistence, Faye eventually became a walking poster child for poise and confidence. She started marching through life pretending she had a book on top of her head and throwing her shoulders back and her chest forward. Step-by-step she marched on. The new behaviors were awkward at first, then they became natural. Faye became a pro at "putting on a face" and complimented herself on her ability to do so. Faye was surviving.

Two years later she was taken in by her Aunt Pauline when Edie chose to skip completely out of her life. Having Pauline enter her life brought unbelievable happiness and security. Aunt Pauline had the habit of consistently calling Faye by her first and middle name, Faye Louise. Flourishing under her aunt's tender care and love, Faye Louise dreamed of one day becoming involved with young children as an educator and teacher in her own kind of place, one that would recognize all children as worthy and enough in their own right. It was something Faye Louise passionately wanted. Pauline committed to investing all she had in Faye Louise to guarantee the fulfillment of such an opportunity to celebrate children. Pauline also knew her niece would continue to heal her own heart by pouring into the hearts of little people. At such a tender age Faye Louise had an amazing desire and capacity to love others. The little girl who had been denied love and value wanted to give it to others. Pauline knew Faye Louise would one day do just that.

After a lunch of homemade white-cheddar macaroni and cheese, fresh hot-ham sandwiches, fruit cups, and miniature root beer floats in frosted mugs, the students spent the first part of the afternoon resting, then enjoyed a wonderful time in the sunshine at Cranston Park. At the end of the day Josie supervised the children as they finished their chores, and then she helped them find and collect their things to take home. Tommy Wynn dropped something into his bag that landed with a thud. Josie investigated. Lo and behold there was his mini root beer mug from lunch.

"What have we here, Tommy?" Josie asked.

"I don't know. Nothing," he replied. Why could kids yank on your heart when they were being mischievously evasive?

"I think you do know. Does this look like nothing?" Josie asked as she held up the tiny mug.

"Ummm . . . it might be something. Maybe," Tommy stammered.

"What do you think we should do with this thing that may or may not be something?" asked Josie, trying to keep a straight face. His face twitching, Tommy looked adorably helpless, as if he might cry.

Then out of nowhere he firmly declared, "I think you should return it, Miss Josie!"

"Okay, let me see if I understand what you are saying, Tommy Wynn," Josie said. "You want me to return your root beer mug to whom?"

"You know who. Miss Nola," he said confidently.

"But I didn't take the mug. I returned mine, and you were supposed to put yours on the tray too. Just like everyone was told to do. I am wondering why you did not do that." Josie hardly had time for this hiccup. She needed to leave as soon as she could to get to church on time. "Okay, Tommy, let's figure this out. You did not return the root beer mug. Either you take it to Miss Nola now and tell her what you've done, or we will have to talk with Miss Faye about what to do next. It's your choice!"

"Okay," said Tommy.

"Okay what?" asked Josie.

"I'll do what you said."

"And what did I say?"

"I will take the mug to Miss Nola." Gently taking it out of Josie's hand, he headed toward the kitchen. Quickly trotting back, he reached for his backpack. Josie asked him if he spoke with Nola, and he assured her that he did.

"Did you tell her you were sorry for taking the mug?" Josie asked.

"You didn't tell me to tell her that," Tommy sincerely replied.

"I guess I didn't." Josie wasn't sure anything was accomplished, but it was time to get Tommy lined up for pickup. Feeling outsmarted by a four-year-old, Josie shrugged her shoulders and let it go.

Arriving home after school and catching up with Ellie and the girls was refreshing. Having little children sure did make big people continuously busy. Josie never realized how much the women in her life had done for her on a daily basis and was reminded of that when she saw Ellie in action. Later, as they rode in the car together on their way to church, Josie marveled at how these people she hadn't known very long were becoming an integral part of her life. God was blessing her, and she was counting on Him to see her through the Challenge, the apparent crisis with Penny, and back to Birmingham. At church Josie ran into Dr. Decker right off the bat.

"Could evening, Doctor, how are you doing?" Josie asked.

"I couldn't be better, young lady. I was glad to hear that your Agnes is now on our schedule," he cheerfully replied.

"Thank you so much for seeing our little angel. You will enjoy her. She is the tiniest little thing with the biggest heart," Josie gushed. "And really well behaved too."

"She surely sounds special. It's my pleasure. We'll make sure everything is okay, and if not we'll see if we can do anything to fix it," Dr. Decker stated.

"Her family and the Fiesta School cannot thank you enough for this," Josie said. "We feel blessed to know someone so generous and willing to assist our students."

"Congratulations on your new staff position at the school. Ellie had us praying for you. They are lucky to have you."

"Oh boy, it's me who's the lucky one, Doctor. Thanks for everything. See you soon." And off they went in their separate ways.

At newcomers' class Josie was eager to meet with Carl Watkins. Second Baptist Church had sponsored his release from prison and was overseeing his probationary period. His being involved in the church was a must, and Carl and Josie again found common ground. Carl was a gentle giant. A huge brown teddy bear of a man, his gentleness was one of his most admirable traits, yet Big Carl had been quick to explain he had a temper he occasionally wasn't proud of. *Who doesn't?* Josie thought. It had to be one of his few vices. But the anger thing had gotten Carl in some big trouble. He shared with Josie that prison was a hands-on education he hoped never to repeat. Now a free man and attending ongoing anger management classes as part of his release requirements, Big Carl was still learning to understand himself and control his impulses. *Good luck with that,* Josie had thought, as she was still trying to figure out how to control her own off-the-cuff reactions. Auntie Birdie frequently encouraged Josie Bee to take her weaknesses to the Lord, and Pearl advised her to slow down and simply think before she spoke or acted out. But Josie, both spontaneous and undisciplined, was bound to make mistakes.

With just the two of them still participating in the class, both felt free to talk about whatever was on their minds. Nothing was off-limits. The last six weeks had allowed Josie to get to know and be comfortable bringing up almost anything with Carl. Talking with him was a weekly highlight. Josie thoroughly appreciated his banter and sense of humor and learning more about his story. He was becoming like a brother, and Josie Bee only wished Pearl could be a part of this blooming relationship. Carl made Josie feel secure, and she felt safe spending time with him. Josie was sure that Carl felt their closeness was special too. He had commented, more than once, that she was the closest thing to a family member he had. Josie Bee had always thought that if she had a brother, Pearl wouldn't have needed to work so hard to keep her out of trouble.

Knowing some things about Big Carl's past, Josie felt confident he would be a sympathetic and confidential listener to what was on her heart. She still didn't know all the details of the Penny White situation, but she was beginning to sense that Frank White was the culprit and had been in control far too long. He could be a huge problem. Josie also knew she could not handle this horrible situation on her own. She was still puzzled about Faye's and Nola's reluctance to figure out a solution for Penny. So many questions and hardly any answers. Who else could have seen the bumps and bruises? Certainly, if the Fiesta had seen anything, they had an obligation, a responsibility regarding the well-being of their students, to report their findings or their suspicions to *somebody*. At least Josie presumed that to be the case.

Tonight, Big Carl shared about the job he was trying really hard not to lose. Josie could certainly relate to his concerns. He had a huge amount of issues on his plate. Carl's primary and only job in prison had placed him in the kitchen. He found that he enjoyed learning all the different aspects of everything that went on in that hectic place. It became Big Carl's saving grace, as his job left him very little time to sit around and think or get into trouble. Because of Carl's enormous size and strength, he was the perfect candidate for unloading the large delivery trucks that arrived daily. It was quickly discovered that there was nothing the big guy didn't mind doing, couldn't do, or wouldn't do to help out. His humble ways and friendly manner made him a favorite among his peers.

When Carl first began sharing about his kitchen experiences, Josie remarked how much the Hallelujah Circle would appreciate someone like him working in their kitchen back home. Josie giggled to herself as she wondered what that would look like for the dominant, all-female group, having a big man in their midst. They would probably adore bossing him around. Maybe too much, and that made Josie smile inside.

The restaurant where Big Carl was employed was not giving him his full wages. Basing it on a probationary period due to his past incarceration, they were withholding money that he was entitled to. Carl felt used and taken advantage of, but jobs for felons were few and far between. He had been lucky to get the position at Chuckie's Grill and didn't want to let the church down, as they were solely responsible for this opportunity. Carl was grateful but struggled with the unfairness of what was expected of him and what was unfairly being withheld from his checks. Josie always seemed to be able to help him balance out the problems of the day, and he depended on her input and listening ear.

But tonight, Carl Watkins could sense that Josie was doing her best to focus on what he was saying but that she had something else on her mind. Her faraway look gave her away.

"Mind me asking what is going on in your head, little sister?" Carl asked. He could tell Josie was touched by his referring to her in this way as she began nodding.

"I have a serious problem, and I really want to tell you about it. I dare not openly discuss it outside these four walls, Carl," Josie said, looking around as if someone might overhear them.

Carl understood that area of concern. "Roger that. I hear you loud and clear," he replied.

"I'm dead serious, Carl. It looks to be something really, really bad. You're the only one I can tell this to," Josie said.

"Go ahead, you have my undivided attention."

Josie launched into the specifics about Frank White, at least what she already knew. She was glad not to have to rein in her anger or think before speaking her mind. She knew Big Carl would hold nothing against her and would appreciate her sincerity and directness. He let Josie be Josie, the beauty of true friendship in a nutshell. And he didn't correct her.

"Big Carl, I don't know what to do. I have no idea who to tell or where to go with this critical situation. I am scared to death for one of my students, Penny White. She is such an itty-bitty thing. Penny has gotten pretty banged up, lots of deep bruises and welts. Gets that deer-in-the-headlight look when I so much as glance at her arms. I don't know how much she has endured or how much more she can take. The abuser appears to be her father. His name is Frank White. He definitely seems to have everyone spooked. I don't have a clue as to where to begin let alone how to end this nightmare. He's a monster. Truth be told, it's just now coming to me. I urgently need your help. Your thoughts. I have no one else to turn to, Carl," cried Josie.

"Miss Josie, I know I can help you," Carl said, patting her hands.

"I hope so, Carl," sighed Josie.

"How about you and I start figuring this out right now so you can let go of some of this worry?" he suggested.

To an outsider peering in, it would have appeared that Josie and Carl were fervently praying for something special, and indeed, that much would be true. Josie already knew they could be heading toward uncharted waters and had no idea what might happen.

"Josie, you know I would do anything for you, I swear! I give you my promise, I will help you in all ways possible. We probably shouldn't be going on about this here, if you know what I mean." And as Josie had done, Big Carl cautiously scanned the room.

"For sure," Josie replied. "It looks like our time slot is over. We probably should get moving. In the meantime, I will get more information, and then we can figure out where we go from here."

"Wherever we go, we go together," Carl said.

"Like salt and pepper," Josie replied.

"Brother and sister," Carl added. Josie nodded.

"Okay," Carl continued. "Next, you find out where this guy works, what time he goes in, when he gets back home, where he goes to hang out with his buddies. Stuff like that. Just do what you're able, and we will start with what we get. Bad idea for me to start nosing around, so it's gotta land on you for now."

Josie liked Carl's reasoning and insight, clearly understanding the need to stay under the radar. "Got it, Boss," she said. She could see this reference pleased Carl to pieces, making it clear she was now looking to him for direction. He probably didn't realize Josie had no other friends or connections that she could tap into to work on something like this. Down South just whispering about white people could get you into a lifetime of trouble, but here Josie felt her dark thoughts rising up to solve a bad situation that knew no racial barriers, let alone potential legal ones.

After telling Big Carl that she would be in touch, Josie left.

12

VODKA AND KOOL-AID

*After the first glass of absinthe you see things as you
wish they were. After the second, you see things as
they are not. Finally, you see things as they really are,
and that is the most horrible thing in the world.*

Oscar Wilde

AFTER HER MEETING with Big Carl, Josie was grateful to be home and
have time to settle down. Grabbing a cold Coca-Cola from the refrigerator, she went to her room. The bedroom was the closest thing to
the safe haven back in Birmingham, and she relished her sweet space.
Propped up on the pink-and-green-embroidered rose-covered pillow
was a letter from Pearl. Josie clutched the envelope to her heart, wishing for cheerful and uplifting news. Gently opening the flap, she lifted
out the pale-colored stationery.

My dearest Josie,
    I am the bearer of very sad news and wish it weren't so. Our
beloved Auntie Gertie peacefully passed into the loving arms of

Jesus. I know I should have called you. It was Auntie's sincere wish that there be no service other than a simple and quiet one at her home church. She especially did not want to put Auntie Birdie through the expense or emotional experience of coming here to say her final goodbyes. The last tender phone call between the two brought me to tears. I was relieved to know that they were able to share their hearts and have that final time together.

You know how practical and no-frills Auntie Gertie was, and she departed with instructions. I must tell you I followed them exactly, as they were entrusted to me. Auntie wanted me to tell you how much she loved you and was extremely proud of how you had accepted God's work to help others. She did not want to worry you and left a letter here that I am to mail "after the dust has settled." Auntie Gertie kept her dry sense of humor to the very end.

Josie, I am very sad. I fear I will cause you to be sad too, and that would never be my intention. My tests came back, and the results are not at all what I expected. But am taking things one day at a time. My coo-coo sounds melodic but is actually maybe a symptom of tuberculosis, which has to do with the lungs. It looks serious, but my doctor is still in the process of trying to evaluate my options. I did not see this coming, and since I couldn't have prevented it, I'm just trying to adjust to whatever unfolds. Josie Bee, I am sorry to put this burden on you. I know how much you love me, and you are the best sister I could ever have hoped for.

I will keep you posted, but never forget how much I love you. You have meant the world to me for as long as I can remember. You were the bright sun in my sky, the biggest star in my universe. I have always believed in you and always will.

Selfishly, I want to walk the beach with you, and make that snowman, and have you catch my tears. See Josie, I am not nearly as strong as you have imagined me to be. I am so sorry.

Please keep your head on straight, sweet sister, and do what you know you have been designed to do. Your heart and commitment to the girls is incredibly important, and I need you to promise me, please, that you will do all that is possible to complete this good work you have begun.

    I will be calling soon. I need to hear your voice.

    I love, love, love you very much.

    Your Big Sister,

    Pearl

Josie went straight to the phone knowing she should ask permission to make an expensive long-distance call, but she would pay for it later. The Prices would understand. Josie had to talk to Pearl. What was she missing here? What was Pearl saying? She must be so tired. Was it for sure tuberculosis, or was she still waiting for more results? Pearl was not an overreactor or drama queen. Her words sounded dramatic to Josie. But for goodness' sake, Pearl had just been through the loss of Auntie Gertie and probably had spent a good amount of time consoling Auntie Birdie. It had surely taken its toll on Pearl.

Grabbing the Florida number and picking up the phone, Josie carefully dialed the numbers at hand. The phone rang and rang and rang. Josie Bee was ready to panic when on the twelfth ring someone whose voice she did not recognize picked up and said hello.

"Could I speak to Pearl Johnson, please?" Josie asked.

"May I ask who is calling?" the new voice asked.

"It's her sister, Josie," she said.

"I am so sorry, but Miss Pearl is already in bed for the night. May I give her a message?"

"Who is this?" Josie gasped. She thought she could hear something in the background, someone speaking.

"I am a friend of Gertie's—here's Pearl now," the woman said as the phone was handed off to Pearl.

"Hello," said her breathless sister. Pearl's voice sounded different. Josie was on high alert.

"Holy moly, it's me, Pearl. It's me, Josie. What's going on down there? Are you okay? Are you feeling sick? Have you heard anything new from your doctors? Are you gonna be okay? Oh my, you have been through so much and I haven't even asked about Auntie Gertie. I wasn't surprised or anything, but it was still very sad. Gosh, were you alone with her when she passed? Now what, Pearl?" Josie had pent-up questions and wanted to know everything. She had been so bottled up. "Did you—"

"Josie, please slow down. I can't keep up with you," Pearl interrupted. "Some of what you are asking I just don't have answers to," she practically whispered. "I'm just really glad you called me."

"What's going on, Pearl? What's wrong? Tell me," Josie persisted.

"My doctor thinks I have probably had this lung disease since I was quite young. He is consulting with other physicians on my behalf, and it's a wait-and-see situation. But I think I will know something more definite rather soon. And I'll tell you everything, I promise," Pearl said.

"Oh Pearl." And that was all Josie could get out before breaking down and releasing all the tears she had been holding back.

Her big sister was crying too. Sobbing in tandem, the girls somehow reached out to one another through their tears. Wishing they were back on the floor of their childhood safe haven, they clung to the sound of each other's voice. Neither Josie nor Pearl could speak. They were unable to get a single intelligible syllable off their lips. They carried on that way until there were no more tears.

"I love you, Josie."

"I love you too, Pearl."

"Miss you, Josie Bee."

"Miss you more, Pearl."

"Josie, I know this is hard. All we can do is pray for each other and hope for the best. I really do miss you and I am so sorry," said Pearl.

"I'm the one who is sorry. I should be there with you, Pearl. We've always at least had each other. No matter what, it was always you and me," Josie murmured. "So what are you thinking, with Auntie Gertie gone? What's next, Pearl?"

Pearl sighed. "I haven't had time to think about what happens now. I just don't know. You'll be the first to know when I figure it out, I promise. Keep your head up, baby girl."

"I love you, Pearl . . ." Josie said one more time.

". . . to the moon and back. Nighty night," Pearl whispered.

"Don't let the bed bugs bite."

"Good night, Josie." And Pearl hung up.

The lump in Josie's throat felt as though it would burst. Not only did she feel incredibly sad but she was also lonely. Even though they had been discussing difficult things, Pearl and Josie were again having a one-on-one conversation, something Josie deeply missed.

She could, however, sense Pearl's fatigue and heard something that was different in her sister's voice. And yes, Pearl had been tired and sad when she wrote that last letter. She had just lost Auntie Gertie and was heartbroken. But at least they had gotten to talk and cry together. Pearl had calmed Josie enough to lull her into feeling that tomorrow could be a better day.

Josie Bee did not sleep well after her phone call with Pearl. When she peeked over at the clock and saw it was 5:30 a.m., Josie knew she should rise and shine and start making a list of what needed to be done for the day. Her thoughts would have pleased Auntie Birdie.

Instead she turned over and decided to do exactly what she had told herself not to do: think about Pearl. Feeling a rush of sadness and homesickness, she planned to indulge herself, get it out of her system, and get to school earlier than expected. Josie didn't particularly want to reflect on the letter or the phone call, and she did not want to worry about what she didn't know. But Pearl seemed ill. Her words came softly and painstakingly, the sobs uncontrolled and coming from down deep, the kind of cries that indicated total release and unrestraint, maybe even a sense of resignation. Josie couldn't be sure. Josie did know Pearl was acting very un-Pearl-like, expressing sadness and allowing her emotions to rise to the surface. Josie felt the release of months of loneliness and separation from the one with whom her childhood memories were intertwined.

Funny how Josie's first recollections were of being held by Pearl in their grandmother's creaky rocker. Back and forth until the resistant Josie would finally fall asleep. It was Pearl who read her story after story to keep her down and entertained when Josie was sick with the measles. Tiny Pearl would go to the kitchen and push the metal table chair across the cream-colored linoleum, landing it smack against the refrigerator ice box. She would then climb to the top, grabbing lime popsicles for Josie when she cried due to her aching sore throat. Pearl had to be quick and quiet, as the girls were not allowed to eat in their bedroom. So big sister would herd baby Josie with a finger-shush to the secure haven of their magical closet. Young Josie always felt secure, realizing now that it had less to do with the closet and more with Pearl's presence. Josie Bee would never forget those sweet times and how contented Pearl had made her feel.

It was Pearl who did everything for little Josie, and as she grew, so did the depth of Pearl's nurturing and never-ending care. Momma was there, but many times she really wasn't. Painful headaches could sideline Momma at the drop of a hat, and they could last for days. She had experienced severe headaches as a child and then appeared to outgrow them. But after having children the migraines sprung back up, and Momma was always trying one remedy or the other. Monique Johnson was in dreamland more often than not, and although very creative and whimsical, Momma was not a hands-on parent. She was always hoping to be discovered by the colorful entertainment industry, getting that "big break." Hopes of being placed in a play or movie or declared the country's next singing sensation remained high on Momma's wish list.

Daddy was more resigned than permissive with regard to his wife's infatuations. Marcus Johnson, hard-working and responsible, was the disciplinarian in the family. Inclined to let many things slide, he seldom found it necessary to reprimand his oldest daughter. He could bring tender Pearl to tears just by looking at her sternly. She was that near-perfect child, while Josie Bee was the one who tested everyone's limits. Pearl could be ferocious in protecting and defending her baby sis. As a negotiator, the quiet and meek Pearl played on the sympathies of her audience, always urging for leniency. Everyone thought she would one day go to law school and become the first in the family to graduate from college. Then Momma and Daddy walked off a curb on that Friday night after a movie, both being struck, killed in a hit-and-run. A white driver was spotted by moviegoer bystanders but to no avail, and with no concrete leads or arrests, their deaths remained unsolved. The girls were crushed, confused, and grief-stricken beyond comprehension. Auntie Birdie instantly swooped in and carried the sisters off to her nest. Josie and Pearl had always enjoyed time with their Auntie, but there is a big difference between visiting and living permanently in someone's home. What had been a playful and fanciful time became a permanent reality. Not that the girls weren't truly grateful for their dear Auntie's provisions, because they were. But together the sisters became a force of two brokenhearted girls, trying their best to recover from the tragic loss of parents and readjustment in a new home with a new set of circumstances and rules. Life certainly wasn't a bed of roses, and the thorns were mighty sharp. The church stepped forward, and a multitude was involved in the delicate journey toward healing and a sense of peace for the afflicted Johnson girls. Josie and Pearl were surrounded by generous and caring people. All that love and encouragement that had been poured into the girls would be valuable and put to good use sooner or later. Every single bit.

Glancing over at the clock, Josie couldn't believe an hour had passed. Jumping up and out of bed, she scrambled to get ready for the busy day ahead. Josie had a job to do, and it was going to take all she had to stay focused and do what was expected from her.

Josie still managed to arrive at school an hour early, taking Faye and Nola completely by surprise. Josie dared not mention anything about Pearl or her unsettling night. She walked in with a smile on her face and cheerfully greeted Faye and Nola.

"Hello there, sunshine," said Faye.

"Are you okay, Miss Josie?" Nola asked.

"I sure am! C'mon, you know the early bird gets the worm," said Josie.

"Really, Josie? Since when? Shall I have Nola dig up some fresh worms for tonight's dinner?" asked Faye. She couldn't help but giggle.

"You are really perky and funny early in the day, Miss Faye. Didn't know you could be so comical, a real Phyllis Diller!" Josie shot back.

"Who? Yeah, well I try. Seriously, what are you doing here this early? Not like you, dear," said Faye.

"Give me a break! I couldn't wait to get here. The reward for my efforts? Seeing your smiling faces and hearing your hilarious accusations," said Josie.

"Oh please," feigned Faye.

"Let's just say I am deeply motivated to put in as much time as possible at this glorious institution. What more can I say?"

"Ah, that is soooo nice, Josie." Faye seemed genuinely pleased.

Having a slice of coffee cake and a large mug of coffee topped with frothy cream, Josie enjoyed her tasty breakfast. Not able to drink black coffee, Josie allowed Nola to entice her into trying it with the rich cream, and Josie thoroughly enjoyed it. Now she was hooked on her own cup of crazy.

With light and jovial banter in place and everyone's tummy contented, Josie and the others began the day. With confirmation from the ladies regarding dinner plans and Josie's staying over for the night, Josie focused on her time with the students. Charlie was one of the first to arrive at Fiesta, allowing them to share while doing a puzzle together. Charlie didn't do puzzles at home and really enjoyed getting the pieces to fit in. It seemed that Charlie and her four stair-step brothers got along well, and they considered her one of the crew. Charlie played kickball and baseball after school with them. Josie quickly surmised that this girl didn't know anything different.

Josie's new thought was to bring in magazines, simply pointing out what some girls liked to wear and see if any of the styles or colors stood out or appealed to Charlie. Maybe they could play a little dress-up and find out if Angel Three would take interest in the new types of clothing. If not, that would be okay too. But Josie did want to work a little on her hair or accessories. Completing the puzzle, Charlie was thrilled with the picture of kittens in a basket. Josie found out that this little girl really liked cats, but the ones that had been brought home disappeared rather quickly. No doubt being in a house with all those boys proved too chaotic for the little furballs.

Sharing time always amused Josie. You never knew what the kids were going to tell you. But it was advantageous today as she wanted to touch base with Patty-Jo to see how things were going with Eggy and find out whether he was still in one piece. To Josie's surprise, Patty-Jo brought Eggy to sharing time to introduce him to all the students. It was fascinating. She had wrapped him in Kleenex to keep him from being seen until she was ready to show him off. Patty-Jo slowly and carefully unwrapped the little egg, holding him up so he could see everyone's faces in the class. The tissue box was close by but not in Patty-Jo's hands. Josie couldn't wait to compare notes with Faye and Nola to see how they viewed the experiment so far.

During snacks, Josie chatted with Agnes to see what was new. She said her grandmother was really happy she was getting to see an eye doctor and wished she had had that opportunity when she was a child. Agnes was so excited. It made Josie's heart swell to see her upbeat and looking forward to seeing Dr. Decker. Riding the bus together would be nice, and Josie was going to ask Nola to pack each of them a surprise snack bag just for the fun of it.

Lunch was pigs in a blanket and cheesy hash-brown potatoes. Ketchup made the rounds, and each child seemed to dress up the hot dogs in their own special way. Helping Nola clear the tables and clean up the ketchup that seemed to have landed on everything, Josie heard about upcoming school activities that she wasn't aware of. As Josie was finding out, no one got more excited than Faye Lewis when it came to lights and bells and the magic of Christmas. In fact, Josie had recently asked her to explain why she liked Christmas so much.

"For me it is all about the twinkling lights," Faye quickly answered. "I love all the colors, but those little clear ones really float my boat. They are sooooo bright! Like tiny sparkling promises on a string. They radiate a magic that makes me think everything is good and if it's not, it can be. Lights have picked me up ever since I was a small child wishing and hoping for my life to be different. Then I wanted it to be better, and ultimately, I just needed a source of real hope in my life. They do that for me," Faye confirmed.

"Well, that's quite a response, Miss Faye. It certainly answers my simple question. Lights it is. Might you be able to order me a quadruple load of them and throw in a handful of stardust for good measure?" Josie teased.

"If only it were that easy, I certainly would," Faye responded wistfully.

Faye was currently planning a field trip to take the kids to see Santa at Wolf & Dessauer in nearby Fort Wayne. She was keen on celebrations, and the holidays provided her with ample opportunities for merriment and cheer. Faye also wanted to work on the kids' table manners and had a couple of tea parties planned in which to practice them. She wanted the students to go over placing their napkins on their laps and saying please and thank-you while not speaking with food in their mouths or chomping like horses. Faye loved these types of exercises with her eager students, reveling in the compliments bestowed on her and the Fiesta School during their past holiday experiences at Murphy's Five and Dime Luncheon Counter.

The weather was cloudy and rainy most of the morning, but going into the afternoon the downpour was torrential. Even Mister George, the ever-adventurous cat, had no intention of stepping out into the heavy rain. So instead Faye recruited Archie Wilson for a special activity. Archie was more than happy to provide the kids with something special to do since they wouldn't be going out to the park. Faye had closets full of construction paper, poster boards, crayons, paints, scissors, and glue. Archie was a natural with the kids. He enjoyed himself and the kids adored him. The break in routine seemed to speed up the afternoon, and before you knew it, it was time to clean up, pick up, and get ready to go home.

As soon as most everyone was loaded up and walking out with parents and guardians, Josie switched gears and wondered what Nola would be whipping up in the kitchen. She also was contemplating much-needed time with both the ladies. Josie heard chicken sizzling and knew it was cooking in a pool of lard in Nola's oversized cast-iron skillet. Her mouth watered. Quickly popping her head into the kitchen, she tried to see what else Nola might be preparing for their supper feast. Josie enjoyed chicken so much she thought she could do without any trimmings, but Nola's side dishes changed her mind then and there. Yes, bring on the potatoes and corn and black-eyed peas. She could handle it.

Faye was already sitting at the yellow table sipping on the Kool-Aid. She made a point to ask Josie if everyone was gone, and when Josie replied, "Almost," Faye got up and shooed her out.

"Back soon, I promise," said Josie, winking at Nola, who also was motioning her out.

Josie Bee remained at the yellow sunshine door until the last two kids departed. As soon as Jupiter and Ernie trotted out the door and down the walkway, Josie closed the door and practically skipped to the kitchen. When she got there, Faye was pouring from the green Mosser pitcher. This time it was lime Kool-Aid. It looked remarkably mystical, the stream of bright green flowing from the iridescent glassware. More eye-catching were the two bottles of vodka sitting on the counter between a can of Crisco and a crock of whipped butter. Usually she was more controlled, casually sipping the "kiddie juice," but this evening Faye appeared to be on her own mission of sorts. Josie had tried alcohol here and there with her friends but wouldn't turn twenty-one for several more months. Of all the things in the world, consuming alcohol wasn't a biggie for Josie. She wasn't against it and didn't particularly care one way or the other if others drank. Josie was more interested in the "why" when one drank such large amounts so quickly. Faye was in a sullen mood, and yet she had been so upbeat and chipper earlier in the day. What was eating at her? Josie selfishly was thinking that she didn't really need this unknown and alarming behavior out of Faye right now.

Josie's main purpose of staying over was to talk about her angels and learn more about Frank White, but she was worried that Faye might be on her way out of this world before dinner even got started. Good grief, she needed to talk to Nola and get her take on Faye's drinking. She had questions and concerns that were imperative to address so she could move forward in helping the girls and meeting the Challenge. Then out of the blue, Faye started firing off questions. Josie wasn't sure if they were addressed to her or not, but she was stunned. Faye had her attention!

"Question number one: Did you know I started drinking around the age of twelve? Question number two: Did I mention I didn't finish high school and I was a dropout? Question number three: Guess who is in prison but possibly will be out in six months? I will give you the answer to this one: his name is Earl Carter, one of my mother's many boyfriends. He was the most vicious and nastiest one of all. A real piece of work. Edie probably wants him out, but me personally, I want him locked away forever. He's more than earned a permanent life sentence. And that, Josie Bee Johnson, is a selection of the things I want you to know about me." Faye said all this without much emotion.

Josie looked at Nola, who said that dinner was hot and ready and that they should eat now, talk later. That sounded reasonable to Josie, and she gave it two thumbs up while Faye shrugged her shoulders as if she didn't care one way or the other.

Nola talked to Faye as Pearl would have spoken to Josie—with the softness and care of a mother. "Please, dear, try and eat a little bit before we talk about things."

Faye was determined to polish off the doctored Kool-Aid, making herself another pitcher with a grape-flavored packet.

"C'mon, Faye, do you have to drink this much? You'll be sick in the morning for sure," Josie said quietly.

"I'll have you know I have done this for many years and have never once missed getting up in the morning. Not one time. Are you judging me, Josie? 'Cause if you are, you can march yourself right out of here and be done with *my* school! Do you hear me?"

And with that last comment out of Faye's mouth, Nola stepped in, telling her inebriated girl that she knew she didn't really mean what she just said. The alcohol was causing Faye to say dreadful things, and it needed to stop. Telling Faye she was to quietly stay put, Nola began serving dinner. Josie could tell Nola understood Faye as the hurting child she was, and did not relish the task of trying to rein her in. Josie was hungry and planned to eat but also frustrated and disappointed. She didn't know how far to push her agenda. Maybe Nola would be sympathetic and pick up the slack, giving Josie what information and direction she desperately needed.

Nola placed small amounts of food on Faye's plate, encouraging her to eat. Faye went from defiance to sincere sadness, and Josie ached for the pain that was surely haunting her spirit. They ate to satisfy the need for nourishment, but there was not much joy in the wonderfully prepared meal. For that reason alone, Josie felt sorry for Nola, Faye, and herself. Josie had planned to share with the team the heartache she was feeling for Pearl, but now wasn't the time. She still wanted to ask somebody about Frank White.

Faye was silent. Barely picking at her food, she seemed unaware of her surroundings. Her eyes were glazed over, and she was on her third miniature Mosser pitcher of vodka and Kool-Aid. Hopefully Faye wasn't intent on trying the orange and fruit punch too, but Josie felt somewhat assured that Nola wouldn't allow it.

Thinking it was safe to bring up Penny and her father to Nola, Josie leaned in and half-whispered to her friend, "So what's up with Frank, and how do we help our sweet little Penny?"

Then Faye jerked forward and, looking half-crazed, shot back, "What do you want us to do, lose all we've worked for? And then what happens? You get to walk away, Josie, and I will be left with nothing. Absolutely nothing. My life will be left in shambles. And what about Nola, Josie?" Faye asked. "Can you think outside the box?"

"What do you mean?" said Josie.

"Frank White is a racist. He runs with Klan members. Yes Josie, the Klan is everywhere. We have our share of haters too!" Faye snapped.

"I don't get what you're saying. We're talking about Frank White!" Josie argued. "He can't be above the law. Aren't you worried that he is going to really hurt one of your precious and most fragile students?"

"Yes, of course I am, but if we aren't here to work with the kids, then what good are we?" Faye said. "He knows about me, Josie. He knows I never finished school, and yet I hold myself up as a director and child advocate for education and success! He promised he would make me the laughingstock of Sand Haven and take everything from me, kicking my lily-white butt to the curb." Even though Faye was drunk, Josie was positive Frank White would say exactly that. "And he'll hurt Nola, because he said he would enjoy that," Faye cried.

"And what else has he done, Faye? Tell me. Has he physically hurt you?" Josie asked, fearing there was more. There just had to be something.

"Just let it alone, Josie. Please. For me, for Nola, for you and everyone else. You can't fight men like Frank White and not get badly hurt, do you hear me?" she said, pleading with the eyes of one who clearly understood what it meant to be damaged.

Nola sprang into action, prying Faye's shaking hands from the juice glass as she spilled the last sips of grape Kool-Aid. "No more, sweet baby, no more," Nola cooed into her ear. Faye let Nola console and hold her, calm her down, and then lead her to her room. When Nola got back to the kitchen, Josie had started picking up.

They put away large amounts of leftovers and did the dishes side by side in silence. Each was lost in their thoughts and fears, wondering what would happen next. Nola understood Faye, knew her story, and allowed her the nightly time to escape her difficult childhood hauntings. Nola comprehended all too well the desire to check out. After witnessing horrendous Klan activities and practices, Nola had literally been scared out of her wits and feared she would certainly end up in the nuthouse. And that was only if she survived at all. A nervous wreck, her big brother encouraged Nola to take a type of medicinal drink that would surely calm her down at the end of the day, allowing her to sleep at night. Nola became attached to her bottled friend in a relatively small period of time. She would look forward to the slow burn of the reliable and smooth whiskey. Nola welcomed it into her life with open arms. But when her sweet mother caught on, there was an urgent coming-to-Jesus-moment which resulted in Nola being sent up North for her own good. Yes, Nola fully understood Miss Faye and she would care for her as long as she was needed. Faye was caught between a rock and a hard place, the adult woman who kept trying to move forward and the broken child who wanted to give up.

Starting slowly, Nola told Josie that Frank White had recently threatened Faye, and the stale smell of beer on his breath and the force he used to push her against the garage wall jerked her back into the past. Faye began remembering things about Earl Carter that she had wanted to forget. Frank even threatened to make Mister George disappear, and the combination of all those factors made something inside Faye snap. Faye had been struggling ever since that conversation, and Frank knew he'd gotten to her. She was scared.

"He thrives on hurting women and little girls," Nola said. "Nobody has been able to stop him. They call him Teflon Frank. Everyone is terrified at what he is and what he is capable of doing. Believe me, we have tried to figure out how to stop him, but we don't see any way out of this right now. Maybe never. And now when Faye looks at Penny, she sees the victim she was as a child, and she hates that she can't protect her or stop it. Faye is a victim too, and she has given her life to serve children in order to give them a safe and secure space to be. She took money given to her by her aunt to invest in others in order to give these kids a happy and healthy environment. None of this is fair. There are no winners, and we all have the potential to lose everything."

"He is a damn locust," Josie said. "Frank White should be eliminated from the face of this earth. Where there is a will there is a way, and Nola, we cannot give up faith that we can change evil for good. Surely God is on our side and our tears are His tears when it comes to His tiniest creations. Please, Nola, work with me, and we can leave Faye out of this. What is stopping Frank from hurting her even if she doesn't rock the boat? She can't go on living like this. Faye will drink until she can no longer function. The locusts will tear her apart. They will infect all parts of her life. They will devour her. It's what they do. They are ravenous. We can't let this happen. Frank White is a locust, and he will kill someone or something. We have no idea how close he has come to already doing that. The damage may already be irreparable. We have to try and stop him, Nola! We can't afford to turn out heads and look the other way."

"I know what you say is well-intended, Josie, but I also know that if there was something that could have been done, we would have gone that route. Our dear Faye is in dire need of a break. Please don't go stirring this pot, and promise me you will back off. We're not the only ones Frank will go after. He is a violent racist and would enjoy hurting you too. Believe me, he is not to be toyed with. I know this to be absolutely true. Please don't doubt my words. Leave this be. Promise me," Nola pleaded urgently.

Josie was aware of the severe trembling in Nola's swollen hands. Josie was conflicted. She needed time to think and get back with Big Carl. Oh, dear Lord, what could they do? Josie vividly remembered Auntie Birdie's heavy words after that dark day in '63: "Do what needs to be done and then drop to your knees and ask forgiveness." Could it be interpreted as the end justifying the means? Time would tell.

Josie Bee peeked in on Faye, and she appeared to be in a state of peaceful slumber with Mister George curled up on her chest. He was a charming creature that dearly loved his mistress. His lovely lady would be lost without him. Mister George meant the world to Faye, and Faye meant the world to her students. What were they going to do?

The next morning, Nola and Josie were careful not to mention anything about the previous evening's discussion. They didn't know how it would affect Faye's disposition and hoped she didn't remember any of it. It was enough that they were distraught and concerned for Faye. Frank White's aggressive threats were causing a collision of Faye's past and present fears. There was a lot to worry about, and even more that needed to be sorted out.

As the get-togethers increased, so did Faye's drinking. Chugging glasses of Kool-Aid was routine. Drinking the beverages from her cherished Mosser glassware made Faye happy, but only temporarily. It was a beautiful set that she had inherited from her dear Aunt Pauline. Faye felt grown-up and classy when she grasped the heavy-leaded luminous glass, remembering how special she felt the first time she held the pieces with her Aunt. She thought it was too beautiful to save only for holidays or special events. So Faye used the miniature green pitcher and luminous juice glasses daily to hold the vodka-and-Kool-Aid mix. Only there was less Kool-Aid and more vodka going into the mix and down the hatch. It didn't take Faye nearly as long to become inebriated as it had when Josie first started coming around. Faye seemed loopier and, not surprisingly, more combative with each sip. But Faye was aware and fearful of Frank White. She had no idea what else to do to neutralize his abuse. And Faye knew Nola understood her coping methods and let her excessive drinking go. Now was not the time to challenge Faye's old habits. Nola fully understood why Faye drank. It was Nola's job to tuck her into bed each night, pray for her, and love her unconditionally. It was her privilege. And Faye would be forever grateful for her faithful friend and nurturer. They took care of each other.

This particular evening Faye appeared to have an appetite, picking less and eating more of Nola's homemade beef and noodles with mashed potatoes and scalloped corn. It hit the spot as the three of them managed to get through the meal comfortably and without incident.

Josie wasn't sure why things were going so well but she was immensely thankful. The night had been thoroughly pleasant. Sitting around the table wrapping up the day's business, the ladies were startled when at 9:00 p.m. the doorbell rang. The unexpected ringing was followed by excessive knocking. Nola jumped up and, limping toward the door, firmly instructed Faye and Josie to stay put and she would take care of it. Ringing at that time of night was never a good sign of anything.

13

A Showdown

*Crying is all right in its way while it lasts.
But you have to stop sooner or later, and then
you still have to decide what to do.*

C. S. Lewis

NOLA HIGHTAILED IT to the front door as if someone had shouted fire. When she opened the yellow door, there stood Sand Haven's notoriously mean lady, Edna Higgins. It was hard to believe this brutally boisterous woman had one of the gentlest little ones in the school, soft-spoken and shy Dee-Dee Higgins, who was a true delight. Staff had hoped she wouldn't one day evolve into her brash and opiniated mother. The ladies couldn't imagine living life in the Higgins household. "If Momma ain't happy, ain't nobody happy" carried a frightening new depth of meaning when thinking of Mrs. Higgins. Edna's face was not capable of breaking a smile.

Nola had specifically told Josie and Faye to stay put. But Josie overheard that Dee-Dee had forgotten her well-loved pink-and-white knitted blankie, Binky. Josie beelined it to the playroom and picked up the worn blanket. It was rare that Binky wasn't in Dee-Dee's hands when she walked out the door. Somehow Josie had missed it at the end of the day. She was supposed to check and clear the play area before the kids left and had intended to brush through after dinner. Josie failed to be on top of her duties and now, because of her carelessness, Edna Higgins was standing on their very doorstep. Dang! Dang! Double dang!

Josie Bee zipped back with Binky in tow, hoping Faye would stay in the kitchen as Nola had firmly instructed both of them to do. Mrs. Higgins had already launched into a sermon on the school's lack of responsibility that resulted in this unnecessary and inconvenient situation. The woman was incredibly agitated and loudly letting them, along with the entire neighborhood, know the level of her annoyance. Josie bounded into the foyer space just in time to witness Faye's clumsy entrance, stumbling toward the commotion at the door.

Oh boy, this was not going to be pretty. Josie wanted to close her eyes. Faye was madder than a wet hen, and Josie presumed she had no filter. But then, like a marionette whose strings had abruptly been severed, Miss Faye Lewis, director of the Fiesta School, crumpled to the floor like a discarded rag doll. Josie wanted to freeze the frame, stop the action, and garner a do-over, but there was little she could control. However, quick-witted Nola helped the toppled woman to her feet, exclaiming, "Surely you must have the flu and need to get back into bed, Miss Faye."

"Quite frankly, Missss Nola, we both know I do not have the flu and was feeling quite fine until this ruuude person practically knocked down our door," Faye stammered.

"Well, I have never been treated like this before, and you will come to regret this, Director Lewis," Mrs. Higgins sneered.

"Are you sure? You've had something like this coming your way for years, and for the record, you don't scare me one iota," Faye declared. She was spittin' feathers!

Mrs. Higgins got directly in Faye's face while simultaneously peering into the kitchen area. She could clearly see the lineup of vodka bottles with the striking green glass Kool-Aid pitcher sitting on the counter.

"Those glazed-over spooky red eyes of yours are a dead giveaway,

Miss Lewis," said Mrs. Higgins, furiously wagging her chubby index finger in the air. "I always suspected the supermarket rumors were true. But because the children are looking forward to the special holiday activities and field trip, I will certainly let this go for now. It is the Christian thing to do. But mark my words, you will not get away any longer with this type of behavior on my watch. I will be coming after you and you can best count on it! Now give me that blanket." Jerking Binky out of Josie's tight grip, Mrs. Higgins turned on her heels and darted out the door like a scalded cat.

"You don't scare me, you old hag," Faye sputtered in the air.

"I told you to stay at the table, child," Nola said, clearly frustrated. Nola and Josie were beyond themselves with disbelief and overwhelming worry. It wasn't a question of what Edna Higgins would do next, but when. As if they weren't dealing with a whole ton of chicken poop as it was, Josie had somehow brought a fresh pile of it into the school. Now it was affecting the professional and personal lives of the very folks she had come to love and adore. They didn't deserve this kind of harsh judgment. Josie felt God should shoulder some if not most of the blame. Wasn't it all His idea anyway? Didn't He know this was gonna happen? What would Auntie Birdie and the Hallelujahs make of the developments in the mission and Edna Higgins's promised showdown?

Nasty Mrs. Higgins just had to have a change of mind. It was possible, wasn't it? After all, weren't all things supposed to be possible with God? Why on earth was Mrs. Higgins so worked up and angry? Probably not a soul in the room, including Mister George, who remained crouched under the "red-for-stop" time-out bench, believed Edna Higgins could have a change of heart. Another locust in the school's sandbox with the potential of growing in numbers and developing a vicious swarm that would attack its core. All the good that had been done for children, including countless hours of instruction and encouragement, was now compromised. Faye Lewis could lose her license and the purpose if not the redemption of her existence. The school was everything, and Faye was at risk of losing it all. The Fiesta had been a safe haven for preschool children, a precious commodity that did not deserve to be tried in the court of careless gossip and community prejudice. Poor Faye and poor Nola. And Josie felt sorry for herself too. Overwhelmed with stress and fear, Josie wanted to drop everything and run. Run to Pearl, take them both back to Birmingham, and stop this continuously building nightmare.

Observing Faye grab another glass of Kool-Aid and trot off toward her room, Josie wanted an escape too. She desperately wanted to leave, but the buses weren't running at this time of night, and she knew she would regret it. You don't desert your teammates when they are in the midst of a struggle. Even Josie knew that. She needed to keep her head on straight, as Pearl would tell her to do, and get to helping Nola clean up the leftovers and dirty pans. Her heart ached so much as she watched Nola look in on Faye with tears trickling down her cheeks. Nola loved her like a daughter, and their mutual love and friendship ran deep.

Faye had effortlessly fallen asleep when her head hit the pillow. Mister George, in spite of all the drama, was wrapped around her neck, peacefully purring. To be able to rest no matter how bad the circumstances appeared was a gift that humans could only wish for. Peace that passes all understanding seemed, at least for the time being, a stretch for Josie's faith. She wasn't completely sure of what it looked like or how it was supposed to feel. Josie Bee felt stronger and more assured of herself when she was piggybacking on her sister's and auntie's convictions. Feeling depleted, Josie couldn't wait to go to bed and get back to the Prices' the next evening. Josie wanted to get an encouraging and upbeat letter off to Pearl, sparing her any of the stressful details of this new situation. Josie needed to make good with Nola, letting her know how sincerely sorry she was for her carelessness earlier. However, Nola indicated she had little to say, and Josie, feeling defeated as well, let it go. The two women tidied up the kitchen in silence. It was neither uncomfortable nor odd; both were lost in their own thoughts and feelings. When they were finished, Josie and Nola hugged, needing no words at all.

Coffee time the next morning was slightly strained and somewhat awkward. Once the team got going, the ladies put aside the events of the previous evening and focused on the students. Josie reminded Faye and Nola that she would be off and running after lunch to take Agnes to her eye appointment with Dr. Decker. They discussed the approaching tea parties so the kids could practice table manners in light of their upcoming holiday lunch experience. The school would be going to G. C. Murphy's Five and Dime to eat, located in Fort Wayne, close to the iconic Wolf & Dessauer Department Store. The kids would be going to W&D's for their annual Christmas field trip to visit Santa and see the amazing magic window displays. The holiday lights and animated figurines were a source of colorful excitement, and the children would fondly remember and cherish this magical experience for the rest of their lives.

Faye Lewis had never known what it was like to celebrate Christmas or go to church to see the baby Jesus lying in a manger filled with straw. As a young child she didn't experience the twinkling lights on a decorated tree like most normal families. Faye's Christmas stocking was not hung by the chimney with care, or anywhere else for that matter, because she did not have one. If not for the thoughtful kindness of a whimsical next-door neighbor, Faye would never have sampled any special or festive foods at the holidays. This sweet neighbor woman always arrived on Christmas Eve, carrying a red plastic plate containing two tangerines, apple and cheese slices, several Ritz crackers, a small dab of peanut butter, one large sugar cookie covered in sparkly green sprinkles, and three miniature candy canes. This was the one thing Faye looked forward to during the holidays, but each December she feared it would end. Faye sat by a drafty and cracked window for hours while watching for the long-anticipated delivery. The plate was always covered in red plastic wrap with a big green bow on top, accompanied with "Merry Christmas, dear Faye."

"Merry Christmas, Mrs. Claus, and thank you," Faye replied. Yes, Faye believed the white-haired jolly woman must be Santa's wife. She vowed to someday pass on this kindness to another wide-eyed child needing a handful of magic.

The little girl grew up, and the big girl genuinely wanted to share the wonder and the glory of the magic of Christmas with others. Now Faye had an entire school to bring into the circle of holiday fantasy and fun. Building up the anticipation and delivery of celebratory splendor filled Faye Lewis with delight. She made the hearts of kids happy, and along the way she gathered a bit of healing stardust to place in her own. Each year, the celebration eased the hurts of Christmases past, those forgotten by others yet remembered by a thoughtful and kind lady who knew Faye's name.

Faye got excited and animated every time she explained to the students about the upcoming holiday field trip to the big city of Fort Wayne. She wanted the children to get swept up in the festivities too, as she delighted in spinning and retelling her tale. As Josie Bee listened to Faye talk to the kids, she began feeling a change in mood and welcomed Faye's ability to get them on board and thinking the merriest of thoughts. Nola was humming "Jingle Bells," and the kids were chirping in like a choir of holiday songbirds.

The morning seemed to fly by for everyone but Agnes, who was so excited she could hardly stand it. She kept looking at the big clock on the wall, asking staff how many more minutes before it was time to eat. Agnes knew they were leaving the school after lunch. She couldn't sit still without fidgeting. Josie reminded her they would be riding a bus, and that seemed to give Agnes something to think about other than the time. Things were feeling more normal and routine as the class broke for lunch.

"Hey, do you two think you can hold down the fort in my absence?" Josie asked Faye and Nola.

"I certainly hope so, Miss Johnson. Somehow, we have managed to do that without your assistance the last, say, five years or so," Faye said.

"I'll be gone for a few hours and know you have kinda gotten used to me being around," Josie chuckled.

"I think you misunderstand, dear. Getting used to and tolerating one's presence are two different things," Faye said kiddingly.

"Ouch, that hurt, Miss Faye!" Josie cried.

"Get over it and get moving if you want to catch that bus, Josie," Nola said.

"Since you put that so nicely, Agnes and I will get going," Josie replied.

"Good luck, Agnes. Do good on your tests," Faye said.

"I'm going to take tests?" Agnes asked.

"No, baby girl, the doctor will do the tests," Josie explained.

"Oh good, because I haven't done no studying," said Agnes.

"That's 'any' studying, Punkin'," corrected Faye.

"Just have fun, Agnes," Nola said with a grin.

"And we're keeeeping our fingers crossed," Faye said.

Agnes and Josie gathered their Fiesta backpacks and headed out the door. Agnes enjoyed the bus ride downtown. They arrived fifteen minutes early to fill out papers and wait their turn. Agnes wasn't exactly sure what was happening but clearly enjoyed Josie's jovial mood. Dr. Decker's assistant made Agnes comfortable, showing her the sticker box where she would be allowed to pick out several of the colorful items after the exam. Josie appreciated being included in the testing room. Still excited, Agnes didn't seem to be anxious or particularly curious by what was about to happen and marched into the examination room like a trooper. Dr. Decker was waiting for them, and he greeted Josie before turning to Agnes.

"Hi Agnes, my name is Dr. Decker. How are you today?" he asked.

"I'm fine, thank you," she replied politely.

"Today I will be checking your eyes. It won't hurt a single bit," he reassured Agnes with a warm smile.

"I know. Miss Josie told me too," Agnes said.

"Good. Let's get started. Can you climb into this big chair for me?" he asked.

"I can do it all by myself," said Agnes.

The Snellen eye chart, made up of big and little letters, dominated the wall in front of the large, cushioned chair that moved up and down.

"I am going to cover up your eyes, one at a time. Is that okay with you, Agnes?" the gentle doctor asked. The little patient nodded, and Dr. Decker proceeded to cover her right eye.

"Do you know all the letters of the alphabet?" the doctor asked.

"Yes," said Agnes.

"All our students do," Josie said, beaming.

"That is excellent," said the doctor. "Agnes, can you tell me what letters you see on that top line? . . . How about the next one? . . . Great. And the next? . . . Now let's switch and cover up your other eye. You are doing a good job, Agnes. Do you want to take a break and rest?"

asked Dr. Decker as if he had all day to spend with his newest patient.

"No, I'm good." Agnes continued on until the exam was completed and Dr. Decker was finished writing notes on his yellow legal pad.

"Thank you for being such a wonderful patient, Agnes. You may go out with my helper, Mrs. Jansen, and see what's in the sticker box," he said.

When the door closed, Dr. Decker shared what he had discovered. Agnes's right eye wandered, and she had extremely poor eyesight. Both appeared reasonably fixable with eye exercises and a pair of new glasses. Everything in Agnes's world, he said, had to have been confusing and blurred given her severe lack of vision, but it was a simple fix. To be able to purchase what she needed and level her playing field made Josie swell inside. She could hardly contain herself. Because Agnes had spent so much time with her blind grandmother, it had become normal for her to work around obstacles. Agnes had naturally learned ways to navigate at home, but school and other places presented unexpected and unpreventable run-ins.

Calling for Mrs. Jansen to bring little Agnes back in, the kind doctor wanted to explain to his miniature patient what would be happening next. "Come back in, young lady," Dr. Decker said as he motioned her back in through the door. Agnes marched into the room with a fistful of stickers and a grin on her face.

"I have stickers I'm going to give to my friends at school," she proudly exclaimed.

"Indeed, you do," said Dr. Decker with a smile and a wink. "Agnes, we are going to work on one of your eyes that gets tired and is always looking for a place to rest," said the doctor, explaining the situation to Agnes with his pad of paper and bright blue magic marker in his hands. "We are going to have Miss Johnson work on eye exercises with you each day, and before long that right eye won't get so tired. Agnes, you will need glasses, and today we are going to have fun picking out a special pair just for you. These will help you see so much better. It will make everything brighter and easier for you, young lady."

Josie felt blessed and grateful that God had placed this kindhearted and gentle practitioner in the midst of the church Josie had been directed to attend. If Josie Bee could recognize God's hand in these little things, then maybe she could trust Him to get her through what was to come. Josie was frightened on many levels, and this block of time with Agnes had given her some much-needed encouragement. *Parakletos* was one of the Hallelujah Circle's most favorite and commonly used words, because it meant "comforter" or "encourager." The ladies felt holier-than-thou using it to talk about pouring encouragement into someone who needed it.

The best part of the eye appointment was being able to give Agnes something she needed to improve her life and help her to progress in her own journey. It was a truly glorious moment. Josie's next part in assisting this little angel was to help choose the perfect frames for her tiny face. With the technician's help and expertise, a pair of cat-eye frames were chosen. The slender, off-white frames looked adorable on Agnes. She was thrilled. Dr. Decker popped his head into the small room telling Agnes the glasses were "on the house."

"How are we supposed to get them down?" Agnes asked, looking puzzled. Everyone chuckled.

Josie was stunned. "Thank you, but I have money to purchase them, and it was never my intention not to pay for these," Josie sputtered.

"It is my joy. Keep up the good work, Miss Johnson," said the good doctor, and off he went. Josie was choked up. She hadn't seen this generous act of kindness coming. Josie had already been deeply thankful for the free examination. But something in Dr. Decker's telling her to keep up the good work took her breath away. Maybe this was a sign of sorts, an indication that in attempting to move forward for the sake of the Challenge, there would be unknown graces sprinkled along the way. Josie couldn't wait to get back to the school and deliver their good news. Glory! Now if only those glasses could arrive before the Fiesta kids went to Fort Wayne to see Santa, it would be perfect.

Leaving the medical building downtown, Josie and Agnes practically skipped to the central bus stop. Waiting for their bus, Josie spied the gentle giant himself, Big Carl, hopping off a bus. He would have been hard to miss. Carl had been on Josie's list to contact, but the drama with Edna Higgins had jammed everything up.

"Hey Carl, can you stay put for just a minute?" Josie shouted.

He turned around and was surprised to see her. "I sure can. What's up?"

"I need to apologize for not getting back to you sooner. Wondering if it would be okay to just connect at church in a few days?" she asked.

"Sure, no problem. I've been kind of busy too, trying to keep my job," he joked.

"Just keep mulling our options around in that humongous thinking tank of yours, okay? I trust you, Carl, and know that together we can work this situation out to our advantage. We've got to do something for Penny as soon as possible, Boss."

Big Carl nodded and the chance meeting was over. On the bus heading back to school, Josie was feeling somewhat positive but by no means overly hopeful regarding Penny. Mostly she was excited to share Agnes's good news with Faye and Nola, for now she was in the moment of success. One step closer to returning to Birmingham. Josie couldn't wait to see their reactions. She certainly owed them some snippets of joy.

When Josie and Agnes returned, they were beaming. Catching Faye's and Nola's attention for a quick minute, Josie gave them two thumbs up, and both flashed big grins. Josie wanted to share the various details of Agnes's good news, but it would have to wait. There seemed to be a minor crisis in motion. Josie noticed a sobbing Patty-Jo, who had just minutes earlier dropped Eggy, cracking his pointy head and skinny face. Nola, who generally kept boiled eggs on hand, was trying to convince Patty-Jo to swap in her injured egg for a new one. But double-fisted Patty-Jo, inconsolable and clutching the tissue box for dear life, was not about to let go of either item. Tearfully, she was wanting to know if Eggy was dead and if they were going to have a funeral and bury it. Kids seemed to be obsessed with burying things. A dead worm, a smashed fly. Faye and Nola suggested Josie take Patty-Jo to the playroom to get the situation ironed out.

The good news about Agnes temporarily on hold, Josie Bee, Patty-Jo, and the damaged egg trotted off to the playroom for a resolution. Once Patty-Jo calmed down, Josie was able to convince her that Eggy wouldn't want her not to have someone to care for, and surprisingly it made sense to the grieving child. She carefully accepted the new egg with plans to put clothes on it to keep it safe and warm. Going to the toy box, Josie was able to locate a random itty-bitty dress that would work perfectly. Patty-Jo was thrilled with her new girl Eggy and happily returned to the group. Mister George leisurely strolled across the room as if to announce it was almost time to wrap things up. He always tried to slip out the door when folks started coming in and out and was pretty good at doing so.

After school Josie shared the details of Agnes's good news. Josie told the ladies about her lazy eye, which was correctable with daily exercises. Best of all, they had already picked out and ordered adorable glasses. It was no wonder that little Agnes bumped into things and was insecure when moving around. Fortunately, both issues could be easily taken care of, and it would make a night-and-day difference for Agnes. Faye and Nola were ecstatic. They had figured the news was good when Josie and Agnes returned with huge smiles on their faces. Faye offered to call Mrs. Jones and give her the positive results, profusely thanking Josie for all her efforts on Agnes's behalf. Josie made sure every single one of her chores was completely done and, apologizing for needing to take off so quickly, explained that she had hoped to stay but had things to do at home that couldn't wait. Josie Bee still hadn't shared her concerns about Pearl, but the time hadn't been right either. Josie promised to arrive earlier than normal in the morning to catch them up and enjoy Nola's wild-blueberry-oatmeal muffins and creamed coffee.

"Oh, and one more thing, ladies," Josie said. "Not only did Agnes receive a free examination, but Dr. Decker made those super-cute glasses free too! Can you believe that?"

"God works in mysterious ways," Nola said.

"He sure does, and I am really glad," said Josie. "It gives us that much more to share with the others."

"God's like that," Nola said. "Full of surprises."

"No one knows that more than me," said Josie.

"Well, you do know what that means, right?" Faye said. "Someone, actually two individuals I know, will be writing thank-you notes tomorrow. Prompt and courteous."

"For sure," Josie promised.

At home Josie pulled out her stationery to write Pearl. Time had passed quickly since their emotional phone call, and Josie remained unsettled. She wanted to share everything with Pearl but knew it best to mention nothing other than her declared love and admiration for the sweetest sister in the world.

My Precious Sister,

I do not have the words to express my forever love for you, nor would I know where to even begin. All my life's memories encompass you, and without you nothing would be worthy of remembrance.

Who is taking care of you, Pearl? It wouldn't be fair if there weren't someone looking out for you.

Have you spoken with Auntie Birdie?

What would you have me do?

I love you so much. It is my wish that you are trying something that will make you better. I am making progress, and as soon as I can wrap things up here, I will come as fast as I can to take you home to Birmingham, where we both belong. I promise, Pearl.

Please don't ever worry that you could make me sad. You have given me nothing but happiness and strength my whole life. I will never forget your sacrifices and determination to help others, beginning with me, certainly your most challenging but rewarding project, right?

I hope that makes you smile, sweet sister of mine. Because I owe you a lifetime of thanks and care. I could never begin to return to you what you have given to me. But I will try.

I love you. I love you. I love you.

Always have, always will.

Josie Bee

Josie would wait and see what she heard back from her sister. In the meantime, she would keep forging forward with the Challenge so she could keep her promise to get them both back where they belonged. Together and in Birmingham was always the plan. Josie felt good about refraining from current events and not putting anything in the letter that would cause more worry or stress for her big sister. Josie presumed that the woman who answered the phone when she called was most likely one of Gertie's closest friends. Someone she trusted to watch over her precious Pearl. Auntie Gertie was a real planner and probably had things covered.

The next few days at school passed quickly. The long-anticipated Fiesta tea party was a hit from start to finish. "I am soooo proud of each of you!" Faye exclaimed. "You have worked really hard and are simply amazing!"

Miss Faye meant it. The students had done everything that had been asked of them. The many practices had really enabled the kids to learn the basics, and their table etiquette appeared effortless. Faye then announced the plans to have lunch at Murphy's after the visit with Santa Claus at Wolf & Dessauer. The kids clapped and cheered, and the countdown to the exciting event began. In just one week Fiesta School would have the luxury of riding in a yellow school bus that Archie Wilson had secured to transport the school's most precious cargo. Archie had requested the favor from a friend, and Miss Faye jumped up and down and wildly clapped her hands like a child with a new toy when he delivered the news. Archie never missed an opportunity to provide for the school, especially if it made his two favorite ladies merry and bright. It was the season for extending goodwill.

A week later the big day finally arrived. The kids showed up at school an hour earlier than normal, dressed in their best. Excitement and anticipation filled the air. Josie looked into Faye's eyes and, seeing the childlike wonder, again realized how important this holiday outing was to her. Josie Bee was grateful to be a part of this festive, memory-making time at the school and looked forward to seeing the sights in downtown Fort Wayne as well. She wanted to believe in so many things too: Believe that after the holidays there would be nothing to worry about. Believe that Frank White would fall off the face of the earth and take Edna Higgins with him. Josie desperately wanted to believe in a perfect ending for everything. Ah, to be a child and live in the moment and feel free, not captive but captivated. Her thoughts quickly turned to Pearl, who had provided her with countless times of extraordinary fairy-tale charm. Now it was someone else's turn to receive. Josie appreciated being part of making the moments magical.

The only drawback was that Josie was disappointed that Agnes's glasses hadn't arrived as expected. She had asked Nola to call the eye office, and they had confirmed that the glasses were in transit. But that had been days earlier, and they still hadn't received them. Agnes really didn't know what she would be missing, so not having the glasses didn't affect her one way or the other. But Josie and the ladies knew it would be a life-changing event when it happened, and there could be no better time than this holiday trip to Fort Wayne.

Faye, Nola, and Josie were allowing the kids extra playtime as they finished preparations, packing snacks and gathering what may be needed on the bus. The kids all clutched pictures they had colored for Santa and were excited to hand over their crinkled masterpieces. Patty-Jo was insistent on taking the new Eggy, and Josie made the off-the-cuff decision to allow it. They had made a cute, fuzzy cap for it earlier in the week. Josie figured Santa would get a chuckle out of it, but mostly Josie didn't want to set Patty-Jo's tears in motion. You never knew what would get those tears flowing, and Josie didn't want to take any risks. They had enough on their minds.

Mr. Wilson had generously offered to act as a chaperone, assisting the students throughout the entire day. Miss Faye thought it fabulous to have another set of eyes and helping hands, and she readily accepted his offer. Faye also let "the Arch" know that they would be dressing up and wearing their Sunday best. When Josie overheard their conversation she wanted to bust at the seams. These white folks didn't have the kind of "Sunday best" the women back home in Birmingham did. Black women dressed as if they were going to a party hosted by the king himself and as if your attire would be scrutinized and screened by an army of saints before entry was permitted. Josie didn't expect that same level of dress-up anywhere in Sand Haven, but she was reasonably sure Faye would look spectacular and no doubt be a real knockout.

Arriving early, Archie was gussied up in a navy blue suit that made him look prominent and distinguished. Faye made it a point to let Archie know how handsome he looked. Beaming from ear to ear, he quickly made himself useful by carrying the bagged snacks and drinks to the waiting vehicle, already parked in front of the school. Having Archie Wilson load the backpacks and other personal belongings spared the ladies extra steps in their heels, allowing him to run the show. It was a real treat to have a man in their midst, let alone one who was willing to do anything they wanted or needed. He was definitely in his element. Archie was a man of many talents: a wonderful neighbor, gifted handyman, a reliable and thoughtful friend. The ladies started laying it on thick, enjoying themselves profusely.

"What would we do without you, Archie Wilson?"

"Superman, is there anything you can't do?"

"Are you reading our minds? You are spoiling us rotten!"

Oh, what fun they were already having together, and Santa wasn't even in the picture yet. It was going to be an unforgettable day.

Faye dressed like the movie star she looked to be, with an upswept hairdo and bright crimson lipstick matching red-heeled shoes. Faye Lewis could have been a flawless mannequin in one of the windows at Wolf & Dessauer or one of the models roaming the department-store floors. Josie was impressed with the way Faye carried herself. Looking classy and impeccably poised, she exuded confidence and purpose. She praised the students on how nice they looked, and they were all enamored of their teacher and advocate. Faye was about to give her go-ahead to board the bus, just like she always did before they jumped into the sandbox, when the doorbell rang followed by a loud knock at the door. Standing there was one of the employees from Dr. Decker's eye office, holding a small package in her hands.

Josie squealed with delight and practically ran Archie over to grab the case of eyeglasses. Josie pulled Agnes in and told her to close her eyes. Carefully opening the glasses case as if it were a delicate treasure, Josie gently slipped the tiny pair of spectacles onto the face of Agnes.

Little did she knew her life was about to change in the most delightful way possible.

"You can open your eyes now, baby angel," Josie whispered. As she placed her in front of the mirror, the look on Agnes's face as she tried to take in what was happening was priceless. Unexpected tears of joy trickled down Josie's cheeks. When she looked up, Nola and Faye were both teary-eyed and hugging one another.

"Well I dooo declare, this is a Christmas miracle of the best kind," cooed Faye.

Agnes Jones silently tilted her head from side to side. Josie grabbed both her hands and squeezed them. "This may take a few minutes to get used to, but tell me, Agnes, what do you see?" Softly, Agnes said, "I see everything." The forgotten errand girl stepped forward and told them they probably would need to come by the office and get the frames adjusted. But for the time being Agnes should wear them for as long as tolerated. Josie profusely thanked her. The students gave Agnes and her new glasses a Fiesta hand, clapping as hard as they could. Then Faye blew the whistle and said her five magical words: "Now go and be free." The kids headed to the door to line up and then walked single file to the waiting bus.

The retired bus driver, a close friend of Archie's, was an affable guy who greeted the chattering students, joking and speaking with each one as they came through the doorway of the bus. Mr. Wilson was on the top step extending a hand for those kiddos who needed it.

The ride to the big city was filled with a symphony of spirited voices in a variety of ranges. Everybody had a song in their heart, and they let it out. The short trip to Fort Wayne from Sand Haven took less than twenty minutes. Unloading in front of Wolf & Dessauer, Miss Faye led the group as Archie brought up the rear. They made a great team. From the get-go the kids were in awe, fascinated by the bright lights and the movements in the window displays. Eventually the ladies, with the aid of Archie's sharp whistle, were able to get the wide-eyed students' attention in order to move them toward the elevator. The youngsters definitely would have preferred taking the moving staircase, but Faye did not feel confident that the escalator was the safest route for them to the second floor, where Santa and his elf assistants were located.

The preschool's youngsters were sectioned off into three groups of seven as they patiently waited their opportunity to ride the elevator. When the mysterious doors opened, the colored operators with white gloves and wide smiles welcomed everyone in. It was the first time riding an elevator for most of the kiddos. Excitedly they tried to figure out how the box moved up and down. Where were they going? When would they get there?

They "landed" at Santa's North Pole, exiting the elevator into a place of frozen fantasy. The dazzled youngsters entered Santa's area with gusto. There was a tremendous rush of glittering scenery and enchantment and Christmas joy.

The kids were placed in line, where they were entertained by a cluster of elves. Each child's artwork for Santa stated what they most wanted for Christmas. Miss Faye told the kids they could tell Santa what they hoped to receive, but they also had to tell him something they wanted that wouldn't cost anything. There was a wide variety of answers but it was never the ladies' intention to manipulate the responses. They wanted the kids to truly think about all the gifts one can receive that are free. A hug, a bedtime story, petting a cat, a compliment. The beauty was in writing down exactly what the child said and having them pass it on to Santa. It sparked a sincere reflectiveness among the youngsters. Most of the responses were thoughtful and touching, while some were flat-out hysterical.

Of course, the answers that Josie paid the most attention to belonged to her four little angel girls. Sweet Agnes wanted her grandmother to someday see a lighted Christmas tree. Patty-Jo said she wanted "everyone to get along and never be sad." If this just wasn't like Patty-Jo to be concerned about others and to not have them fussing with one another. Taking staff by surprise was Charlie Harper's answer, which was "to get a hand-me-down dress from somebody because it wouldn't cost anything." While Josie had been questioning whether this young girl was interested in fashion magazines, rough-and-tough Charlene had actually been thinking about dresses. You just could never tell what kids were contemplating, and Josie realized these tiny sponges absorbed everything around them, consciously or unconsciously, something she had not previously considered. Penny White's answer struck

Josie's heart; she clearly enunciated seven powerful words: "I want to be loved," and then came the last two words, "that's all." The troubled eyes haunted with past hurts and pain seemed to implore Josie for help. Josie wanted to say, "Yes, little one, I will find a way to rescue you, I can promise you that," but instead, a quivering Miss Josie wrapped her arms around a bruised Penny. In holding her close, Josie wanted Penny to feel safe and protected. Later she would figure out how to make it permanent.

Santa spent three minutes or so with each of the students as they discussed what they wanted. Each child gave the jolly man their response cards and went into detail regarding their artwork. Patty-Jo shared Eggy, giving Santa a jolly good laugh. Twenty-one kids collectively chatted with Santa Claus for over an hour. The school had carefully chosen a time slot that would not typically be very busy, so Santa and his elves had plenty of time for them. After walking around the North Pole, the Fiesta's time ended with the much-anticipated train display and Engineer John.

Josie had seen *The Engineer John Show* on TV at the Prices' home. It showcased children, making them the stars of every one of his shows. If they were visiting the television station, Engineer John made sure each child got their turn to be on the air. When kids sent in drawings, he displayed every single one received, putting the child's name out to the television audience.

Now after seeing the big tunnel and the train setup, most of the boys wanted to try on Engineer John's famous striped conductor's hat. Ecstatic to see the real-life television star, they also wanted to go back and change their "want list" to include a train set. Miss Faye warmly thanked Engineer John for his knowledge and enthusiasm, promising they'd be back next year for sure just to see him. He was right up there with Santa in popularity and charm.

Miss Faye let her class know it was time to leave the North Pole to walk to Murphy's Five and Dime and have lunch at its well-known horseshoe-shaped luncheon counter. After that they would view its celebrated doughnut machine and be allowed to choose one delicious treat before leaving the store. Everyone was enthralled by the spectacles of the city, but no one had been more captivated with the sights of the

downtown's holiday decorations than Agnes Jones. On the way out of
Wolf & Dessauer, Agnes stopped in front of the huge display of Santa
and his reindeer on the east side of the building.

"Whatcha think, Agnes?" Josie asked.

"It is beautiful. I think Santa's suit is beautiful. It is red and white,"
she remarked as if it were the loveliest thing she had seen so far. "And I
can see Santa's reindeer."

"Can you count how many there are?" Josie asked.

"One, two, three, four…" she began, and then looked panic-stricken.

"What's wrong, Agnes?"

"Where did the rest go? There's s'posed to be . . . eweven or twelve,"
Agnes said as if she couldn't believe her eyes.

"Agnes, 'eleven,' not 'eweven,' comes after ten and before twelve.
You counted every single reindeer that's up there," said Josie, reassuring
here there were only four up there on the building.

"Oh, I thought I couldn't see the rest," she said.

"How many Santas do you see?" Josie kiddingly asked her.

"Miss Josie, there is only one Santa Claus. He is just really fat," she
stated innocently.

"We are so happy you can see better now," Josie said.

"I see everything, Miss Josie . . . everything," Agnes almost whispered. As if she spoke too loudly, she would scare what she was noticing
away.

"What do you like best so far?" asked Josie.

"I like the pretty lights. They sparkle like stars. And I like the little
things that move in the big windows," Agnes said. This little one was
not at a loss for words. Agnes was fully locked into the sights around
her as if she was memorizing every detail.

"The magic windows are really special, aren't they, Agnes?" Josie
said. She herself couldn't believe all the details and movement in Wolf
& Dessauer's outstanding windows. She had never seen anything like it
before. Pearl would've loved the holiday displays and these works of art.
She would have been mesmerized. And her eyes would have twinkled.

Not missing a beat, Agnes went on. "I liked the little raccoons ice
skating. Someday I'm going to skate like that with my own friends,"
she proudly declared.

"I'm sure you will," Josie mused. "I bet you liked Santa feeding his reindeers too, right?"

"Are they Santa's pets?" Agnes asked.

"Yes, I guess they are, sweetheart," said Josie. "Anything else you really liked?"

"In that window there is a mommy making cookies for her kids," Agnes said, pointing. "She moves. The mother moves. She's taking cookies out of the oven on a tray. The children can't wait to eat them. They're very happy."

"You are exactly right. I am so glad you can see all those little things, Agnes," said Josie.

"Thank you, Miss Josie," said Agnes.

"What for?" asked Josie.

"I am happy," Agnes said.

"You are a special young lady. I am proud of you," said Josie.

"Miss Josie, I'm proud of you too," Agnes said back, squeezing her hand.

Josie Bee felt an unexpected lump in her throat. This was such a tender moment. But at the same time, Josie realized she had only facilitated getting Agnes a pair of cat-eye glasses. She couldn't give her the protection she might one day need, and Josie couldn't promise her a life without harm. It hurt her heart to think about what could happen to any one of these children tomorrow or the next day, exactly like what happened to the girls in the church basement in Birmingham. After that, there were no more celebrations. They were gone forever. It made Josie sad.

As Josie walked into G. C. Murphy's Five and Dime with the Fiesta school entourage, her mind immediately jumped back to Birmingham, where she knew she would not have been welcome at a place like this. It was strange to her that she could then enter the restaurant and even sit wherever she wanted. Josie was feeling neither jubilant nor sad, but there was a definite sense of unease. Right now, however, she had twenty-five hungry people to think about, and she let her unsettling thoughts go.

The students had a designated area with a placard labeled on a pedestal that said FIESTA SCHOOL. Faye had contacted the restaurant beforehand so they would be prepared for their large number of twenty-five. Murphy's hostess had previously narrowed down the choices to grilled-cheese sandwiches, hot dogs, or hamburgers with fries. The students had made their selections at the school the week prior after thoroughly discussing the three available options. They practiced exactly what they would say when asked to order, with pleases and thank-yous firmly in place. Faye was intense, watching and listening to each one as they gave their responses. She was a proud mother hen, and Nola beamed continuously as well. They loved and adored their precious youngsters to pieces. Josie figured Nola had to be happy not to be in the kitchen but to be served by others for once. Plus, Miss Nola looked surprisingly different all dressed up with her hair down and not pulled back into a bun. Josie hadn't realized how pretty she was. The students were doing a marvelous job, and their impeccable behavior was being noticed by other diners. Talking in hushed voices with napkins perfectly placed in their laps, they silently chewed the food with their mouths closed, for the most part. Beanie Barker and Tommy Wynn belched almost simultaneously after knocking down their entire Cokes, but they quickly recovered after a stern look from Faye. Putting their hands over their mouths, they both said, "Excuse me." The waitresses were delighted with their young customers. Archie Wilson remarked several times that, simply put, the ladies were miracle workers.

The kids finished off their sandwiches and fries while quietly sipping fizzy Coca-Colas. If that weren't enough sugar for the little people, they would soon be leaving to go to the doughnut-machine demonstration at the front of the store. Josie and Nola couldn't decide which kind of icing to have on their cake doughnuts: brown caramel, chocolate, vanilla, or the girl-pleasing hot pink. Murphy's doughnuts were known to be the best in town.

Sensing the kids' tummies had to be full, Nola suggested they place everyone's selections in a to-go box and enjoy them once they returned to the school. Archie seconded the motion. Although this caused an initial murmur of disappointment, the kids quickly rebounded, becoming excited for another ride in the bright yellow school bus.

Heading out of the department store, Josie noticed the cutest black-and-white checkered dress on display. She didn't have the time or the means to go back to Fort Wayne later, and she found herself wanting to purchase the dress for Charlie. It was perfect—not too girly but sweetly fashionable, with a cluster of cherries pinned to the center of the white starched collar. Grabbing Nola's arm, Josie told her what she was planning to do and promised to hurry back to the bus.

Once Josie returned, they headed back to the Fiesta School. The ride was quiet. Their big day catching up with them, the tuckered youngsters snuggled down in their seats. The staff basked in the immense satisfaction of all that had been accomplished. The day had been wonderful and memorable, one of the biggest and brightest days of the school year for the students as well as the staff.

It was the week after Christmas and, the holiday season completed, Faye, Nola, and Josie were ready for one week off before New Year's. The last four weeks of school between Thanksgiving and Christmas had been a whirlwind of activities and responsibilities culminating in the wonderful and glorious holiday field trip. The exhausted staff had done what they set out to do and were feeling victorious, basking in the sweetness the season encourages and now looking forward to the promises of the coming New Year. In just a week's time they would be ready to start up again and move forward toward the second half of the Fiesta school year. Nola had wanted tonight's dinner to be celebratory, a reward for all their hard work and excellence in finishing strong.

Josie Bee could not figure out the aroma drifting out of the kitchen, but it smelled incredible. She exclaimed, "For goodness' sake, Miss Nola, what on earth have you created in there? Is it about ready?" Nola had wanted it to be a surprise and had not allowed either Faye or Josie to help in any way, let alone be in her kitchen during the preparations.

Nola didn't even have a chance to reply before all of a sudden, the front room of Faye's beloved school and home was filled with an array of flashing colors: Red, white, and blue. Red, white, and blue. Everything was red, white, and blue.

14

SANDBOX LESSONS

*Grief is like the ocean; it comes on
waves ebbing and flowing.
Sometimes the water is calm, and
sometimes it is overwhelming.
All we can do is learn to swim.*

Vicki Harrison

CONTINUOUS FLASHING RED, white, and blue lights had filled the room and were bouncing off the walls. Faye gasped, and Nola steadied her from behind, preventing Faye from dropping to the floor. Josie, temporarily silent, found her voice and cried out, "How can this be happening?" As the knocking on the door escalated, so did Josie's inability to move toward the commotion. Policemen outside your door was never a good thing back home. And it was just as frightening here in Sand Haven.

Looking at Faye, who appeared dazed, Nola started calmly talking to the both of them. "Pull it together, girls. We have to answer that door, and the sooner the better. Step aside and invite those nice officers in. We have nothing to hide, and we can't be completely sure why they are here."

Josie sensed Nola knew exactly why there were policemen outside. Threatening Edna Higgins had brought law enforcement to their doorstep, and true to her word she was coming after Faye. She was a locust, and Edna wanted nothing more than to damage everyone and everything in her path of revenge and destruction.

Nola promptly went to the door and opened it. There stood Officer Larry Finch, whom both Faye and Nola knew. Nola politely asked him to come in. Faye regained enough composure to approach the officer and asked softly, "Why, Larry, what brings you to my door during the suppertime hour?" Her innocent approach seemed so genuine. Officer Finch disregarded protocol and took Faye aside while reassuringly holding her hands.

"Faye, I am sorry about this official visit, and I apologize, but I had no warning it was going to go down like this tonight." Although his kindness and honesty were comforting to the ladies, he continued somberly, "I have papers and complaints signed by Mrs. Edna Higgins. She is accusing you of drunken behavior during school hours and on school property. Faye Louise Lewis, you are hereby officially charged." Larry Finch looked like he couldn't believe his own ears, serving trumped-up charges to this lovely lady. It was absurd.

"Larry, I couldn't be notified by a more considerate or kind person than you," Faye tearfully replied. "You have been a good friend and sounding board. I thank you for that. Is there anything else?"

"I also need to inform you that your court appearance in two weeks is required, Faye. It is part of the legal process, but it might be best to hire an attorney to represent you. Mrs. Higgins means business, and she is out to destroy you. I'm sorry, Faye. Protect yourself. Try to lie low, okay? Don't give her any more ammunition to use against you."

After the two police cruisers pulled out of the driveway, Archie Wilson burst onto the scene like a crazed papa bear, defensive and ready to strike.

"Good gravy, what is going on over here?" he nervously asked. "Everyone all right?"

"We're fine, Arch, thanks for checking on us," Faye said. And with tears rolling, she filled her neighbor in on the unfortunate details, and then began to bawl.

Archie became visibly upset. "That wicked, wicked witch," he said with clenched teeth and tight fists.

"Only someone like Edna Higgins would do this," Faye said. "This will undoubtedly affect the students more than anybody else."

"Are you sure I can't do anything? I'd be more than happy to stick around."

"No, the excitement is over," Faye said. "I think I can speak for all of us when I say this has been a gut-wrenching moment. One always wants to believe that people can have a change of heart and that things will actually turn around," Faye said. "But we have just been headbutted by Mrs. Edna Higgins, and we are going to have to give this some serious thought," she calmly said. There were no more tears, just a reluctant sense of figuring out what to do next.

"I see you have a lot on your mind," Archie said. "I'll excuse myself. Do not hesitate to call if you need me. I'm always here for you, and I mean that."

Faye then poured herself a drink and announced plans to retire early. Neither Nola nor Josie had much of an appetite anymore either, but for lack of anything better to do they headed to the comfort of the kitchen for a quick bite to eat. Josie was still unsettled. The lights and sirens had taken her back to her days in Birmingham, ones filled with unpredictability and violence. She bitterly regretted her part in what was unfolding. As she wondered how she could have prevented this mess, she heard Auntie Birdie firmly saying, *No use crying over spilled milk. But you do need to clean it up.*

As she got ready for bed in her room at Miss Faye's house, Josie Bee, besides being jumpy and edgy, reflected that this unfortunate turn of events could spoil the progress she had been making with her four little angel girls. If this situation with Mrs. Higgins ultimately brought down the school, what would become of Josie's efforts? She didn't have the time or desire to start over again, and she needed to get to Pearl in Jacksonville and take her back home to Birmingham. Josie was desperate too. The Challenge needed to move forward or else God would need to reconstruct His original plan. Did God even create a Plan B? She wondered about this as she stretched out in bed and pulled the blanket over her. Thank goodness Josie was about to meet with Big Carl. The thought of him eased her anxious spirit. Hopefully he had options ready to lay out for her consideration. As she began to drift off to sleep, Josie Bee was glad of the trust she could place in her big-boned friend's instincts on effectively dealing with the elusive and abusive Frank White.

Josie woke up in the morning feeling unrested and groggy, yearning for more hours of real sleep. When they arrived at the breakfast table, Nola said she had tossed and turned throughout the night too. Faye was already sipping her coffee, immediately expressing how embarrassed she was. She wondered what her neighbors knew or might be thinking. She said she felt like a condemned criminal already, with no hope of a fair hearing. Nola urged her to continue doing what she did best: keep her head up and take care of the kids she dearly loved.

As soon as school came to a close for the day and everything was completed and accounted for, Josie departed to catch the bus. It felt like it had been a long time since she had been in her little bedroom at the Price home, and she was eager to see if there might be, hopefully, a letter from Pearl. There wasn't. Josie was sorely disappointed. Changing gears, she shifted her thoughts to Big Carl, realizing the importance of their next meeting. Josie, wanting to move forward, knew that everything hinged on what Carl had figured out.

Connecting at church, Josie gave Carl a warm bear hug. She hadn't realized how much she missed her burly friend the past two weeks, nor how safe he made her feel. "What have you got for me, Carl? I am all ears," Josie carefully whispered.

"Miss Josie, there is nothing good to say about this guy. A real bad dude. Sounds as though he has been on the law's radar for years. He's been hauled in and out of jail, accused of about anything you could imagine, but convicted of nothing. The fear of this maniac is what nightmares are made of, and nobody wants to go up against him. He's hurt a lot of folks bad. His daddy wasn't as lucky as Frank. He spent most of his adult years in county lockup, then moved on to the state penitentiary when Frankie was a young boy. His momma couldn't control him. After he roughed her up one time too many, Wanda White packed her bags, grabbed Frank's younger sister, and skipped town. My guess is that Frank thinks his wife might do what his momma did, so he keeps Alice White on a very short leash."

"So, what are we going to do about this?" Josie asked, her eyes fixed on her friend's face.

"We need to fight fire with fire. We have to scare the living daylights out of Frank White, and if that doesn't work, we need to eliminate him altogether," Carl calmly stated as if they were discussing whether to pick up juice or a gallon of milk from the local supermarket. Carl had connections with a small group of former inmates, a few of whom had given him the scoop on Frank. One went to school with him, and another had briefly worked with White on a dairy farm. With a short fuse and uncontrollable temper, Frank White was abruptly fired for mistreating a milking cow. No one understood how he continued to latch on to employment, but he did and was generally dismissed from a job within a matter of months. Over the past year, Frank had been working at a brickyard where his boss, Hank Billingsley, seemed to tolerate his rough behavior. Determined to give this perceived disadvantaged man a chance to feed his family and develop into something worthwhile, Frank's boss took him under his wing. Frank seemed to have a decent amount of respect for the fairness and appreciation Hank afforded him. In turn, Frank was on his best behavior at the plant, but after hours was another story. "The jerk is continuously looking for a fight and fights anyone who gets in his path."

Carl was on a roll. He continued, "Me and the fellas thought we could watch him for a few days and see where he goes after work and who he associates with. We considered paying his boss a visit but decided we wouldn't want to tip our hand, depending on the direction we go in. If we thought there was even the slightest chance that getting his boss involved would help . . . well, the boys and I just don't see that happening."

"This thing about your boys kinda scares me. I thought this was just between you and me, Carl." Josie was beginning to feel jumpy and agitated, not at all in the mood to begin trusting anyone new. "This will just complicate things," she snapped.

"Wait a minute, Josie girl, you gave me the go-ahead to figure this out, and I took the bull by the horns. I am not taking this lightly and am protecting you at all costs," Carl answered, looking a bit taken aback. He took his commitment to help very seriously. He intended to be extremely cautious and careful, not planning to ever see the inside of a prison again.

"Sorry, Carl. I didn't mean to bite your head off," Josie apologized as she squeezed his arm.

"We pretty much figured out that one person standing up to Frank wouldn't do much, but if he felt threatened by three or four others he might get the message we're trying to send. My guys know how to intimidate and inflict some serious pain on this type of cockroach psycho. Violence is the only thing he can relate to, and if he feels his life is in danger, then we may have a chance at stopping him. If not, he is going to have to disappear, Josie. There are no other options with men like this. He is going to permanently hurt that little girl whether it's intentional or not. I saw guys like this in prison and they can't be fixed. Others believe this too, and to be completely honest with you, Josie, no one is gonna care. Trust me when I say there will be no tears shed, only sighs of relief, if someone disposes of this piece of human garbage. But it will take skilled planning and execution, and the less you know about this the safer it will be. Those are the only two options we feel will be worth the investment, so to speak, to accomplish what needs to be done. There is nothing else, Josie. It is what it is."

"And you think this will work and no one will know what happened? I can't have this come back on Faye and the school. They can't ever find out, Carl. Can you promise me that? Their hands are completely full over at the school and this is *my* obstacle. I am convinced it is solely my responsibility to work this situation out. It rests on me to save Penny from any further damage and hurt. Hopefully Alice will be strong enough to continue on."

"What do *you* want to see happen, Josie?" Carl firmly asked.

"I want you to threaten him, and if that doesn't work, put him down, Big Carl. Far, far away, where he can never again lay a hand on anyone or anything."

"Yes, ma'am," said Carl, and with the solemn nods of their heads, they exchanged no further words and went their separate ways. Both felt the gravity of their conversation. But now they had a plan.

As Josie rode home with Ellie and Del, the girls were loquacious chatterbugs, but Josie had very little to contribute. Josie had expected to feel a sense of relief, a release of sorts from the consuming worry of not knowing what to do. Reassurance of the path forward. But that feeling was not washing over her. What was holding her back? This solution was to be the last big piece of the puzzle, and with all the other elements starting to drop into place, the Challenge would be on its way, eventually, to a successful completion, and within a decent time frame. Josie could live with that.

"Cat got your tongue, Josie?" Ellie kiddingly asked as they bounded out of the vehicle.

"I guess," she said, and explaining how tired she was she said her good nights and headed to her room. Still no letter from Pearl. Josie figured she'd give her a ring in the morning when she got up, starting the day off hearing the familiar voice of her sister. Josie was excited that she could share with Pearl the life-changing progress her fourth and final angel girl, Penny White, would soon be experiencing. Precious Penny. She could hardly wait. Josie didn't dare think this wouldn't work. It had to.

The next day Josie woke up far too early to put a call into Pearl. Auntie Birdie had ingrained in them the importance of not using the telephone before nine in the morning or after nine in the evening. Josie laughed, knowing Pearl wouldn't mind one single bit, but she couldn't bring herself to break the rules. Anyway, it was no biggie to wait an hour or so. Planning to call Pearl collect from the Fiesta, Josie was skittish that Nola or Faye might overhear the conversation and know she was hiding something. Josie hated to keep this from them but had convinced herself that in doing so she was sparing them from worry and concern on her behalf. Both friends had plenty on their plates. Josie knew the formal accusations were tearing Faye up, and the scene with the lights and sirens had lit up the gossip mills, causing many tongues to wag. And it had affected them all.

Arriving at the school with plenty of time to spare, Josie got set up for the day before breaking away to ring Pearl. Once the call had been made, she came back into the main room with a puzzled look on her face. "Everything okay, Miss Josie?" Faye asked.

"I guess so, but the call was really odd. The lady staying there with Pearl, Frieda Brown, apologized for not being able to talk and said it was urgent that she speak with me right after work. It was somewhat noisy in the background. I'm not sure what it was, but I could hardly understand Miss Brown. Then she abruptly hung up without offering me the chance to talk with my sister." It felt strangely awkward. Something was wrong.

Josie was confused and disappointed. "Might it be okay if I leave early today? I promise to make it up." Josie knew Faye was serious about starting to work on details for the upcoming talent show and that she had thrown herself into the process to keep busy and prevent herself from focusing on the obvious. Come to think of it, just about everyone Josie knew was acting distracted and indifferent, including herself.

"Sure, Josie," said Faye. "We'll give Archie a call, and he will be happy as a clam to pop over here and fill in for you. I guess we have come to depend on you! We'll be fine. Why don't you plan on leaving after lunch? Sounds like you need to get a handle on whatever has you unsettled."

The bus ride home usually allowed time for dropped shoulders and peaceful thoughts, but with Josie's head spinning like a top, there was no respite from what was going on in her life. Josie Bee had to wonder whether her plan with Carl could really be one without repercussions. The last thing Josie wanted to do was bring more hurt and complications to Faye and Nola. What would the others think if they knew Josie planned to deliberately break the law to accomplish her goals? Without hesitation, Josie had been willing to go from acceptable to unacceptable behavior in the blink of an eye. She was beginning to feel like she was in over her head. Confirming the plan to do away with Frank White had been too easy.

The bus came to a sharp and squeaky halt. Josie Bee was home.

Walking down the driveway Josie could hear the telephone ringing, and it seemed noticeably sharp. Dropping her bright yellow backpack on the doorstep, Josie fumbled with the keys, trying to unlock the door. Once inside she raced to the gossip bench table and grabbed the shrill-sounding phone. Out of breath, Josie managed to say, "Price residence, may I help you?"

"Josephine Johnson?" asked a somewhat familiar voice on the other end.

"Yes, it is, may I ask who's calling?" she asked, but Josie recognized the voice as belonging to Frieda Brown. Trembling within, she intuitively knew something was very wrong.

"It's Frieda. I have been staying here at your Auntie's house with Pearl. I took a chance you might be home. This is one of the most difficult things I have ever been asked to do, and I wish there was another way to share what it is I must tell you. But there just isn't." She paused.

Fear and panic flooded Josie's heart and mind. "Please continue," Josie heard herself say. She felt like she was shutting down and watching herself from a distance. She could hardly hear the sound of her own voice.

"After your dear Auntie Gertie passed, Pearl began letting go as well. She had been so fastidiously strong for your Auntie, but collectively everything took its toll and Pearl was worn out. Several of us tried to offer support, but Pearl would have none of it. Your sister was adamantly faithful in her care for your Auntie Gertie, and she was intensely worried and concerned for you as well, Josie. Never for herself, always for others. Pearl loved you so much with all she had." Frieda took a deep breath and struggled on. "The medical situation with Pearl drastically worsened within the last two days. We didn't reach out and contact you or your Auntie Birdie because Pearl insisted that we not call until she bounced back. She felt the potential severity of her illness would push you over the edge, and she couldn't have that on her heart. It would have been too much for her to bear. She truly believed she would recover." Josie couldn't process what she was now hearing.

"What are you saying, Miss Brown?" Josie was drifting away but still reluctantly part of the spiraling conversation.

She heard Frieda say, as if from a distance, "Pearl is gone, Josie. She has passed into the loving arms of Jesus. I am so very, very sorry for your loss. It happened so quickly."

The voice on the other end was filled with sorrow, but Josie could barely hear it.

"I want you to know I loved both your Auntie and your precious sister deeply," Frieda said as her sobs overlapped with gasps from Josie, a duet of shared pain and sadness.

And now there was silence between them. After a few seconds, Frieda continued.

"There are other details we can discuss at a better time. I am sure you have many questions, and I can only imagine your shock. Pearl reminded me very much of your Auntie Gertie, never wanting to be a bother or a burden for others. Their time together had been rich and tender."

"Thank you, Miss Brown," Josie heard herself say.

"I am so sorry for your loss," she repeated.

Josie hung up.

Dazed, Josie Bee sat at the phone table unable to move. She didn't know what she was supposed to do next. She felt like she was having an out-of-body experience. She knew what she heard, but didn't know what she believed. Josie tried to put her head around the stark reality of being present in a world that no longer included her sister. It wasn't even possible. Gone? Where? She was numb on every level. Was this a cruel, sick joke? Were the locusts teasing her? How could this be God's perfect will? What was Auntie Birdie feeling? She had to be devastated and heartbroken. Had she been in the loop? Josie Bee knew she should be calling her Auntie right now, but she just couldn't. She was not sure she even wanted to. With so many questions and no answers, Josie felt hollow and depleted. She felt no purpose for her afflicted life, no desire to go back to the school, no desire to continue the Challenge. For the most part, everyone Josie had ever loved had been taken from her. How could this be possible?

How could she go on without Pearl? Hadn't her parents' death been tragic enough? She only got through it because of Pearl. Life without Pearl wasn't going to work. Life was worth it because of Pearl. Everything good Josie had was because of Pearl. Pearl was everything.

If this was indeed real, Josie had no reason to go on. She couldn't. She wouldn't!

"Pearl, Pearl? Can you hear me? I love you. I need you."

Josie felt broken. It wasn't even so much that she was broken because that suggested the possibility of being fixed. Josie was damaged goods, and the anger in her soul was seething. What do you do when you can't do anything? You run. You shut down. Josie wanted to take off and keep running. She was done. Finished. It didn't matter what God wanted next. Josie wasn't interested. Ripped apart, overwhelmed, and out of control. And angry. Very, very angry.

"Do you hate me, God? Are you punishing me for something I did? You take away the one person in the whole world I love more than anyone and now what? Are you even listening?"

Josie sobbed.

No one has loved me like Pearl, she thought. *I'm here because of her. Pearl is why I came. She always believed in me, and I wanted to make her proud. I did what you asked of me. God, I have nothing more to give. Not a single thing.*

Click-click. In the midst of her weeping, the mail slot opened, and a few pieces of mail dropped into the foyer. Josie could see a familiar Swiss-dotted pale-pink envelope on the floor. Slowly she pulled herself up from the uncomfortable bench and walked the few steps to retrieve the letter. Then, as if temporarily forgotten, a slender white box was pushed through the slot. Josie picked it up. On the outside of the small package was Pearl's beautiful slanted-to-the-left cursive writing. With clammy hands, she held the letter and box to her chest and ran to her room. Dropping onto her bed, Josie held tight to what Pearl had sent, weeping uncontrollably.

She dared not open them. Not yet. This would be the last communication she would receive from her sister. She lay down on the bed, clutching the items, and cried herself to sleep.

Several hours later Josie awoke feeling the presence of someone in her bedroom. Opening her swollen eyelids, Josie saw Ellie in her prayer shawl bent over in conversation with God, praying for her. The tears started all over. Just as Pearl had and Auntie Birdie before that, prayers were being lifted up on Josie's behalf to Almighty God. Had she known the true seriousness of Pearl's illness, she would have been down on her knees interceding for her very life, begging God to heal her. Pleading for a miracle. Josie was failing on all accounts. Everything in her life was falling apart as if broken into a million bits. She was ready to give up and check out.

"If you really knew who I was, you would spare yourself the time and trouble to pray for me, Ellie. There's really no point," Josie whispered. Josie was speaking the truth, and she didn't feel the need to sugarcoat. With Pearl, the one person who loved Josie better than she loved herself, now gone, so was Josie's desire to function in any meaningful manner.

"I'm going home, Ellie. I am not staying here. I'm done," Josie said clearly.

"Josie, I can't say I know exactly how you feel," Ellie said, "but your Auntie knows. Birdie's heart is shattered too. She lost her beloved sister. And she loved Pearl like a daughter. Your Auntie feels that way about you too."

"That's good because then maybe she will be really happy to see me come home. It's where I belong."

"This has been a terrible, terrible shock. I can't take this pain from you, but if I could, sweet sweet Josie, I would." Ellie whispered. "God knows I would do anything to spare you this agony."

"I don't want to go on without Pearl, Ellie. I just can't," Josie whimpered. "I can't."

"I know, baby. It will take time, but Pearl wouldn't want you to be sad forever," said Ellie.

"Why would God take her?" asked Josie.

"I can't answer that, Josie, nobody can," Ellie said.

"I know," said Josie.

"I know you can't imagine getting past your pain and sadness. But trust me, your broken heart will heal," Ellie said gently. "Take it one day at a time. It's about the only thing you can do." Ellie cupped Josie's cheeks in her hands and kissed her on the forehead.

"We love you." And Ellie quietly left the room.

Josie stared at the pink envelope and the white box lying next to her on the quilted bed. She didn't know whether she had the strength to open either item. Although curious, Josie Bee remained unsure whether she could even handle the words or what was in the package. She desperately ached for Pearl and wished only to be enveloped in the arms of her sister.

With trembling hands Josie reached for the letter and slowly and carefully opened the flap, hardly wanting to disturb it. Seeing Pearl's carefully penned words once again moved Josie to tears. She was a mess. After her eyes cleared, Josie began reading.

My precious Josie,
I love you. Totally. Completely.
Forever.
Please forgive me. This will be important and necessary in order for you to be able to continue moving forward. Where you go from here is crucial. I never meant to keep you in the dark about my condition, but I was surprised and initially in denial myself.
Busy attending to Auntie's failing circumstances, I had little time to reflect on what I was thinking or going to do. I must note, had it not been for Gertie's conscientious doctors, this condition would never have been discovered and diagnosed. And that would have been, somehow, much worse, Josie Bee.
A very slow-growing bacteria identified as tuberculosis gathered in my lungs, and my unknown condition worsened once I arrived in Florida. Apparently, my immune system had been defending and fighting the infection for a long time until it could no longer keep up. I guess my cute little coo-coo wasn't that adorably innocent after all. You always liked the tiny hiccup and tried to imitate it until Momma put a stop to it. You always made me laugh.
Reflecting back, I continue to be grateful that I came to watch

over Auntie Gertie and heeded the call to make a difference. I believe it would have been beyond painful for Auntie Birdie to have you gone and me in Birmingham preparing for this journey, wherever it leads me. I believe God was in the details, arranging a perfect plan, and I remain in awe of my Creator and Savior.

I am still hoping to bounce back and will call you soon. The doctor is optimistic, but you never know, so I am writing this letter to you now, should I not get a chance later. I am back and forth on this and not fully convinced I can beat this disease. I am tired, baby sister.

Please, Josie, don't let the possibility of my passing cause you to become bitter. Should anything happen, know that we will one day be together again., holding hands and looking up at the shining stars wondering how to hang on the bright moon.

We share a lifetime of rich memories that are filled with love, heartbreak, and loss, and here we are. Sisters, survivors, and souls that will live on. That's how it works. You know that, right?

I desperately love you.

I will need you to keep that pretty little head on straight, something I have repeated over and over. I mean it now more than ever, should anything happen to me. Please, please choose to do good and make a difference. My spirited Josie Bee, do it when and where you can. I know you can choose this path and stay on it. If you stray, understand that will happen from time to time, but at all cost find your way back, sweet sister. God is in your corner and is your eternal advocate. Remember, when God is for you, who can be against you?

I have loved you more than life itself, and Josie Bee, I believe in you.

I cannot say goodbye because I cannot predict the future. This is not final. Should God see fit to take me home, you will continue to know my love. I promise to stay in touch. I will see you again on the other side of our moon and among the stars.

I love you always,
Pearl

Josie Bee felt peace washing over her, and once again Pearl had somehow managed to calm her heart and troubled spirit. Josie graciously felt included, valued, and deeply loved by her only sister. Strengthened by Pearl's precious words, Josie then opened the package from Pearl. It was beautifully graced with her delicate, flowing handwriting. Gently Josie removed the brown outer paper, which revealed a lightweight silver jewelry case. Cautiously Josie opened the box to discover an inside lining of navy blue velvet. She was looking at a strand of pearls. Tears fell off her cheeks. Josie Bee was completely overtaken. There was not a single thing in the entire world that meant more than being given Pearl's necklace, the one she had received for graduation from Auntie Birdie. The strand that she wore to important occasions and routinely to church on Sundays. Pearl wanted *her* to have them. Josie had admired them continuously, one day hoping to have her own set. Pearl saw it through to personally give the pearls to her little sister. The special delivery meant more than Josie could put into words. Then to top it off, there was a note from Pearl that simply said:

I will be smiling each time you put these on.
You are as lovely as these pearls.
I love you.
Pearl

As she carefully placed the pearl necklace back into the jewelry box, Josie noticed a raised area underneath the right corner. Pulling back the cotton, Josie removed something wrapped in white tissue. What she uncovered was a mint-colored piece of sea glass. Josie knew exactly what it was: Pearl's first find. She ran her fingers over its smooth surface as tears fell from her eyes. Was there anything Pearl would not remember? She had been so excited and sincere when she told Josie about finding her very first sea-glass treasure and that it had been for her. Pearl said it was an offering, that she hoped they would hunt for sea glass together one day. It was remarkable that a broken piece of glass could be refined by water, wind, sun, and sand. Somehow the sea glass survives in spite of, or maybe because of, the harsh elements it finds itself engulfed in. Jagged edges become smooth. The surface becomes polished. Pearl had often marveled at the uniqueness of each piece, and wondered aloud what its journey had entailed. She compared it to the lives they had lived. That was classic Pearl. Always seeing the beauty in the broken. Josie vowed to carry this treasure with her always. A stunning reminder of Pearl and of how being broken doesn't have to be the final chapter of one's life. Hopefully Josie's sharp edges would be smoothed, her character renewed and refurbished like sea glass. Somehow, she felt Pearl wanted her to see those possibilities. It was exactly like her.

Josie Bee doubted it would ever be possible to think of Pearl and not have eyes filled with salty, stinging tears. Too much to take in, she was bewildered. Having loved Pearl passionately for as long as she could remember, it surely meant Josie's grief would be equally as intense and long. Already the sweet moment of calm while reading Pearl's words was giving way to the deep sadness that had sprouted heavily in her heart. Josie wanted to go home, but first she had to go to Fiesta in the morning and share Pearl's passing with her two special friends. Then Josie needed to get ahold of Auntie Birdie and make plans to go home. Surely this would be the practical and agreeable thing to do. And that's about all Josie could figure out for the time being.

A few days later, Josie arrived at the school at the break of dawn, earlier than expected. Ellie had garnered her some time off without explanation. When Josie walked in, Faye was still getting ready for school. The woman looked like a crazed racoon. She had dark circles around her bloodshot eyes, a direct result of her increased drinking and sleepless nights with never-ending worry. It would be difficult to know who was more surprised, Faye being startled by unexpectedly seeing Josie so early or Josie observing Faye minus the makeup and with a head filled with hot-pink curlers.

It was quite a contrast to the classy Faye that Josie had witnessed on the field trip to Fort Wayne. Now the reality of what was happening appeared in full view on the face of Faye Lewis, and it spoke volumes. Faced with the reality of Edna Higgins's accusations, Fiesta School could no longer hope for a miracle that would wipe their slate clean. Already fragile, tears flooded Josie's face and swollen eyes. When she saw Josie, Faye's coffee mug slipped from her hands and shattered to bits. Nola ran into the room as they stared at the floor. The possibility of the school not recovering from the lawsuit was their new reality. In another week they would have a better idea of what the future held or didn't hold for them, but now it felt like everything was falling apart. Deep down in their hearts, everyone knew it did not look good.

"I'm sorry, I'm sorry," Josie babbled. "Please forgive me, this is all my fault. And I don't know what to do about it. Everything is a mess."

"We take one day at a time, and we finish what we have started," Nola said with authority. "Faye, you need to get yourself fixed up before you scare anyone else, myself included!"

"Stop, please stop! I need to tell you something," Josie said. "I . . . want to tell you about my precious Pearl, my sister . . . she's gone." And just like that Josie was down on her knees, falling apart like the broken cup.

"Oh my gosh, where did she go, Josie?" Faye cried out.

"Pearl died. She's passed away. Pearl is gone."

"What do you mean, child?" Nola asked.

"Why didn't you tell us she was that sick? You said everything was going to work out. Didn't Pearl tell you that, Josie?" Faye asked. Eyes wide open and clouded with tears, mouths gaping, both Faye and Nola were stunned. And neither knew what to say.

"I didn't know how sick she was. I guess I couldn't, I didn't want to believe that Pearl couldn't get well. I didn't know. How did I not know this could happen? But now Pearl isn't here, and I wasn't there. I've been in Sand Haven messing things up. I don't know what to do. I don't. I don't know what to do next. I just don't know. What am I supposed to do? What good is there in my being here?"

Faye and Nola rushed to Josie and joined her on the floor. They threw their arms around her, encompassing their friend with compassion and love.

"It's going to be okay. Pearl loved you so much, sweetie," Faye whispered in her ear.

"We are deeply sorry, baby," Nola said in hushed tones. Josie heard no more than that, but she felt consoled and safe in their arms, as if everything *would* somehow be okay. But then Josie knew she had to tell the girls what she was thinking, and she needed to do it right now.

"I am going back to Birmingham. I am going home," Josie cried out.

"We understand, and expect you to take some more time off. Whatever you need," Nola reassured Josie.

"Home for the funeral?" Faye asked.

"I didn't even think to ask. I don't know. I can't even imagine Pearl gone," Josie sobbed.

"Why don't you let me drive you home, Josie," Nola offered.

"No thanks, the bus is fine. I need to go back to the Prices'. I have to call Auntie Birdie and see how they are going to get me home and how soon."

"Home for a visit, Josie?" asked Nola.

"No, for good. Nobody here needs me and I gotta go," said Josie. "I just wanted to come over and tell you about Pearl and that I would be leaving." Josie got up.

"Josie, we love you," said Faye.

"And please don't forget that," said Nola.

With her head down, Josie nodded on her way out.

Josie was glad to be sitting on the phone bench in an empty house. She preferred privacy at the moment as she tried to think what she wanted to say to Auntie Birdie. Apparently, Auntie had called just minutes after Josie left for the Fiesta. Ellie had left a note on Josie's bed requesting Josie return her call immediately when she returned. Ellie said she would be praying for her, knowing how hard the conversation would be. Josie was procrastinating because she didn't really know if she could even speak at all. Taking a deep breath, Josie dialed her Auntie, preparing herself to hear the familiar voice.

"Hello, Josephine, is that you?" Auntie Birdie asked.

"It is, Auntie," Josie said sadly.

"Josie Bee, I am so sorry we have lost our precious Pearl," said Auntie Birdie.

"I know . . ." Josie immediately began sobbing. Auntie Birdie was crying too. They gave each other the time needed to cry. It was a relief to grieve together. When they had finished, Auntie continued on.

"Josie Bee, are you able to take some time off?" Auntie Birdie said.

"I have lots of time off. I can't stay here, Auntie Birdie. I'm coming home," Josie said.

"I know what it means to lose one's devoted sister. I just lost my Gertie—"

"And I am so sorry, Auntie, for your loss, please forgive me for not mentioning it sooner," Josie moaned. But nobody could love a sister more than Josie loved Pearl.

"So I fully understand the depth of your sadness, but we must be somewhat practical, Josephine, and not get ahead of ourselves," Auntie Birdie said.

Josie was shocked. She had never even considered that Auntie would not want her home.

"But I want to come home, I planned on it," said Josie. "I can't stay here knowing Pearl is gone."

"What would you do differently, Josie, if you were to come home?" asked Auntie Birdie.

"I don't know," Josie said.

"That is exactly the point, dear. The Circle and I have discussed what options there might be now, and after much thought and prayer, we think it is in your best interest to take a break and work on things as you feel you are able. You have many good friends in Sand Haven, and you will gain strength and solace in them as you begin to heal," said Auntie Birdie encouragingly.

"I don't understand how that would work, Auntie. I don't want to be here any longer," Josie said. "I just don't want to be here at all."

"But we think in the long run, it is the best choice for you, dear," Auntie Birdie said.

"Don't you want me to come home, Auntie?" Josie said.

"I would love nothing better. It has been most difficult without you and Pearl. I have missed you so much. I had to love you both enough to let you go. And one day soon, it is my prayer you will come back to me, Josie Bee," Auntie Birdie whispered through tears.

"So, I can't come home?" Josie asked, her voice small. "Please, Auntie? Are you really saying you're not going to allow me to come home?"

"This is very difficult for me. But not quite yet. There are things that need your attention, Josephine," said Auntie Birdie. "God will see you through this. You need to trust me."

"Is there going to be a funeral for Pearl?" she asked. Josie surely would get to go home for that.

"Pearl left instructions she would appreciate a celebration service when you are finished in Sand Haven and can return to Birmingham," said Auntie.

Pearl had turned into one of those practical Thomas sisters, leaving plans and far-reaching instructions, and ironically expecting them not to be questioned.

"I love you, Josephine," choked Birdie.

"I'll be in touch. I love you, Auntie."

Josie was stuck in Indiana. And she was not a happy camper.

If that wasn't a kick in the bucket, Josie didn't know what was. Being told to stay put wasn't what she had expected to hear from Auntie Birdie. Josie wanted to get home even faster now, but with her life being turned upside down, she wasn't yet thinking straight. Josie Bee felt she was once again being forced to do what she hadn't wanted to do. Josie wondered if Auntie Birdie knew about the big check Pearl had sent her or if Auntie even had a vague notion Josie Bee now had a bunch of her own money. And was somewhat independent. Josie could pack up and get herself home, but her return would certainly not be met with the approval of the Hallelujahs, let alone Auntie Birdie's blessing. Josie felt she had no choice but to stay. And if she could do what she had always done well, put her head down and block out her emotions, she could stubbornly forge ahead. How else could she deal with the loss of Pearl and manage to accomplish anything? Only God knew whether she could stay and complete the Challenge. Momentarily, Josie connected a little more with her mother, who had viewed life as a stage and that all its participants were mere actors studying their parts. Yes, Josie would have to do some fine acting to get through this. Like Faye had done at one time in her life.

Everyone was being extremely nice to Josie. The Prices told her to take time before going back to Fiesta School, if and when she was ready. Faye and Nola said the same. After a week Josie had slept more than she had in a long time and was clearly missing Faye and Nola and the kiddos. She missed the routine of acting normal. Giving them a call, she asked if they were ready to have her back. Josie was told they had work to do and needed her if she felt up to it. She guessed she did.

Arriving earlier than expected her first day back, Josie walked into Nola's waiting arms. The embrace was tight and reassuring, and Josie felt loved. Now back, she couldn't help but ask how things were going and if anything was new.

"Now that is a loaded question, Miss Josie," Nola said lightheartedly. "There have been some pretty wild tales going on at the supermarket, but I think we have been in a holding pattern."

"What are we going to do, Nola?" Josie said as they walked into the kitchen.

"We still have a job to do, and we will continue until we are told differently," said Nola. "We are adults. We have a responsibility and a duty to look out for our children. Apparently, there are many who have forgotten that. No one is thinking of them, which breaks my heart. And this will destroy Faye. I am worried to death about her."

Josie knew that to be true.

"But the best we can do right now," Nola continued, "is to keep working. The talent show is our highest priority. It may very well be our final gift to the kids and their families. And we will do it well. And if you are up to it, we need you on our team. We are so deeply sorry about Pearl. You loved her dearly. She would be very proud of your efforts in trying to remain here until things get resolved. Thank you."

"I wanted to go home. But they wouldn't let me. I really felt like I didn't have a choice. Auntie Birdie and the Hallelujahs thought it best to remain here," Josie said.

"Well, let's keep that our little secret as Faye was hoping you missed her and the kids enough to want to come back," said Nola.

"There's a lot of truth to that too. And maybe I missed your cooking some, Nola," said Josie.

"That's our girl. Welcome home, Josie. We are here for you. The kids have missed you a great deal too," said Nola.

As Faye popped out, she looked drastically different than she had the last time Josie had seen her. Confident, ready to tackle whatever the day had in store for them, perfectly applied bright fuchsia lipstick and mascara her secret weapons. Josie assumed Nola had given Faye the same pep talk she had just received and that they would be focusing on the end-of-the-year talent show and finishing strong. Faye appeared determined to do whatever it took to carry on.

The students, filing in, were busily chattering like chipmunks, happy to be at school. It lifted Josie's spirits to see their sweet faces. Their innocence, their sincere condolences. Pure concern with no hidden agenda.

The first activity of the morning was a surprise for Josie. Faye gave her a giant poster-board card. Every single child showed her where they had signed their name next to their traced handprint. It meant so much to Josie, and she grinned from ear to ear. The kids were precious.

Mid-morning, they started discussions about the talent show. Trying to figure out the assignments was a hoot. Just about every child wanted to sing an impossibly difficult song or attempt to imitate circus acts or movie stunts. Realistically there were a number of things each child would be good at. Helping each child to choose the best option was the trick. Dancing and singing were always crowd-pleasers, but with twenty-one children it was best to mix up the routines. On the list so far was jumping rope, hula-hooping, hand clapping, juggling, cheerleading, tumbling, and somersaulting. Also, there were magic tricks, garbage-can drumming, a singing duet with Nola on the piano, tapping with ballerina moves, and a yearly favorite, bell ringing. Things were certainly moving along, but the key to taking the stress off the kids when performing was practice, practice, and more practice.

Although they had been talking about it off and on, a few students still either didn't know what they wanted to do or couldn't narrow it down to a specific performance.

One of the most interesting ideas came from Patty-Jo Tucker, who wanted to know if she could put one of her pictures in the show. Patty-Jo was artistically inclined and very serious about her artwork. Exactly why she reminded Josie of Addie Mae Collins. It was a perfect way for Patty-Jo to display the early stages of development in her God-given talent. Always thinking about others, she had demonstrated her nurturing tendencies while taking care of Eggy. The tissues eventually fell by the wayside, possibly because no one mentioned or focused on them. Patty-Jo found out that caring for something or someone else made her tiny heart happy. Then Faye officially introduced Patty-Jo to Mister George, allowing her to feed him in the morning and comb his fur before naptime each afternoon. Delighted, Patty-Jo soon forgot about Eggy and started drawing pictures of the black-and-white cat. Showing and describing her creations would be wonderful for this tender child. Her parents were going to be thrilled not to see the Kleenex box up there on stage too. In fact, they might find themselves looking for a tissue to dab their tears of joy, which were the most unexpected kind.

Petite Agnes Jones, promising to let Miss Josie know soon what it was she wanted to do, had been blossoming before Fiesta's very eyes. The new glasses were a big success, and once they had been adjusted and tightened, Agnes was very comfortable in them. Several of the girls remarked how much they liked the cat-eye frames, and that made Agnes feel really good about herself. The few incidences of playful teasing earlier in the school year had dropped off significantly. Agnes displayed a gentle fearlessness, and it was rewarding to watch her glide around the class with certainty and purpose. Her confidence had grown.

Josie had been playing with Charlie Harper's hair when time allowed and had a few ideas about how to style it for the production. Charlie wanted to do a dance or sing or do both, but more surprisingly, she also wanted to dress up. Josie was still ecstatic that she had picked up the checked dress at Murphy's, and it was all she could do not to pull it out of the box and show it to her. The ladies had decided it would be best to keep it a surprise and give her the dress right before the show so she would feel special that night.

Knowing that Carl and his boys were going to be visiting Frank White soon gave Josie a badly needed surge of hope. She desperately hoped that the bruises on Penny's arms would be faded if not almost gone before the talent show, with no fresh ones being added. Josie was becoming resigned to the fact that it might cost her far more than she had bargained for or could possibly afford. But drastic things needed to be done to control this depraved man, and the sooner the better. This was the driver. Every time the telephone rang, Josie jumped in anticipation of news about Frank. Carl assured Josie they would scrupulously take care of every detail, that he had it covered, and not to worry. She knew Carl was going to get the job done with the utmost discretion to protect her as well as himself. Big Carl had voiced several times his desire to never return to prison. He was committed to doing whatever needed to be done to help Josie out because she had become like a sister to him. The feeling of family meant the world to Big Carl. In his heartfelt acceptance to be there for Josie he had once again given his support before thinking it through. These were the kind of off-the-cuff actions that had gotten Carl into big trouble in the past. The fact that he needed to be perfect and careful in every way was an understatement. As time went on, Carl began to realize the depth of his allegiance to Josie and an innocent little girl who needed help. He continued forward.

And Josie needed to believe that this *event* would go precisely as planned so Penny and her family might live a better and healthier life. Josie wished never to lay eyes on Frank White, let alone see him appear at the talent show. The mere thought of it caused Josie to quiver. This needed to be Penny's time to shine and be recognized, a time for her wishes to come true. This brave survivor knew exactly what she wanted to do, and her starry-eyed excitement was contagious. Penny wanted to be a singing princess performing her favorite song, "A Dream Is a Wish Your Heart Makes." Princess Penny had a nice ring to it, fitting for a little girl who believed in fairy tales and so badly needed a happy ending of her own.

After a refreshing and productive day at school, the reunited team of four had accomplished everything they had set out to do. With Archie's assistance, several of the boys had made progress figuring out exactly what they were going to do for the show. Given how preoccupied and busy they all were, it was hard to imagine how much dirt was about to fly in the direction of the Fiesta School.

As Nola plowed through the last of the scattered backpacks, the telephone rang. Nola pleasantly answered. The call was short, but the look on Nola's drained face when she hung up was long and filled with angst. Once the last student was out the door, Nola motioned for the girls to come sit down.

"For Pete's sake, Nola, just tell us," said Faye impatiently as she dropped down with a thud. "Now what?" She was reading Nola well and knew something awful was heading their way.

"There is a group of parents spearheaded by Edna Higgins who are requesting the Fiesta School be permanently closed at the end of the school year. They also want you removed from your position without delay. They are prepared to take their case to court should you not comply voluntarily. And immediately," replied Nola. It pained her to share this message.

"We're done," Faye cried out. "The damage is already done, and recovery is not even remotely possible. But I will fight the action to have me removed. They can't do that. I have never drunk during school hours, nor would I ever."

"Of course, you would never do that, Faye," said Archie, taking everyone by surprise.

"We thought you had slipped out with the kids," Faye said.

"Nope, right here. Sorry, but this really is eating me up. I want to shake some sense into that Higgins woman. She is a menace, and someone should try to settle her down. I can do that," said Archie.

"No, Arch, it would make no difference getting down in the mud with that . . . sow," Faye sputtered.

"Please, Faye, let me do something to help you. I can't sit idly by any longer and have them wrongly attack you!" Archie persisted. "They just can't get away with this."

"Thank you, I truly appreciate it, but the damage is irreparable. I've been through this before. Don't involve yourself. It would make no difference. This isn't going to stop Edna. She and her group will keep accusations coming my way to tie me up in court in order to tear me down financially and emotionally. I don't know how to fight these kinds of personal attacks. I'm not built for this. However, I am smart enough to realize when it's time to go. A lady always knows when her time is up. And I cannot begin to thank you enough for doing so much for us, Archie."

"I'm not in your position, but I hope you give this some thought, Faye. Don't let them run you out of town. We will fight it with you," Archie vowed. "If you ladies can think of anything I can do, you know where I live," he said on his way out.

It was unbelievable the destruction the local gossips had caused to Faye and the Fiesta School. In light of what Faye and Nola had done over the past five years, it was undeservedly ludicrous. Faye had pitched in when Jupiter Martin's mom had emergency surgery and he was sick with the flu and nobody offered to help out. She stepped in when Alice White, courtesy of Frank's angry blows, was in the hospital with a broken arm, a shattered jaw, and severe concussion, welcoming Penny into her arms and home. And when bed-wetting Tommy Wynn and his younger twin brothers, Timmy and Teddy, needed a place to stay, Faye and Nola provided for them too. Paying for their single's mom's train ticket to Wisconsin, they got Tanya back to her father's house before he passed from pneumonia.

These dear ladies were known for their kindness and generosity, had given and given, and had never asked or expected anything in return. Reaching out with love and genuine concern to care for their students, Faye and Nola did whatever it took to cradle their extended school families, with not so much as a speck of controversy. What on earth had gotten into this swarm of women to want to do away with their children's happy and safe haven? Did they honestly believe Faye would harm her students, or had they been carefully coerced into standing with Edna Higgins on her crooked mission? What hold did Edna have over these people?

Faced with the likelihood of the school closing, Faye had a lot on her mind. She also had her reasons for thinking it best not to fight. But she absolutely would not walk away from her students before the school year ended. Hurting and angry and afraid, Faye turned to her only practiced solace, Kool-Aid with a kick. Nola remained silent. She did not try to encourage her shattered girl to first eat or bother any attempts to slow down her consumption.

Between mourning for Pearl and grieving for Faye and Nola, Josie felt the oppression of loss and death all around her. She felt as if she couldn't breathe and was on the verge of losing control, maybe even her sanity, or what was left of it. Josie wanted to run. Nothing felt right. She sorely needed to get some fresh air. Sensing, as Archie had, that it was a reasonable time to split, Josie stood up, promising to return first thing in the morning.

Faye snapped out of her drifting daze. "I know what it feels like when you feel you have lost everything. I really do, Josie," she said. "I am so sorry, I truly am."

As Faye returned to her sweet lemon-lime beverage, Josie envied her friend's ability to reach out but then escape from the commotion and pain. Josie was up and down like a yo-yo. She had no idea how to process the exit of all the people she had loved so much. They left her. She had been really busy being mad when Momma and Daddy were killed. Why did that have to happen? Josie had always done her share or more of naughty things, but wasn't that an expected part of growing up? Learning from one's mistakes? Or was God punishing her? Was there a grave lesson here? Why her bigger-than-life sister?

Everything was now capsulated in the loss of Pearl. Josie Bee deliberately pushed her brokenness away, knowing full well she couldn't handle it. It would be a very long time before she'd be able to wrap her head around the loss of her sister. Always begging Pearl to carry her around, Josie was now carrying Pearl in her heart. Heavy as a brick, Josie felt the weight of Pearl's absence. She wondered if she'd ever be ready to deal with it. Without an understanding of how it would work, Josie disconnected.

Shutting down her feelings, Josie wanted nothing more than to escape to Cranston Park. She asked Nola if she could borrow the variegated yellow sunshine blanket, the one Nola had knitted for Faye when the school first opened years earlier. Nola's painful arthritis had affected her hands to the point where she could no longer hold a knitting needle. It was just a matter of time before she would not be able to play the piano either. Ben-Gay could only do so much. With no questions asked, Nola limped to the hall closet, brought the afghan back to Josie, gave her a hug, and told her to be careful.

"How much trouble can you get into at a sandbox?" Josie asked.

Quietly shutting the sunshine door, Josie was alone with her heavy, sad thoughts, with very little hope of any light breaking through the darkness. She clutched the warm blanket to her chest and hurried to the familiar nearby park. Once there Josie briskly walked to the deserted sandbox. The winter weather had been mild, but a cold front was coming through and the temperature was dropping to near freezing. As if the entire wonderland belonged solely to her, Josie, alone in the park, felt overtaken by its hushed beauty. So many important and memory-filled events had happened in a sandbox. Josie Bee had learned countless life lessons from those sandy childhood experiences. Her first recollections of learning about Jesus took place at the big box of sand behind the Rosewood Street Baptist Church in Birmingham. Pearl would watch over her, helping her get in and get out, while Momma casually dozed off at a nearby picnic table. Josie broke into a smile at the memory, feeling the cold muscles tighten in her wind-chilled face. The sandbox was a safe place filled with thoughts of family, friends, and God, and a sense of undefined confidence and security. Now Josie wouldn't trade those times of learning and growth, good habits and carefree thoughts, for anything. The shared memories with other children on Sundays, her sister throughout the years, and now with the Fiesta students, were priceless. Josie found herself climbing into the Cranston Park sandbox by herself, shivering from cold and permeating fear. How had things gone so terribly wrong, and when had Josie Bee deliberately stopped trusting God? Or had she never really trusted Him from the get-go?

Feeling convicted, Josie realized that when she had arrived in Sand Haven, she was focused solely on what she had to do in order to complete her assignment. Written correspondence with Pearl met her emotional needs, eased her homesickness, and gave her a sense of accountability. Josie reached out to Auntie Birdie and the Hallelujahs only when necessary and to please their requirements for keeping the group posted on her progress. Josie loved Auntie Birdie and didn't mean to shut her out, but she had allowed it to happen all the same. Churchgoing as an obligation did not feed Josie's spiritual growth as expected. Instead she had developed an intense bond with Carl Watkins, which was what made Wednesdays meaningful and fun. Carl was a gentle, recovering soul, and Josie had convinced him to partner with her to commit a crime that—now that she was thoroughly thinking things through—would unavoidably put him in prison for the rest of his life. Surely destroying the dreams of the kindest and most selfless woman, next to Pearl, that Josie had ever met was one of her most regrettable acts thus far. Faye was dedicated to giving back all that she had lost as a child. Investing in the developing lives of the youngest kids in her community was all Faye ever wanted to do. Central to Faye's ability to serve and follow the path of her heart, walking with her every step of the way, was Faye's best friend in the whole world, Nola Greene. Nola was the mother she never had, the one who loved Faye unconditionally and who had never failed her. And in coming North with her own tragic memories and brokenness, Nola had connected with another hurting soul and together they helped each other. Then there were the Prices, who had taken Josie in, providing her with room and board practically for nothing and, more importantly, giving her a sense of family. The Prices were giving back in exchange for all the Hallelujahs had done for them in their time of need. But the desire to assist Josie went deeper than that. They genuinely wanted to bless her with a safe haven. Even Archie Wilson had given Josie the gift of friendship, not to mention his gifts of time and talents at the school. All these people, an integral part of Josie's life, had become her community, and they were doing life together. A fellowship of sorts.

Auntie Birdie and then Pearl continuously encouraged Josie to seek solitude when there was a conflict and to realistically—not emotionally—define the negatives and the positives, the pros and cons of the situation. The visible good Josie Bee was experiencing in her frenetic months in Indiana was with the designated angels. Agnes was seeing a beautiful new world through her glasses and doing remarkably well in school. Patty-Jo was learning to emerge from herself and care for others, which made her feel happy. Charlie, once a rough-and-tumble bully, had been choosing gentleness and kindness in her interactions with others. She was learning that her actions could be chosen and controlled, and that she could be whatever she wanted, not what was handed down to her and expected. These three young girls encouraged Josie to want to be better, to do better in her own life. But when Josie started thinking about Penny White, panic filled her body. She shook in agony and disbelief that she had given Big Carl the go-ahead, the affirmation, to take Frank White down. Oh Lord Almighty, what had she done in the name of protecting precious Penny? How could she be so stupid and naïve to think this would solve the problem of Frank White? "Returning violence for violence multiplies violence." Josie had heard this from Martin Luther King during a rally. He said that it thrives on hate, and Josie knew that to be true. She hated Frank. She had never even laid eyes on him, but she vehemently despised who he was and what he stood for. Josie did not want to stop hating him because she didn't want to stop the plan of removing him from the picture permanently. But ultimately, Josie knew how wrong it was. Auntie Birdie had repeatedly stated that you cannot sit down in a pool of hate and not be pulled under. Josie was having a difficult time grasping air, recognizing that her deliberate actions and thoughts of hate went directly against everything she was supposed to be doing. Her entire body writhed in shame. Hate could not rule. God had to be disgusted with her. Is this why everything was falling apart? She had become part of the problem by proposing a flawed solution. Now she had to try and retrieve whatever there was left to save. Was it too late to find Carl and halt the beating, stop the killing? Or was the initial desire of a dark heart going to have the final say?

As a child in the sandbox, Josie learned about God and love that surpasses hate. How to play nice, to share whatever it is you have, to never want to hurt or shout at anybody, and how important it was to spend time with those you care about. Josie and Pearl had loved how the sandbox made them feel. They felt happy and secure when they were together.

Now Josie was scared to death with each passing minute about what the next day had in store for them. The papers regarding the school's closing would be delivered tomorrow, and Frank White could possibly be dead by morning. Faye and Nola were about to legally lose everything they had worked for and cherished. Josie could only imagine the damage the school closing was going to generate, not only with Faye and Nola but with the preschool community as well. Josie was most alarmed at her own actions, which could destroy the futures of Big Carl and his recovering cohorts. Pearl would be heartbroken and filled with shame at what her little sister had impulsively done and what Josie had become. Letting Auntie Birdie and the Hallelujah Circle and the entire church back home down would prove their investment had been ill-chosen and reprehensible. The church ladies assumed they were walking hand in hand with Josie, but it was what they did not know that would shatter their hearts. Everything was desperately wrong and about to get worse. Josie, foremost, had failed God, and failing God had failed her sister, Faye, Nola, and innocent children. Would God have mercy on her jaded soul? Was she worth saving?

Pulling the yellow knitted blanket tighter and tighter around her shivering shoulders, Josie started rocking and rocking. Back and forth, back and forth. At first, she was in the closet that Pearl had meticulously painted, floating among the clouds of blue and white. Next Josie was in Grandma's oversized rocker, enclosed in her sister's arms, snug and secure, tenderly moving forward and backward. The gentle movement transcended time and space. Josie Bee, encircled by the calming silence accompanied by snowflakes dancing in the air, became acutely aware that she most certainly was not alone.

15

LOVE BEATS HATE

Through violence you may murder the hater, but you do
not murder hate. In fact, violence merely increases hate. .
. . Darkness cannot drive out darkness: only light can do
that. Hate cannot drive out hate: only love can do that.

Martin Luther King Jr.

THE GENTLE PRESENCE of God was all around Josie Bee. She felt safe and protected. Sitting in the sandbox amid the peaceful silence of the park allowed Josie to clear her mind of the accumulated clutter that had taken up residence and was overflowing into her compromised heart. She had lost her way on this journey toward making the lives of others better and had jeopardized her own. Josie Bee had denied the Source His rightful position. Had Auntie Birdie and the Hallelujahs not been in God's service, Josie Bee would have been dead in the water before she even got started on the Challenge. It was her selfless sister, Pearl, who had always been by her side since the very day she was born. Josie Bee didn't know or couldn't remember all the help and care that had been given her throughout her days.

Looking back, Josie could visualize Auntie on her knees praying for her, sometimes accompanied by Pearl. Then there were the ladies at church faithfully gathering to intercede on her behalf. Bless Ellie Price's heart. She had been present and wrapped in her prayer shawl after receiving the news about Pearl's passing. Josie had been naïve, fooling herself into thinking she was in control of her world. Not thinking about how every action and every word spoken has a consequence, Josie Bee had now landed herself in a pit. At the bottom of this dark place Josie was unable to see a way out. She had been so sure she was invincible and stupidly (a word Auntie Birdie preferred she not use) forged ahead as if she were a free agent. But even that wasn't true. It was Pearl who continuously rescued her as if it were her designated purpose in life. Without big sister and lifelong guardian angel, Josie Bee felt abandoned and lost. Stumbling on her willful path she had tumbled into a trough of destruction. Why didn't Josie realize that you can't toy with the lives of others without consequences? And in planning to take out another's life, you will ravage and unravel yours in the process. In her immaturity and carelessness, Josie Bee had seen no other way to save Penny, and had easily accepted Frank's elimination as the most convenient solution. But flippantly doling out death sentences was never her job. Josie in that moment of acceptance and confirmation with Big Carl had herself become the locust. Burying her face in her hands, Josie had the most contempt for herself and what she had become.

Reaching for God, Josie cried out to Him and begged for His mercy. She wondered how a holy God could even stand the sight of his wayward child, let alone begin to forgive her. Josie wondered how this process was supposed to unfold. Verses she had memorized all those times Auntie had taken her and Pearl to Vacation Bible School and Sunday school began running through her mind. Josie had been more excited about the cookies and Kool-Aid, but now those experiences were serving as a roadmap to reach the throne of God's grace.

"If we confess our sins God will forgive us." Grasping onto those words for hope, Josie Bee began talking to her newfound Father. Initially wondering where to begin, the words started to come naturally. Moving to her knees and tilting her face to the heavens, Josie said, "Jesus, please forgive me. I am truly sorry for everything I have done wrong. I need, I really want You in my life. I love You, Heavenly Father."

Unexplainably released from her burden of separation and wrongness, Josie was filled with an indescribable feeling of peace. She felt free, and in her heart, Josie just knew the things she had done wrong had been forgiven. She felt the weight she had been carrying slide off of her.

Then Josie realized snow had been gently falling for some time, and a blanket of white covered the ground. She looked up in wonder and delight. A fluttering of magical flurries drifted through the air. Catching snowflakes on her tongue, Josie ached for Pearl. Together they were supposed to share sea glass and snowflakes. Tears of remembrance intermingled with tears of loss. Looking up, Josie clearly saw Pearl with her head thrown back, softly giggling, tossing down the flakes of snow.

"I told you I'd keep in touch, baby girl."

"I can't believe it's you, Pearl," Josie cried. "Please don't go away again. Can't you just stay?"

"You know it doesn't work that way, baby sister," said Pearl. "Nice try, Josie Bee. Remember you can't always have your way." She smiled.

"But I still need you, Pearl. Please."

"This glimpse has meant everything, but you know I have to go," said her gentle sister.

"Bye Pearl. I love you," whispered Josie, still nodding her head as the encircling snowflakes thickened around her.

Josie was mesmerized. She had not been able to look away. The tender experience left her unable to move. Josie Bee had gotten to see Pearl. She profusely thanked God for whatever had just happened. She wasn't sure she could put it into words. A vision? A dream? Hallucination? Heavenly intervention? It didn't matter. Josie was able to connect with Pearl, and her heart was full. She was thankful to God for His grace and gift of the never-to-be-forgotten moments with her sister. Josie's heart was new and different. And it would lead her to make some immediate changes. Even Josie was baffled by the urgency of her about-face. She had been headed for *bad* trouble and needed to change course. Right now!

Walking home, Josie knew exactly what she had to do next. Urgently

praying there was time to stop Carl, she ran for the bus stop. Josie Bee
was confident she'd be able to talk to Big Carl during his evening shift
at Chuckie's Grill. She'd probably have to wait until he took his break,
but that would be fine. She had plenty of things to figure out and
could put the time spent waiting to good use. In fact, Josie was hungry
and thought one of Chuckie's pork barbecue sliders loaded with grilled
onions and peppers would hit the spot. A side of homemade fries and
a big Coca-Cola would be her reward if she was able to stop Big Carl.
If that was even possible. *Ifs* always carried so much uncertainty. You
can't predict an *if* situation.

Josie observed that the dinner hour at Chuckie's Grill was insanely
busy. She also knew standing in line was the only way she could weave
to the front of the restaurant, in order to talk with someone who could
get a message to Carl. So Josie got in line. Hopefully, she would be
able to quickly grab a spot at the crowded counter. Most of the tables
throughout the popular establishment were full, but as Josie saw it, she
might as well be eating during the wait. When she reached the front of
the line, Josie eagerly approached the manager, who was wearing a cap
with the image of a pig on its bill.

"Could you please check with Carl Watkins to see what time he
may be taking his supper break?" Josie asked.

"The big guy? He ain't here, little lady. How else might I assist
you?" He grinned as if he had said something clever.

"C'mon, is this his night off or what?"

"I guess it depends on who's asking."

"Please tell Carl there's someone here to see him and it will only
take a minute," said Josie, attempting to be sweetly persuasive.

"No, it won't," Piggy Head replied.

"And why is that a problem?" asked Josie.

"Because that dude quit two days ago."

Josie was stunned. She could have been knocked over with a canary
feather.

"Well, where did he go?" Josie asked louder than she had intended.

"Your guess is as good as mine, little lady," he said.

"Thanks for nothing," Josie mumbled under her breath. Losing her
appetite, her fear catapulted and her patience waned.

"Any time, little lady," the guy said with a smirk. It set Josie off and her mouth in motion.

"Shut up, pig head." In a huff, Josie stomped out of the crowded greasy dive.

Josie Bee was back to square one. Out on the street, she quickly realized she had no idea where to go next. Other than Big Carl's nameless pals, she wasn't aware of anyone he might hang out with or turn to for help. Maybe someone from his support group, which he had been required to attend after his release from prison, would know something about his whereabouts. Telling herself to think, Josie tried to remember where Carl said they met for their meetings. It seemed like it was in a church downtown somewhere. Maybe next to Papa's Pantry, which fed the homeless and downtrodden from the area? Yes, that was it. Josie knew exactly where it was located. She had taken notice of the place as she passed it on her way to that phony government job interview when she first arrived in Sand Haven. Or at least that was her perception. Once you have eyes on you, you never fully shake that feeling off. And the food ministry reminded her of the Hallelujahs back home. They would have had a field day in a place like Papa's.

Hopping off yet another bus, Josie had both the church and Papa's Pantry in view. When her feet hit the ground, she was running. Everything had changed. Approaching the Freedom Missionary Church, Josie found the full parking lot a positive sign. She hoped by some miraculous coincidence to find Carl or at the very least someone who knew him. Josie walked through the heavy double doors and encountered an empty foyer and a dark sanctuary beyond it. The owners of all those vehicles in the lot must be meeting in one of the other rooms. Josie didn't relish going in search of a classroom full of ex-cons having who knows what kind of a discussion. But Josie Bee had to see whether Big Carl was there, and that meant looking around, whether it creeped her out or not. She proceeded through the poorly lighted hallway. There at the end, she spotted a light and heard voices coming from the room. Without thinking to knock first, she barged into what turned out to be an emotional AA meeting moment. Embarrassed,

Josie apologized and practically flew out of the church, feeling defeated and more than slightly light-headed.

Josie needed to grab something fast to satisfy her growling stomach before she fainted. She zipped into Papa's, feeling certain the pantry people wouldn't refuse to serve her. Josie was hungry and in need, not to mention exhausted. She entered the building and was warmly directed to stand in the hot food line.

Out of the blue the sound of Carl's deep voice rang in Josie's ears, and she thought she would melt into a puddle of butter. "Hey Josie, fancy meeting you here. What's up?" Carl looked genuinely happy to see her and at the same time puzzled.

Josie clutched the big guy as if her life depended on it. Relieved and in a state of disbelief, Josie stood silent for a moment to regain her composure. "Carl, I have been looking for you all over this town! We have to talk. Now!"

Carl led Josie to a table where a few others had finished up and were leisurely sitting around chatting.

Josie looked Carl straight in the eyes and said, "Alone!" The others got the drift that she meant business and left.

"Calm down, little sister. What's up? We got this, remember?" Big Carl looked perplexed.

"No, we don't got this. We don't have anything, Carl. Zero. Nada. Have you done anything yet?" Josie held her breath, afraid to hear his answer, but needing to know.

"Now listen to me, Josie, we're running a little behind our original timeline, but things are going down very soon. My guys are in place and patiently waiting for the right moment. You don't need to know the exact details. They are fully aware of what needs to be done. No need to rush anything at this point. Relax! We got this. All this worrying is making you look . . . kinda crazy, girl." Carl was as cool as a cucumber and looked as if he didn't have a care in the world, even with what was about to explode on his plate. It was as if everything was routine.

"You want to see crazy, Carl? Hang with me for just a second. We've got to stop this! Are you listening to me? I am going to flip you like a pancake if you're not hearing me, bro," Josie sputtered.

"Josie, you are hissing like a snake. Check yourself! You're talking to *me*. Pull it back."

The annoyed and volatile look on Josie's face said it all. She was about to blow up, and Big Carl clearly read her like a book. He needed to calm the stormy waters.

"Let's go outside and talk," Carl said, looking confused. "I'm working here at Papa's, and I don't want the staff to think I could be a problem. You know what I mean?"

"Okay. We've got to call off this thing with Frank White, Carl."

As if he hadn't heard a thing she said, Big Carl stated, "Atta girl, Miss Johnson, let's go out and get some fresh air." Carl nodded at the friendly lady in charge, the same one who instructed Josie where to stand, and said, "This young lady isn't feeling well, so I'm going to help her out by getting her some much-needed fresh air. The quicker the better, if you know what I mean. Back in a few, Miss Brewster."

Once they were both outside and out of earshot of anybody else, Carl said, "Okay, Josie, what are you saying? You're not making a lot of sense. You want me to call off tonight's event? It isn't possible, Josie. I have absolutely no way to make contact with the guys. If you're concerned that we're going to get caught, I can promise you that—"

"It's not about getting caught or not," Josie said, cutting him off.

Josie was nearly hysterical, with tears streaming down her tormented face. "It's beyond wrong, Carl. It's insane. We are all going to pay for this, and it is my fault. I am the bad seed. You were just trying to solve my problem, help me out. I wanted that. I get it. But I have now created a lifetime of potential punishment for you. For you and your friends. And for me. Being sorry isn't going to fix it. We have to try to do something or we have no chance of preventing this ill-conceived disaster and the consequences that will follow. We will all be found guilty of murder, no matter how I try to keep you out of it. And we will pay the ultimate price for committing this crime. Dear Jesus, what have I done? What do I do now?"

Josie was beside herself. And then it started coming to her: the only thing that made an ounce of sense was to get help. Right now. This very minute.

"We can go to the police," she said. Josie could hardly believe the words she had just spoken. Police. Back home you ran from them, and now she needed their help! "I will tell them I hired those guys and will take the fall if the officers don't get there in time. I will keep you entirely out of the story, Carl. I'll do for you what you were gonna do for me. I'll convince them that those guys had no idea what I had gotten them involved in. I will tell them that I wasn't thinking straight because of my fear of Frank White. You know, Carl, that I was desperate to help Penny White, and in doing so I made the worst possible decision of my life."

All Carl could say was, "Josie, you're really not playing with a full deck." But this was no attempt at humor. Carl understood what was at stake. He saw the panicky look Josie had on her face.

"I think we should pray to Jesus and ask Him to have mercy on Frank and your guys, not to mention you and me. We messed up, and we need His help, Carl." Josie shook her index finger like Auntie Birdie. "Where is the closest police station?"

"You really are crazy, girl."

"Tell me where it is, Carl!"

"I will! I will! First, I need a split second to run in and tell Miss Brewster there has been an emergency and we are headed to the police station. I can't afford to have her think I have walked off the job. I need to keep this one, Josie!"

"Make it dang quick, Carl. We don't have much time!" Josie all but shouted. She was really close to totally losing it.

"It's done! Let's move!" Carl barked.

Grabbing her arm, he told her the local precinct was only a block and a half away. Scratching his head, he started to mutter something about it not being a good idea, but Josie tore off to get to the station as fast as possible, with Carl scrambling to keep up. Every minute and every single second counted. Josie continued to pray that they could get the help they needed to place officers at Frank's place of employment at the brickyard. They needed to get there before his shift ended and before Carl's guys could snag Frank.

As Josie and Carl got closer to the police department, they noticed that a crowd had gathered nearby. There was a lot of commotion, with several police cars and two ambulances in the mix. Racing red, white, and blue moving lights flashed, sirens pierced the air, and uniformed officers shouted left and right for everyone to stand back. It was a mob-like scene. Josie could not get to the front stairs to enter the building.

Then she grabbed Carl's arm to pull him back. An intoxicated and angry man was in the center of the fray, shouting foul language, which came through clear as a bell.

Carl looked at Josie with a grin.

"What are you grinning at, you weirdo? We need to get in there," Josie said, tugging on his arm.

"Josie," Carl said, "that's Frank White."

Josie stopped in her tracks. It was like hitting the jackpot. Stupid Frank White was here and alive, and the best part: he was being tackled to the ground and handcuffed by the Sand Haven PD. Glancing around, Josie now saw more police cars from Fort Wayne, the Allen County Sheriff's Department, and even two state vehicles. Wow, whatever Frank did this time finally stirred up the wrong kind of attention for himself. And he skipped work in order to do it!

As they would learn later, Frank White had fatefully decided not to show up at the brickyard the entire day. Instead he spent most of the time at Benny's Binge Bar, where he began drinking right off the bat, and drank continuously throughout the day. Watching the establishment's big mounted Magnavox TV, Frank became angry and belligerent as he learned there was a visiting civil rights leader who would be speaking at Sand Haven's Civic Center. His city. Downtown. Tonight. He muttered things about moseying on over to the center and presenting his concerns on all the hogwash being circulated. By then, Teflon Frank was visibly irate and out of control. When the bartender warned him that the drinks would no longer be forthcoming, Frank hit the roof. Shortly thereafter the ranting bully was ushered out the door. He promised he would be back to settle the score with the bar at a later time. No one was sad to see him leave. And the regulars would be relieved to know later that he would not be returning either.

Now here he was, spewing racial hate and venom like the vicious snake he was known to be. Without even knowing the details, Josie knew God was in them. The lights of truth and glory were popping around Josie and Carl like it was the Fourth of July.

"Carl, hey Carl, this is our God working!" Josie shouted above the ruckus. "Can you hear me, friend? Only God knew how to take Frank out. He did this!"

Josie was so thankful. God let Frank take care of Frank! Auntie Birdie always said, "Trash will take itself out," and as Josie was finding out, her Auntie usually knew what she was talking about. Frank certainly took himself out, as if he had dug the hole and dropped his sorry self into the ground.

Some of the onlookers were hooting and cheering. Gleaning what they could, Josie and Carl learned there had been a terrible car accident and that Frank had been behind the wheel. Allegedly, Frank had attempted a deliberate hit-and-run, but literally dozens and dozens of eyewitnesses had seen the cowardly act, and all confirmed it was Frank White in his souped-up blue sedan. Two men had been hurt. One was on a stretcher being loaded onto an ambulance, and the other was walking beside it. Shortly thereafter, four patrol cars and two unmarked vehicles accompanied the departing ambulance. It was headed to Parkview Memorial Hospital in nearby Fort Wayne.

It was Officer Larry Finch who addressed the remaining crowd and spoke with the group of reporters. Urging people to go home and watch the evening news for up-to-date coverage, Officer Finch shared what information he had permission to release, making it clear he had no news on the status of the injured parties. He did clarify, however, the two men involved were Mayor Jeffrey Bower and civil rights activist James Barnes. Former college classmates, the two had met to walk to the Civic Auditorium downtown together before the evening's forum on equal justice. Barnes, a renowned lawyer and guest speaker, had generated a lot of excitement with a record-breaking turnout predicted. Barnes had spoken in Fort Wayne the previous night, and Mayor Bower arranged with his old college friend to bring his timely message to Sand Haven while in the vicinity.

But less than two blocks from the auditorium, a slow-moving car pulled up alongside the pair, the driver screaming racial epithets. As if that weren't nasty enough, the vehicle's operator backed up and drove as if he intended to run Barnes down. Mayor Bower pushed his friend out of harm's way, taking the brunt of the hit. Frank White plowed right into the mayor, hitting him head-on and causing severe injury. Barnes was only minimally hurt. Frank was arrested and booked.

As the crowd dispersed, Josie caught Officer Finch's attention. He thoughtfully walked over to Josie and Carl, inquiring how Miss Faye was doing. First introducing him to Carl, Josie thanked him for being so nice the night he had to pay the visit to Faye. Replying to his question about Faye, Josie acknowledged they were expecting the other set of papers in the morning and that, under the circumstances, Miss Faye was holding up but was badly shaken and hurt by the accusations. The fact that the school would most likely be forced to close was a blow to them all.

"Honestly, I think both Miss Faye and Miss Nola thought they would be running the Fiesta into their golden years," Josie mused.

"It's not over until it's over if you catch my drift. Miss Faye is stronger than she realizes right now. Give her some time and she could very well weather this storm too," said Officer Finch.

"I get the feeling she thinks she has already been convicted and hung out to dry," said Josie.

"Perceived public opinion can do that to you. I'm sure it feels that way," he said.

"Thanks for your support and thinking of Miss Faye," Josie said.

"She's a real nice lady, and the community is lucky to have her in it," said Officer Finch.

He nodded thoughtfully and then put on his hat. "Nice meeting you, Mr. Watkins. Good seeing you, Miss Josie. Give Faye my best, okay? Been a really long day and I need to get going. But maybe I could stop by and personally give her the news on Teflon Frank. Take care." With those words Officer Finch was gone.

Josie thought it odd he would, at this time of night, think it a good idea to drop by and tell Miss Faye about Frank. She wondered what condition her sweet friend might be in by then or what her relationship was with Larry Finch. They seemed pretty tight.

"What are you smiling at, Josie?" Carl asked. "You look like you got some perky thoughts running around in that head of yours. It's good to see, little sister."

"I was thinking about being a kid and drinking Kool-Aid at

Vacation Bible School," Josie said with a smirk.

"Really?" asked Big Carl.

"Nah, actually I don't know what I was thinking exactly, bro," Josie said. She felt like a cat who swallowed a canary and happy as a lark to know Frankie Boy was behind bars and likely headed to the big house. That was something to celebrate! Glory!

Josie also felt as if she had lived a lifetime in the past eight hours. What a day it had been. Her first impulse was to run to Faye and tell her everything, but looking at her watch she was fairly certain Faye was on her way to la-la land. With Nola watching over her like a mother hen, Josie knew everything back at the ranch was as good as it could be under the circumstances. Popping over there wasn't necessary. She could, however, surprise them by getting to the school extra-extra early in the morning.

Josie was famished, so she easily talked Big Carl into accompanying her to White Castle for burgers and fries. "My treat, Carl," Josie said as she dangled a ten dollar bill before his face.

"Hey, you know I can never say no to you," he said, grinning.

"You're telling me."

Relieved to be home and headed to her comfy bed, Josie Bee nevertheless knew she had to share with Ellie and Del all the things that had happened. How she found God while sitting in the sandbox at Cranston Park. How she had confessed and apologized to the Lord for all the things she had done wrong. And how God had forgiven her, loved her, and had a plan for her life. Ellie and Del hugged Josie while praising God over and over. Josie had more than one lump in her throat as she delivered her conversion message from beginning to end. Sparing none of the details, Josie released everything—except for the interaction with Pearl. Josie felt that gift belonged solely to her. She would hold on to it forever. Thanking the couple and telling them how much she loved and appreciated them, Josie was off to bed. She went to her room and crawled into bed, falling asleep without changing her clothes or removing her scuffed shoes.

Josie was elated as she stopped by Barney's Bakery in the morning. She picked out a dozen doughnuts to celebrate the arrest of the infamous Frank White. She could hardly wait to get to the school and deliver the news. Josie began with Faye's favorite, the raspberry-filled jelly ones. Four of those with vanilla icing; four mixed long johns, two white, two chocolate; and Josie's personal pick, the fluffy glazed yeast ones. Mr. Barney placed them in a large bright white box with a rainbow-colored cardboard "B" and tied it with a yellow ribbon. Josie felt the day would be off to a glorious start when she appeared with a big purchase from the best bakery in town. That along with the thought of Nola's yummy brew and Josie was already flying high. It was a win-win combination.

Josie bounded in with a song in her heart and the biggest grin ever on her face. "What's up with you, Miss Josie Bee Johnson?" asked Faye. Did you just win the Reader's Digest Sweepstakes?"

"Ummmm . . . not exactly, but something even better. Much better, in fact," Josie teased.

"Do tell," Faye responded rather flippantly, almost more interested in the doughnuts than in the tale to come.

"Okay, I want to make sure I have your utmost attention. And you are getting pretty curious, right? Get your listening ears on, ladies. Let me know when you're ready," Josie directed while still holding on to the beautiful and fragrant box of goodies.

"Really Josie, nothing can be as good as what you have in your hands. And we surely could use the sugar. Can't we continue the jest while sampling the sweets? And I'm just saying for the record there best be some custard-filled creme sticks, 'cause you know thems my favorite, young lady." Nola grinned, with a wagging finger. "And I don't think you would want to disappoint me these days, if you know what I mean." Unfortunately, Josie did.

"Now who is using poor grammar? And here in Indiana, they call them long johns, Nola," Josie reminded her. "And fine, I know exactly what you mean so go ahead and grab what you want because I will not spill the beans until you are settled and focused."

"This better really be juicy, Josie," Faye said while eagerly grabbing a raspberry jelly doughnut. "Might I put an extra one on my plate should this forthcoming information take a while?" she said.

"Whatever." Having snatched a quick bite herself, Josie attempted to reply with a mouthful of the sweet dough.

"Not pretty, Josie. Why don't we wait until you don't have half a gnawed pastry hanging out of your mouth, shall we? I wouldn't want to lose my appetite at this point," said Faye, rolling her eyes and pretending to be disgusted.

"Probably a good idea, Miss Lewis, thank you for the suggestion," said Josie. "You two look happy as clams eating your sweets, but honestly, I cannot wait one more minute to tell you my news," she added, somewhat anxiously.

"Then don't! We have been waiting on you to tell us what has you higher than a kite and bringing us Barney's to boot! Go, girl!" said Faye.

"I witnessed Frank White being hauled off to jail last night and it was the best thing I've ever seen!" Josie exclaimed. "I wish you had been there!! Carl and I were so dang excited we didn't know what to do but we about popped our corks." The words just flew out.

Then suddenly it was so quiet you could hear a pin drop. Yep, Josie certainly had their undivided attention now. Funny thing was, she had not once considered how she would even begin to explain being there—in the midst of downtown Sand Haven on the steps of the police station. And then their questions began full force. The doughnuts in the lovely box were all but forgotten. Faye and Nola wanted to know everything.

"Explain this to us, Josie. Why were you at the station in the first place?" Faye shot off like a rocket. "And how did you know it was Frank White? Have you made contact or seen him before? I think you have some explaining to do," said Faye in a no-nonsense tone.

"Hey, I almost forgot but I need to tell you how nice your policeman friend was. Introduced him to Big Carl and he even remarked that he should run by and give you the scoop on what had just happened. Seemed real concerned about doing that. But I told Officer Finch that you were probably already asleep. I was really kinda puzzled about why he would want to rush over to tell you at that time of night, you know? I wanted to be the one to tell you all about it first thing this morning. It was so cool. Isn't this one of the best things that could have happened?" asked Josie. Even though she could think of a few other things as well. One miracle at a time.

"Tell me you're not trying to flip the conversation here, Josie," said Faye. "Or are you?"

"Of course not. Not at all. I just now remembered to tell you about talking to Officer Finch. He was trying to keep the crowd in check because there was a lot of commotion and hooting and hollering, if you can imagine. Everyone there seemed pumped about Frank being arrested and all. I'm sure it will be on the front page of the paper and probably the top story on the news 'cause there were cameramen everywhere. Like I said, it was really something to see. The best part was that everybody was happy to see Frank handcuffed." Josie found herself rattling on, wanting to share what she knew and could. This was definitely not the moment to break down and share anything that she would come to regret later. She had to be smart. It was enough that a bad man was removed from the community and taken away where he surely belonged. There was no harm done on Josie's part as far as she and Big Carl were concerned. She planned to keep the not-so-pretty stuff to herself.

Nola was intuitively wondering what Josie was *not* telling them. Biting at the bit, itching to launch her own set of questions to get some clarification. There certainly had to be more going on than Josie was putting out. But as Nola noticed the muscles in Faye's face relax the longer Josie jabbered on, Nola, too, was deeply relieved that Frank White was behind bars. This cruel human being might actually get his due after all.

The time of sharing and euphoric sugar-high feeling came to an abrupt halt the minute the doorbell rang. Like a jack-in-the-box, Nola popped up and Faye placed her hand forward to let her know she would answer the door. It was the court courier. The revised papers arrived, as Nola's source had forewarned, and the messenger finished his delivery process with, "You have been officially served, Faye Louise Lewis, Director, Fiesta School."

"Yes, I certainly have, thank you," she said quietly as she closed the yellow door.

As they looked it over, they were surprised to find that Edna Higgins had completely dropped the first stipulation of the suit. The original part had centered on requiring Faye to immediately resign, having no further contact with the Fiesta School after the hearing date. Through their trusted "source," Nola let it be known that Faye was not about to let that happen and in fact would be instructing her lawyer to fight it. Mrs. Higgins had presumed Faye would instantaneously buckle and was not prepared financially to have this court action drag on. Contingent on Faye Lewis agreeing to accept the permanent closing of the Fiesta School by or on June 1, Higgins and her group would then be inclined to drop the first condition for no contact. This allowed Faye time to figure out her options and give her some control over the situation. It would have absolutely broken Faye's heart to be prevented from having further contact with her students and to abruptly be forced to turn her back on them. She couldn't have done that.

Faye's lawyer had been in the process of reevaluating whether she could be forced to close the school based solely on the initial allegations. There just wasn't time to address this and fight it in a timely manner before the end of the school year. So now it made perfect sense to agree to the closing in order to pacify Edna Higgins and temporarily prevent any interruptions to the Fiesta's remaining days. One issue at a time, her lawyer had advised from the start. And in light of the papers in Faye's hands, it seemed like a good strategy.

Just as Faye was putting the papers away, Archie slipped into the kitchen through the back door. "Archibald A. Wilson, reporting for duty, ma'am," he said as he saluted Faye. "Awaiting today's classified assignment." He grinned.

"Seems like somebody this morning is feeling their oats," said Faye. "What might the 'A' stand for, sir?"

"Why, it stands for 'adorable.' Adorable Archie, that's me." His playfulness made Faye giggle. It was so unlike the Arch, it made Josie and Nola laugh too. He refused Josie's offer of a doughnut, saying they all seemed to be spoken for and he didn't want to start any infighting among his girls. With that being said, the ladies each generously donated one of their four treats to adorable Archie. With the offer of a cup of Nola's coffee accepted, they all got down to the day's business.

Faye mentioned that with the talent show only a few weeks away, it would be taking top priority. It was time to divvy up the kids, figuring out which adult would be responsible for whom. Archie graciously offered to take on all nine boys, and Josie, hoping it was okay, wanted her four angels. She couldn't wait to show off Agnes, Patty-Jo, Charlie, and Penny. That would leave four girls left for Faye and four for Nola. It was absolutely perfect.

Next they went over general rules and protocol. Starting with how the kids would move from backstage to their place in the spotlight, Faye emphasized that the kids needed to understand and constantly be reminded that there is to be no running whatsoever. That alone could prevent a stampede. Also, they needed to remember to smile, smile, smile. Nobody wanted to see unhappy or crabby-looking kids onstage. From here on out it would be practiced daily what the children would be expected to do before and after their performances. Whether they chose to bow or curtsy, the preschoolers needed to understand that they were to do it only once. If you gave them free rein, some wouldn't know when to stop.

"So, we nip that one in the bud. It's always something," Faye said, but down deep everyone knew those surprises were a hoot. The entire class would be involved in the opening song, "Twinkle, Twinkle, Little Star," as well as the closing number, "What the World Needs Now." The production itself would be divided into two parts with a fifteen-minute punch-and-cookie intermission in the middle.

The children were to be dropped off at the Parkwood Baptist Church auditorium, thanks going to Josie for reserving the space. Parkwood would be large enough to comfortably hold the expected crowd of one hundred, give or take a few. The parents would be told to bring their children one hour before start time, dressed in their Sunday best and having had something to eat before their arrival. Oh, and this year (Faye was on a roll) there would be no need to enlist parents or volunteers to help out. Frankly, she didn't know who was on what base with the group action viciously trying to dethrone her. With the additions of Josie and Archie, they were more than adequately prepared to do all aspects of the talent show on their own. This possibly being the final show, there was no need to promote applications for next year or push for donations. Josie Bee was in a position to underwrite all expenses and had said that the sky was the limit, so it would be a real dazzler. Pearl would be pleased that her generosity had gone on to serve so many others. The decoration for their show's theme, "All Our Stars Twinkle," was almost complete. Nola had finished painting the poster boards bright yellow and was ready to cut out the three-foot stars. The students would write their names on them, add a bunch of glitter, and then they would be handed over to Mr. Wilson. Archie's job was to reinforce and string them together with wire. The banner would serve as the backdrop for the kids on stage, representing all twenty-one twinkling performers.

"And one more piece of instruction," Faye said. "Please hand in by tomorrow morning your children's acts. Their names will be listed in the program in the order they will be performing, complete with information about each star and why they shine so brightly at the Fiesta School. I will enjoy writing about what makes each one special but welcome your insights as well. We will also be allowed to use the church for a practice session during school hours one day prior. This will allow the kids a full dress rehearsal, the opportunity to walk the stage reinforcing the no-running rule, and the chance to accustom themselves to the bright lights. Staff will be expected to set up the night before practice, and that way we all know exactly how it will look. And trust me, it will be a rush for the youngsters. We also get an indication about who might tend toward stage fright, and we have a strategy that has worked well for that situation. As important as this event is for the parents and family, we must remember, foremost, that it is the kids' time to celebrate who they are and what they can do. We make this fun by practicing now what they need to know, alleviating excess stress and confusion later. Any questions?"

Josie dutifully raised her hand and with a big grin asked, "Does anybody think we might be able to use more muscle and an extra pair of legs?"

"What—or should I say *who*—do you have in mind, Josie?" Faye asked.

"My great giant of a friend, Carl Watkins. Carl enjoys children, has flexible free time, and has an unlimited supply of energy!"

"Sounds like a winner if that is agreeable with you, Archie," Faye replied.

"A friend of Miss Josie's is a friend of mine," said Archie, who was clearly excited to have another guy helping him out.

"All righty then, it's a done deal," said Faye, as she closed out the session by telling them to have another great day at the Fiesta, *where all things are possible*. She just loved saying those words.

As they dispersed to greet the kids and get them ready for the morning activities, Josie knew that someday she would sincerely miss hearing the kids reciting the Pledge of Allegiance, followed by "The Star-Spangled Banner." The young students not only knew every single word, they actually understood the importance of both sentimental pieces. It was refreshing how the sweet and pure voices of the little ones reached out, putting a melody in their hearts, even when staff knew these were tough times, with more disappointment and heartache to follow. The atmosphere at the Fiesta School changed drastically within minutes once it filled with happy chatter, song and dance, the sound of drums, and unfiltered excitement from the arriving children.

Days and weeks of preparation were behind them and the end-of-the-school-year finale before them. The most anticipated event of the year was about to occur, and the excitement at Fiesta School was bubbling like a brook. Other than a few routine hiccups at rehearsal the night before, the young students were well-prepared for the big night. The run-through was almost flawless thanks to the excessive practice and dedication on the part of the students and the staff. The kids were eager to perform. Miss Faye would be front and center before her accusers, but she wouldn't let them rob her of what wasn't theirs to take. At least not yet. Director Lewis's message was more important than any of the drama behind the scenes because it was her stars who were center stage and about to shine. She had been successful in avoiding any confrontation, staying totally out of any crossfire. Nola, on pins and needles, continued to worry about how Faye would hold up, suspecting she had to let down sooner or later, but she had done exceedingly well thus far.

Josie was emotional. For her this was the culmination in honoring the lost lives of her Birmingham friends. Addie Mae Collins. Denise McNair. Carole Robertson. Cynthia Wesley. And Faye was generously allowing her to talk about them toward the end of the program. Josie Bee couldn't be prouder or sadder at the same time. She was going to be able to share their names. She wanted everyone to know those names. Her four chosen cherubs were representing the four girls that were gone, in a wake of heartbreak that never fully heals. However, their memories were going to live on, and they would be remembered in new hearts, hopefully kinder and gentler ones.

For the ladies, Saturday morning started off with an unexpected delivery from Posie's Flower Shop. The carrier, a chipper young gentleman, remarked that there must be three very special women to receive an order like he was delivering, saying that the last time he had an order this large was for an in-home funeral. Making a couple of trips to the van, he returned with a total of twenty-one individually wrapped sunflowers. Each was enfolded in a bright, yellow wrapper complete with a matching colored bow and a sparkly blue star attached. Archie's intent was to have these presented to the students right before their final song. He was sure that Faye would be on board.

It took both Faye and Nola to unload the generous bouquets. The delivery man returned to the vehicle to pick up an oversized vase filled with two dozen fragrant alpine sunset roses. They thought that was the end of the order and began closing the door, but the carrier said, "Not so fast, ladies," and, pushing the door back toward them, handed over three more packages tied up in miniature roses and baby's breath. Already feeling choked up, the ladies unanimously credited Archie with the surprising and thoughtful barrage of flowers.

As if on cue Archie knocked before he entered the area permeated with the sweet scent of fragrant and plentiful blooms. "Good morning, dear ones," he said with a knowing grin as he playfully bowed. "At your service." The women rushed in for a group hug, knowing Archie was the one behind their unsuspected joy. Faye even sneaked a tiny peck on his cheek. No one was more taken aback or pleased than Archie himself. Opening the small envelope tucked underneath the ribbons, Faye read aloud the message attached to the bouquet: "A rose representing each beloved student and the three women who have loved them well."

"Oh Archie, if you aren't the sweetest man on the face of this earth," Faye softly cooed. "I don't know—we don't know what we would have done without you, friend. We thank you from the bottom of our hearts. Archibald A. Wilson, you *are* adorable, but I think 'A' must stand for 'angelic.' You have always been an angel to me."

"Okay, well, I think 'A' is for 'appreciated,'" said Josie. "Nola, what do you think?"

"I think maybe I have too many words to choose from," Nola said. "Accomplished, admired, and adored come quickly to mind. Shall I go on?"

"Please do," Archie said, bobbing his head.

"Affable, amusing, and authentic. Okay, I think I'm done," said Nola.

"Anyone have anything to add?" asked Josie.

"Astute and adventurous. Now I'm finished too," said Faye, smiling.

"Enough of this silliness, let's get to opening your packages. We don't have all day," said the Arch.

At his prompting, they opened their personalized packages, which contained wrist corsages made of bright smiles and canary bird roses. The three women reacted as he hoped they would: with squeals of delight and jubilant hugs all around.

Archie prepared to leave and get over to the church to make the necessary last-minute set changes. Faye, Nola, and Josie Bee were heading out for their beauty shop appointments at a local hair salon. Before leaving, Faye shouted back at Archie, "You are not going to recognize us tonight. We plan on looking *gorgeous!*"

"*You* already are," Archie gushed.

For Archie it wasn't about the abundant flowers, although they were exquisitely beautiful. It was the personal letters he had enclosed within each box. Archie had been inspired to tell each woman what she had come to mean to him. He wanted to take this opportunity to thank them for enriching his life and challenging him to be a better person. These sweet ladies had encouraged him as he was trying to navigate a life that had become meaningless and empty after the loss of Althea. The purpose he had found in the school had revitalized Archie's spirit, sustaining him through the last difficult months and years. His time and contributions at the Fiesta School had brought him a new joy and sense of satisfaction. The evening's talent show was going to be a bona fide celebration for everyone at the school, and Archie was grateful to be a part of the festivities.

Faye had plenty of experience with these talent shows, but Josie had butterflies in her stomach fluttering at full speed. Nola was her dignified self, calm and collected, keeping everyone else on track. It looked to be an exceptionally packed house. The excitement in the air and throughout the entire church was undeniable. This was certainly going to be a memorable evening.

Strikingly attractive on her worst day, Faye Lewis looked flawlessly beautiful in her sparkling yellow evening gown and top knot. The elegant chignon bun was perfect to complete Miss Faye's classy look. A ray of sunshine, she illuminated the entire auditorium with her beauty and charm. Nola complemented the festive atmosphere, displaying a midnight blue maxi chiffon dress that trailed beautifully when she moved. Her teased high bun gave her a sophisticated look. The one most drastically affected by the salon's services, however, was Josie Bee. Beyond stunning, with a smooth upswept hairdo and dangling pearl earrings, Josie's crimson red dress offset her slender bare shoulders. Stylishly wrapped around Josie's neck clung her sister's exquisite cultured pearls. Josie, wanting to honor Pearl, her departed friends, and the school, was overcome with emotion. She thanked God for His vision in giving her a role in the joyful Fiesta School, culminating in this opportunity to share her mission.

At last all was ready, and it was time to begin. The stage looked professional with the banner of glittery stars and shining lights in the background. Miss Faye rang the traditional school bell to mark the beginning of the show. The kids walked onto the platform and stood on their designated colored circles. Red, brown, yellow, black, or white. Standing there waiting for the music to start with the lights dimmed and the spotlights focused, the radiant students looked like little angels. When "Twinkle, Twinkle, Little Star" began, the kids sang their hearts out and danced with unrestrained joy. It was a perfect beginning.

After the group opening, Miss Faye encouraged everyone to show their appreciation and clap for the shining stars. Scanning the audience, Faye was surprised to see Officer Finch at the back of the stadium standing near the door. Previously he had asked both Faye and Nola if they were anticipating any trouble and told them that he would certainly be happy to attend and make his presence known. Faye assured him they had it handled and to enjoy a Saturday evening off. Both women had an inkling that he intended to be there and, assuming it was out of concern for the kids, thought it was a generous gesture.

The first act involved Jupiter and Ernie singing a cowboy duet while proudly sitting on a large sawhorse Archie had meticulously created, the horse complete with flowing mane and long matching tail. The boys wowed the crowd with their black-and-white cowboy hats and enthusiastic singing.

Joey Links dressed as Superman and, rapidly flapping his arms up and down, flew onto the stage and rescued a kitty stuck in the top of a tree. He then took a victory lap around the stage with the stuffed animal cradled under one arm so he could still soar. Johnny and Beanie followed up with a number on metal trash-can-lid drums. Elijah Cross juggled. Tommy and Josiah did a circus act, with Tommy as the ringmaster and Josiah as the lion. Moshe Miller did somersaults, cartwheels, and forward rolls.

Two more acts with the girls were left before intermission. Polly Schmidt performed a cheerleading routine, and Etta Redmond sang "You Are My Sunshine" with Nola accompanying her on the church's baby grand. Etta curtseyed, and as her applause died down, Faye took to the stage.

"Thank you, you have been a wonderful audience. Don't we have stars that shine bright and sparkle? Now, please help yourselves to Miss

Nola's homemade cookies and punch. We will look forward to meeting back in our seats in roughly fifteen minutes. We have an outstanding second half prepared. Thank you!"

Everyone was excited to have Nola's ginger ale punch with lime sherbert on top and her array of homemade cookies. There were platters of oatmeal scotchies, old-fashioned peanut butter cookies, soft molasses chewies, snickerdoodles with extra cinnamon and sugar, almond ginger snaps, Mexican crinkle cookies, maple whoopie pies, apricot pinwheels, double-chocolate-chip delights, lemon snowdrops, raspberry-jam thumbprints, and frosted spice cookies. Nola had been baking and freezing her specialties for months. She was the Fiesta's renowned Cookie Queen.

Miss Faye grinned, thrilled at how wonderfully smooth the night was progressing. And she knew the best was yet to come. She was still smiling when a sharp, familiar voice stopped her in her tracks. Like a hot knife cutting through butter, Faye's soft heart was exposed, her feelings of happiness dissolved. It never even remotely crossed Faye's gentle mind that Edna Higgins would dare have anything to do with her at the talent show. But right off the bat, Faye instinctively knew this hellbent woman was set on creating a scene of shame and embarrassment for her. This renegade locust had pulled away from her swarm to single Faye out.

Miss Faye Lewis was not prepared for, nor could she have even remotely imagined, what would happen next.

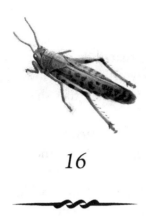

16

Putting on the Ritz

Never let anyone—any person or any force—
dampen, dim or diminish your light.

John Lewis

THANK GOODNESS FAYE Louise Lewis had an alert guardian angel waiting in the wings to swoop in and save her. From the minute Archie Wilson spied Mrs. Higgins sashaying down the aisle, he instantly got a queasy feeling in the pit of his stomach. He wouldn't put anything past the miserable sourpuss. Archie intended to put an end to whatever crazy thing Edna was up to. In the past few weeks she had been busier than a rabid squirrel, stirring things up for Faye and the school. The Arch couldn't do much about all that nastiness, but he was in a position to remove this current threat—the quicker the better. Faye certainly didn't deserve another ambush, let alone one in public and on her big day.

Just as Edna was about to grab Faye's sleeveless arm, Archie rushed up from behind. Lifting Edna's thick bulky body off the ground as she kicked and hollered like a pig in a poke, he whisked her backstage.

It was a timely blessing that the audience was firmly hovering over Nola's outstanding display of goodies. However, at the first indication of trouble, Nola, the mother hen that she was, had also hightailed it toward Faye.

Normally reserved and courteous, Miss Nola would gladly have muddied her spotless reputation for the opportunity to slap Edna Higgins upside her thick skull. Thankfully Archie got to her first. Out of the lights and behind the curtains, the Arch was joined by Beanie Barker's dad, Bear, doubling up the efforts to control the nearly speech-less but hostile woman. Archie threatened to deliver Edna directly to her vehicle should the battle-ax decide not to settle down and control herself. She would be forced to miss her only daughter's performance. Archie also recounted how hard Dee-Dee had worked to perfect her act, and in doing so, wanted badly to please her mother. Gentle DeeDee was the second act after the intermission, taking place in a matter of minutes.

"Get your hands off me!" Edna hissed at Archie with a voice filled with venom. And she certainly didn't much care for Bear Barker either. He was a wimp, a loser, in her opinion. When she had gone to him to sign the petition, Bear had flatly refused. He and his wife had taken a real liking to Director Lewis. Edna Higgins was told to mind her own business and "get a life," which infuriated her to no end. The gall of some people! She intended to never forget their lack of support and understanding in the future.

"You have real problems, lady, that's all I can say," said Archie. "But here is not the time or the place to go into it. If you don't sit down and mind your p's and q's, you are leaving. I mean it. And I would think that would just about break your little girl's heart."

"She has worked really hard, and I think you will be quite proud of Dee-Dee," said Nola, who was still standing by and watching Edna like a hawk. Nola wasn't ready to relax quite yet. She was fixin' to make sure there were no more surprises from the likes of Edna Higgins.

"And I don't need your two cents, Nola Greene. Who do you think you are anyway? You don't belong here either. You don't seem to get that. Maybe you, too, can go back where you came from when the school is legally forced to close," sneered Edna.

"I know how you feel about me, and I don't care. You aren't worth a response." Nola turned away before she did say something that she might later regret. She wouldn't let Edna tarnish the night or its twinkling stars and families. Edna didn't amount to a hill of beans.

"Do you need my assistance getting back to your seat or would you like Mr. Wilson to escort you to your vehicle?" asked Bear. "Your choice. And we'll be keeping our eyes on you!"

Turning on her heels, Edna Higgins stormed back to her seat as the lights dimmed. Trekking back to check on Faye, Archie need not have worried. Calm and collected, Faye Lewis was already sharing what could be expected in the second half of the Fiesta talent show production. She was delighted to report that not a single cookie remained.

"Isn't our very own Nola Greene absolutely phenomenal?" Miss Faye gushed. "Kudos to the family and friends of the Fiesta's stars for completely finishing up the dessert table. Nice job!" In her element and feeling a sense of control, Director Lewis basked in every moment of what was going to be the school's final show.

Esmeralda Hill, starting off the second half, was one of Nola's last two girls. As she walked across the stage, she looked adorable in her navy-blue-and-white sailor outfit, complete with the nautical white hat held in place by a small army of bobby pins. As Esmeralda sang and danced to "On the Good Ship Lollipop," several remarked how much the little girl resembled Shirley Temple in her younger years. Once finished, Esmeralda tossed out lollipops. When her bucket was emptied there were several playful boos and calls for more. Proud of herself, Esmeralda took the wrapper off the one sucker she had left in her pocket and popped it into her mouth, waving as she walked off the stage. Forgetting her curtsy, she quickly ran back out and, to make up for it, curtsied twice.

Deidra Delilah Higgins was up next. The entire staff was on pins and needles hoping Mrs. Higgins would stay put in her chair and not make a commotion. Josie glowed with satisfaction as Dee-Dee Higgins absolutely nailed her performance. Many were wondering how a child so sweet and pure could have existed in the belly of such a wicked and rigid woman. The most caring prayed for the little one, bending a knee for the darling Dee-Dee. Edna had only one thing right: A mother is supposed to be her child's number-one cheerleader. To be there and walk with them every possible step of the way is what mothers are supposed to do. What Edna had terribly wrong was that a mother cannot build their loved one up by brutally knocking others down. Nor could you replace encouragement with sharp criticism, and not seriously wound your child's spirit. Sadly, that was how Edna operated, and it wasn't nice or pleasant. Sooner or later these deeds would come back to haunt her. Most things like that usually did. Go figure.

After Dee-Dee's performance, Director Faye once again took the stage to explain how the children's performances were chosen, emphasizing their complete involvement from beginning to end. "We have been so proud of the performances given by our first nine talented boys and Miss Nola's four accomplished girls. A total of thirteen amazing young children. That leaves us with eight remaining presentations. Now it is my great joy to present the program's next four youngsters. I have had the opportunity to spend countless hours and precious moments with these girls on the program, and I'm extremely proud of each of them," said Miss Faye, filled with emotion. "More importantly, I have been tremendously blessed to work with them, and getting to know what is in their hearts has been the very best part. Parents, I cannot say it enough: be thankful you have children who want to be kind. Thank you for giving me the privilege to witness and celebrate their goodness. It has been humbling and very much appreciated. Sooooo . . . here we go."

And there was that twang her staff adored, as Faye playfully exaggerated her words.

"Let's begin with Miss Tabytha Baker and Miss Peggy Lawson singing together, 'Star Light, Star Bright,' with Miss Nola accompanying them on the piano. Take it away, girls," Miss Faye said as she stepped away from the podium.

Tabytha sang the first round, Peggy the second, and they sweetly finished off the third together. They curtsied confidently and walked offstage, hand in hand and to much applause. Faye beamed. Next was Rosita Perez. She eloquently recited the "Itsy Bitsy Spider" first in English and then in Spanish, complete with hand motions. The looks on her family's faces were ones of great pride. Their baby girl was proud of her heritage.

The last of Faye Lewis's four girls was Judy Flack, and she was one funny kid. From the very beginning Judy insisted on doing "I'm a Little Teapot," planning to fall over at the end of the song, pretend it was an accident, run off the stage, and then run back on to say, "That's all folks" like Porky Pig. It all came off perfectly.

Once the audience calmed down, Miss Faye went back to the mic to prepare the way for Josie and the remaining four girls.

"The final young performers have been working with Miss Josie Bee Johnson, who has been a breath of fresh air and youthful vitality at the Fiesta. It is my privilege to turn the stage over to Miss Josie, who would like to share a few words before her girls lead us into the home stretch of tonight's activities. Miss Josie?"

Josie Bee climbed the few steps to the stage and turned to the audience, smiling. "Thank you, Director Faye. You are certainly one of the nicest and kindest people I have ever met. I mean that with all my heart! You have been a driving force in expanding my life experiences, challenging me to do better, and giving me tools in which to learn to work with others. Your courage has given me courage, and I am indebted to you for the investment you have made in my life. I am forever grateful." As Josie pushed herself to stay focused and keep moving, she brushed away the tears collecting in her eyes. Turning her attention to the audience, Josie cleared her throat.

"My name is Josie Bee Johnson, and I was born and raised in Birmingham, Alabama. Over two and a half years ago, Sixteenth Street Baptist Church was the site of a bombing by the Ku Klux Klan. It wasn't my home church, but I was on my way to attend there the morning the bomb went off. The Klan purposefully attempted to destroy that church and those in it. To this day I cannot get my head around how human beings could do such tragic things to other members of the human race, but the Klan notoriously did. These racist people were driven to damage and destroy others based solely on the fact that they didn't like the color of their skin. I hear myself telling you this true story, and yet it remains painfully surreal. You all have children here at the Fiesta School, and you are truly blessed because of the diversity this school represents. Your kids see all the skin colors, but in their world, they view this with curiosity, not with disdain. They see hearts. Your students would never be taught any form of hate here. It's not acceptable, and we know it is wrong. Your kids are encouraged to appreciate and care for one another. This safe haven celebrates differences. You can be mighty proud of what Fiesta School stands for. It is one of the most remarkable places I have ever been. As you look around, you can see that your kids can become whatever they want and go wherever their dreams could possibly lead them. However, it would be in vain if the hearts of these students were to become compromised and tainted by racism and other prejudices. At the Fiesta School their precious hearts have been protected and combined with positive thoughts and good experiences consciously day in and day out. We have a job to do and fully understand the importance of its purpose. Director Faye has created an environment structured to reflect the contributions and worth of each child based on who they are. It has been fun. And rewarding because every child here feels accepted and celebrated. And that makes us all feel good." Grateful for her notecards, Josie felt her confidence increase as she continued.

"Thank you for being in this room. Your support and love for these youngsters means everything to them. And isn't that what this is all about? You are their world, and they learn the very most from you. In providing your children with the best tools and opportunities for growth, Fiesta is leveling their playing field so that in the future they may continue to be as successful and happy as they are tonight. It has been our honor to serve these students and a privilege to watch them grow this past school year. At the conclusion of the next four students' performances, I will return to briefly explain what it is that brought me from Birmingham to Sand Haven and ultimately the Fiesta School. Thank you. Now, on with the show. Let's bring out our remaining stars!"

First of the final four was an animated Agnes Jones. It was hard to believe this was the same little girl who had initially hunched over her desk and shied away from others. Agnes had reminded Josie of Carole Robertson from the very beginning. Something about Agnes reached out and tugged on the strings of her heart, reminding her of Carole's strong beliefs. Having identified the problem with her sight, Josie learned that this child nevertheless walked by faith. Even when she stumbled, Agnes never took anyone else down with her. Although dealing with an obvious handicap, she remained available and ready to help others. Sporting fashionable cat-eye frames and having the ability to see all that she had been missing, Agnes simply blossomed. Confident and secure, she wanted to do something peppy, delightfully choosing to do a happy dance. This was really going to come as a surprise to her family, who had become accustomed to a shy and somewhat reserved Agnes.

Once the music started, Agnes popped out from behind the large flowering magnolia tree. Archie had constructed the tree out of real branches in honor of Nola, who, being born and raised in Mississippi, frequently spoke of her affection for her state flower. As Josie watched Agnes's act unfold, she noticed a rare tear rolling down Nola's cheek. Josie understood the strong effect Southern touches had on those far away from their original homes, and she knew it made Nola homesick.

Agnes was encircling the magnolia tree, singing and swaying to the rhythm of Sam Cooke's "It's a Wonderful World." Agnes beamed as she, dressed up as a tree fairy, gracefully danced to the music. But the happiest faces belonged to her parents and her very proud grandma. Although Agnes's grandmother couldn't see the dance, she felt her granddaughter's spirit and clearly heard each and every word she sang, flowing clearly out of her mouth. Agnes gave a lovely curtsy and basked in the audience's generous applause.

The most sensitive of all the students, Patty-Jo Tucker patiently awaited her cue. Patty-Jo had experienced a remarkable year of growth and adjustment, demonstrating quiet strength as she embraced difficult changes. Josie and the others had discovered that Patty-Jo's intense desire to make everybody happy was the real cause of her pain and that the tissue box and the constant fountain of tears were just symptoms of this. With her discomfort with perceived conflict, Patty-Jo had been chosen by Josie to represent Addie Mae Collins, who avoided disagreements and squabbles whenever she could. Both were genuine peacemakers and gentle people. Josie knew Addie's sweet presence was missed. She had always been helpful to her friends. And Addie liked to draw, too.

For tonight's talent show, Patty-Jo had prepared the most unusual of presentations. The staff marveled at her ability to know what best suited her and to recognize her own blooming talents. Knowing she would not be comfortable looking out into the crowd and seeing all eyes on her, Patty-Jo chose to share her favorite piece of artwork. It was the picture she had meticulously drawn and painted of Mister George. Patty-Jo adored the black-and-white feline and had an amazing ability to sketch him. Her portrait was a tribute created from a place of love and joy for her newfound companion. Patty-Jo enjoyed feeding him and brushing his silky coat. Mister George returned these favors by snuggling up beside her, purring loudly, and allowing her to hold his paws.

An easel had been set up center stage with a cloth draped over the picture. Patty-Jo walked across the stage, then Josie met her and kneeled to the left of the display. Patty-Jo stood on her right. They had decided to allow Patty-Jo to share through questions and answers.

"Patty-Jo," Josie said, "could you please remove the cloth and show us what's underneath it?" Removing the yellow fabric, Patty-Jo took a step back, absorbing herself in the face of Mister George. Josie provided the audience with background information surrounding Patty-Jo's special relationship with the cat, emphasizing her caring tendencies. Patty-Jo, she said, thoroughly enjoyed drawing, coloring, and painting, but most of her joy came from sharing what she had made with others.

"Thank you," Josie continued. "This is a beautiful painting of a very special cat. Can you tell us the name of this cat?"

In a deliberate and concise way, Patty-Jo responded, "This is Mister George, and he is a cat who lives at the school. He is my friend and likes me very much. And I take care of him."

"How do you do that, Patty-Jo?" Josie asked.

"I give him what he needs every day," Patty-Jo said.

"And what is that?" Josie probed.

"He needs to be fed his crunchies."

Josie nodded for Patty-Jo to go on, as she pretended to take a brush through her hair.

"Mister George needs to have his hair brushed, just like I do. I brush his hair." Getting more comfortable Patty-Jo warmed to her subject. "I talk to him a lot. And I tell him I love him very much. He is a good boy. And he is my friend." The sincerity and affection in her voice was touching.

"I know that means a lot to Mister George. You are very kind to him. And you know what, Patty-Jo? You are Mister George's friend too. He loves you right back. What do you think about that, young lady?"

"I think it would be a more wonderful place if everyone took care of each other. And was nice to each other." Truth from the mouths of babes.

Josie then asked Patty-Jo a final question. "Is there anything else you would like to share with all these nice people out there?"

Nodding yes, Patty-Jo said, "I hope people say, 'I love you.'"

"Because?"

"That would make people feel good and maybe not cry so much," said Patty-Jo.

"Thank you, Patty-Jo. Thank you for sharing Mister George and your wonderful talent. We want to bring someone out who has been waiting to thank you in his very own way," Josie said. Out strolled Miss Faye with Mister George snuggled in her arms. Faye handed the ball of fur into the waiting arms of Patty-Jo Tucker. The squeal of delight that came from the surprised little girl prompted the audience to cheer. "I am so proud of all three of you," Josie said with a quivering lower lip, knowing full well this was near the end of the Fiesta's existence. It was a visual memory she would never forget. Love that had traveled from an adult to a child to a beloved pet, like a rippling stone.

Hearing Pearl's voice prompting her to hold it together, Josie continued on to the lectern to announce the next performer. Onto the stage walked Charlie Harper, a striking vision in her crisp checked dress and sparkly red shoes. She looked very different. When she had first been dropped off, Josie whisked her to the dressing room to finally give her the dress she had picked up in Fort Wayne at Murphy's. Every time—and there were many—Josie wanted to bring it out and give it to Charlie, Nola would say it was best to wait. "Imagine how special she will feel to be so wonderfully dressed on show night." Nola also pointed out that it would have been asking far too much to expect the young child to keep the surprise to herself. Later Josie spied the crimson shoes in the window of Martin's Footwear and couldn't resist them either. They completed the transformation.

When Josie had handed Charlie the wrapped package, she was baffled. With her tiny fingers she lifted the dress from within the white tissue and said, "For me?"

"Yes, silly, for lovely you," said Josie, giggling. "Of course for you!"

"It can't be for me, Miss Josie! It just can't be!"

"And why not?" Josie asked.

"Because it is for a girl. It has tags on it . . . it is brand-new and nobody has ever worn it," she whispered.

"It is yours, baby girl. It is all yours." Josie wondered how something so small could mean so much. Her heart was doing flip-flops. The only one happier was Charlie. Josie couldn't imagine Faye being forced to walk away from this kind of pure love and appreciation. Maybe Josie was thinking of Nola and herself too. Numerous times over the past eight months, she hadn't been able to envision staying in Sand Haven another month, week, or even one single day longer than necessary, she so desperately missed Pearl and their life together. But God allowed, and most likely directed, all the encouragement and support that came her way, giving Josie what she needed to stay.

But at this moment, the night was about Charlie Harper demonstrating entirely new thoughts and feelings, relishing the opportunity to stretch her wings while also showing her family something they didn't expect. To dance in the moment as kids naturally do. Nola had placed red ribbons in Charlie's hair and curled her newly cut bangs. She looked totally different, and Charlie was comfortable with her new look.

"I would like to present our next performance, by Charlene Harper," Josie announced. "Charlene will be singing 'Over the Rainbow.'"

Charlie practically floated across the platform and came to a stop in front of the sheeted rainbow backdrop. She lit up the auditorium. The audience could hardly believe their eyes. One of Archie's boys asked why a new girl got to be in their show. Performing in the magic of the moment, Charlie lost her old identity but claimed a new one. The most momentous response, however, was found in the looks on the faces of the entire Harper family. It took a second or two for the four boys to recognize their beautiful tomboy sister, but when they did, they erupted into a symphony of whistles and high-pitched catcalls. Recognizing that the noisy commotion was coming from her brothers, Charlie flashed them a big smile. Tears ran down the stunned faces of both her parents, each overwhelmed at what they were seeing in their little girl.

Taking a deep breath, Charlie was ready to soar. She gave the standard head-nod, counted to three, and flew into the song. Taking everyone over the rainbow, she convinced her entire audience that dreams really do come true. Charlie Harper received a standing ovation. She curtsied and with both hands she effortlessly blew kisses to her family. She had practiced her ending many times over.

As Charlie looked out on the audience and saw the reactions from the staff and the families of the students, she was euphoric. But Edna Higgins was not among them. She had practically dragged her daughter out the minute she had finished her part, despite Dee-Dee's begging her mother to please let her stay. As Edna stormed out with her reluctant hostage in tow, Nola and Josie looked at each other, feeling bad for Dee-Dee but relieved that Edna was on her way out.

Miss Faye again took the stage. "And now ladies and gentlemen, family and friends, we come to our last single performance of the evening. Without further delay, we proudly present Miss Penny Ann White," she announced.

Josie was praying that sweet Penny, nervous and distracted, had calmed down. Backstage Nola instantly discovered that something was bothering Penny. She feared that her father was going to show up and punish her, as he had done in other instances. Thank God Almighty there had been no new marks and bruises, but it was the invisible scars that ran deep and would take the longest to heal. Apparently, before leaving for the church, Penny unfortunately answered the ringing phone. It was her Daddy, Frank, calling from jail, going through the roof threatening to come take care of her and her lousy mother. Alice, seeing the look of sheer terror on Penny's face, grabbed the phone and told Frank where he could go. She slammed the phone down as hard as she could, saying, "Good riddance," and picked it back up, taking it off the hook. Alice wasn't even going to give him the opportunity to call her back. She felt the resolve in her actions. The determined mother would make it a point to contact her lawyer and level another complaint.

In the meantime, Mayor Bower had been making progress from his injuries after having been struck by Frank White's car, but then he developed pneumonia, delaying Frank's day in court. Either way, depending on what the charges ended up being, Frankie Boy was going away for a very long time, probably for the rest of his natural days. Connecting Frank to a series of violent burglaries, witnesses were happy to come around and share what they knew now that there was no chance of his getting out of jail and coming after them. Alice had gotten her first job and was doing things she had only dreamed of someday attempting. Frank had controlled every single facet of her life from day one, and only now was she learning how to live free. Friends that had been run off by Frank were back in her life. Neighbors who had been afraid to approach her were speaking now in passing. Best of all, her children were flourishing. Rediscovering God and being able to attend church, Alice White gave Him the glory for saving her and the kids. Now she was going to see her little girl have fun and twinkle like the star she deserved to be. Shouldn't everyone get an opportunity to sparkle?

Alice confided the incident to Nola as soon as they arrived in the church. Instantly Nola talked with Penny, reassuring her that her father would not be coming to the talent show. Nola told her not to worry because her daddy was in a place that didn't allow him to go home or ever hurt anyone again. And if there *had* been a chance Frank would barge in, it would be over Nola's dead body. And she would have put up the fight of her life. Nola had seen racist and deranged Frank Whites in Mississippi, and she was not the same woman she was back then. No longer would she stand by in silence, paralyzed by fear while hideous cowards performed brutal acts of terror. She had fled once, but now Nola would hold her ground and demand the right to be heard, and to be treated equally and fairly.

Faye and Nola and Alice shared a special bond. All three had been intimidated, mistreated, and abused by cruel men in one way or another. They recognized in each other the evidence of such treatment and could understand one another's insecurities and scars. There wasn't a magical salve for their wounds. This they knew. But they had an unspoken kind of awareness and support that provided a measure of healing. Alice had shared with Nola how they were handling the situation of Frank's arrest and incarceration. Based on that, Nola felt confident that what she was saying to the vulnerable little girl would be consistent with what she had already been told. Nola knew it was important to reassure Penny that she was safe, and there was absolutely nothing to fear. And she succeeded in doing just that as Penny seemed to have changed gears, appearing animated and excited about the night, forgetting all about the disturbing phone call.

"Penny," Miss Faye continued, "will be dancing and singing 'A Dream Is a Wish Your Heart Makes.'"

Dressed in a sleeveless baby-blue chiffon gown, Penny was the princess she had dreamed of being. Princesses got rescued, not hurt, and that was why Penny wanted to be one. Josie cringed inside at the pain Penny had suffered and endured at the hands of Frank, and she thanked God for His protection. This moment was possible only because of the Challenge, and Josie was a better person because of it too. Looking out and seeing the peace on Alice White's relaxed face was an unexpected blessing. Not to mention how drop-dead stunning she looked. Alice had discovered God and Maybelline at practically the same time. Looking fantastic, Alice watched her Penny Ann dance without reservation, releasing the hidden song that had been secretly tucked into her fragile heart. Best of all for Faye, Nola, and Josie was that Penny was up there in full view with arms fairly free of visible bumps or bruises.

Princess Penny finished her song to another standing ovation. Josie couldn't help but wonder how many people in the audience had been aware of what the White family had been dealing with. Tear-streaked faces and emotions betrayed the silences of two women who quickly dropped their faces into their hands. Afterward Josie would remember seeing those same folks embracing Alice. She hoped they were sharing some very nice things with that sweet lady, who exhibited a renewed spunk and grace.

Frank White could rot in the slammer like a decomposing rat. And

Josie knew she was not alone in her sentiments, her thoughts reverberating in the minds of others who had been recipients of Frank's hot temper and deliberate cruelty.

Returning to the front, Faye enthusiastically congratulated the shining stars and thanked them for their hard work in making this talent show the best ever. The students had one more song to do as a class, which would then bring the evening's activities to a close. Miss Josie would now be returning to share a few remaining thoughts. Turning the podium over to her anxious friend, Faye said, "Miss Josie?"

Josie had to calm herself and stay focused on exactly what it was she hoped to accomplish this evening. She needed to make clear what brought her to this particular moment in time, and she was not going to skirt around the church bombing. It claimed the lives of four wonderful girls. As Nola had once said to Josie, sometimes there are no words, and yet we attempt to describe the indescribable. Josie knew she needed to try.

"Thank you so much," Josie said. "I realize we are at the tail end of a long and rewarding evening, but it is really important for me to take these few minutes and share with you what brought me here to Fiesta School. It is a journey that began with tragic life-changing circumstances. But even hope and goodness can eventually emerge from the deepest despair and darkness.

Secretly, Josie prayed for justice to be served with a conviction of those responsible for the bombing. She knew she had done her part to bring closure by honoring the four girls, knowing full well that the families back home were still longing for restoration. "I guess it would be like seeing a beautiful rainbow and trusting that its promises are really going to come to fruition. Let me begin…."

17

RESOUNDING REMEMBRANCES

I have a dream that my four little children will one day
live in a nation where they will not be judged by the
color of their skin but by the content of their character.

Martin Luther King Jr.

"AS I MENTIONED earlier," Josie said, "I am originally from Birmingham, Alabama. On September 15, 1963, there was a bombing in our sister church, Sixteenth Street Baptist Church. It was on a Sunday morning. It was meant to hurt as many children and adults as possible. It killed four girls I knew, and it is extremely important to me that you know their names: Carole Robertson, Addie Mae Collins, Denise McNair, and Cynthia Wesley. Because they should never be forgotten. This act of brutal persecution hardened my heart in ways that are hard to describe. I began spiraling down a path of destruction and despair. I watched the parents of each of these children, and I couldn't process how they were supposed to handle the loss of their child in the manner in which they died. What do you do when you lose your beloved daughter to the hands of hate? I didn't have any answers, and my own heart screamed for retaliation. I was becoming like the haters, the damaging locusts that wanted to destroy anything and everything in their paths.

"The Ku Klux Klan, like the locusts, created intense fear and attracted others of like mind to join their racist organization. God loved me enough to offer me a way out of my compromised state. He knew I was headed for serious trouble and that I could end up harming others, including my own family. In His way God issued me an opportunity in which to begin healing my heart while remembering these four girls. The Challenge was designed for me to choose four young children, each representing one of the deceased girls, and make a difference in their lives in remembrance of Carole, Addie, Denise, and Cynthia. Can you remember these names please? Carole. Addie. Denise. Cynthia." Josie repeated the names slowly.

"My church back home, Rosewood Street Baptist, sponsored my journey here to Indiana. In Sand Haven God placed Faye Lewis and the Fiesta School in my life, giving me the opportunity to be in the midst of children. My church group placed me with a wonderful family, Ellie and Del Price and their two young girls, themselves relocating here from Birmingham a few years earlier. I didn't realize that there had been several safety nets in place to catch me should I not be able to handle all the changes I was facing. But God was indeed in the center of my new life here in Indiana, working out details to make it possible for me to meet the demanding requirements of the Challenge. I am only beginning to get a handle on how everything has been coming together. I guess I really needed to be away from those I loved in order to appreciate and love them better. I needed to start growing up, and to become more than what I was.

"I had the opportunity to meet Director Lewis, and she graciously allowed me to visit Fiesta to see what her preschool was like. She was so proud and excited when she told me about this school. Once I arrived, I had the sincere pleasure of meeting Miss Nola Greene, and her Southern kindness connected with me. Not to mention her fine cooking! Once I got to see your children in action, I knew this school was special and unique. It was something I wanted to become a part of. It was like nothing I had ever been a part of before. There was so much happiness and joy, and the students were delightful. After twisting the director's arm"—there were a few chuckles in the audience—"I was allowed to come on staff at Fiesta. Then I knew I had to really get to know the children in order to start figuring out what it was I needed to learn and do.

"It was extremely difficult to figure out which four children I was supposed to focus on. As you know, every child in this school is remarkable and worthy. Eventually, I had to relinquish control and trust God to show me which children to select in honor of Carole, Addie, Denise, and Cynthia. My choices were Agnes Jones, Patty-Jo Tucker, Charlie Harper, and Penny White. It has been humbly rewarding getting to know these girls, and I am incredibly proud of them. I am equally as proud of every single student that attends Fiesta School. Director Lewis and Miss Nola have provided an empire of kindness and acceptance here, and that should make each of you equally as proud. Hate is a learned behavior, and it is *not* taught at Fiesta. What your children have learned about acceptance and unconditional love will serve them for the rest of their lives. This is the really important stuff. This will make a difference in their lives.

"In reviewing my time here at Fiesta School, I am just beginning to understand how much I have learned about the students. Your children have been amazing teachers. I could go on for days on end, but it is most likely things you already know, and we are nearing the end of a full night," Josie said, and grinned as she saw heads nodding.

"So, at this time I want to narrow down for you my thoughts and insights in respect to my following chosen four angel girls," Josie firmly continued without hesitation and with a genuine sense of pride and accomplishment in her selections.

"First, I chose to honor Carole Robertson by picking Agnes Jones. Agnes's charming face reminded me of a young Carole. It quickly took me back when I first laid eyes on Agnes and her adorable big brown eyes. Carole was absolutely lovely too. She had been such an outgoing and friendly personality who reached out to others beginning at an early age. She was confident and eager to learn, playing instruments and routinely going to dance classes. Carole enjoyed interacting with others and was always personable. This same form of genuine helpfulness and care can be seen in Agnes Jones. I would come to learn from Agnes that even if things aren't perfect in your own world, that's not an excuse for not helping and looking out for others. Like Carole, Agnes is very giving. Eventually we here at the school came to realize she was being held back by vision issues. Once that was taken care of, Agnes instantly became more confident and outgoing. Just like Carole, this girl is now ready to tackle anything that comes her way.

"Second, Patty-Jo Tucker was chosen to represent Addie Mae Collins. Addie Mae was one of the gentlest and sweetest little things on the face of the earth. She had always been a peaceful spirit, from the time she was a little one. Addie just cared for everyone and wanted to see those around her get along and not be at odds with one another. She was a true peacemaker, and I immediately saw the same tenderness in Patty-Jo from the get-go. She is a tender sprout, too. And Patty-Jo is artistic as well, liking to sketch and draw just like Addie Mae had done. With a gentle song in her heart at all times, Patty-Jo was perfect to pair with Addie. They could have been best buds. Patty-Jo demonstrated to me that we are all built for service. If we do not care for others, it will chip away at our hearts and wound our spirits. Then we can't be all that we were designed to be. And this would be sad.

"Representing the youngest of the four girls killed in the church bombing and my third choice is Charlene Harper. She caught my eye because of how different she was from Denise McNair. I know that must sound a bit odd, but they were drastically different on the out-side. Denise was a sharp little dresser from the time she was first dressed by her mother. She enjoyed pretty outfits with matching pieces: a hat, a purse, the shoes. Denise was always classy and full of style. I laugh when I think back on my first encounter with Charlene. Called "Charlie" by her family and raised with four brothers, she appeared to be most com-fortable being dressed like one of the boys, which was just fine. She was a rough and tough youngster, and there was nothing wrong with that. It made Charlie every bit as strong-willed and dominant as Denise McNair had been. Denise was affectionately called "Niecie." Both girls were balls of fire. Spitfire Charlie taught me that sometimes we have to figure out and define who we are and want to grow up to be. We do not have to accept the views others, intentionally or unintentionally, hand down. It's more than okay to be different. We have been created to be enough in our own right. And this is true for each of these students. They are all never-to-be-repeated, one-of-a-kind miracles."

Josie took a big breath as she rounded the corner.

"And this brings me to my fourth and final selection, and that would be Penny White representing Cynthia Wesley. I chose to honor Cynthia with this sweet little girl. Penny's delicate face reminded me of my young friend. When Cynthia laughed, the corners of her mouth tipped up in such a contagious way, you just wanted to join in somehow. When I first observed Penny, I saw her face do a similar thing at one point, and I wanted to see more of it. But then I began seeing a timid little person appearing to struggle with a certain measure of . . . I didn't know what. Somehow, I wanted her to be more carefree like Cynthia, just happy and well taken care of in all those ways that nurture and sustain you. Although each of these girls, Penny and Cynthia, at points had difficult childhood experiences, there would be positive changes for both in the most unexpected ways. Cynthia had gained a wonderful life with loving and doting adoptive parents. I certainly wanted, in the worst way, the same security for my final angel. Penny demonstrated bravery and hope in dreaming of a better tomorrow, learning along her young journey that it is never okay for one person to hurt another. And I learned it is always important that we stand up for others when we see mistreatment of any kind. Together we can make a difference. It's never about what we want to do for others, because ultimately, they give back and teach us so much more." Josie felt her voice soften considerably. She did not speak these words lightly but gently. There was no condemnation, only affirmation. Things really can change.

"I am humbled by these opportunities to meet your children and to learn lessons from them that I could never have grasped on my own. Their insights will walk with me forever. They are truly shining stars whose sparkle reaches down into our hearts, minds, and spirits. And we are never the same.

"As we go into our final selection, please remember to tell your kids how proud you are of them. They live for those words. Never forget to hug and squeeze them, telling them you love them, because someday it may not be possible. We can lose our loved ones in a split second, and there are no do-overs. And sometimes it's not about the do-overs at all, but about not being able to do anything new. Please remember, in a corner of your hearts, to pray for those who have suffered such losses and tragedies.

"If not for the grace of God, the parents of Carole, Addie, Denise, and Cynthia could not have gone on. You don't ever get over the loss of a child, but you have to figure out how to exist in your world without them. There is not a parent on the face of the earth who wants their child to be taken from them and then forgotten. It has been my humble privilege to remember four inspirational and unforgettable lives that tragically and abruptly ended too soon at the hands of hate. My hope is that we, each and every one of us, choose to purposefully walk in the light of acceptance and love for others. Just like the kids naturally do, we need to see hearts first and not get hung up on the other things. Thank you for sharing your children, and thank you, Fiesta, for providing a safe and happy environment that celebrates uniqueness, diversity, and love in action."

Josie was finished. What she had just spoken was not going to change the world. Josie thought that was more in God's line of work anyway. She was a novice, a broken vessel herself, and not an experienced speaker to boot. She thought she may have seen several nodding heads here and there throughout her talk. But between the bright lights, occasional watery eyes, and trying to keep her place on the notecards, Josie wasn't absolutely sure. For goodness' sake, maybe not even a handful of folks out in the audience were even listening at this point, let alone moved. But Josie couldn't let her fear of failure and ridicule prevent her from sharing her heart and the journey she had been on. If one person listened and had second thoughts about anything, that was all she could hope for. She was not going to erase hatred or wipe out racism. The locusts wouldn't be destroyed. But Josie did believe she had an opportunity to speak truth by starting a conversation—with neighbors, friends, family, someone in the community. Josie needed to share in order to be obedient and responsible to God and her supporting team.

She was at Fiesta School because of what had tragically happened to Carole, Addie, Denise, and Cynthia. Josie was also learning that if you don't stand up for others, then you are standing down. There is no resting spot between right and wrong.

Josie Bee had done what she had set out to do, and yet there was so much more she could have shared on a variety of levels. She would have told those listening in the audience that it was her prayer that these four chosen girls would forever have a connection to one another. That they would somehow walk through life together in one way or another because they shared this distinction of being part of the Challenge. The Birmingham girls had been incredibly tight, had shared more than most kids given a full lifetime. Inequality. Racism. The Children's March. Bombings. The continuous locusts of hate. Those girls were a formidable foursome! There was never any question about that. And now there were four others in life with one another and wouldn't it be something if they stuck together? If they grew into a strong friendship? Because of the fatal tragedies. Because they too were young girls. Because they shared the honor of being one of this chosen four. Because together they would also be a force for what is good and right in the world. Josie would have to enlist the thoughts of others much smarter than herself in order to purposefully encourage the possibility of such an outcome. And probably God should be first on her list.

Unclasping her still-clutched hands, Josie moved back to her spot at the side of the stage.

"Leave well enough alone," she could almost hear Auntie Birdie's voice whispering in her ear. "Stop changing what is already good enough." *I hope so*, Josie thought. It was the best she could do.

Pearl, what do you think? Josie instantly thought to herself. She had tried so hard to block Pearl from her thoughts, keeping her head up and pushing forward to do what she had come to do. But she painfully missed her sister and wanted to please her. *Did I do okay, sweet sister? Are you proud of me?* Sighing, Josie refocused on Faye and what was left to accomplish on this remarkable and progressive night.

With tears in her eyes, Josie admiringly watched Faye stroll back to the podium with courage and grit. She spoke clearly into the mic. "Thank youuuuuu, Miss Johnson, for sharing from your heart and trusting us not only with the lives of the students but with your life too. It has most certainly been a wonderful, wonderful year, now, hasn't it?" The audience applauded enthusiastically, and the kids were jumping up and down.

"At this time, I would like to thank Miss Nola Greene for her continuous support and never-ending love. My best friend, I wouldn't know how to do life without you. You inspire me. Mr. Archie Wilson, you have done so much for the school and our students. We can never repay you. You have given countless hours, painted many objects—especially with yellow—and continuously surprised us with your thoughtfulness and creative ways. Miss Josie, you came to us as a child and have grown before our eyes into a woman who has great compassion for children. Thank you for challenging our spirits and values, keeping us accountable and authentic. Last but not least, Mr. Carl Watkins, your strength is obvious. I do belieeeeve you could move mountains if that is what you wanted to do. Your renewed pledge to do good by helping others makes you our very own giant teddy bear. Thank you." As Miss Faye was about to announce the closing song, Archie walked up and gently took over her space.

"Parents, family, and friends, our shining stars, tonight we also want to celebrate our one-of-a-kind director, Miss Faye Lewis. Miss Lewis's intense devotion to the youngsters in this community is highly recognized. She has brought her shining light into the lives of dozens and dozens of children over the past five years. Miss Lewis's passion to teach, guide, and nurture these youngsters has always been exemplary. It has always been Director Lewis's mission to serve impressionable youngsters, providing them a happy environment in which to develop as young human beings. From the manners they learned while eating at the table to the lessons learned in the sandbox, it has been the driving force in Miss Lewis's life to provide for children the very best she could. Miss Lewis gave them what she knew they deserved, the very best possible, and for that we say thank you. Thank you for being an example of kindness, love, and commitment. You are loved, Miss Lewis, and we couldn't be prouder of who you are and what you have accomplished. Thank you." As Archie Wilson stepped back, the audience erupted into deafening applause as several began standing up. Then there were more. With a good part of the auditorium on its feet, Faye unexpectedly was overwhelmed with emotion, big tears running down her face. Nola and Josie were on their feet clapping as well.

Once the applause died down, Faye Lewis thanked the audience, her staff, and most of all the precious children. "I will forever cherish each and every one of you, and all the memories we have created and collected together. The show must go on," she continued. "As our brilliant sparkling stars are taking their spots on stage, finishing with the iconic song 'What the World Needs Now Is Love,' let's stand together. We'd love to have you join in."

Jumping on the designated floor circles in black, brown, yellow, red, and white, with sunflowers in hand, the kids happily sang and moved about with everything they had left. Forming a line, the youngsters grabbed one another's hands, and together bowed several times. Faye was in a swaying frenzy along with the others, families and friends moving back and forth to the magical rhythm of the song. It was a time of unity and confirmation that the world needed love and a whole bunch of it. Not just for some but for everyone. It was a beautiful close to a wonderful celebration.

It was time for the traditional ringing of the school bell to officially signal the end of the cherished event. It would then be rung again later when it was time to leave the building. Both honors belonged to Director Lewis. The familiar sound also led to scattered chaos as the kids were up and running wild. They had been sitting for a long time and were ready to move. With Faye no longer in charge, the students were released into the care and control of their parents and families. Staff grinned. It was now their time to visit and mingle with the guests.

Tonight, however, there was an elephant in the room. Several of the parents appeared to be uneasy and apprehensive. What most of them couldn't have known was that Director Faye Lewis had refused to look at the petition of signatures demanding her ouster. Nola had always been as wise as an owl, suggesting Faye not review the list of names as she didn't need any more hurt piled on her plate. Word had been that several neighbors signed the formal papers along with a few employees from Marshy's Market who had consistently witnessed Director Lewis's carts filled with Tom's and the colorful packets of Kool-Aid. Although Faye had a pretty good idea of whose names most likely appeared on the document, she did not know for certain, and that had been okay with her.

Immediately, Esmeralda's friendly mother, Rosita, speaking a mile a minute in very broken English, took Faye's hands warmly in hers, promising that the new papers would fix everything. "What papers?" Faye asked.

"Mrs. Barker, she tell you," she tried to explain.

One name that would definitely not have been on Edna Higgins's petition was Rosita Hill's. She had expressed nothing but overwhelming gratefulness for Nola's English lessons when the Hills first arrived in Sand Haven from Mexico. She continued to express her thankfulness with large platters of tacos delivered to the Fiesta every Thanksgiving and during May in celebration of Cinco de Mayo. A deeply religious woman, Rosita had given both Nola and Faye beautiful hand-beaded rosaries that had been in their family for a very long time, priceless treasures that touched their hearts and indicated the depth of their ongoing friendship with Rosita and her dear family.

Approaching Faye directly after speaking with Rosita, Alice White hugged Faye tight, thanking her for everything. Josie watched the intense embrace in wonder, the beauty and grace of two transformed women.

"I will never be able to thank you for being in my corner from the get-go. I think I always knew, but when Larry—excuse me, Officer Finch—explained what the two of you had been working on and trying your hardest to do"—her tears dropped like heavy rain—"ummm, I don't know what to say." Searching for a tissue in her handbag, Alice grabbed some and dabbed her wet face.

"Oh Alice, I wish it could have been more and that things had moved quicker," Faye said.

And then it suddenly struck Faye. She and Alice White could very well have been close friends had circumstances been different. Alice could have been that girlfriend Faye had initially longed for in Sand Haven where new beginnings had initially looked promising. Tupperware parties, Beeline in-home style shows, cups of coffee or late evening cocktails. Faye felt a kinship with Alice and was relieved and ecstatic to see her moving forward. Rebuilding a once-shattered life was not easy, and it took courage, guts, and persistence. Faye understood that, and Alice possessed an abundance of all three.

Then Miss Faye continued, "You have said plenty, dear, and I appreciate it. I only wish you and the kids the very best. You deserve it."

"And one more thing," Alice said shyly. "I have to admit that I've always admired you from a distance. I dream that someday I can become a well-dressed and classy lady like you. And that melon-colored red sweater, just striking!"

Faye gasped. "Shooooot, that ole thang?" she said with the exaggerated twang of a true Southern belle. "You can have it, Alice! It would look much nicer on you. This is an ideal time for me to clean out my overstuffed closet. I'll bag up some things and drop them off to you. My sincere pleasure!"

Alice was beyond surprised. "Thank you, Faye! And I am so sorry about what has happened to you. It isn't fair. You don't deserve any of this," Alice whispered.

"As we both know, dear, it's those locusts we never see coming that try to take us down," said Faye.

"But Officer Finch and I were talking. You don't have to go. You know that, right? Faye, you can fight those allegations," Alice said. "Not everyone believes them!"

"Maybe, maybe not. But I am beginning to think it might be a good time in my life to move on. I'm in the process of trying to figure that out. But when we get knocked down, we just have to figure out how to get back up, right? You take care of your family. I'll be fine. You take good care of yourself, and trust me when I say you are worth it, Alice," Faye reassured her.

"You too, friend," said Alice.

Alice's words touched Faye's innermost spirit, making it soar higher than a kite. Who would have guessed that the cruelty of others would create for them a fortress of support? Life could be unpredictable like that sometimes.

And Josie found her spirit pleasantly surprised as several of the parents had let her know, in their own ways, that they had appreciated her efforts in sharing her heart. Pats on the back, a couple of hand squeezes, and some heartfelt words from the mothers in particular were reassuring to Josie that she had spoken well enough to get a response from others.

But the gestures and sincerity of the parents of her four angel girls took her over the moon. Josie had come to thoroughly enjoy their children, loving them for who they were. It made her smile that the girls from back home were being remembered and that she clearly saw each of them in her Fiesta chosen four. She felt blessed and incredibly thankful.

Nervously, Beanie Barker's mother walked up to both Faye and Nola. She wanted them to know that a new petition was being circulated to reinstate Fiesta School, as Rosita Hill had tried to explain. Barbra Barker hoped this unfortunate misunderstanding could be corrected and rectified. They would know the township's decision within the next thirty days. Profusely thanking the Barkers for their concern and action, Faye let them know that what's done is done, and that they would most likely not be interested in reopening the school.

Close by and overhearing Mrs. Barker's comments, unable to control herself, Josie instinctively rolled her eyes. She wondered where these concerned parents had been throughout Edna Higgins's locust campaign to destroy their beloved Fiesta School.

The Prices, bless their hearts, waited patiently to get to all three ladies, Faye, Nola, and Josie. Everyone was tickled pink that the entire Price family came to the show; they wouldn't have missed it for anything. Paula and Patsy, dressed in their Sunday best, were excited to be around the young entertainers from the production.

"We are so proud of you, Josie Bee," Ellie said. "And Miss Faye and Miss Nola, how can we ever thank you? It has taken a village, now hasn't it?" Ellie said with a chuckle.

There was a chorus of "Amen!" accompanied by Ellie's "Glory!"

Carl approached the group just as Archie joined them. He thanked everyone for their support and for giving him a chance to have a blast with Mr. Wilson. "I thought you needed a worker and understood there would be some labor involved, but I have been the one blessed by your labors of love. It was a beautiful thing seeing those kids do what they did. Never knew what little kids were capable of," Carl admitted.

Carl Watkins sincerely appreciated his time at the school and being treated and readily accepted as one of the team. Assisting Archie had meant the world to him. Never knowing his real father and suffering horrendously at the hand of an abusive stepdad, he had never been befriended by a nurturing male. It also explained how easy it had been for Carl to feel a part of other types of alliances whether they were good for him or not. Carl would never forget how Archie took him under his wing and treated him like something special. It felt good and made the big guy think he could do about anything he put his mind to. Archie thoroughly appreciated time spent with the young students, and Carl was like any one of those children, only a whole lot bigger. Big as a bear with a tender heart to match, if opportunities came his way Carl would go far in becoming an upstanding member in any community.

"Mr. Wilson, it's kinda hard to put into words how much the time you've spent with me has meant. I never knew a man like you. How you treated me is something I will never forget," Big Carl said.

Archie's father had been a wonderful man. Each day Archie had with his parents was the best gift a child could have received. Archie grew up feeling loved and valued, and he knew his parents were always there for him. It would be years before Archie realized that not all families were like his. He didn't know any different. But as he got older, he realized that one of the greatest gifts his father had given him was the example of the love and respect he demonstrated to Archie's mother. It was a neat thing now to be able to pass along to Carl some of those special things Archie's dad had done for him.

"Hey, no problem, my big man. I had a good teacher. I have enjoyed our time together as well. If ever I had been blessed with a son, I could only have hoped he would have possessed a heart as big as yours," said Archie.

"That means a lot coming from you, Mr. Wilson. You've taught me a lot that I didn't even know I needed to learn," Carl said.

"You have many talents, and I hope you keep developing those woodworking skills you displayed for the school. You can do whatever you put your mind to, Carl. Your helping me out made a tremendous difference! We all appreciated your willingness to do whatever needed to be done," said Archie. "And by the way, women notice and are particularly grateful for such actions, if you know what I mean," Archie said with a wink.

"I hear you. I can definitely see that," Carl said, grinning back.

"And what are you two sharing that would put such smugness on your faces?" Faye curiously observed from a short distance.

"Oh, just man-to-man stuff, Miss Faye," said Carl. "You know how that goes."

"You two look pretty tight," Faye commented.

"We are, and this friendship is solid," said the Arch.

Carl beamed.

Looking from the outside in, everything appeared lighthearted and nonchalant, normal conversation after a successful production among the staff. But with a tremendous amount of work, sweat, and tears behind them, this marked the beginning of the end for Fiesta School and its dedicated team. Everyone knew it. Maybe it would be a win-win for Faye, Nola, and Josie eventually. But it would not be good for the community. They would lose an outstanding school, a brilliant director, and an exemplary staff dedicated to the education of young preschoolers.

As folks began heading for the doors, students were still in their glory, high-fiving and giggling with each other. Everyone was having a ball, and nobody wanted the evening to end. But the time was nearing to ring the final bell for probably the last time. Faye didn't have the heart to do it, and quietly asked Nola if she would perform the honor. Nola suggested staff stand together, side by side, and with lumps in their throats and stinging tears in their eyes, they took turns ringing the bell. It was a bittersweet moment, and they all wondered, what on God's green earth happens next?

18

CONTEMPLATIONS UNEXPECTED

When it looks like the sun isn't going to shine
any more, God puts a rainbow in the clouds.
Each one has the possibility, the responsibility, the
probability to be the rainbow in the clouds.

Maya Angelou

AFTER SATURDAY EVENING'S show, everyone (with the exception of Archie) attended Second Baptist Church per Ellie and Del's invitation. With dinner following at the Prices' home, Nola knew what to expect: a Southern-cooked meal second to none. She spoke with Ellie, offering to bring several of her finest dishes. Ellie of course said absolutely not, that this was their pleasure and that they were to bring only themselves. So, while the school had been working up to the last minute getting ready for the production, Ellie had been busy preparing a meal worthy of Hallelujah standards. Carl had come to understand that "Hallelujahs" was synonymous with fabulous food and plenty of it. He had been fascinated from the first time Josie affectionately spoke of her Auntie and the group. Carl had learned from working in the prison kitchen the importance of the abundance of good food and how to present it. It became a game to try and stretch basic ingredients while inventing new and different results. Big Carl worked hard to please his prison peers, and when serving always double-blessed as many as possible. Studying cookbooks in his free hours, Carl had hoped to find a job in line with his abilities and imagination once his incarceration was over, but Sand Haven proved to have little to offer. Working in a restaurant where piggy caps were a must fell below his expectations, but needing a job, Carl gratefully accepted the placement attained through church connections. Someday he hoped to be in a position to live out his passion while at the same time using his cooking skills for some type of service to others. The one thing Big Carl recognized was his need to help others, and he valued the insights he had gleaned during his imprisonment. About to have dinner at the Prices' and being served exquisite Southern foods was a double bonus in his book. Carl was on cloud nine.

Josie, too, was pleased as punch and looking forward to this time together surrounded by her chosen family and friends. Ellie and Del were family in Josie's book, and she was thankful for all they had done and given her. She loved them dearly.

Eventually, Josie would need to start figuring out her options, seriously contemplating what she might be doing in the near future. Everyone presumed that Faye would choose to close up shop without putting up a fuss. Something had changed inside her head and heart, which Josie assumed she would discuss with them when she was ready. Josie had promised Auntie Birdie she'd be calling after the noon meal with several things to share. The Challenge's success was a victory for everyone involved, but it was now completed and the school would be closing. In fact, it was Faye's intention to close the school the following week, on the last day of their school year. Josie felt her work in Sand Haven was "officially" completed. She still wanted to go home, but it was more complicated now with the deep feelings she had developed for her friends, compounded by the loss of Pearl. On a monetary level Josie Bee no longer expected or needed financial support from the Hallelujahs and felt good about that. They had given her plenty and could use their monies to help someone else in need. The check from Pearl was more than enough to carry Josie's current expenses until she figured out what she was doing next, and then some. The scheduled phone conversation with Auntie Birdie was sadly overdue. Josie Bee looked forward to talking with her beloved Auntie and catching up with whatever was going on back home. She hadn't been so much out of the loop as she had been sitting primarily in her *own* loop.

The guests' arrival at the Price home felt to Josie more like a homecoming. There was lighthearted chatter, with dinner expectations running high. It was enough for today not knowing what tomorrow would bring. As Auntie Birdie would have said while feverishly shaking her index finger, "Tomorrow will take care of itself, so let it alone and allow it to do its job." In principle it sounded fine, but in application it was more difficult. How they were going to fit into the movement of change was puzzling at best and unpredictable at worst. Auntie popped back into Josie's mind. "Oh, ye of little faith." Had she not learned a single thing? And what about the faith of that tiny mustard seed she always heard about?

Putting her thoughts and those of Auntie Birdie aside, Josie knew only that she was really hungry. On the verge of experiencing an ultimate down-South meal, her immediate physical and spiritual needs would be met in the best way possible.

For Nola, too, the aromas drifting out of the kitchen prompted memories of being back home. Food from the South provided nourishment for the soul and touched her in the depths of her very being. With eyes closed, Nola drifted back home, and in those few moments she was at peace.

Josie saw her face and knew just what she was thinking. There continued to be an unspoken connection between Nola and Josie Bee. Neither one of them shared the specifics of their upbringing in light of the violence and fear that came with growing up in the South. Sometimes there was purposeful silence in order not to dig up old ghosts. It was what was not said that spoke volumes. Josie felt the pull of Birmingham tugging on her heart, releasing memories that were good while suppressing those that were too painful to let out.

"Where are you two? Are you in the same place?" Faye gently

prodded Nola and Josie. "You have the same kind of look on your faces, I'm jealous," Faye playfully whined.

"Don't worry, we wouldn't go anywhere without you, Miss Faye! Promise!" Josie said with a Girl Scout finger pledge.

"You never made it into Scouts, Miss Josie, so that doesn't count. Don't you remember telling us about that, dear? A Brownie flunky," Faye teased.

"No time for that as we best get to the kitchen and earn our keep," Josie hollered over her shoulder as she trotted off. There was quite a spread laid out: platters of pork chops stuffed with apples and onions, Dixie chicken shortcakes with fresh mushrooms, and scalloped sweet potatoes with pineapple. There was enough food for a small army. Still to come were bowls of mashed potatoes, sautéed corn, candied yams, fried okra and tomatoes, and of course, creamy pork gravy. The raisin and buttermilk biscuits, corn sticks, orange-fruit nut bread, and cracklin' bread lining the elongated glass trays were almost too pretty to eat. My oh my, Ellie had outdone herself. Dishes of butter pickles, deviled eggs, and candied beets completed the feast. Standing at the bountiful table with the others, Josie painfully felt the absence of Pearl. Her sister would have enjoyed this gathering of chosen family and friends, the time of sharing and being together. And Pearl's presence would have made this celebration perfect.

As if on cue, Ellie reentered the room with a flowered bowl of creamed peas and pearl onions, which was Pearl's all-time favorite vegetable dish, a fact that Josie had shared with the Prices the first time she had peas in their home. Thinking the dish had been named in her honor, the good girl Pearl always ate her peas and pearl onions first. Every single one of them. After all, her name began P-e-a . . . They had come to grow on Josie too, even though she had spit them out as a youngster. Surprisingly, it was exactly what Josie needed, and she thanked Ellie for her thoughtfulness in acknowledging Pearl. While still standing, Del asked that they take one another's hands and together thank God for His love and grace in bringing them together. With a chorus of hearty amens, everyone sat down to the much-anticipated celebration.

Josie looked up and down the length of the extended table of eight.

After Pearl passed, Josie had felt like an orphan. But actually she had never really been alone. Every person at this table had been there for her. They understood things Josie hadn't even figured out. God had put together this ensemble of love and support, and Josie Bee was full of gratitude. Josie wondered how many more times she would sit at the Price table sharing a meal. She had a sticky lump in her throat. She feared her strong sense of belonging here might later become a sad sense of longing. Here she finally fit in and had found a place and *knew* it was hers. It was something she hadn't expected, nor could she have known how good it would feel to be wanted and accepted for who she was.

Pushing the thoughts aside, Josie vowed to melt into the moment and stop worrying about what was coming next. These people were her community. She loved each person in a mighty way, and they loved her right back. Josie had gained some valuable insights to her character, and yet none of these folks tried to "fix" her. They let Josie be Josie.

Carl chuckled and said he was thinking about getting a bus ticket to go South so he could eat food like this on a daily basis. Nola commented that his waistline would not be able to contend with his desire to overeat, which could be problematic for him.

"Hey Bro, that would make you bigger than you are now," Josie said playfully.

"Those are the kinds of problems I could only dream of having," Big Carl shot back with a wide grin.

After the meal, Paula and Patsy were eager to pitch in clearing the table. Dessert was next, with three choices: black walnut cake with creamy chocolate icing, old-fashioned bread pudding with vanilla sauce (on this occasion omitting the traditional whiskey flavoring), or Grandma's deep-dish apple pie. Although stuffed to the gills, no one wanted to take a chance at offending Ellie. She had spent countless hours preparing her best to serve this circle of loved ones. It was decided wholeheartedly they would need to sample all three options.

After desserts and coffee, the ladies put together doggie bags for those willing to aid in reducing the leftovers. With many hands pitching in to take food and tidy up, the kitchen was neat as a pin in no time at all. Carl finished off the efforts by sweeping the floor and taking out the trash, as it was his pleasure to do whatever he could to express the thankfulness he literally felt in the pit of his stomach. He, too, felt validated, not to mention stuffed like a big Thanksgiving turkey!

With everything finished, Faye and Nola announced they were heading out. The ladies had arranged two plates of leftovers for Archie, who had been invited but regretfully needed to decline. Even Carl mentioned missing his new friend.

Anticipating meeting for breakfast the following week, Archie and Carl planned on routinely staying in touch. Big Carl offered to give Archie cooking lessons in exchange for woodworking instruction. The two men discussed possibly starting a small birdhouse business, complementing Archie's woodworking talents and Carl's flair for detail. Pearl, with her love for enlightening spaces, would have appreciated Big Carl's desire to make things colorful and interesting.

Carl decided to stay afterward to help Del complete a project he was working on in the garage. Ellie proclaimed it was naptime and, after saying her goodbyes, headed directly to her room. Patsy and Paula planned on spending the afternoon reading. Josie Bee, for her part, expected to spend a lengthy period of time talking to her Auntie and eating her fair amount of crow. Ready to tackle the conversation, Josie went to make the call.

Auntie Birdie picked up the phone on its first ring. It was wonderful hearing her greeting. Josie realized that she took it for granted that Auntie would always be there to answer. She had never considered the possibility of this not being the case. Yet another thing taken for granted.

"Hi Auntie Birdie, is that—is that really you?" Suddenly hearing the sound of her Auntie's voice, Josie felt hers breaking up. "I am so glad to speak with you, Auntie. I've really missed you." Before Josie realized it, she had launched into a one-sided monologue apologizing for the many times she had failed to contact her Auntie, include her in conversations, or share the important things going on in both their lives. Out of breath and between tears, Josie paused, and Auntie Birdie immediately interrupted her.

"I need you to come home, baby girl. Please, Josie Bee, it's time to come back to me."

Josie heard this strong woman breaking down and sobbing. It struck Josie that her Auntie seldom cried. But she wept at Daddy's and Momma's funeral, and again after Pearl died. And it hit Josie hard. She got it. There had been so much loss in the past four years for everyone in their lives. Auntie Birdie was probably the only person in Josie's world who could fully understand her grief. Losing Pearl was life's greatest shock and, for Josie Bee, a hundred times harder to accept than the loss of her parents. But Auntie knew. She understood her niece's pain, as she had lost her baby sister too. Instead of reaching out in unity, Josie had closed up tight, building a wall of silence and separation. She hadn't even considered how difficult the loss of her older sister, Gertie, must have been for her Auntie. Josie could only imagine how deeply Pearl's death had devastated her. Loss on top of loss, she had to be so worn down, and where was Josie? What faraway planet had she been visiting?

"Please forgive me, Auntie, I never meant to shut you out," Josie implored. "I love you so much. There are times I think I can't continue on without Pearl. And I know how much you loved her. I'm sorry for you too." Josie was relieved to have shared her deepest feelings of sorrow, fear, and regret. Auntie Birdie let her sob, allowing her to release her pent-up feelings before speaking again.

"Come home, Josephine. It's where you belong," Auntie whispered. "It's time."

"Wow, I was hoping to hear those words some time ago. Many things have changed since then, haven't they, Auntie?" Josie said.

"I can't argue with that. I know we are both exhausted presently, but when we can reconvene, I have something to share. I need you to take some time to think about it, but right now it is top secret and something we must keep between ourselves," Auntie Birdie said.

"You have my ear, Auntie. I'm curious. How about I give you a call in the next day or so when I have some phone time alone. And maybe we'll both be more settled. Would that work?"

"The sooner the better, Josephine," replied her Auntie Birdie. "And remember, for the time being it is strictly confidential."

The days following the best talent show ever in Fiesta's five years of existence were busy and full. The school was much like an active hive with buzzing kids weaving here and there, continuously turning to their Queen Bee for one thing or another. If Faye Lewis said anything once, she most likely said it a dozen times or more. Staff had been sending things home for weeks with the end of school just around the corner. Now down to the nitty-gritty, watching the kids clear their desks was quite emotional for the Fiesta trio. All three women got choked up from time to time. It was priceless how much the items in the little desks meant to the students. They wanted to keep everything, eventually placing their things in the big brown bags that had their names written on them, which were compliments of Marshy's Market. It was like a major close-out where everything needed to go.

Helping the kids pack up was emotional but not difficult. The challenge was then sorting through the accumulation of large items scattered throughout the school. There were a variety of tables, chairs, and cabinets, not to mention several bookcases and a small army of desks. In fact, Faye didn't know if she would ever have a need for her beloved rolltop desk in a teaching setting ever again, or any of the other furniture for that matter. But Faye was sure she would take Archie's big clock with her wherever she went. It had meant the world from day one when she was first gifted the enormous tick-tock. Frankly, Faye just had no idea what to keep nor what to part with because she didn't have the foggiest idea what she was going to be doing next. Not one single clue. No notion whatsoever. It was bewildering. However, there was still much that needed to be done.

The next biggest issue at hand was where to place the gigantic sprawling props used in the talent show. Parkwood Baptist generously offered to temporarily store them, strongly suggesting they also wouldn't mind acquiring the pieces permanently. The bustling church was known for its intricate plays and talent-filled musicals. They were confident that they could put to use every single object handcrafted by the talented Archie Wilson. Nola immediately refused to part with her cherished magnolia tree, insisting it be the first thing carefully removed from the auditorium. Now it sat in the front room of the house that was no longer considered a school. Faye had placed twinkle lights on its upswept silver branches, adding a lovely warm glow to the space now filled with sadness and uncertainty. Faye chose to view the tiny flickers as snippets of hope—hope for what, she did not know.

THREE WEEKS LATER

Edna Higgins was currently the talk of the town. She had finally lost her mind. Edna was not the son her father had originally hoped for, but she sure was acting like a madman now, exhibiting horrendously erratic conduct at Marshy's Market. And no less on a hectic busy Saturday morning. The busiest day of the week, and she was creating a serious disturbance.

"Hey Boom-Boom, Boom-Boom Lewis, over here," she yelled, ridiculously waving her arms like a bumbling traffic cop.

Already the center of attention she continued, "You and your entourage know the way, center stage. C'mon now, Director, let's get a move on!" Edna shouted.

"For Pete's sake, now what?" Faye said in disbelief. "What are you doing, Mrs. Higgins? Give it a rest, dear," as she continued walking through the produce section. Edna looked like someone who had sipped too much happy juice. Edna was combative, trying to stop Faye from moving away from the unwanted attention and confrontation.

"Not so fast there, sweet cheeks. I want to have a few words with you," Edna boisterously announced as she grabbed hold of Faye.

"If you don't remove that chubby stranglehold of yours off *my* arm," Faye said, "I swear I will take a swing at you, Edna. You are a miserable cluck, and it would be my pleasure to knock you out." Faye was horrified she had allowed the ugly white witch of the Midwest to get under her skin. She had no intentions of striking her but found satisfaction in throwing the words out there, hoping they would stick in her foggy mind. After all, Faye Louise Lewis was a classy woman with fine manners, and a catfight at the local market was beneath her. Totally.

Before Faye had time to make a decision regarding what to do next, Archie was there and standing between them. Nola arrived then too, and patted his shoulder, thanking him for getting there so quickly.

After she caught a glimpse of Mrs. Higgins marching through the store, she knew it was not a coincidence. Nola asked the manager if she could use the store phone and, mumbling something about an emergency, made the call to Archie.

Aware of Faye's Saturday-morning routine, Edna had gone to Marshy's to set up an ambush in order to retaliate for the talent-show fiasco and to flat-out embarrass her. Even though Edna felt she won the showdown, just about everyone had recently turned on her, regretful that they had supported her allegations in the first place.

Normally Faye would have done her shopping alone. Today, however, Nola and Josie had accompanied her with plans for the three of them to go out for a late breakfast afterward. Nola needn't have worried. Faye seemed more than capable of handling the wildcat. Edna had met her match, lady or not.

Stepping forward, Archie tried to disperse the group of onlookers that had collected, hoping for a good brawl between the two women. "That's all, folks, nothing more happening here. Have a nice weekend and remember, Marshy's is *the* only place to shop," he said, covering both the grocery's motto and the crowd's shopping preference at the moment.

Once again, for the second time in six weeks, Archie took the mean Edna Higgins out of the fray, speaking to her calmly but sternly. Erupting into a verbal rage, Edna hit the roof after Archie Wilson suggested that he would prefer driving her home in his car.

"Why would you do that?" she asked.

"How about, *you* are not fit to drive at this point," Archie suggested.

"You think I'm the drinker here," Edna stated in disbelief.

"Maybe you are fit to drive or maybe not. Either way, I feel it would be safer for others if I were to drive you home, Mrs. Higgins," Archie said reasonably.

"Or what, you stupid man?" Edna hissed.

"I will have Mr. Marsh call the authorities and tell them it is very possible that you have consumed a heavy amount of alcohol, leading to obnoxious and unpredictable behavior," said Archie. "And that you *are* dangerous!"

"You wouldn't dare!"

"Just try me, Edna. We're going now, or I will have Miss Lewis get Manager Marsh's attention. I think we both know how interesting that could be." Archie couldn't help but smirk. As did the girls, all three of them. Mr. Marsh couldn't keep his eyes off Faye on a normal day, let alone one filled with commotion.

Josie placed her hand over her mouth to stifle herself. Oh boy, this might be the best thing ever. She was actually kind of hoping Edna would continue making a stink.

"Here we go again. It's your choice. You have ten seconds, or I will make it for you," Archie threatened.

"Fine. Peachy. Fine," she mumbled. Edna couldn't stand Martin Marsh and vice versa. The slithering snake would side with Boom-Boom, that much she knew.

"Byeeeeeeee, Mrs. Higgins. Have yourself a nice day, do you hear me, sweetie?" Faye cooed as Archie directed the flabbergasted menace out of the supermarket.

Faye continued to shop, picking up several bottles of Tom's and a couple boxes of Cheez-Its. There was a surplus of sugar and Kool-Aid at the house, a reminder of the absence of the kids. Nola decided to follow Archie and Edna to the parking lot just to make sure Edna didn't have a change of mind. If Nola had been making the decisions, she would have left Edna Higgins in Marshy's sputtering like a fool. But Archie was a decent guy and only wanted to get Edna home safely and be done with her. It was the kind of excitement he did not relish. One thing Archie knew for sure was that if you struck at one of the Fiesta ladies, you'd have a handful of trouble with the remaining two. It would be a dirty shame to see the dynamic trio broken up when they were so good together. But life sometimes worked that way. You had no idea what was around the corner. And Archie was as curious as the rest to see what was in store for all of them.

Finally finishing up on the last aisle of the grocery store, Faye and Josie spotted Larry Finch and Alice White in the back of Marshy's picking up a few items.

"Oh, my goodness, can you believe that?" said Josie, pointing at the two.

"It's not polite to point, Josie! Put your finger down, dear, immediately please. But ya know, I did think it was a bit odd that Larry was at the talent show. Now it's beginning to make some sense," Faye remarked.

Looking at each other the two smiled. It was nice seeing the possibility of a little romance budding. Alice was a free woman. Everyone felt sorry for what she had weathered. Alice White had been granted a speedy divorce from Frank, mostly due to his extremely rapid departure into the penal system. Alice certainly deserved some overdue happiness, and both Josie and Faye hoped whatever it was she wanted, it would work out well for her and the kids.

After their initial conversation the day after the talent show, Josie got mighty curious about what it was Auntie Birdie might be wanting to share confidentially with her. That was the part that really started getting her interest up. This was a first. She couldn't recall a single time when she and Auntie had truly shared a secret or a confidence. So, what on earth could Auntie Birdie be wanting to tell her? Getting the best of her curiosity, Josie chose sooner than later to contact her Auntie. Less than a day after their last phone call, Josie reached out.

"Auntie, it's me," Josie said with unmasked excitement in her voice.

"For goodness sakes, I didn't expect such a prompt return call, Josephine," said Birdie. "I must admit I recognize and appreciate your timeliness. Thank you, young lady."

"You're welcome. Your parting words when we last spoke were tantalizing, Auntie. You're not trying to pull the wool over my eyes, now, are you?" Josie asked.

"I really don't have the time or energy to mislead you. Josie, I have a very serious situation to share with you—that is, if you have the time," Birdie teased.

"That's pretty funny, Auntie! As you know, I'm all about having an excess of time these days," Josie chuckled. She was finding that her Auntie Birdie had a dry but fairly quick sense of humor. In their past experiences, neither one of them had felt humorously charmed by the other.

"I am going to take that as my cue to begin what it is I want to share with you. So please bear with me and just listen. Try not to react, and for crying out loud, don't start saying 'no.' That's not going to fly with me, Josie. Those are the ground rules."

"Gotcha, Auntie. C'mon now, spill your beans," Josie impatiently urged.

Berniece Thomas continued, describing in detail the building on of a designated preschool addition at Rosewood Street Baptist Church back home in Birmingham. Birdie went on to describe the need for innovative and progressive quality education for their community's youngest children. In meeting the needs of youngsters awaiting kindergarten, they could also meet the demands of working parents in providing a safe and reliable place for their kids. Auntie Birdie's excitement was obvious and her commitment to this vision of service undeniable. The church wanted to reach out in a new ministry toward meeting the needs of young people with families in their church and community. Birdie and the Hallelujahs were prayerfully, squarely behind offering the new positions to what soon appeared to be the former staff at Fiesta School. Understanding that it was a certainty that Josie's school was closing, they thought it a wonderful opportunity to have the experienced staff consider relocation to Rosewood. Berniece had continually shared what information she had gleaned, primarily from Ellie and Del, with her church group and Board. And she had understood why Josie would be reluctant to give this information over to the Hallelujahs, but it was Birdie's responsibility to have a handle on what was going on in Sand Haven. She didn't need to hear it from Josie. After months of discussions, planning, and the raising of funds, the educational dream once only imagined became a bona fide reality. Things were moving forward and now was the time to consider its workforce. The Hallelujahs had been led to encourage the church to think outside the box and contemplate the group from Indiana as a base for creating something unpredictably unique.

When Auntie Birdie had finished her spiel, Josie was more than blown away. She was interested. Yet she couldn't imagine something like this working out, but it was still quite an idea. For now, she didn't know how to process what she had just heard.

"I know this is a lot to take in all at once. Sift through it, Josie," she heard Auntie say.

"Oh wow, I really don't know what to say," Josie mumbled.

"That is probably a good thing. For now. Let's reconvene when you have had some time to collect your thoughts. I am sure there will be many more questions, or at least I hope so, Josephine. This is a serious responsibility and as you can see, not to be taken lightly or without a good amount of consideration and, of course, prayer," admonished Birdie.

After this conversation, Josie and her Auntie were back and forth on the phone nonstop. The questions came and the answers were deliberated. Whispering and being somewhat secretive, Ellie's sense of playfulness got the best of her.

"What on earth could the two of you be cooking up?" Ellie asked Josie.

"For me to know and you to find out," Josie said, throwing back one of her old juvenile jabs. Josie didn't even have an inkling that Ellie knew much more than she was letting on. "I will tell you one thing. It is a lot easier working with Auntie than against her."

Josie was enjoying the camaraderie she was sharing with her Auntie Birdie. Reconnecting in heart and deed felt right, moving the desires of both their hearts forward in a surprising way. Josie Bee had a creative mind but knew she couldn't have put together a package like this. Maybe not even in a lifetime. If nothing else, Josie was beginning to see Auntie as the incredibly productive person the community had always recognized and adored. She was on a mission, and the only person who could stop her was giving her the right of way, at least according to Berniece Thomas.

Birdie had shared how difficult it had become to accomplish their goals and tasks in the church kitchen, noting that the Hallelujahs were getting older and experiencing the "joys" of mature aging. More and more of them were needing to take time off for family needs and appointments. It seemed to be one thing after another. The Circle really needed younger members, "but today's youth are busy doing their own thing," lamented Auntie Birdie. "Then after that, they seem to settle down, start having children, and don't have the time or energy to do what we need to do. Do you have any ideas, Josie?"

"Not really, Auntie. Not off the top of my head."

"Well, Josephine, do you think you might be able to dig a little deeper and get to the bottom of your head?"

Josie told her Auntie she'd work on it and promised to get back to her later on that one.

Of greater interest to Josie was the progress being made on the development of the new addition at the church back home. Birdie and the Hallelujah Circle had been hosting buffets and fundraisers to bring in money for the project. Feeling it would enhance the mission of Rosewood Street Baptist Church and serve the community in new ways, the church leadership had high hopes for the added space and plans for occupancy. Auntie made it a point to keep Josie in-the-loop regarding specific progress being made towards moving forward. She requested that Josie pray for the ministry and reiterated that God was in charge and His timing would be perfect.

Weekly evening meals continued with Nola and Faye, and were always fun and festive. One evening, when Nola left to take a phone call from her sister back in Mississippi, Josie finally got the nerve to ask Faye about Penny White. Afraid the conversation could blow up in her face, Josie all but chickened out.

"Um . . . would you mind if we skip back to a subject we have kinda talked about before and quite bluntly it didn't go all that well?" asked Josie.

"What do you want to know, Josie? Did you suddenly forget what you have so desperately been wanting to find out?" Faye asked.

"This is really hard, and I wasn't eavesdropping, but I overheard Alice White thanking you at the talent show for being in her corner and working with Officer Finch." Josie went on to explain her puzzlement, wondering what she could possibly be missing.

"Josie, I agreed to discuss this with no one but Nola, and it was for your own safety and well-being that you not know what Larry and I were up to. With every single passing day, I was worried sick that something would happen to Penny. Alice had tried once to get away from Frank, and he all but killed her. We just had to be extremely careful. I knew I looked pathetic and weak. I could see it in your eyes. You thought I was more concerned with my school, my livelihood, than getting help for Penny. But I believed in you, Josie, and I trusted you would know the full story sooner or later."

"I am an awful person! How could I doubt you? I lashed out, I accused you, and you took it, Faye," Josie cried. "You deserved better, and I am so sorry." Josie dropped her face into her hands, shaking like a leaf.

"You didn't know, and I couldn't tell you. I knew you truly cared for Penny, and I loved you for that, dear Josie," Faye said. And then she giggled. "I thought Nola was going to pop her cork. She was equally invested in you and loves you every bit as much as I do. It may have been even harder on her. I knew if we were truly friends, we'd get this worked out at some point, and here we are."

"Can you ever forgive me, Faye?"

"Of course. That's what friends do. I adore you, Josie," Faye said.

Josie was beyond thankful to have this burden lifted and behind her. It would have continued to tie her up in knots. It was the only thing that didn't seem to fit with Faye's selfless character when it came to the kids. It was always about them. It was what made Faye and Nola special. How could she consider leaving them? There was so much to learn. Josie had just started trusting them. It would be like losing her sister all over, or her parents. Would Faye and Nola consider inviting Josie to join them, or did they have plans to go their separate ways? What was God's plan, and who was going where?

Things back on the church home front were moving forward. Everything appeared to be in order, the i's dotted and the t's crossed and ready to go. Josie felt as though she would burst. She now wanted to share the complete game plan with the ladies, hoping the news would be well-received and that they would consider what it was she could offer them. Maybe Josie was too excited and overly optimistic about the results of the many weeks of prayers and intercessions. What she needed was the support of others, those who could contribute to and honor the mission of Rosewood and its vision for the future. Every time she thought about it, Josie's mind tumbled, and there were butterflies in her stomach. They needed a come-to-Jesus meeting immediately. Oh boy, the Hallelujahs would have loved that statement!

It was time to ask Ellie and Del to do what they did best: host another dinner. This time there would be nine in attendance, and something simple would be ideal, the sooner the better. The Prices were gracious and curious about the details but heartily agreed to go light, serving gumbo and fresh-baked bread with Ellie's cinnamon-honey butter. Next, Josie called Faye and Nola and invited them to the upcoming dinner. Eager to find out what was so important, they readily accepted. Josie next dialed up Archie, knowing he would accept, if for no other reason than to get a good, homecooked meal after having to miss the last one. Josie didn't expect him to respond to her pitch, but being a part of their inner circle, she did not want to exclude him either. Big Carl was always hungry and a definite shoo-in. And you just couldn't predict what the big teddy bear might or might not do.

The guest list was completed and confirmed. Glory hallelujah and roll those saints in. Josie was higher than a kite on a blustery day in March. Two days later and with several calls in between from an anxious Auntie Birdie, the guests arrived ahead of schedule, curious to see what Josie Bee was up to. The seafood gumbo's aroma permeated the house along with the breads baking in the oven, setting the stage and suggesting something wonderful was about to happen. Josie insisted that they eat right away so they could then get down to the unresolved business at hand.

"Josie, you are about to explode, so go ahead and let the secretive cat out of your bulging bag," Faye urged her.

"Nope, dinner first and then we can chat. No dessert afterward unless I get my way," she threatened. "I'm serious about that. I just can't know for sure how this is going to play out. I don't know if I am more scared or more excited. I guess afraid for sure. In fact, I'm scared to death. I wanted to tell you what was in the works earlier, but there were no guarantees, and I couldn't make any promises or disappoint you if things didn't work out. No more info. Eat please!"

The shrimp and crab gumbo, hearty and spicy, hit the spot. Filled with the delicious combination of flavorful spices, bell peppers, celery, and onions, the tomato-based soup was out of this world. Sourdough and butter-garlic breads complemented the main dish. Josie couldn't help herself and casually remarked, "Wouldn't it be great to eat like this every day of the week?"

Carl could only say, "No way, sister! That would be a sin of some sort. But that's my dream," he said, flashing a big grin.

Josie looked around the table knowing that what she was looking at, in one way or another, would be changing. She was delighted that Archie was present too. Looking at Patsy and Paula and Ellie and Del, Josie realized how deeply she adored this family of four. Where would she be without them? Nola with her guiding ways and warmth touched Josie's spirit, reminding her of Auntie Birdie, and feeling strangely familiar from that first encounter. Faye, a sister at heart, was a cherished friend, and Josie trusted her. Carl was the brother she never had, who had her back no matter how crazy the ideas in her head. These folks were her community, her family. Josie cared about them so much and wanted to take each one with her wherever she went for the rest of her life. Realistically she knew that the only possibilities for what she was offering would be restricted to Faye, Nola, and maybe Big Carl.

"Okay, let's get started. Is it necessary to start at the very beginning?" Josie teased.

"Come on, little sis, get to the point please!" Carl begged.

"How would you all like to have a fresh beginning in a new place with an opportunity designed just for you, created with each of you in mind? It would be like taking the Fiesta on the road, sort of like a churchy traveling circus. Only this road leads back to Birmingham. We—meaning my Auntie Birdie and her sidekicks, the Hallelujahs— would like to start a school that will serve to help out young mothers who attend the church and for those in the immediate community. Not sure exactly how many students there will be or what the school will be called. It's all still up for grabs."

Josie paused as everyone absorbed the information thus far.

"Did I mention the Hallelujahs would be providing the snacks and meals?" Josie asked. "Great news for you, Miss Nola, right? And Director Faye, you would continue on in the same capacity with a handpicked staff at your fingertips. Carl, would you consider blessing the Hallelujah Circle with that special teddy-bear personality that defines you and your heart? Of course, they want to see you in action. I have bragged you up so much they can hardly believe that you are a real person, and I am not kidding! Archie, we know this would most likely not work for you, but being part of who we are and what we do together, you could not be excluded. You are amazing! And give me your word, you'll all at least think about it. Pinky promise?" Josie excitedly asked as she shook her little finger. "And there you have it in a nutshell. I am available for any and all questions. Please take a day or so before responding. The jobs are yours if you want them, if you're interested. But we have to give an answer within the next week or soon after, as things are rapidly progressing at this point."

Josie giggled and added, "Any way you think we could reconvene tomorrow night? Is that too soon? Not soon enough?"

Seeing the nodding of heads, Josie confirmed they would meet back for desserts the next evening. Ellie let everyone know there was an abundance of soup left over and if it was okay with them, she would gladly heat it up again for the following get-together.

Josie had a hard time figuring out what Faye and Nola thought of her proposal but could clearly see the wheels turning in Big Carl's head. Around and around and around they went. He looked more certain than anyone else. Nobody jumped up and down and said, "That's perfect, sign me up!" But it was agreed. Tomorrow each would come with an answer, but once again it was what Josie didn't see coming that would blow her away. Leave it up to God to do something like that, the thing no one could have expected, not even in a thousand years.

19

GOING HOME

Through many dangers, toils and snares,
I have already come;
'Tis grace hath brought me safe thus far,
And grace will lead me home.

John Newton

THANKING JESUS FOR waking her up, Josie sprang out of bed and headed directly to the phone. Knowing Auntie Birdie was currently the one sitting on pins and needles waiting for information, Josie Bee wanted to let her know where things stood. But at this point everything was in a holding pattern. Anxious but in an upbeat mood, Josie knew her Auntie had been up for hours with God and strong coffee. Considerable amounts of both.

"Good morning, Josephine," the voice on the other end said.

"How'd you know it was me?" Josie playfully asked.

"Aren't you amusing, dear," said Auntie Birdie, chuckling to herself.

Josie knew Auntie B. didn't find her particularly funny on any given day. "What is up with all this 'Josephine' stuff?"

"You are an activist for the kingdom now, and I couldn't be

prouder!" her Auntie replied.

"Yeah, I guess Momma must have had an inkling about that."

Josie certainly was not an exotic beauty, nor did she have the voice of an exquisite songbird. She was not Josephine Baker, but she was trying to become the best version of herself, and that was all she guessed she was required to do. She was trying to become the woman God had created her to be. This was good news for Auntie Birdie, although Josie Bee would always be that special someone who tested her patience and forbearance. Pausing, Josie wondered whether her parents could peer down from heaven and catch glimpses of what was going on. She hoped that if they could peek down between the stars, they would see their youngest daughter trying to fulfill her destiny and sense she was moving in the right direction. Josie's parents, Pearl, and her deceased friends were never far from her thoughts, like a tug-of-war between who was here and who was there. She continued to want to bring honor to those loved ones who were no longer walking the earth but skipping down streets of gold. Pearl was always beside her. Josie didn't know if she'd ever be able to let go of her. Pearl never wanted to hold Josie back, not then and not now. So Josie continued to focus on what needed to be done to move forward, always conscious of what Pearl might think or might want her to do. But there were many times Josie wanted to curl up in a ball and cry until she needed a refill on tears. Josie didn't think she'd ever truly be at peace with Pearl's absence. She expected that the wound would always remain open in some way. Fortunately, Josie Bee had someone pushing her forward. Auntie Birdie intended to keep her challenged and accountable to boot. *Gotta love that,* Josie thought, half smiling to herself.

"Josie, are you purposefully keeping me in suspense?" Auntie asked, breaking into Josie's thoughts.

Ah, that was the Berniece Thomas Josie knew and loved. "No, ma'am! We met last evening as planned, and everyone needed time to think about the offer. I will have answers tonight. One way or another, we will know where we stand then," Josie confirmed.

"And you will call me the minute you know?" Auntie's tone was instructively firm. It was not a question but an expectation.

"Without delay, I promise." Josie prayed for the news they both desperately wanted. It was not enough to expect things to magically fall into her lap. She was clearly learning this through her formidable Auntie, that you keep opening doors until God closes them.

As she hung up the phone and made her way to the kitchen, Josie Bee conceded that she would miss Ellie Price tremendously. Like Dorothy told the cowardly lion in *The Wizard of Oz*, "I'm going to miss you most of all." Ellie had not been feeling well lately, which had sent warning bells ringing in Josie's ears. After glossing over Pearl's situation, Josie wanted to be more aware of others' circumstances, whatever they turned out to be or not to be. Either way, Josie was monitoring the situation. Ellie said it was nothing when Josie asked her several times about it, but in retrospect Josie could see she had been exhausted for weeks. It would be exactly like Ellie, as it had been with Pearl, not to want to be the cause of any unnecessary concern for others. Sometimes selfless people could scare the living daylights out of you when they tried so hard *not* to make you worry.

Josie wanted to check and make sure another mealtime wouldn't be too much on Ellie. Even Josie Bee was capable of reheating a pot of soup, and Nola would love the opportunity to assist. Josie went into the kitchen to see what she could do. Ellie was on her way to lie down for a few minutes before returning to the kitchen, explaining to Josie that she had slept fitfully through the night and just needed a quick twenty-minute cat nap. When Josie asked whether she was feeling up to hosting again, Ellie reassured her that she appreciated her concern but was looking forward to what the evening had in store for them.

You and me both, thought Josie Bee.

That was only one of the things Josie loved about her precious friend. Always encouraging and reassuring, Ellie never wanted to bother or trouble anybody. Yet Josie had not returned the favor, giving her plenty of fretful and uneasy moments over the past weeks and months. She surmised Ellie knew more than she was letting on. Ellie reminded Josie of her big sister, not the least reason being the fact that she watched out for her as Pearl had done. Her heart aching, Josie was coming to realize that leaving and loss were becoming a central theme in her life. With tentative steps forward and unexpected stumbles backward, the process was complicated and at times terribly painful. Why had Josie taken so long to recognize that the good times were there and not celebrated them more? Living in the moment could be a tricky thing. Sometimes finding joy was like looking for a needle in a haystack, but it is always in there somewhere. Trusting God and claiming His promises, Josie was beginning to think like one of the Hallelujahs. Another one of them thar hoots! Shaking her head, she couldn't help but chuckle to herself.

As late afternoon rolled around, Del put the heavy stockpot filled with seafood gumbo on top of the stove, preparing for round two. Somehow it smelled even better than the night before, and Ellie, feeling fine and perky after her little nap, hustled around the kitchen as usual. Arriving promptly, the friends warmly embraced. As the time of decision drew closer, Josie Bee began growing more insecure and anxious. In just the past year there had been goodbyes that had turned into permanent separations. Josie didn't know if she could handle another farewell, which was the part that frightened her the most about all of this. It made her feel vulnerable.

They gathered around the table and held hands. Del asked for God's blessing on the food. The gumbo was comforting and filling. Ellie made fresh cornbread baked to a golden brown with drizzled honey butter on top. Paula and Patsy concocted an interesting relish tray with celery and peanut butter and a side of cherry jam. Finishing dinner, the group jointly decided that dessert and coffee needed to wait until after the big pow-wow.

"Any volunteers? Who would like to share what's on their mind first?" Josie asked playfully, although she wasn't feeling very playful.

"That's so nice and polite, Josie," said Nola, flashing a grin, but quickly reassuming her poker face. At least her sense of humor, consistently dry, was still intact. "I'll be happy to go first," she continued. "Let me start by saying something very important: Alabama ain't no Mississippi. I always thought I would eventually go back to Mississippi to confront my fears and demons. But I have decided I see no ultimate glory in doing so and that they can remain in the closet. That being said, you can count me in. I will welcome returning to the South and closer to my kin. It is time for me to go back." Leaning forward, Nola whispered, "Thank you, baby girl," and her eyes told Josie she was more than ready to go.

"Oh, my goodness, thank you, Nola. Glory! I love you to pieces."

They were off to a good start, and Josie was flying high.

"Yes, Carl, you are next. You can put your hand down now. We're not in school, bro," Josie said, smiling. She was pretty sure he was going to say yes because he was visibly busting at the seams.

"This is the best thing to have ever happened to me, next to being introduced to you and Southern cookin'. Or should it be the other way around? Cooking hasn't been near as complicated as you, Josie Bee. So, this is how I see it, little sis. You know I'm not letting you go anywhere without me. Someone has to keep you outta trouble. I'm in too," Carl proudly announced, giving Josie two huge thumbs up and his trademark toothy grin.

"You're the best, Big Carl! I just knew you'd be in! But I'm warning you, those Hallelujahs are going to be all over you like flies on tar paper, fussin' and asking you to do everything they can conjure up under the sky. And it won't be an easy job to please that many old ladies—er, mature women—who are set in their ways. You will make that kitchen sizzle, bro, in a way it never has before."

Josie was ecstatic.

"Okay, Miss Faye Lewis, have we saved the best for last? What might you have to say? You're seldom at a loss for words," Josie sassed.

"Slow down, Miss Smarty-Pants. It's not quite as easy-peasy for me as it appears to be for these other fine but apparently gullible folks. They seem ready to fly the coop, but this has been my home, the first place I thought I could create and build on my own—no offense, Nola."

"None taken, my sweet girl," Nola mused.

"As most of you know, the school has been my saving grace, allowing me to grow in ways I had always dreamed and imagined. I truly thought I'd be here until the day I died. There are so many things I would miss deeply and so much more I wanted to accomplish. This is going to sound a bit corny, but I love walking to the sandbox at Cranston Park. I have done my best thinking, scheming, and visualizing there in the box, and it's only sweeter when the kids are there beside me. Their laughter and innocence have carried me to heights I never thought possible. I feel safe and contented. I am thrilled knowing

I have a next-door neighbor who watches out for me in a variety of wonderful ways. I adore you, Archie, and will forever be grateful for our friendship, which has been constant and genuine. Men like you are few and far between. You are irreplaceable. Mister George also means the world to me and doesn't appreciate changes to his world. A new environment might be too hard on him. I am totally attached to my little guy, and I can't chance losing him along the way."

Josie began feeling her heart sink, and she felt numb and shut down. Faye continued on.

"I thought I was secure in this community because of the school, and now I am unsettled and bewildered. On some level, I guess I always knew the attack on my character and principles had long been in the making. But the recognition that a number of the parents did not support the purpose of the preschool or what was constructively being taught at Fiesta was a crushing blow. It devastated my spirit and changed how I had come to view myself here in Sand Haven. How can we teach tolerance and respect in working out problems and conflicts when parents choose the opposite? How do kids understand relationships when the adults viciously turn on one another? True enough, it undermines us, but it is more confusing and destructive for our children. These parents didn't understand how badly we wanted to level the playing field for their kids. I ask myself, 'How is this even possible?' Not only with reading, numbers, languages, writing, and reading, but with character development and service to others, and many didn't even recognize what it is we have been focused on doing. Of equal importance, we've always wanted to prepare the hearts of the students for socialization and successful relationship building. Suddenly, I once again grasp the full force of feeling less than and devalued in the eyes of others. Josie, we have had this conversation. And Nola, you know exactly how this feels and the lingering harm it can do to one's spirit. We have been working on resolving our personal and past baggage, only to be kicked in the teeth and wrongly judged and dismissed. Deliberate and vicious condemnation without cause is not only morally wrong, it crushes our hearts. Talk about locusts swarming in and causing devastation and damage. Josie, you have opened my eyes to this analogy, and I can clearly see it. I feel it. I don't know exactly what this means, but I feel a tugging and longing to go to church, to discover your God. You were but a child when you departed Birmingham, and you weren't always sure of yourself, am I right about that?"

Josie nodded. She wasn't sure where this was heading. Locusts, church, God, her wavering ways and inexperience. It was a lot to take in.

"And yet you believed God had a conversation with you, a life-changing one. Pearl supported you, then your Auntie, followed by the Hallelujahs, and with childlike faith you accepted the Challenge. Or maybe you were roped into it? Either way, I am amazed that you left your safe haven and journeyed here. But when you hopped off that bus and arrived in a place not filled with Southerners, you did so with a ton of support. Those people back home had your back. And you stuck it out. That's really something, young lady. I was an adult when I carved out my new life, but you were still a developing young person with a lot on her shoulders. And just loooook at you now, Miss Johnson. Josie, I am so very, very proud of you," said Faye.

Josie's head was spinning now in the other direction. She never expected any of this.

"This was my comfort zone, and the stark truth is, it is no longer comfortable or suitable. God has placed His hands on every single one of us around this table."

Heads nodded.

"Nola has reminded me of this more times than I can count. I was constantly aware of Nola's belief in a sovereign God. She has a peace about her. Nola didn't shame or belittle me but let me discover and learn needed truths along the way. She has unconditionally loved me and has been my rock. I wanted to give you the same gift of being permitted to make mistakes, Josie, and to figure things out. That's what parents do for their children, and this chosen family is no different."

And then Faye paused.

Josie held her breath.

"Nola is ready to go. She loves a good adventure, and I guess I do too. I would very much appreciate this opportunity to start anew, so I will be going South with y'all."

"Really and truly?" Josie asked.

"Absolutely!" said Faye. "This confirms my growing decision to move on." She paused before continuing. "One of the difficult parts of leaving is not seeing my former charges grow up and witnessing their successes and gains. And it is also extremely difficult to let go of those who have come alongside to cheer and support me. Archie, I again thank you from the bottom of my heart. You have blessed me over the years, putting the salve of friendship on my various wounds. I will miss you terribly. Thank you for being my friend, for being Nola's friend, and for all you have done for the kids. You are loved by many." Unable to say the words out loud, squeezing Nola's outstretched hand for support, Faye silently mouthed the words, "I love you, friend."

Josie jumped right in, not realizing what Faye had just said to Archie.

"Ooooh, Faye, you have made me the happiest I can remember in quite a while," Josie said. "We need you so much, and I couldn't bear to leave you behind. I guess we need each other at this point in our chaotic lives. And by the way, this will give you an authentic opportunity to work on that Southern drawl of yours. Just sayin'."

Finding it his time to speak, Archie wanted to share a few sentiments as well. "My love and respect for each one of you runs deep. My feelings completely echo yours. I wish I were leaving with you, but of course it is not workable for me, and for that I am truly sorry. My loss is Birmingham's gain. I would certainly be up for a visit after you good people get settled in. But does that church understand how the four of you are going to rock their foundation? Lordy, Lordy, I question whether they understand what they are getting into with the former Fiesta team. This will be quite the show. And thank you for allowing me the opportunity to have a ring-side seat in such a loving and fun community. Now it is somebody else's turn to experience this incredible unit of do-gooders." Archie nervously chuckled and looked as if he were holding back his emotions.

Breaking the ensuing silence, Ellie and Del jumped up and motioned to the girls. It was the perfect time for dessert. In short order, Paula and Patsy bounded into the room giggling in sheer delight. Each of the girls carried a platter covered with shiny aluminum foil. They asked whether anybody could guess what they had, but of course no one had a clue. Josie secretly hoped it was two different versions of her favorite banana cream pies, but that was one of the things she would request of the Hallelujahs on their arrival home. Each woman in the Circle had their own special family recipe, and how it could be so different from one person to another was insane. The rivalry and bragging rights about them was hilariously competitive.

"Ready? Ladies and gentleman, are you ready?" Paula squealed. Eager to remove their aluminum-foil coverings, each one held a tray of frosted cupcakes in their excited hands. Paula's was completely iced in pink, and Patsy's displayed the blue icing. Both girls were hopping up and down like jumping beans.

A moment of silence ensued, and Josie turned to Ellie and gasped. "You're pregnant?"

"A bun in the oven, well, I'll be!" exclaimed Nola.

"Yes, ma'am!" Ellie said, nodding her head and smiling. "We are a family of four about to become a blessed family of five in approximately six months."

They let the excitement soak in and die down for a moment, and then Ellie continued, "We also have another announcement to make. Del?" Ellie gave him the nod to proceed.

"We're going to have this baby back home in Alabama, where we birthed both our baby girls," Del said with his arms around Ellie. "The kids couldn't be happier, and neither could we."

"What about your job and upcoming promotion?" Josie asked.

"My three-year contract is up this month, and the promotion has been put on hold yet again for whatever reason. It is time for us to go home. After much prayer and church support, we feel it is exactly where we need to be. And as you may guess, we will be well received at Rosewood Street Baptist," Del said. "Oh, and by the way, Josie, before you go getting all puffed up, our situation is actually not about you at all. Birdie has been aware of our thoughts and hopes to return to Birmingham for some time." He paused at the surprised look on Josie Bee's face. Del laughed and then continued, "Our Alabama heartstrings had been pulling at El's and my hearts for over a year now. We have appreciated our time and experiences here in Sand Haven. We met a lot of good people and learned a great deal from my work, which of course is what initially brought us here. But when we realized our family was about to grow by one, it solidified our desires to return home."

"Your being here with us, Josie, probably is what kept us grounded and focused," Ellie said. "The time frame was perfect, especially with the girls' school schedule and all. So, if you want to give yourself a little pat on the back, I think you are entitled to do so."

"Whoa, whoa, whoa. Wait just a minute. Are you telling us this has been in the works? Auntie Birdie has known all along?" Josie dramatically feigned disbelief with her hand over her heart.

"Can't pull one over on you, Josie Bee, now can we?" Del said, joining in the laughter with the others.

"Hey Miss Smarty-Pants, you just figuring that out? Guess your Auntie Birdie has more of a sense of humor than you have been giving her credit for," said Faye.

"I guess so," Josie said. "Wait until I call my dear Auntie, which I promised to do right away after I knew who exactly was on board." Wow, so Auntie Birdie knew about the baby and the move. But Auntie couldn't have known what the others were going to decide, now could she? Josie was perplexed.

"Your Auntie Berniece vows that she and the Hallelujahs had a firm grip on the situation," Ellie said. "And that they had approval from You-Know-Who above that things were going to work out as planned."

"If that doesn't take the cake. Wait until I talk with Auntie. And thank her." Josie was over the moon with excitement and relief. There was a mixture of animated chatter and laughter, congratulations and hugs. Even Archie, smiling and supportive as always, shared their moments with sincere enthusiasm, even though it had to be bittersweet for him.

With an overabundance of anticipation, love, and unfiltered joy dancing in everyone's hearts, the family became tearful as Del spontaneously began delivering genuine thanks to the Almighty God. His emotional expression came from deep, deep inside and flowed on as Del raised his booming voice to the heavens, praising God. Praising Him for His eternal gift of grace, His continued mercy, and His divine goodness in their lives and the lives of those around them. Glory! Glory to God in the highest! Glory to God for His love! Glory for salvation! Glory for that which they didn't deserve but was given to them. No one could have fathomed this coming from the quiet and restrained Delbert Price. The Spirit-filled delivery was articulate and heartfelt. Del's words touched them at their core.

They were all left speechless and humbled after Del's final "We thank you in the matchless name of Jesus, Amen!"

"Whoa there, Brother Price," Carl said. "I think we have ourselves a bona fide preacher in the family."

Those around the circle nodded in agreement.

Josie needed to call Auntie Birdie but wasn't quite ready to thank her for being so secretive. She quickly decided to have a little fun with dear sweet Berniece. Realizing two could play at this game of not sharing everything, she hoped to match wit with wit. After everybody went their separate ways, Josie went to the phone feeling deliberately mischievous and playful, and made the promised call to Birmingham.

Auntie Birdie promptly answered as she always did. The moment she answered, Josie went into hysterical mode. She breathed rapidly in and out, sobbing into the receiver. Josie got the reaction she hoped for. Auntie Birdie was clearly panicked and tried her best to calm her niece down.

"For goodness' sake, Josephine, pull yourself together and tell me what is wrong," Auntie Birdie pleaded.

"You ask me what's wrong? How about everything, Auntie! Nobody is coming to Birmingham! Do you hear me? Nobody. N-O-B-O-D-Y!"

This was almost *too* much fun. Josie Bee was having a ball.

"Stop it, Josephine! I am fully aware of how to spell that word, young lady. Now tell me what is going on up there!"

"They got an offer—" Josie started to say but was instantly interrupted by her Auntie.

"Who got an offer?"

"I'm trying to tell you that, if you'd please let me finish. The Fiesta School got an offer this morning from the Fort Wayne Public School System. You do know where Fort Wayne is, right? This big school system wants to reform preschools to better transition children into their kindergarten program," Josie said, concentrating hard not to give the ruse away. She was having a difficult time containing herself.

Stern and sharp, Auntie demanded, "What else do you know about this sudden offer?"

"Only that Faye said it was too good to resist or turn down. Everybody is going with her: Nola, most likely even Archie Wilson, who would follow her into a blazing inferno, and now for sure, Big Carl." Josie gave a loud, aggravated sigh into the phone. "Now I am beginning to wonder if this isn't a better fit for me than coming back home and starting over at the church."

"Please stop whining, Josie, you're not five years old anymore. It is not becoming or ladylike! Do you hear me?"

Being reprimanded by her well-mannered Auntie was music to Josie's ears.

"They invited me to join them. I feel honored. It makes me happy that they wouldn't go anywhere without me, but I don't know what I should do. Can you help me, Auntie Birdie? Please? You always know the right thing to do, and I need your discretion!" Josie was laying it on thick now and thought it might be about time to fold. Going too far might backfire, but hopefully Auntie Birdie would be a good sport. After all, she started it by keeping the Prices' situation from her. And probably for only a handful of times in her life, Berniece Thomas didn't know what to say.

"Cat got your tongue, Auntie?" Josie innocently questioned.

"I guess I don't know what to say, Josephine. I don't understand what is happening. I am sorry." Birdie certainly sounded befuddled and confused.

Breaking the silence Josie said, "You know I love you with all my heart, Auntie."

"Thank you, Josephine," Birdie said ever so quietly. She was in a daze, and Josie sensed it was time to quit pulling her leg.

"No, thank you for seeing with God's eyes the needs of others. Your vision in seeing those concerns through, constantly supporting, praying, and believing in all of us back here, it is such a blessing. And by the way, surprise! We *are* coming home to Birmingham, and I do mean most of us."

"What about . . . no contract with the public schools in Fort Wayne?"

"Not that I know of!"

"No offer too good to resist?"

"Negative on that one as well," Josie replied sweetly.

"And *who* is coming to Birmingham?" she asked.

"Eight of us! Everyone but Archie for real. But then again you knew about the Prices, isn't that correct?" Josie just had to add that last comment, to which Auntie did not respond. "Okay. I just thought I ought to be a little secretive too and hold back the good news just awhile longer," said Josie.

"Josephine Bee Johnson, you're going to be the death of me yet! I love you, child of mine." And Auntie, with nothing more to say, knew she had met her match.

Crazy as rats in a tin house, the race to Birmingham was on. With so much to do it was tough to know where to begin. One foot was out the door; the other was stuck in routine packing duties. Archie was a pro at gathering the different sizes of boxes, reinforcing them with thick tape and shredded paper, then taping them up for good measure.

Patty-Jo Tucker dropped by unexpectedly to give Miss Faye a going-away present. It was her cherished portrait of Mister George. Faye was touched. Mrs. Tucker, taking time off work to come by, had the painting framed, hoping it would match Faye's new décor down South.

"It suuuurely will," Faye exclaimed. The beautiful and meaningful moment prompted both Patty-Jo and Faye to reach out for the box of Kleenex. Removing several tissues, Patty-Jo explained that she would miss everybody, especially Mister George. Nola saw how deeply the exchange was affecting Faye and asked Patty-Jo if she wouldn't mind grabbing her a few tissues too.

After the Tuckers left, Faye and Nola got back to work. Looking forward to the timely opportunity in Birmingham didn't mean that leaving Sand Haven was any less difficult. Many, many good events and milestones had occurred here, and the unfortunate recent situation did not cancel out any of the good that had been accomplished.

The locusts came damaging Faye's years of service and progressive steps forward, but they did not have the final say. Faye was going to continue moving forward with her own army in tow. What was meant to cripple and destroy would turn into an eventual victory. At the end of the day the Fiesta team knew it was time to move on. The fact that they could do it together was nothing short of an unexpected miracle.

It was always those things you never saw coming that could take your knees out from under you. The same could be said of the amazing, joyful surprises that come around the corner without warning. Instead of breaking down, they were all breaking out. It was a time of celebrating all children, past, present, and future, and knowing they could never forget any of them. They all had their own special places in their hearts.

Faye was eager in many ways to become a part of this productive Baptist church, the spiritual entity that took care of its people, supporting them through the ups and downs of social reform and civil justice, not to mention everyday life. Faye was fascinated with the vision of a church family and excited by the idea of acceptance into a warm community. She knew she would be walking into a sacred space. Faye had always done life very much alone. Becoming part of an overall plan appealed to her in an unprecedented sort of way. To be a part of something bigger than herself with forever benefits was attractive to her mind and spirit.

Thinking about the kids' sandbox, Faye recalled Josie's church's sandbox, which Josie had talked about to the point of bragging. Josie had grown up in it and described it as much bigger and even roomier than Cranston Park's. It was hard to imagine a sandbox more wonderful than the one Faye had visited the last five years. But noting that even Jesus had played in it made Faye giggle. One of Josie's first Sunday school teachers had told her that because God was always with them, his son Jesus got to play in their sandbox too. He was right there beside them, and Josie never thought any different. Josie told Faye she would just have to see the gigantic box with her own eyes and she wouldn't be disappointed.

Josie also told Paula and Patsy that she couldn't wait to take them to the best sandbox in the world. It was the same one that their daddy had played in when he was a little boy. They were excited and could hardly wait. Josie shared stories about learning Sunday school lessons seated in the sandy box with Pearl, memories that would always warm her heart. Pearl would have been thrilled her baby sister was moving back home, but with a stab of fresh grief Josie knew she wouldn't be there waiting for her. Moments like these robbed her of some of the present joy, but Josie was beginning to understand that that was what grief did. No more homecomings together or planned events in the future. Josie would never be in Pearl's wedding or watch her grow a family. At times the grief was so overwhelming that Josie Bee could hardly catch her breath. She could not see it getting any easier but knew in her heart she needed to keep moving. And hope for the best.

One of the last things to be packed at Faye and Nola's place was the gigantic wall clock presented to the school by Archie Wilson. Pulling it from its place of honor on the front wall was too much for Faye. Nola, seeing it coming, was there and ready to catch another round of tears. More tissues in hand, Nola held her heartbroken girl, understanding how hard it was for her to leave the Arch behind, along with all the wonderful memories that had been created.

"I'm sorry, sweet girl," Nola said, gently comforting her. "I know how much our friend means to you. He adores you too, but there are circumstances out of our control, and it is what it is as harsh as it sounds, dear."

"It just hurts so much, and I just know he will be unhappy without us. Or do I just think it's going to work that way? It's not fair," Faye cried.

"And we both know life doesn't always give us what we want or think we deserve. It is not for us to decide what falls on whom. Only God knows that, sweetie." And Nola was silent.

The ladies had seen Archie somewhat regularly, but with the packing nearing an end, his time at the house was much less. He seemed to be constantly busy doing projects around his own house and cleaning out his garage. Big Carl had routinely been over there working in Archie's yard, trimming trees and repairing fencing. Carl was in a good place with spending more time with Archie, and working for his buddy while earning extra money on the side was helpful. Josie was working double duty, assisting a pregnant Ellie in her packing, and popping over to finish up what she could at the school. The Prices were hiring a moving van to do most of their moving, a gift from Del's new employer in Birmingham. Del and his family would be moving four weeks after everyone else to allow him the required time to wrap up commitments at his workplace. The girls were excited for a new adventure and to see the too-good-to-be-true sandbox at the church that Josie couldn't stop talking about. Archie had generously offered to rent a big truck and drive Faye's furnishings to Alabama, which solved the biggest problem at hand. Ellie and Del had also offered to bring whatever didn't make it into Archie's rental back with them. At least Faye, Nola, and Josie knew they would be seeing Archie again relatively soon. It was a gift they would all need and counted on.

Faye, Nola, and Josie decided to take a goodbye trip to Marshy's, where much had happened between the three of them. Faye, unsure about finding Mister George's crunchy food down South, wanted to pick up a few months' supply. If she found they didn't have it in Birmingham, Archie agreed to bring down a few cases on the truck. Faye didn't want to stress Mister George out even more with unfamiliar cat chow. He would be undergoing enough change as it was. He had gotten rather spoiled over the years, and Faye loved his dependence on her. And of course, Faye wanted to stock up on Nola's Ben-Gay because Marshy's routinely had a two-for-one sale. And her Tom's vodka was always well priced. Watching as Faye loaded up the cart with her juices, Josie couldn't help but make a not-so-subtle smart-aleck comment.

"Hey Miss Faye, you better go light on that stuff around the Hallelujahs. 'Lips that touch liquor shall never touch ours,' is one of their favorite lines, dear," Josie teased.

"Funny you never mentioned that aspect of church protocol before now, Josie," Faye cooed. "And I doubt very strongly I will be sweeping in for a smooch anytime soon, so you needn't worry about any of that," she said with her face scrunched up.

"Just wanted you to know you've been warned. Might want to brush up a little on the women's temperance movement is all."

"You are funny, a real comedian, oh, but you have heard that before."

"This is going to be a ball. I am so excited," Josie squealed.

"That it is, funny girl. That it is." What Josie found amusing, Nola suspected wouldn't be that funny later when Faye had to address her drinking frenzy. Nola knew a little something about breaking those horrible habits.

And then Faye picked up a few extra bottles of Tom's for good measure.

Finishing up at Marshy's, the trio zipped home to allow Nola time to put the finishing touches on her last fried-chicken dinner at the house. Archie was coming over for the final meal and to staple down the remaining details for their departures. He had also offered to take care of the house and handle what needed to be done to get it on the market. Archie was thrilled to be able to take this overwhelming responsibility off Faye's shoulders, knowing it would have been next to impossible for her to tackle this on top of everything else. He was happy to do it. Faye was beyond grateful as there had been so much to do and the time had flown by. The girls would be leaving in less than a day now, and that in itself was still hard to believe at times. Archie's plan was to head out in roughly four weeks with Big Carl in tow.

The dinner was bittersweet yet festive thanks to Nola and her great cooking. Nola outdid herself, making everyone's favorites. It was a night to celebrate friendship and the success of their combined efforts. Raising the luminous green Mosser glasses in unison, together they toasted each other and sipped Kool-Aid. Josie Bee, just two weeks shy of her twenty-first birthday, felt she was close enough to the big day to be given permission to join in. She thoroughly enjoyed the fuss everyone made over her. The red velvet birthday cake with cream cheese icing and twenty-one blazing candles was magnificent.

The night was coming to a close, and even though everyone knew it had to end, nobody wanted to make the first move to get up. Finally, it was Archie who handed over a completed checklist, having done all he could to prepare and ensure a smooth transition. Nola was most concerned about the travel arrangements for her adored magnolia tree.

Archie reassured her that they would individually wrap the branches and that it would be riding up front close to Carl and himself in the truck. Confirming all was taken care of, and giving warm hugs to each of the girls, Archie asked Faye to walk him to the door. Being women of suspicious natures, Nola and Josie exchanged glances while quietly getting up and racing to the doorway as soon as Faye and Archie were outside. Peeking out through the windows, they saw Archie motioning them out.

"Afraid you were going to miss something, ladies?" he teased.

"Maybe. Would we? Miss something that is," Josie nervously replied.

"Depends on how you define 'something,'" Archie said.

"Now you have meeeeee curious, Arch," Faye cooed, touching his arm.

"I wanted you to be the first to know, but who was I kidding? I wanted you all to know I am coming to Birmingham too," Archie declared.

"We already know that, silly. Tell us something we don't know," Faye said.

"I bet you didn't know I *am* coming to Birmingham, Alabama, to live. I am moving to the big city," Archie stated.

"But what do you mean? You said it wasn't feasible for you, and that made a lot of sense to us," said Faye.

"Yes, I did, and yes I am. I didn't know financially how I could swing it so quickly, but then I got busy working on the house, and with Carl's help I got it into tip-top shape much quicker than expected. I already have a potential buyer. If this goes through, once it is wrapped up, I will be on my way south permanently. I also welcome the change of scenery and opportunity. Once there, I can assure you, I will be at your service, Faye. Make that all of your services," Archie added as his eyes quickly met Nola's and Josie's.

"Oh Arch, leaving you was the only thing disturbing my heart. It didn't seem right, and I couldn't imagine how it was going to be without you," Faye said. "I don't know what to say."

"Knowing that it makes you happy makes me happy," replied the Arch.

"I think I speak for everyone, Archie, we all feel that way," Nola chimed in, and Josie nodded.

Moving in for a group embrace, Archie mentioned that he, too, was beyond grateful for new beginnings. Nobody saw this one coming either.

20

SAYING GOODBYE

*If ever there is tomorrow when we're not together . . .
there is something you must always remember. You are
braver than you believe, stronger than you seem, and
smarter than you think. But the most important thing
is, even if we're apart . . . I'll always be with you.*

A. A. Milne

AFTER SPENDING HER last night in Sand Haven with Faye and Nola, Josie was up bright and early, packed and ready for the big day of departure. With plans of popping over to the Prices' first thing, she needed to say her goodbyes and give them their final hugs. Knowing she would be seeing the group in Birmingham before she knew it made this part easy-peasy. After that Josie was heading to Cranston Park to spend some quiet moments sitting in the sandbox and talking to Pearl. Josie felt more expressive and articulate when she wrote her feelings down on paper, so she had written her departing thoughts in a letter to her sister. Auntie Birdie had emphasized the importance of doing so when circumstances called for it, and this was definitely one of those times.

Josie knew saying goodbye at the Prices' would be quick, as the family was traveling to the Franke Park Zoo in neighboring Fort Wayne for Breakfast-with-the-Animals. That was okay with Josie. She hated farewells in general, even though this one was more like "See ya later" than "Goodbye." In fact, Paula and Patsy were so eager to get going that they hurriedly brushed by Josie before their parents pulled them back for a proper parting. Ellie and Del were happy to drop Josie off at the park on their way out.

Once the blue station wagon was out of sight, Josie Bee made her way to the sandbox. Pulling the pale yellow envelope from her cherished backpack, she slowly entered the sand. Experiencing the weight of the finality of her last moments in Sand Haven, Josie's heart was expectedly heavy. She carefully smoothed out her place in the sandbox, gingerly sitting down with the papers in hand.

"Hey Pearl, I wrote you a letter, but I wanted to chat with you first. I wanted to share a few things, and I seem to be more organized when I write my thoughts down. You-know-who would appreciate these efforts. Our Auntie always mentioned your notes and sweet messages. What can I say? I guess I am the late bloomer in the family. We can't all be as perfect as you, but I'll keep trying. Ready? Here I go." With that, Josie began reading.

My Dear Pearl,

As you can see, I have been crazy busy down here. I know you have been with me every step of the way, but it hasn't been the same. I am struggling with your passing, and some days are just so much harder to wake up and get up than others. I have this big hole in my heart. Some days I don't know what to do, Pearl. I desperately miss you. And I don't think I'll ever understand the term "passing." Pass where? What does that really mean anyway?

Why can't I be more like you?

I get that everything has a way of working itself out. I really do. But I wonder if things would have taken another path had I reacted differently to the bombing. On top of Momma and

Daddy's death, and the Children's March, it became too much for me. All that nastiness and fear swelled up inside me like a balloon. Hate splashed all over me, and I couldn't wash it off. Its venom poisoned my heart. You put your head up toward the sun and continued to march forward without missing a beat. You deliberately set out to rebuild and invest in others. I only got angrier and angrier. I dropped my head toward acts of revenge, which was the force that directed my heart. It was my rebellious nature that captured God's attention in the first place. And we both know where it went from there.

Here I am and there you are. We are not promised an existence without heartache and loss. Continuing on without you is the kicker. You always told me to try my hardest to keep going. But what if it isn't enough?

I know you don't want me to give in to the locusts and their doom. You wouldn't wish that for me. I know you see clearly the bigger picture, Pearl. I am trying to see it too. I want you to know that what I have learned I will take with me into this new chapter in my life. I feel grateful most of the time. I am still trying to find balance. The Challenge allowed me to understand what you always knew, that we are built for service. I need to remember that. If we don't live out our God-driven purposes, we are cheating others and crippling ourselves. You always said so, as did Auntie, the Hallelujahs, the church. I couldn't have learned that all by myself. Are you smiling, big sister? Humble thanks.

I am going home, Pearl. The best part is that my friends are coming too. Auntie Birdie is beside herself, and the Hallelujahs have huge plans for us, especially Big Carl. With the Prices and Archie on their way soon, it is a complete picture of what our God can do. By far, the hardest part is doing all this without you.

I am returning to my roots. Faye is desperately searching to find hers. Forgiving those roots has been Nola's challenge, while both Carl and Archie want to put down new ones. The Prices are looking forward to expanding theirs, and we rejoice with them. Walking together, this community of friends is going to Birmingham. I have to giggle when I think our church really has no idea what is heading their way. We are a handful. Planning on taking Birmingham by storm. To quote our beloved Hallelujahs, "It's what we do." Doing this without you, arriving home and not having you there, is what scares me the most, Pearl. I hear your voice telling me things will be fine and that I am braver and stronger than I could ever envision. All I can say is that I hope so.

Stay tuned. I have this feeling that many things are going to heat up once we get settled in Alabama. And that could be another story in itself. I can only imagine what we can stir up down there with our accumulated version of love and compassion.

Can you peek down? I'm burying your letter in the right corner of the box just like we used to do when we were little. Don't forget to dig it up, it's down pretty deep. I miss you, Pearl. I guess that is all I have to tell you for now. I'll be in touch, please stay close. You promised.

As always, I love you to the moon and back,
Josie Bee

Josie pulled herself up out of the warm sand, flattening its surface until it looked completely level. Bending over she drew a big heart for Pearl containing the words "I am trying." Tilting her head upward, Josie Bee saw Pearl with hands clasped tight, whispering, "That's my baby girl." Wiping away a stray tear, Josie felt the comforting warmth of the sun on her face. Determined to honor Pearl by moving forward, she took steps away from the sandbox. With renewed faith and courage, and sand in her shoes, Josie Bee began walking toward her new beginning. She also knew it wasn't goodbye because Pearl would be going with her too. They would stick together like that. It's what they did.

SUGGESTED RESOURCES

American Legends: The Life of Josephine Baker. N.p.: CreateSpace Independent Publishing, 2015.

Arsenault, Raymond. *Freedom Riders: 1961 and the Struggle for Racial Justice.* New York: Oxford University Press, 2006.

Barron, Jim, and Kathie Barron. *Wolf and Dessauer: Where Fort Wayne Shopped.* Charleston, SC: The History Press, 2011.

Brimner, Larry Dane. *Birmingham Sunday.* Honesdale, PA: Calkins Creek, 2010.

Chestnut, J. L., Jr., and Julia Cass. *Black in Selma: The Uncommon Life of J. L. Chestnut.* New York: Farrar, Straus & Giroux, 1990.

Cobbs, Elizabeth H., and Petric J. Smith. *Long Time Coming: An Insider's Story of the Birmingham Church Bombing that Rocked the World.* Birmingham: Crane Hill, 1994.

DiAngelo, Robin. *White Fragility: Why It's So Hard for White People to Talk about Racism.* Boston: Beacon, 2018.

Eli, Quinn. *Many Strong and Beautiful Voices: Quotations from Africans throughout the Diaspora.* Philadelphia: Running Press, 1997.

Ellison, Ralph. *Invisible Man.* 1947; New York: Vintage, 1995.

Ferguson, Sheila. *Soul Food: Classic Cuisine from the Deep South.* New York: Grove, 1989.

Haley, Alex, and Malcolm X. *The Autobiography of Malcolm X.* New York: Ballantine, 1964.

Jones, Doug, with Greg Truman. *Bending toward Justice: The Birmingham Church Bombing that Changed the Course of Civil Rights.* New York: All Points Press, 2019.

Kersey, Paul. *The Tragic City: Birmingham 1963–2013*. N.p.: CreateSpace Independent Publishing, 2013.

King, Martin Luther, Jr. *The Autobiography of Martin Luther King, Jr.* Edited by Clayborne Carson. New York: Grand Central Publishing, 1998.

———. *I Have a Dream: Writings and Speeches that Changed the World*. Edited by James M. Washington. New York: HarperCollins, 1986.

Larson, Catherine Claire. *As We Forgive: Stories of Reconciliation from Rwanda*. Grand Rapids: Zondervan, 2009.

Lee, Spike, dir. *4 Little Girls*. 1997; New York: HBO Studios, 2004. DVD.

Levinson, Cynthia. *We've Got a Job: The 1963 Birmingham Children's March*. Atlanta: Peachtree, 2012.

Lockwood, Jeffrey A. *Locust: The Devastating Rise and Mysterious Disappearance of the Insect that Shaped the American Frontier*. New York: Basic Books, 2004.

Mayer, Robert H. *When the Children Marched: The Birmingham Civil Rights Movement*. Berkeley Heights, NJ: Enslow, 2008.

McKinstry, Carolyn Maull, with Denise George. *While the World Watched: A Birmingham Bombing Survivor Comes of Age during the Civil Rights Movement*. Carol Stream, IL: Tyndale, 2011.

McWhorter, Diane. *Carry Me Home: Birmingham, Alabama; The Climactic Battle of the Civil Rights Revolution*. New York: Simon & Schuster, 2001.

Parks, Rosa, with Jim Haskins. *Rosa Parks: My Story*. New York: Dial, 1992.

Phillips, Donald T. *Martin Luther King, Jr., on Leadership: Inspiration and Wisdom for Challenging Times*. New York: Warner Books, 1999.

Sikora, Frank. *Until Justice Rolls Down: The Birmingham Church Bombing Case*. Tuscaloosa: University of Alabama Press, 1991.

Thomas, Kim. *Potluck: Parables of Giving, Taking, and Belonging*. Colorado Springs, WaterBrook, 2006.

Till-Mobley, Mamie, and Christopher Benson. *Death of Innocence: The Story of Hate Crime that Changed America*. New York: Random House, 2003.

Uschan, Michael V. *Lynching and Murder in the Deep South*. Farmington Hills, MI: Lucent, 2007.

Weatherford, Carole Boston. *Birmingham, 1963*. Honesdale, PA: Wordsong, 2007.

Webb, Sheyann, and Rachel West Nelson. *Selma, Lord, Selma: Girlhood Memories of the Civil-Rights Days as Told to Frank Sikora*. Tuscaloosa: University of Alabama Press, 1980.

Wilkerson, Isabel. *The Warmth of Other Suns: The Epic Story of America's Great Migration*. New York: Random House, 2010.

Wright, Barnett. *1963: How the Birmingham Civil Rights Movement Changed America and the World*. Birmingham: The Birmingham News, 2013.

WITH GRATITUDE

*Feeling gratitude and not expressing it is
like wrapping a present and not giving it.*

William Arthur Ward

This book is dedicated to the light of my life:
Gary Wynn Gray

My husband and forever life partner, you continue to amaze and delight me with your heart of grace. You have always been my faithful encourager. Your forgiving spirit challenges me to move forward. Your generous spirit urges me to find ways in which to give more.

You are my Braveheart and my Pooh. You have consistently demonstrated the resolve to move forward and do the right thing regardless of genuine fear, crushing circumstances and difficult outcomes. Your walk is steady and firm. You continue the race in anticipation of the day when you will hear these words from Jesus, "Well done good and faithful servant."

Thank you for your kindness and care. I love you with all my heart. Always have, always will.

My sons:
Bradley Alan Gray
Douglas Adam Gray

You have been the biggest blessings in my life from the very day each of you entered this world. Your kind hearts and walk with Christ

bless me. Your service and care for others humbles me. The husbands
you are to your wives, and the fathers you are to your incredible children, bring me the best joy ever. Your natural and developed character
takes my breath away and all I can say is, "Glory." I am humbled by
your goodness. With love and respect.

My daughter-in-loves:
Shallon Lisette Gray
Valerie Louise Gray

In a league of your own, you hold your own. I couldn't be prouder
to call you daughters or more grateful for the gifts and talents you bring
to our family. I praise God for answering the prayers of a momma who
only wanted the very best for her sons. You are loving wives and amazing mothers. God gave me you—His very best—and so much more. I
am proud of you both. With love and admiration.

My grandchildren are sunbeams that illuminate my life:
I am so proud of each of you. Love you to the moon and back,
Your Nana

Denyon Elijah Gray
Aryah Tabytha Gray
Calyx Moshe Gray
Zion Wynn Gray
Xyler Josiah Gray
Lawson Louise Gray

The women who loved me well for a very long time:
My mother: Dawn Marie Brott
My grandmother: Opal Kirkpatrick
My mother-in-love: Virginia Gray
My auntie: Patricia Kirkpatrick
My mentor: Ruth Merillat
My defender: Donalee Betz
My champion: Sharon Meltzer

My three siblings: Pamela Bryan, Jennair Hanley, Ken Kirkpatrick. In the cookies of life, you are the sprinkles and the chocolate chips.

Jack Gray: my father-in-love who gave me the nickname of Cinderella when I was sixteen, you always made me feel like a princess. Bigger than life, your profound work ethic is legendary. I love you.

Rhoda Faith Hobbs: You have been my lifelong best friend and ultimate cheerleader. You've walked alongside me through thick and thin with unconditional love and understanding for fifty years. Your gentle spirit has soothed my heart and your prayers have lifted me up more times than I can remember. I have always seen the face of Jesus in everything you do. Love you BFF!

Christine Waters: Giddyap girlfriend! Your words of encouragement have been powerful and constant. You have spurred me on with your sense of humor to accelerate and continue the race. You are equipped with excellent advice and kindness, and I am incredibly grateful. You are my hoot! I love you to pieces.

Great friends are gems who continue to support, encourage, and advise. Like the stars I can't always see them, but I lovingly know they are out there:

Eloise Hosken, Teri Faust, Tami Sandifer, Joni LeMay, Roxanne Parker, Peggy Georgi, Tina Drost, Debbie Winstead, Joyce Sprunger, Marie McVay, Claudia LaBarr, Christine Betz, Stephanie Henry, Susie Mansfield, Luanne Rock, Eva Waltz, Pam Dickson, Kimberly Davis, Kyra VanSlooten, Teri Lewis, Lynette Merillat, Julie Storrer, Christy Shaw, Anita Krier, Judy Tiberio, David Tiberio, Sandra VanGilder, Mike VanGilder, Patricia Russell, Cara Jaimes, Terri McFarland, Barb Wagley, Janet Pickard, Janet Brown, Greg Waters, Corbett Day, Jessica Chesser, Bill Chesser, Dr. Bryton Mansfield, Dr. Christina Richardson, Jen Tran, Pooja Jain, Giselheid Everett. And a big shout out to wonderful neighbors and friends on Beaver Island.

Terese Tomko: Being the mother of four girls has given you much wisdom and I appreciate that you have taken me under your wing to share your knowledge and tips. Smiling. Part family, part friend, you are a breath of fresh air. Sweet thanks.

Ryan Lee: I knew what I wanted and you delivered. Your artistic God-given natural talent is truly out of this world. Delighted, and oozing with appreciation, my heart thanks you. You are wondrous.

Seth Borton: Thank you for painstakingly putting up my Christmas tree every year in August. It's the lights-of-hope-on-a-string that mean so much. I am always over-the-moon thankful for your friendship and expertise.

Allison Fallon: You were right when you said the story captivated me. And again, when you said it was confusing. Find Your Voice kick-started the writing process for me. An outline *is* very important, and I thank you for clearing that up for me. Your new book is the cat's meow!

Jeff Reimer: My first editor extraordinaire, I quickly nicknamed you Hatchet Man. You single-handedly went into my manuscript and struck out thousands and thousands of words. Then you hammered the daylights out of my dangling modifiers and anything else that was in the way. I appreciated your superb critical reading and grammar skills, your generous sense of humor. You are brilliant. Thank you.

Jessica Reimer: My second editor extraordinaire, I fondly named you the Fairy Sweeper because you make even a broom look as good as a wand in your hands: you are magical. You swept in to brush up the disjointed parts of my story, and I have been continuously grateful. I've enjoyed every minute we spent poring over content and searching for the right words. Polishing and refining is challenging, but with your wonderful knack for connecting the dots, even that was fun. You are a joy. I adore you.

Jennifer Rush – Thank you for your assistance and patience in working with me. Outskirts Press has a system second to none and you are a well-tuned conductor. Thank you for kindly realizing it IS hard to teach an older dog new tricks and understanding that my laptop and I will most likely never be friends. You have been a bona fide blessing, a book shrink, my friend. Deep thanks—I couldn't have asked for a better agent.

Susanne Smith: When I found out you were born in Birmingham, Alabama, on September 15, 1963, my heart skipped a beat. On the very same day that you came into the world, just down the street, six other children perished. It's hard to get your heart around that. Appreciate your reflections and recognition of responsibility for others, resulting in how you continue to carry out your educational commitment to serve young children. Your Kansas school staff and students adore you and are fortunate to have such a devoted and kind principal. You understand your history and the significance it has had in your life. Bushels of thanks for your generous words and time. You've been most gracious.

Carol & Paul Hoppe: It is amazing all you were able to do in the wake of Barbara's murder. You stated you did not understand how people who don't know God get through something like this. I have often wondered the same thing. By the grace of God and your desire to be of service to others going through this type of gut-wrenching experience, you chose to become involved in the Victim's Assistance Program funded by the Fort Wayne Police Department. Designed to help families navigate the court system, this program enabled you to walk with others, tenderly listen to their stories, and hold their hands. Explaining procedures, sitting with parents in court, you did whatever was needed to help the grieving families keep moving. Volunteering for thirty-four years, you made an astounding difference. You moved forward in the best way you knew. Honoring Barbara, you were among the first set of parents to join a newly founded group called Parents of Murdered Children. You both are superheroes. Love you.

Pauline Dammeier – This dear Aunt worked as a full-time domestic for the Eavey family, owners of Eavey 's Supermarket in Fort Wayne, Indiana, back in the 50's and 60's. On her Saturday mornings off, Aunt Pauline would catch a bus to go downtown to Murphy's Five and Dime to buy us a box of cake doughnuts. Then she would catch another bus in order to deliver them. And hop on one more to go back to work. I will never forget how special she made us feel and how good those doughnuts tasted. Aunt Pauline also saw to it that my siblings and I had spankin' new pajamas each year to wear on Christmas Eve. Aunt Pauline was the perfect example of having little but giving much. I am forever grateful for such acts of kindness.

Patricia Kirkpatrick – You should have been a detective-of-sorts. The way you jumped on every question I sent your way and in such a quick fashion, was remarkable. You truly love teaching and learning and "filling in the blanks." Thank you for being a good human and the sweetest aunt on the face of the earth. Hugs and thanks for all you have done for me throughout my life.

Ms. Irma Tyler-Wood, B.A., Harvard Law School, J.D.: My favorite teacher at Lakeside Junior High School! Your passion for teaching made such an impact on me. You taught American History with fury and civil rights with compassion. Reconnecting and sharing has been such a blessed thrill. You are one of the biggest overachievers I have ever met. Talk about breaking glass ceilings! "If you don't know your history you cannot move forward." Got it.

Sister Peg Albert, OP, PhD, president of Siena Heights University: You have an overflowing love and zeal for all children, big and small. The way you care for and nurture your college students is remarkable. And you make it a point to learn their names. Thank you for recognizing that inside we are all just little kids who have grown big. You have an exponentially huge heart, my friend, that knows no limits. Great for the students! And an example for us.

The Honorable Margaret M.S. Noe, Juris Doctor (JD), Circuit Court Judge, Retired: Your ferocious stance on protecting and defending children made you a mighty advocate. I wish you had been in Alabama in 1963. They could've used your compassion and grit in the struggle for justice for the girls. "I have learned we must commend our children for their courage and bravery. Their words may guide other hurting children who must first walk out of the pain. A shining light that promotes growth. Let's give our children a pathway that is bright, safe, and joyful. A pathway they can trust. Let that path be one that leads away from the shadows of darkness and into the light. Let the children speak!" Amen.

The Honorable Timothy P. Pickard, Juris Doctor (JD), Circuit Court Judge, Retired: Even as a college student years back at MSU in the '60s, you were teaming up with State Rep. Jackie Vaughn III, getting legislation passed to eliminate housing and job discrimination based on race. Your passion for fairness and equality and protection for the most vulnerable—the children—has left its mark. The legislation you developed that passed for children's inheritance benefits was important. "I've seen the very best and the very worst in my court when it comes to children. The best brings enormous joy, and the worst can handicap a child for life."

Adrian Training School: I remain forever grateful for the privilege to have volunteered at this uniquely progressive school for twenty years, serving a population of deeply troubled young girls with heartbreaking stories. I learned a great deal from an exceptional staff of good human beings who demonstrated patience and a level of care second to none. Giving the girls an education, a big safe haven, and huge amounts of fabulous food, was eye-opening and heart-satisfying. Thank you for allowing me in.

Free2Play: A program in the schools that systematically and successfully teaches Movement Literacy® so that all kids are free to play, free to move, free to achieve their goals. Furthermore, it levels the playing field, allowing all kids to be "athletes"—those who move, those who serve others. So proud of this program and the love and respect its creators have for the well-being of children.

Hot Rock Training Camp: This camp utilizes the game of basketball to learn more about the game of life, finding purpose and passion through Christ. Thirty years strong, seeing hundreds of kids laughing and playing and having a meaningful experience in a safe environment with lots of great food and snacks, is priceless. You can do these kinds of things when you live out in the boondocks—in our backyard, it is the highlight of our family's summer. It's what we do.

The H.O.P.E. Community Center: Helping others through projects and experiences, H.O.P.E. exists for adults with disabilities, where when in reality, it exemplifies people with amazing abilities showing us what it means to be an authentic person full of zest for life and zest for others. These big kids are happy, and I thank them for making us smile, too!

192 Food Relief Ministries: Inspired to eliminate hunger, these warriors provide meal packs to our county's students for weekends, extended breaks at the holidays, and during the summer months. Understanding that these recipients need to be nourished and fed is everything. Doing it is really cool. Thank you for recognizing and serving our hungry children. You are making a profound difference and investment in others.

GIFT Community: It's a pleasure to be in your space. You are good people with a magnitude of gifts and talents, but your hearts are what make you unforgettable and unique. Please look at some of those videos since Fluffy loves sign language and teaching it to you has been a thrill for me.

Lenawee Christian School: Thank you for being a place that values education to the fullest, but more importantly, is concerned with what is in a child's heart and soul. A safe haven for fourteen years for each of my boys, it is the best gift you can give parents and families. Because of the vision and pure faithfulness of Ruth and Orville Merillat, and the entire Merillat family, we and countless others have experienced the gift of a lifetime. The jewels in their crowns must surely be innumerable. Salt of the earth, Ruth and Orville set the bar high. We love and will always miss them until we one day meet again.

And to the children: Playing with spirited children in Kenya (Africa Inland Mission), interacting with deaf children in Jamaica (Caribbean Christian Centre for the Deaf), witnessing brave children rescued from the sex trade play freely in Thailand, watching energetic kids play basketball in the streets of Kazakhstan; to Hot Rock, Free2Play, the H.O.P.E. Center, school playgrounds everywhere; I know one thing for sure: Kids gloriously demonstrate in-the-moment contentment and joy when they are at play and that should send a clear message. Play more. Smile more. As Ralph Waldo Emerson once said, "It is a happy talent to know how to play." Thanks for the memories.

Joan Baez – "Birmingham Sunday" – This song has played over and over in my heart since I first heard it. I listen to it frequently. Written by John Farina and sung by Joan Baez, it is tender, emotional and moving.